Pinned!- Story Description

Mark Casey, a native New Yorker; [illegible] his home state and live in another part of th[illegible] a small town Kentucky woman named Roxi[illegible] girl of his dreams - beautiful, sensual, ambitio[illegible] having an extended series of talks via the internet and by p[illegible] decides to visit her at her home in Kentucky.

The meeting is magic. They fall head over heals for each other and decide to live together. He packs up his belongings and moves into her beautiful house. But there are immediate problems as soon as he gets to his new abode. They fight where they never did before. Roxie lies to him constantly. Their once raging sexual relationship has turned sour and they are now sleeping apart from each other. What could have caused this abyss that was once a dream?

Six weeks after moving his possessions and his life away from his home town and into her world, he is charged with a heinous crime and during the investigation by the local police, a large cache of illegal drugs is found. Mark is arrested, charged with this crime and while he is in custody, Roxie packs up her house, takes all of both her and Mark's personal property and moves out of state. Unfortunately, Mark's nightmare doesn't end there.

This is a true story of flagrant injustice in a small country town. These horrifying accusations strain Mark's family and friends trust, while calling their most cherished beliefs into serious question. The story rapidly moves along and tracks the actions of Mark himself as well as the motivations of the calculating Roxie, the local police force and the Kentucky State Police, the County Attorney and the Attorney General, and even the legal tenets of the Commonwealth of Kentucky.

Not only are many truths revealed, but also exposed is the extent that some will go to dominate, possess, hold power and even cover-up their actions. This story goes all the way up to the central characters jury trial, for the crimes that he didn't commit.

For anyone who has ever dreamed of living in small-town USA and getting away from the rat-race of metropolis, this tale of one man's battle against the local 'good ol boys' may cause you to reconsider possibilities in a new light.

Charles W. Massie
www.starshowpublications.com

Charles W. Massie

Book One of the "BlueGrass" Series

Library of Congress Control Number:		2012911575
ISBN:	Hardcover	978-1-4771-3420-7
	Softcover	978-1-4771-3419-1
	Ebook	978-1-4771-3421-4

This book was printed in the United States of America.

To order additional copies of this book, contact:
Xlibris Corporation
1-888-795-4274
www.Xlibris.com
Orders@Xlibris.com
118527

Contents

Introduction

It is really hard to write a crime novel in the 'first person' mode. For one thing, the reader knows that the narrator didn't die as a result of the actions in the book. For another thing, it's sometimes hard to stay objective when you are writing about events that you are personally involved in.

But I believe that I have done it in this story entitled, PINNED! This is a true story. I know it's true, because I lived it; correction, am still living it. All of the events in this book happened between March 2009 and March 2010, taking place in a little town located in the Cumberland Valley of South Central Kentucky. Burkesville is a sleepy little farm community, where people keep their doors unlocked, where there are no gangs, and where practically every corner boasts a church. It's in a dry county and so the public does not have to contend with bar patrons. It has an eclectic mixture of Christian, Mennonite and Amish congregants.

At the same time, this area is rumored to be home to several members of the infamous 'Cornbread Mafia' tribe. These are renegades who used to run illegal whiskey, mainly Hooch and Moonshine, during the depression and now run illegal drugs. What was once an empire that dealt mainly with production and distribution of marijuana is now into the production and distribution of methamphetamine, better known as 'Meth'. Every week, the local papers are sprinkled with tales of arrests in little, 'out-or-the-way' towns. And every week, the number seems to grow.

Like I said, I am still living this story. It won't be over until the resolutions of the court cases that are at hand are done and 'justice', by legal definition, has been served. Until then, I have opted to put these words to paper, based upon entries in my daily journals and the mounds of handwritten and typed notes that I have kept. The names of the characters have been changed to protect the guilty. They know who they are and I can expect a flurry of threats for defamation of character or slander or some other irrelevant charges. I don't care. I know this story is true. They know this story is true. Official documents can be shown to prove the story is true.

Now it's up to the reader.

There may be people who are put off by certain chapters containing graphic sexual scenes. For this, I apologize if I offended anyone. I didn't do this to entice prurient interests. I did it because much of what happens in this book is tied inextricably to sexual motivations and the physical entanglements that happen between two people in love. Or I should say, at least one person in love.

My goal in writing this odyssey is to let people know that however safe and secure you feel in your personal sphere; No matter how many friends you believe you have; No matter how smart or dumb you are as you stumble through life; There are people out there just waiting in the wings, to take advantage of you. Maybe you will be lucky. Maybe you will never have to face what is lurking around secret corners. Maybe you are in good standing with your guardian angel.

Or maybe God, in his infinite wisdom, will call you up, to prove your worth.

My word to the wise is this. Keep ever watchful of those who would do you harm. Keep ever watchful of devils with pretty angel faces. Keep ever watchful for those who would have you . . . .

PINNED!

* * *

The Definitions of Pinned

To give a woman a fraternity pin
She was pinned as a token of attachment.

To transfix or grip
The butterfly was pinned to the speciman wall.

To fasten or secure with a pin or pins
The seamstress pinned the cuffs of the pants.

In Wrestling, to win a fall from a move
The challenger won with a Cradle pin.

To place in a position of trusting dependence
He pinned his faith on an absurdity.

To utilize in Bowling or Golf
He really pinned that ball.

To hold fast or rivet
The bicycle rider was pinned under the car.

To completely immobilize someone
All options were gone and he was pinned.

* * *

Part One

Dream a Little Dream of Me

"What deceives, can also be said to enchant."

Plato (Greek Philosopher)

Prologue

The Arrest—Burkesville, KY—July 8, 2009

"Honey, open the door," I pleaded. "I don't have my keys or anything. You're being totally unreasonable."

I heard no movement from inside the house. I stood next to the front door hoping that Roxie would come to her senses and let me in. Not that it was chilly or anything, but I didn't relish spending the night on the porch because of a stupid argument.

I knocked again to no avail and then I peeked in the front window. The living room was empty as a tomb and I didn't see any shadows of movement throughout the house. I went down the porch and looked in the office window. The lights were on but no one was in the room.

"Where the hell could she have gone?" I thought. I knew she got pissed real easily and with all the drinks she had earlier that day, she probably wasn't thinking straight. I hoped she hadn't pass out or hurt herself. I didn't want to have to break in a window to get in just because she had a wild hair up her ass.

"Fine, be that way," I yelled, "I'll sleep in the RV."

With that I went down the stairs and opened the door to the RV with all good intentions to climb inside and spend the night but I was irritated by her attitude. I thought if we could just talk it out, I could apologize for yelling at her and we could make up. Besides, I was starving; not having eaten all day.

"Screw it," I thought again, "I'm going to wait her out."

I snuck quietly up onto the porch and ducked down to avoid being seen through the front window. I stood next to the front door, between the doorjamb and the stainless steel grill and even if she was right next to the front window looking out, she couldn't see me. I remained there, silent, waiting, hoping that she would come looking for me.

My mind kept reviewing our conversations over the last couple days. Since moving here in early June, we had had an argument almost every other day about some trivial bullshit. Petty, meaningless things would end up getting all blown out of proportion until I would break down and argue with her. I had enough of this crap last month when I decided to leave, but she sweet-talked me back and told me that it was because she had not been taking her medication.

I thought things would change but after the incidents surrounding our trip to Pigeon Forge and the constant bickering, I decided on the 4th of July to pull the plug on the relationship. The only thing that I should have done differently was to not tell her I was leaving until we were on the plane back to New York. That was what had really set off this latest volley between us. But her performance in the shower the other night had caused me to drop my guard again.

"Click," I heard the dead bolt unlatch. Finally she was growing some brains and going to let me in. The door opened up slowly and I was ready to put my arms around her and hug her. Boy did I get a surprise. The first thing coming out of the door was the barrel of her shotgun. I reached down and grabbed the barrel midway and yanked it out of her hands.

"Boom!" was the resounding answer. The shotgun was loaded. Immediately the door slammed and I once again heard the distinctive click of the dead bolt. The heat from the barrel was getting uncomfortable and I immediately dropped the shotgun to keep from burning my hand. I couldn't believe that I had been standing there holding a shotgun by the barrel and thinking how lucky I was that I was not standing directly in front of it. I took the shotgun, opened up the side door of the RV and placed it on the floor. Now I was pissed.

"Hey moron," I shouted. "Open the damned door now, or I kick it in."

Silence.

"I'm not kidding . . . open the door. Your little shotgun is put away and I'm still here. I want to talk it out and I'm not going away."

Silence.

I looked in the front window again and still couldn't see any movement. She must be hiding in the bathroom. I went around to the back of the house and looked in the kitchen and the bathroom windows. There was still no sight of her. I tried opening the back door of the house, even though I suspected it was locked. It was. I went back around the front and looked at the aluminum molding around the front window. How in the hell was I going to pull that molding off the window, without having any tools? Opening the window was easy but getting the molding off was another story. I could break the front window but I knew I would just end up replacing it tomorrow and I didn't want a houseful of bugs. I was just about to use one of the heavy spatulas from the grill to unscrew the strips of molding when I saw the distinctive blue lights of a police cruiser coming over the driveway rise.

"Mark!" was the command from the cars PA speaker. "Come out with your hands up."

"Son of a bitch," I muttered.

I thought about it and realized that she must have called the police when she first locked me out, before getting her shotgun. I figured it would take the police at least fifteen minutes to get here from town and there were two cars. That told me that they must have hauled-ass all the way out here and that this was not a 'garden variety' disturbance call.

"I'm right here," I said as I proceeded down off the porch out into the yard.

"Turn around with your hands up," a voice said.

A Cumberland County Sheriff came up behind me and placed me in handcuffs. He then loaded me into the back of his cruiser and slammed the door. I figured that Roxie had called the police and given them some kind of bullshit story about me threatening her. I wanted to tell my side of the story but the cop left me in the car and went into the house. So I sat there, pissed off and trying to figure out what she could have told them to warrant sending two cars, fourteen miles out of town on a Wednesday night. After about twenty minutes went by, the policeman came out to the car and let me out.

Hmmm, maybe things aren't going to be so bad after all, was my thought. He took the handcuffs off and spun me around to face him. Then he put the cuffs back on.

"I don't want you to be uncomfortable when you are giving your statement." He said. "If I leave you here, do you promise not to run away?"

"Where the hell would I go?" I said. "I'm out here in the middle of nowhere."

With that, 'Officer Friendly' told me to stay there and he went back into the house. I guess he must have trusted that I wouldn't be running away because we really were in the middle of nowhere. I was dressed in shorts, sneaks, and a light summer shirt and had about $ 1.50 in my pocket.

Momentarily, two more police cars pulled up. One of them was from the Burkesville City police; and the other, a Kentucky State Trooper.

I'm thinking, something is definitely not right. This is way too much action for a domestic violence call; even if it really did happen. Then up over the rise comes an ambulance from the medical center. What is going on?

As I stood there, two officers escorted Roxie across the lawn and into the waiting ambulance.

The sheriff came back over to me and I asked him "What's going on with the ambulance?"

"You beat her up pretty good boy," He replied. I stood there with my mouth hanging open.

"I didn't touch her!" I shouted. "How could I; I was locked out on the porch when you guys showed up."

"Well boy," he continued, "we want to talk to you about some other things. Come with me."

As the two of us got up on the porch, a third deputy came out of the house and asked me "Where is the shotgun?"

"It's right inside the side door of the RV," I pointed. "I didn't want her trying to take any more potshots at me."

"That's funny," he said, "we heard that you were the one firing off rounds."

"Wrongo," I protested, "just do a gun shot residue scan on her and you'll find out who had the gun."

I followed the officer into the house. He led me down the hallway to my office space where three more cops stood. As I entered, he asked me, "Would you mind explaining this?"

I stood there looking in amazement at a large, one gallon size baggie of pot, sitting in my open briefcase. Beside it were 3 smaller, 1-ounce baggies. I felt like I had been hit with a brick because all four officers of the law in the room were glaring at me.

"I have no idea officer." I stated, "I have never seen that shit in this house."

"This IS your office, is it not?" The lead detective asked.

"Yes, it's where I do my work. I just launched a medical website. But I can assure you that my work does not include any kinds of drugs. I am selling medical related equipment like hearing aids and breast augmentation, nothing illegal."

"We found the rest of your stash too," He said. With that he lifted an ashtray that contained an assortment of rolling papers, cigarette butts and a couple of roaches from previously smoked joints. I didn't like his inference that this was my stash.

"Honestly," I said, "I haven't smoked reefer in years; at least 30 years. Roxie smokes and I didn't care. But as far as all this that you have found, I've never seen that amount in this house before and I cannot lay claim to it. It's not mine. I can only think that it was planted here because I don't think Roxie had this just laying around. I believe that she is just a recreational smoker."

"We found most of the money upstairs," the officer stated, "but we want the rest; where is it?"

"If you found money upstairs," I said, "then it must have been from rubbing a magic lantern, because it's not mine, and from what Roxie has been telling me, she doesn't have any money either. Just where did you find this other money?"

"It was in the safe," John Law, one of Officer Friendly's coworkers said. "Now where is the rest?"

"First of all, the safe is over there across the hall," I said and pointed to Roxie's office space. "And as far any money goes, I wouldn't know. If Roxie had any money around, she didn't tell me and I don't pry into her personal banking habits. I have my money hidden where she does not have access to it, because I just pulled it out of the bank two days ago and hid it."

"Prove it . . . we want to see it," he said, "and if you just pulled it out of the bank, we're not going to take it."

With that, I lifted up the leaf of the table in the office and pulled out a plain white business envelope that I had taped out of sight. The officer took the envelope, opened it up and proceeded to count out a total of seventeen $ 100 bills; Two hundred dollars less than I had pulled out of the bank on Monday.

"Log this in as evidence," the detective said to his companion, "$1,700 in drug proceeds."

"That's bullshit!" I shrieked, "I just pulled $1,900 out when I was at the bank on Monday. I kept $ 200 out for shopping today, of which I have about $ 1.50 left. I stashed that $1,700 so that Roxie would not find it. I have the withdraw slip from the bank to prove it."

"As far as we're concerned," he sneered, "this money was taken during a drug bust and it will be logged in as evidence. We also found plants growing on your property. We are taking you down to City Hall to be processed. Do you have anything you want to say before you go?"

"Officer, I am telling you," I pleaded. "This is not my pot. This is not my property. Up until 6 weeks ago, I lived in New York State. I came down here to live with Roxie, but that is proving to be a pipe dream. We met on the internet but after living here with her, I've decided that she isn't the kind of person that I want to spend the rest of my life with. This is her property and if you found pot plants, they're hers. But the money that you just took is mine. It came from my bank and this whole thing is a setup."

"So you are saying that all this is her stuff?" He asked.

You have to understand that this was my lover. And even though I was innocent, I'd be damned if I was going to put any blame on her, not knowing what was going on in her mind. I desperately wanted to talk to her. So rather than directly agree with his accusations about her and to push the blame off of me, I elected to be vague in my answer.

"I can't say definitively that this is hers or not, but I've never seen it before and it's not mine." I continued, "We were gone today since about 11:00 this morning. We spent the day in Bowling Green and supposedly no one was here. I can't tell you who the owner of that pot is, or where it came from. For all I know, you put it there when I was locked in your car."

Officer Friendly looked at me and said "Sorry, but I just don't believe you. We'll sort this all out when you get downtown." He asked another officer "Is the canine unit here yet?"

The other deputy said that they had just arrived and were proceeding to bring the dogs in the house. As all this was happening I was taken out through the living room and the officer was nice enough to let me grab a couple of packs of cigarettes from a carton that I had there. I was loaded into the police car and off we went, leaving the rest of the officers to finish searching.

During the 14 mile trip back to Burkesville, I sat in the back seat with the cuffs on as the sheriff drove quietly, listening to the police radio and a classic rock station. When we got into town I asked him what happens next.

"Both of you are probably going to be arrested," he said, "it depends on how extensive her injuries are."

"Officer . . . she definitely needs help," I stated, "but as God is my witness, I did not beat her up."

"I'll agree she needs help," he said, "but this whole matter is going to be in the hands of the court."

We arrived at City Hall and I was taken in and placed in a holding cell. Officer Friendly took my wallet and disappeared into the other room. I wondered if I would get my one phone call when it dawned on me that I wouldn't know who to call. I didn't know a soul down here except Roxie and I vaguely knew the two neighbors on our road. I sure as hell didn't know their last names, much less their phone numbers. That meant that any bail arrangements were going to have to come from my friends and family in New York and Pennsylvania. Great! . . . I'm in a bucket of redneck shit and 900 miles away from home. Suddenly this get-a-way with the love of my life wasn't looking so good.

Twenty minutes later the investigating officer came over to the holding cell and asked me to hold up my arm. I did so and he asked if a small scratch on my right arm was a result of beating Roxie.

"I told you," I said, "I didn't lay a hand on her. We got into an argument and I slapped her on the face, open hand. That was it. I went outside and she locked me out. That's why I was on the porch when you guys pulled up."

He didn't say a word but went back to the other room. In about ten minutes, two guys came over and opened up the cell, placed me back in cuffs and escorted me outside to a waiting van. I asked where we were going.

"We are transporting you to Adair County Jail." He said.

"On what charges?" I asked.

"You'll get a complete transcript when we get there."

I couldn't wait for this tall tale.

* * *

1) Profile and Contact

Syracuse, NY—March 29, 2009

"Hey Maggie," I shouted, "I'm sending you my Craigs List profile. Check it out."

Maggie Cavanaugh was my friend, happily married, the director of the local library and she was always interested what I had up my sleeve. I had been coming into the library everyday for the last year because I did not have Internet access at home.

As a matter of fact, I didn't even have a home of my own. When my parents went into the nursing home, I was forced to leave their house because my sisters, executrixes of the estate, wanted to put the house up on the market. I lived with my friend Les Johnson for about a year but then he decided to reconcile with his wife, and I had to move again.

After that, I went to live with another acquaintance, Willie. But that situation was crazy because he was so jealous of my relationship with Michelle his girlfriend, and he kicked me out after only three months. There was nothing between Michelle and me, other than being friends. I had known her for a long time and we just had fun together. But Willie didn't like the fact that her and I laughed all the time and he never laughed. He just bitched. Here's a guy that has more money than God, a fairly successful business, two Harley's and a Subaru in the garage and the best he can come up with is to bitch about anything and everything. He definitely fit the role of an obsessive Virgo.

Being broke sucks.

I was barely able to cover my expenses when I was living at Willie's house and now I didn't know what I was going to do. I had applied for and was granted Social Security disability because my legs were clogged up with Calcium deposits and I could not walk very easily. That was one of the reasons I had to give up my company that I had with a partner. My partner wasn't interested in keeping it going alone and I just couldn't do it anymore.

So I was waiting for my Social Security disbursement to come through because it had been approved. But money was very tight. I had made a few bad investments and had squandered savings that I had and I didn't really have anything to fall back on. In fact, money was so tight, that I was forced to live in my storage bin for two months. That had to be the lowest point in my life. Every night, I would park my car in the lot, sneak into the facility and lay down on a stack of blankets nestled amongst my boxed-up possessions. For hygiene, I relied on friend's houses, the Rescue Mission and bathrooms at Wal-Mart and Target. People who knew my situation started calling me "The Boy in the Bin" as a joke.

Like I said, it sucked.

It wasn't like I was used to living in high style. As a temporary shelter, the bin was fine. But the fact was that it was getting cold at night in Syracuse, NY and soon the snow would be flying. I had no idea what I was going to do but somehow I trusted that God would take care of me. The answer to my prayers came when I won $3,000 playing lotto. With three grand, I could get a little efficiency apartment and make it through the winter. But, as with every silver lining in my life, there was a snag. In the same week that I won the money, my friend Les got a DWI charge.

It was the night of my birthday and Les offered to take me out for a drink. He was celebrating that he finally made the break with his ex-wife and threw her out of his house. We agreed to go out and he would be my designated driver. That didn't work out so well because as soon as we hit the first bar, he started pouring down the Gin and Tonics like he had a fire in his stomach. I realized then that I didn't have a Designated Driver anymore, I was at the mercy of a drunk; in a bar I'm not familiar with and the weather outside was a blazing snowstorm. Great! On top of that, Les had decided that he was going to pick up this chick at the bar.

"Hey man, I thought this was MY birthday treat," I said, "if you're going to get lucky, I need to get back home before it really starts snowing."

"I got this chick all hot for me," Les claimed, "How about if we take you over to my house and you can sleep in the garage instead of the storage bin? Then I'll go out with her. You and I can go out anytime."

So I agreed and the three of us drove through the flurries back to Les's house and he dropped me off. I was glad because the snowstorm outside had really picked up and even though sleeping in the garage wasn't the Ritz; but it was better than the storage bin.

It wasn't until the next day, after Les hadn't come home that night, that I found out that he had been stopped for driving without headlights and when they did a field sobriety test, he registered 2.2; over double the legal limit. Naturally, he spent the night in jail and called his daughter the next morning, who in turn called me on my cell phone. The two of us went down to the jail to pick him up. He was lucky enough to get out on his own recognizance.

"Son of a bitch," Les moaned, "what am I going to do?"

"Hey," I said, "You've got a good job. Can't you just pay the fine and be done with it?"

"No, I'm a repeat offender. I've had 4 DWI charges in the last 9 years. They consider this a felony and I may go to jail. I talked to my lawyer and he needs to have a $3,000 deposit, just to represent me."

"What about your wife?"

"Screw her," he said, "I got fed up with her pissy attitude and kicked her out." "Do you really think she is going to lend me any money?"

Les had no room to get fed up with anyone's pissy attitude. Les was obnoxious. He had diarrhea of the mouth, he was a pathological liar and worst of all, he was totally mercenary when it came to doing things for people. There was always a price tag. I got along with him alright as long as I could keep distance between us but when he started babbling his bullshit to me, it was time to walk away and let him talk to himself; which I did a lot.

Les was the kind of guy that everything happened to. He never did anything, according to him, to deserve the abuse he took from other people. To listen to Les, he was a sensitive, caring man. Just as an example, he bought a red-hot SS Camaro last year, just so he could pick up women. That was his intent anyway. But because of his attitude, I don't think he ever had any chick's ride in the car. As soon as he opened his mouth, any girl could figure out he was just trying to get in her pants. There were two topics that he always had comments on; Cars and sex. That was the extent his conversations.

He was a pretty good mechanic and did side work for anyone who would pay. But as far as any social grace, it was practically non existent. He had a penchant for going to strip clubs and hitting on the dancers. I had seen him in action a number of times and I always thought he could walk into a whorehouse with $ 20 bills hanging out of his pocket, and still get nothing. So anyway, his car just sat there in the garage, collecting dust, while he made payments on it. That was a shame too because this 1997 Camaro was a car that needed to be shown off. It was a 30th Anniversary model with every factory option available, including an LT-1 Corvette engine. It also had an SLP Engineering aftermarket package that included a special hood, stainless exhaust and upgrades to the lighting and handling systems.

"Les, here's what I'll do," I said. "I won some money this week. I will give you $2,000 for your defense and I'll keep $1,000 of it. That should be enough to let me sleep in your basement for a while; What do 'ya say?"

"You pay the taxes on your winnings and you've got a deal. I'll let you stay until July."

"NOT! . . . You pay the taxes Les," I replied. "You have the house and expenses and can write all the taxes off against losing lotto tickets. I don't have that luxury."

"Ok, but make it till the end of May. By June 1st, you promise to be out."

"No problem. I'll probably be out sooner because I want to move down south as soon as my SSI disbursement comes through."

So that is how I found myself in the current situation. I was living in Les's basement and using the public library for my internet access. It actually wasn't too bad. I made it through the cold winter, I had the run of the house for cooking and showering and most of the day I was either running around or doing research at the library. In addition to looking into starting an online business, I decided to put a profile up on Craigs List, looking for a possible relationship.

Originally, I had in mind to go to either Knoxville, Tennessee or somewhere in Virginia when I got my disability award from Social Security. I knew that it was going to be around $13,000 and I also knew that I could make a good start somewhere else with that money. I absolutely hated living in New York State and anywhere would have been fine . . . Really.

The idea of advertising for a relationship was sort of a joke. I just thought I'd throw it out there and see what might happen. I had been without a girlfriend since June of last year when Grace and I split up. Grace was also my business partner at one time and I loved her dearly. But the pressure of running a business got in the way of our love life and things went sideways.

Another factor was that Grace was an excessive drinker and because of this we could never just go out and have one drink. It was always 4 or 5 or more. I had had a couple of DWI convictions in the past and was bound and determined that I would never get another. So that situation also affected the relationship. I hurt because of her and I figured the best way to forget about her was to find someone else. Maybe I could hook up with one of those southern belles I had heard about.

"Hey Maggie," I shouted again, "Do you know the difference between a Northern girl and a Southern girl?"

"No Mark," Maggie answered, "but I suppose you are going to tell me."

"A Northern girl sez 'you can' and a Southern girl sez 'yall' can."

I could see Maggie grinning as she said "You are not right . . . sick, sick, sick."

"Ah, but you love me."

I was pretty happy with the profile I had put together. The intro line read 'Looking to get my soul kissed' and I thought that this might provoke some ladies to at least read it. The ad went on to give my physical description, a few details of what I liked, disliked, what I looked for in a woman and what I didn't want; all the usual stuff. I attached a recent photograph of me wearing a green St. Patty's day wig, so that the reader knew that I wasn't a troll or anything, but still had a sense of humor, and I sent it to Maggie for her review.

"Mark," she said, "you're Irish aren't you?"

"Half Irish," I answered, "the other half is Heinz 57."

"So why do you have down here that you don't want any drunks or druggies?" She asked.

"Shit, after the last couple women that I've been with, I need a break." I said. "First Paula and then Grace; I figure if I stay away from the drunks, I might have some money for a new car or something."

"Well Mark, I've got to say," she continued, "the profile looks pretty good. And I like your smiling face in the picture. But why are you sending the picture of you in the wig? Do you think someone will say anything about you being challenged in the head-hair department if your send that really good picture of you?"

"I don't want to show all my goodies right out of the box. If they can get by the green wig and still contact me, they might be someone with a sense of humor."

"I think you should hide the fact that you are not quite right," Maggie said with a smile. "They will find that out soon enough."

"Nah, I believe in Shock and Awe, like George Bush," I quipped. "Besides, there's plenty of time to send a real and serious photo when I get to know them better; and if anyone says anything about me being bald, I'll just tell them that the more hair I lose the more head I get."

Maggie just reiterated her former comment, "You are just not right."

I posted the profile on Craigs List and went back to doing my research work. I wasn't sure what kind of online business I wanted but I knew that if I could set one up and start making money, I could work the business anywhere I decided to live. For years I had worked basically in the sales field; first running an Engineering and Testing Company and then more recently as CEO of an Information Technology Company. I thought I was going to retire in 2004 when I sold the IT Company but after sitting in bars all day getting drunk, I decided after 6 months that this wasn't my path in life and so Grace and I started a small Catering Company. That worked out fine until my health issues crept in and forced me to go on disability.

I stayed at the library for a couple of hours more and then I left to do my running around and maybe stop and have a drink. The more time I was away from home, the less I had to deal with Les and his highly developed lines of SNIFF.

That's short for Singular Non-Interesting Fantasy Fodder.

I went to the library the next day. It was April Fools day and I was trying to think of some prank to pull on my friends. I love jokes, pranks, cartoons, anything to get a laugh from people. I think that if you can make someone laugh and relieve them a bit from their daily worries, you've done a good deed for the universe. Of course, it depends on the other person. They have to have a good sense of humor anyway or you find that the energy is sometimes wasted.

So anyway, I decided to wear my novelty contact lenses. These are a non-prescription contact lenses, that from the outside look bone white in color. Since I have deep blue eyes, the bone white color really freaks people out when they see them. I slipped them in and walked into the library.

"Hi Girls," I said.

"Mark, your eyes," Maggie said.

"What," I replied, "don't tell me I look like I've got a hangover?"

"No, they're all white," she said, "and you look like a zombie."

"April Fools!"

"You goofball" Maggie retorted. "What kind of a stunt was that?"

"Just for you Maggs," I replied, "who else would know what a zombie looks like?"

"You are sick, sick, sick, Mark . . . SICK!"

With that interchange, I went into the computer room and set my laptop up. I was using and older Dell unit that I had salvaged from a recycling bin. I replace the hard drive and it worked fine so I was a happy camper to just be able to have all my important documents in one convenient place.

Once I got logged on, the first thing I did was check my email. I had 18 messages that morning, 9 of them in response to my Craigs List posting. The other 9 were from my contacts, product registrations, password confirmations, things like that.

Because the Craigs List profile was a new thing for me, I proceeded to go through my responses first, one by one. Of the 9 responses, 5 were from girls that had a link to a porno website.

Click . . . Delete.

Of the remaining 4, none of them had a picture attached. I read the first one from a girl in another upstate New York town. She was currently going to a community college there and working for her father in his construction company. She liked my profile and thought she would like to 'hook-up' with me.

Click . . . Delete.

I don't do hook-ups like I did in my younger days.

The next was from a girl who must have gone to the Vinnie Barbarini School of grammar. Every other word was 'dees' or 'duhs'. I thought I was back in Brooklyn by the time I got done with the posting.

Click . . . Delete.

The third one was interesting. It was from a girl living in Kentucky, Roxanne Patrick. She was originally from New York and was thinking of moving back. She had a 23 acre organic farm down there and an online business. I filed that one away for an answer later.

The last one was from a local girl who was just going through a divorce. She said that she had never been on Craigs List before and her friends coaxed her to give it a try. She wasn't interested in one-night stands or anything right now except possibly dating. I filed this one away for a future response.

I went about doing my daily computer chores like researching online businesses, checking my bank account, and answering my other emails. After an hour, I went back to the 2 Craigs List responses and re-read them. I answered both of them with the same email by cut and paste method. I gave them a brief description of myself, highlighted my work, hobbies and other personal information and sent them off.

Maggie came in the computer room and asked "Did you get any responses to your ad?"

"As a matter of fact I did," I said. "Half of them were ads for porno sites but I got 2 that I answered."

"I think you are crazy, looking for a date on Craigs List," she said, "You never know what kind of nutcases are out there."

"Hey, I'm right here."

"No, you know what I mean," She continued. "Some girl could be an ax murderer or something, you never know. Remember the last ad you placed; the one for your birthday escort?"

I had placed an ad on Craigs List last year looking for an escort to a birthday party my friends were throwing for me. It was simple; I just wanted an escort. No girlfriend, no sex, no relationship; just an escort. No strings attached. I started getting emails from some girl in Russia who wanted to come to the US. She sent all kinds of pictures of herself and God, she was a beauty. I carried on an email communication with her for about 2 weeks until she asked me to send her $ 900 via Western Union.

Click . . . Delete.

"Well Maggie, what can I say?" I replied. "I'm not going to do anything stupid. I just want to see what is out there. Besides, nothing really bad can happen to a careful person like me. Since Grace and I broke up, my horns have been growing at a rapid pace and I don't cruise the pick-up bars anymore. I just want to see what kind of person might find me interesting and then I'll go from there."

"I thank the Lord I'm not in the dating game anymore," she said as she left the room, "be careful."

"Maggie, I'm so cautious, that whenever people tell me to drive carefully, I put a condom on."

"Sick," was the only word I heard.

I went back to the task of researching internet businesses. I already had a domain name for a medical business. It seemed logical to see what kind of products were out there to sell online. I looked at hearing aids, breast augmentation products, male enhancement products, wrinkle removers, vitamins, herbal supplements and countless other 'get paid big bucks' ideas. All this research took me into the afternoon hours when I checked my emails again. And there they were; answers to my latest postings to the Craigs List girls.

The local girl sent a nice letter saying that she was 5'7", 135 pounds, has 2 kids ages 10 and 13, liked dancing, cuddling, and was looking for a serious relationship.

"Hmmm," I thought, "Here's a woman that is just going through a divorce and already looking for a new target for heartbreak. Besides, 5'7" is a little taller than I like because I'm 5'5." Also, I was not really looking for a ready made family, since I've existed all my life without one. I'll save this one for later."

The girl from Kentucky, Roxanne, also sent a nice letter.

"I've lived down here in Kentucky for about 3 years." She said. "My divorce was final last fall and I'm trying to decide whether to stay here or move back up north to be with my family. I'm 5'1", 115 pounds, red hair, blue eyes; I like computers, music, nature and a lot of other things. I don't have a picture right now but I'll try to find one if you are interested."

"Wow," I thought, "She sounds great. No pitch for a relationship, into the same things I like and a huge bonus, she is a redhead."

I've always had an affinity for red hair on a woman. It's not a prerequisite, but something I've always found attractive. When I dated Grace, she went out one day and had her hair dyed, just for me. That was one of the things I loved about Grace and would still be with her if it hadn't been for the booze and business problems. She did things just for me. And I did things just for her. I still wished we were together but that was all water under the bridge now. It was time for me to move on and get on with my life.

I sent back another email to Roxanne. I gave her a little more information about myself, talked about the fact that I had been an astrologer for about 30 years, told her how much I hated New York State and wanted to move south and told her about my love for Progressive Rock music.

"Yikes," I said, "Why would anyone want to move to New York? The job market sucks here, taxes are high, the social scene is nil and the winters are brutal."

I went on to explain how I pretty much liked all music except RAP and how progressive rock was music that had sort of a spiritual meaning; Music that talks to your heart.

"Progressive Rock is groups like Genesis, Alan Parsons, Yes, Moody Blues, Spock's Beard, Saga and a lot of others" I wrote. "This is music you listen to. Not music you put on when you are vacuuming the rug."

I finished the email and attached another picture I had; of me dressed in a nice suit. It was taken during a time that I was going out on business calls or something. I added the line, "This is just to prove that I clean up well."

Click . . . off it went.

Win, lose or draw, I thought, we'll see if I get an answer.

* * *

2) Pictures

Syracuse, NY—April 3, 2009

I spent the last two days doing my usual; running around on errands, visiting friends and going to the library for research. I got a couple more responses from the Craigs List ad but there was nothing that really made me want to jump up and holler. I hadn't heard anything from the local girl that wrote me and I was kind of glad about that. I wasn't really interested in her but if she had sent a picture and she was a real fox, I would have had a problem. Even though I didn't have a current relationship, my normal thinking patterns have been known to have been misdirected in the past by the essence of a beautiful woman. In other words, where I normally consider the total package of a person before making judgment, when beauty enters, logic has sometimes flown the coop.

By mid-afternoon, I had narrowed my decision on an online business down to either selling medical products or building a website to sell computer generated astrology products. I liked both ideas but both of them were fairly well saturated on the web. I decided to check my mail one more time for the day.

The first email in the box was from none other than, the girl from Kentucky, Roxanne. I opened it up and read:

"You must have a lot of confidence to wear a silly wig like that. I like that in a man. I laughed when I saw it and thought to myself that this was a guy who must be a lot of fun to be with. The picture of you in the suit is nice too.

Here's a little more about myself. I'm 54 years old; all my kids are grown; my youngest is graduating from Syracuse University next month, my other daughter lives in Verona, NY and my son is in the army in South Carolina.

I found a picture of myself that was taken at my house. I was frantic because I can't remember the last time I wasn't camera-shy but I did want to prove to you that I don't live under a bridge or something like that.

If you don't respond, I'll understand. By the way, my friends call me Roxie. I hope to hear from you soon."

I looked at the picture. She was beautiful. She was standing in some sort of hallway with a pair of slacks and a white knit sweater on. This wasn't a hi-definition picture but you could see that she had a figure, a very beautiful face, and that stunning red hair. My pulse rate jumped about 10 points as I stared at that face.

I must be out of my mind, I thought to myself. I'm going ga-ga over a girl I've never met; one that lives 900 miles away. What's wrong with me?

But I kept thinking about it. Here was a woman who looked like my dream girl, owned a farm in approximately the same location that I wanted to move to, had no baggage to speak of, had an online business and knew people up here in New York. I couldn't keep from looking at that face and fantasizing. I immediately dashed off another email to her:

"Roxie; Got your email and picture. Thank you so much. I got a laugh about the 'living under a bridge' part. But looking at your picture, I don't think you have too much to worry about."

I wrote a few more details of my life, things that I thought she might like to know, attached another picture I had of me and sent her a joke, just to get a read on where her sense of humor was. It was a simple one-liner, but it was the kind of joke that could gauge laugh sense and IQ:

"What do gay termites have for breakfast?"

?

?

?

"Woodpeckers"

Click . . . off it went.

I called Maggie into the computer room. "Maggs, what do you think of my dream-girl?"

She looked at her picture and said "Where did you get that?"

I told her this was the girl from Kentucky; one of the responses I got from the Craigs List ad. I gave her a brief overview of what Roxie had told me about the farm, the online business, being divorced and the rest.

"She's cute. How old is she?"

"She says she's 54, but she looks younger, don't you think?"

"Well don't get all squirrelly over a picture, Mark" she said, "you can do a lot with Photoshop."

"I know" I said, "but she's got the looks, the body, a business, a home. Can't I just have a little fantasy?"

"I guess," she replied and went back to her desk.

The next couple of days were the same. We emailed back and forth. With every email, she would add her phone number and tell me to call her. I didn't jump on that option of calling her because (1) I was enjoying my fantasy and (2) it cost me minutes on my cell phone and I'm cheap. I thought it better to get to know one another better before we actually spoke.

She told me a bit more of herself. How she and her ex used to own a construction company down in St. Augustine, Florida and even though they were divorced, she had kept the contracts for maintenance on some of the bigger apartment complexes. Every once in a while, she would have to go down there to make a bid or oversee a current project. She also had her Real Estate license in New York and Florida, which was one of the reasons she was considering a move back to New York.

I thought to myself what an industrious woman this was. Running an organic farm could not be a piece of cake, but to have to deal with construction crews and keep up with the codes had to be a positive nightmare. I asked her how she kept up with it all.

"I'm a naturally healthy person" She wrote. "I believe hard work tends to keep you young and that you will have plenty of time to slack off when you finally die. It's not the organic farm or the construction that makes me tired. It's not being able to relax. There is always something that has to be done; has to be done by me, because I'm all I've got."

I liked that attitude. In fact, it was very similar to my own. I was industrious also, but I learned a long time ago not to bite off more than I could chew. I thought about what we had been talking about and finally, I got up the nerve to give her a call.

The ring tone in my cell phone went on and on for about 8 rings. I was just ready to hang up when the call was picked up.

"Hello," a beautiful voice answered. I have a sharp ear for tonal quality and this was a very soothing, beautiful sounding voice. My pulse rate jumped another 10 notches.

"Hi Roxie, it's Mark; how are you doing?"

The conversation was magical. She said that she was so glad that I called and thought that maybe I hadn't called sooner because I didn't like her. We did a lot of small talk about her family, my family, life in New York, life in Kentucky. And we made a pact to talk again. With that I hung up and pondered the experience I had just been through.

I have to admit that after that initial call, I was hooked on Roxie. I didn't care how many other responses to my ad I got, I liked this woman. I liked her looks, her voice, her sense of humor, everything.

I went home that night and put the TV on. But every 5 minutes or so, her voice drifted back into my head. Maybe it was because I had not had an intellectually stimulating conversation with a female in a while, or maybe it was that deep, down inside, whether I wanted to admit it or not, I was lonely. But the fact remains that I could not get my mind off this woman. Finally at 11:30, amidst thoughts of the day's events, I fell asleep.

And I heard singing.

* * *

3) Falling Too Fast

Syracuse, NY—April 8, 2009

It had been a week since I first had contact with Roxie. I followed my day-to-day exercise of going to the library and taking care of all of my errands. The past weekend had been a bit of a break because I took time out to go to a local psychic fair. Being an astrologer, or at least a student of astrological studies, I'm always interested in having readings done to gauge whether my predictions are genuine. I have found over the years that I am good at prediction for other people, but when it comes to me, my emotion and intellect get in the way and basically, I suck at it.

I went from booth to booth, looking for an astrologer to do a reading for me but for some reason, they were not in evidence at this show. All I saw were tea-leaf readers, runes readers, tarot readers and the obligatory booths that sold healing potions, magical charms and other occult junk. I know that there are some real psychics out there in the world who are sensitive to hidden things. But I also know there are some real charlatans who are just in it for the money. I wanted an astrologer because they are the only ones who, in my Christian beliefs, follow the path of God. There is a lot of occult entanglement that comes from negative or satanic sources. I am aware of that and try to stay as far away as possible.

But astrology is God given. It is not fortune telling as much as it is an assessment of the character of the individual and his response to planetary vibrations. Astrology only deals with potential and free will is always involved.

But for some reason, I could not find one who practices the cosmic craft. Maybe it was fate or maybe they all stayed away because they had more important commitments. I guess I'll never know. Looking back, I should have left too, but I had this $ 50 bill burning a hole in my pocket and I really wanted to know if, by chance, someone might be able to tell me something about Roxie. I finally selected an open set at a psychic reader who claimed to be a specialist in the ways of a Medicine Man. He was, supposedly a 4th generation American Indian with an extreme sensitivity to coming events.

As I sat there listening to him tell me about my life events, none of which I could remember because they probably happened in a past life, I couldn't shake the image of a field full of cows. The reading continued for about 30 minutes and the overall assessment by this reader, was that my life would never change until I moved down south. At that point, it would take a radical turn for the better, according to the medicine man.

Again, the image of cows kept coming back and as I paid my money and left, I realized that I was thinking what a bunch of bullshit this was.

When I finally got back to the library on Monday, my email box had another 12 or 13 posts from a variety of sources. My eyes immediately caught 2 from Roxie. The rest of them would have to wait as I gave her my undivided attention.

There were emails, of course, but also lengthy phone calls. We always talked at night when I got home and it was private. But more and more, Roxie was calling me during the day to tell me the weather or ask me a question or something. If she caught me at an inconvenient time I would just let the phone take it and put it into voice mail. Then I would return the call to her as soon as I got free. She knew I always had my cell phone with me and could reach me at all hours; so she did. She told me that she was growing very fond of our conversations. That they were the highlight of her day and even though I was burning up minutes, she just loved to hear the sound of my voice.

"You don't know what that voice does to me Mark," she said, "I had forgotten how nice it was to hear a soothing tone. I just wish you were here so I could look at your handsome face at the same time."

I liked talking to her too. She had a nice, soothing voice and even though I had seen the few pictures she had sent me, I could close my eyes and visualize her being in the room with me. And because I was not opposed to another romantic relationship, I thought about how nice it would be for me to feel a woman's touch; the smell of her hair; the caress of her lips. I had to admit, I was lonely. I was about as dissatisfied with my love-life as a greyhound on a leash. I definitely wanted change and Roxie was making it hard to not want to just pack up and move to Kentucky. She was definitely making it hard.

We talked about her business interests there and how difficult it would be to just shelve everything and move up to New York. She agreed and said that it would take some doing but she was going to make some changes in her life and that was just one option. She admitted that with all of her antiques that she sold on EBay, doing the construction trips and taking care of her animals, it might be a year before she could do anything.

"Animals?" I asked. "What animals are you talking about?"

"I have a dog, a cat, chickens, goats and I board race horses on my property."

"Do you mean race horses like Kentucky Sorenson race horses?" I said.

"Exactly . . . My neighbor has horses at the Sorenson and whichever ones weren't up in Lexington, he boarded here. He pays me to feed them, board them and brush them out once a week,"

"Jesus," I said, "don't you have enough on your plate?"

"Oh, it's not bad." she said, "right now there's only two there. In the fall, he may have 2 more, but it depends on whether he sells them or not."

Being a Sagittarius, I have natural love for horses; horses and unicorns. But I hadn't ever seen any unicorns. So hearing about her boarding them on her property pushed her ratings up another couple of rungs.

I had sent her some listings of my favorite musical artists. These included Porcupine Tree, ELP, Genesis, YES and Pink Floyd. She had already gotten the email from me about my love for progressive rock and she said that she was a music lover too.

"I know all those bands except Porcupine Tree," she said, "and there was another one that you sent that I had never heard of before either; Spock's Beard, I think. As a matter of fact, I have YES on my Facebook profile."

Wham . . . The killer comment. My favorite band, above everyone else, was YES. I had been in love with their music since 1970; had seen every tour they ever did except one and had all their CD's, including some rare import pressings.

"YES is my favorite band," I said, "I've followed them for a long, long time. I can't believe you have them on Facebook."

"Oh, I really like them too," she continued, "they make such good music and they are excellent musicians."

"Have you ever seen them 'live'?"

"No, I've never been in the right place at the right time."

Well, this was a new wrinkle in our conversations that I had not expected or could have even anticipated.

So let me just review the situation: Here's a woman; a very beautiful woman with a beautiful body. Who is also a natural Redhead, that I'm into; Who owns an organic farm, that I'm into; Who has an online business, that I'm into; Who seems to be very motivated, that I'm into. Who has a good communication skill and a pretty good sense of humor, that I'm into; who boards horses, that I'm into; And on top of it all, loves my favorite band, YES.

"Honey," I said. "I can't believe how many things we match up on. Do you feel energy between us, or am I the only one who's in la-la land?"

"Mark, I felt a connection the first time we spoke." she explained "When I lived in Syracuse, I was the understudy of Chief Shenandoa, head of the Onondaga Indians. I studied under him for 3 years. If you didn't know it by now, I am very psychic."

"I'm not psychic, but I am an astrologer," I said. "I did your horoscope and couldn't believe the synergy between us. But until we began talking, I never realized how potent the connections were. It's almost like a gift from the universe that we met."

"Oh, Mark," she breathed "I feel the same thing too. I didn't want to say anything because I was afraid of scaring you away. But it's there. I used to read Tarot Cards and Runes to look into the future. As soon as I began talking to you, something told me to throw them away."

"I also used to read Tarot until I realized that the energy was so negative. Now I just do my astrology because I try to follow the ways of a good Christian. But, I'm not throwing anything about you away. I think you are a definite keeper."

We continued our conversation until about 11:00 p.m. The topics included more about life in Kentucky, her children, music and what the next step in our relationship should be.

"Mark, I want you to come down here and visit." she announced, "No commitments, No drama; just a visit so that we can meet face-to-face."

"Roxie, I would love to do that but right now, I've budgeted all my money out for the rest of the month. I get paid again on May 3rd and I could probably do it then."

"OK," she said with a sullen voice, "make me suffer. It's just that our conversations are so lively and fresh. I haven't had this much fun talking to someone in years. All the people down here have the intellectual agility of small soap dishes."

"Ha," I laughed, "Great line."

"No, it's true," she continued, "there are some truly dumb people here and I think I've met every one of them. That's another reason I was thinking of moving back to New York; just to get away from it."

"Tell you what, Roxie," I said. "Let's table this discussion for now and think about everything. If we still feel the same way about a visit in a couple of days, I plug it into my social calendar."

"Oh, you're too kind." She bubbled.

"Really, I'm serious. I don't want to build you up or me up, by promising a visit and then have a change of heart. I want to think about it and let you think about it."

"All right," she said, "we'll talk again, I'm sure. But I have to tell you something."

"What would that be, my dear," was my reply.

"Every day, I'm feeling more and more attracted to you and every day I want to see where this will lead to," She blurted. "There, I've said what's on my mind."

"Roxie, I'm feeling the same and I can't wait until we talk again . . . Until tomorrow?"

"Tomorrow it is," she said, "but tonight is going to be restless for me. Goodnight Honey"

"Goodnight Honey."

We hung up and I sat there holding the phone in my hand, mesmerized. What had happened? My stomach was all butterflies and I felt like I was walking on Holy Water. Why was I feeling this way about someone whom I had just started talking to a week ago, and had never met? I never felt like this in my entire life. I had to stop and go to bed. I had a full day the next day and not only needed my sleep, but wanted to dream about what could be when I finally met Roxie. Would she look like her pictures? Would she really be as nice as our conversations said she was? Is she a soul-mate? What would my friends say when I told them I met this girl on the Internet. There were a million questions, but for now, I needed to rest and it was bedtime.

I didn't bother to admit to myself, that I'd like to go to bed with her too.

* * *

4) Phone Madness

Syracuse, NY—April 11, 2009

The week went by as usual. I did my research routine at the library, followed up on my appointments, visited friends and talked to Roxie at least 3 times a day. Even though I had asked her to hold her calls to me until after 9:00 p.m., when I got free cellular minutes, she kept making 'Quickie' calls during the day. It might be something as simple as just asking how I made out at the doctors' office or how my day going, but the fact was, she kept calling. Her excuse was always the same.

"Honey, I just love to hear your voice," she said, "and I'll keep it brief until tonight."

It seemed petty for me to complain about something so simple and actually I liked the attention. I thought to myself that if she was like this now, what it would be like when I finally met her. One of the things that was on her mind was getting me down to Kentucky 'post haste'. I already had planned to go down there in May when I got my Social Security check, but she kept insisting that she needed me now.

"Baby, I just can't afford it right now," I said. "May is only 3 weeks away and we'll see what happens then."

"How much would it cost to take a bus?" she asked, "I'd be glad to advance you the money for that."

Now that sounded like an interesting proposal. A bus ride would be a pain in the ass but I really had nothing else pressing to do. Besides, I could go down there, meet this gal and if it didn't spark between us, just grab another bus back home. Since she had offered to advance me the money of the ticket, and I intended to pay it back to her, worse case scenario is that I'd only be out a couple of hundred bucks.

"I don't know," I said "I've never even thought of taking Greyhound. Is there a bus station in town?"

"No," she replied, "but there's one in Bowling Green. It's only about an hour away and I could drive and pick you up. It's really not that far."

"Ok, why don't you check into it on your end and I'll check here to see what kind of schedule I can get."

"I'll find out and call you back tonight," she said, "Can you feel the smile on my face?"

"Keep smiling, I'll talk to you later."

Since I was online anyway, I went to the Greyhound web page and entered in the departure and arrival information they requested. There were several options available for schedules but the long and short of it was that the trip would be a minimum of 19 hours. Ugh, 19 hours on a bus.

Oh well, as Tina Turner would say, 'what's love got to do with it.'

The thing that caught my eye was that if you book with a one-week advance notice, the ticket is only $ 65. I thought that was an excellent price and I decided to take a chance and book passage. I would be leaving on April 22nd at 7:00 p.m. and arrive on April 23rd at about 4 in the afternoon. That way, I could sleep most of the night and be 'fresh as a daisy' when I saw my honey for the first time. Except for a shower . . . maybe we could take one . . . no, stop that Mark.

I put in the required credit card info and got a confirmation. I could pick the ticket up anytime at the station but could not board luggage until departure. I immediately pulled up my astrology software and cast a chart for the time of my departure.

Libra rising in the chart indicated a question about relationships and this certainly fit the bill. All of the planetary aspects looked good and that made me happy. It told me that I would have a great trip to Kentucky. To say the least, it was difficult to contain my excitement. Roxie called later that night and told me essentially the same thing about the bus schedules. I didn't mention that I had already booked passage because I wanted to see if her offer was still open about advancing the money. $ 65 wasn't a great amount but it cut into my walk-around money, which I didn't like to do since I was on an austerity budget. I also didn't mention that it was 7:35 p.m. and not 9:00 p.m.

Another call that was costing me money.

"There are busses that leave Syracuse on Monday next week," she said, "it's between 19 and 23 hours depending on which route you take. You could be here on Tuesday."

"Well, that's all fine and well, but it's a little rushed for me. I don't even have the funds to get a one-way ticket, much less a round trip."

"I told you I would loan you the money, honey," and then she followed with "Did you think I was joking?"

"No, but that's only 4 days away," I said. "I don't want you wiring money or anything like that. How about if you just send me a check. I can pay you back when I get there."

"Ok, I'll send the money tomorrow only if you promise to reserve a trip tomorrow."

"I promise," I said. "I have to look at the schedules and figure out what's best. Let me call you back around 9 tonight. There is a show on History Channel that I want to watch and as soon as it's over, I'll give you a call."

"Oh, don't go," She pleaded.

"No, I'm serious. I really want to watch this show and after 9, I get free minutes." I insisted. "Besides, you will have me all to yourself then."

"Alright, but call, OK?" again she sounded forlorn.

"Yes Dear, I'll talk to you soon." and I ended the call.

I clicked on the History Channel and started watching a show on the history of the Freemasons. My dad was a Mason and I had thought about joining a long time ago, but just never got around to it. I really didn't know anything about them except that they were a secret society and had been around a long time. I was about 10 minutes into the show when the phone rang. I looked at the caller ID and guess who, Roxie.

"Yes, Dear," I answered.

"Do you know that you are so sexy?" She asked. "I was just looking at your pictures that you sent and a thrill ran down my spine."

"Honey, it's not 9 yet. I told you, I'd call."

"But I miss you," she said, "and I want to be with you."

"I'll call. Now let me watch this show till then."

"Ok, bye," and she hung up.

I went back to the show and was starting to get intrigued and no more than 5 minutes passed when the phone rang again. Son of a bitch, I muttered as I picked up the phone and looked at the ID. It was Roxie again.

"What!" I said as I answered the phone.

"Are you enjoying your show?" She asked.

"I was. Now leave me alone until 9 dammit," and again, I hung up the phone.

I was starting to get a little pissed. What part of no didn't she understand? I went back to watching the show and over the course of 45 minutes; she called a total of 22 times. I never answered again and just let the voice mail take the calls. I figured that if I ignored her, she would quit calling. But the calls kept coming in about every 2 or 3 minutes. I finally turned the phone off so that I didn't have to listen to that incessant ringing. Promptly at 9:01 p.m., I called her. She picked up the phone and I could tell that she had been crying.

"Roxie, what's wrong?" I asked.

"When you wouldn't answer my calls, I figured that you just wanted me to send you money and I would never hear from you again . . . It hurt."

"Honey," I said in a soft voice, "I told you that I really wanted to watch this show and I told you that I would call. When you kept calling and interrupting me, I just turned off the phone. What would you have done?"

"I don't know," she sniffed, "I just miss you so much and I'm afraid that if I don't keep reminding you, maybe you will lose interest or something."

"No, I'm not losing interest, but give me a break. I asked you to hold the calls off until after 9 and you still call me during the day. And I wanted to catch this show and nothing was going to get in my way. I'm sorry if I upset you, forgive me?"

"Why can't you get out your teleporter and come down now . . . I need you."

"If only it was that easy, I'd do it in a heartbeat."

We continued the conversation for another hour and finally I said I had to go. We ended the call with mock kisses on the phone and then she told me that she would try to behave in the future.

"Ok, I'll let you go for tonight," she said, "but you know I'm going to be having some vivid dreams tonight."

There was a pause and I said, "You're not the Lone Ranger."

"I love you," she told me, "do you love me too?"

I had to think a minute with what I had just heard. I know that she could sense the pause in the conversation as I tried to weigh the consequences of whatever answer I gave.

"I'm starting to feel that way Roxie," I said. "I've never felt so strongly about a person in my life."

"I wasn't going to say anything" she continued "but it's just something I've been feeling for a couple of days and I know how much you admire honesty. That's why I said it."

"It's great being loved, isn't it?" was my reply.

"Good Night my love," were her last words that night.

I told her good night and hung up. What was going on? Am I under some kind of spell or something? Thirteen days ago, I had never heard of Roxanne Patrick. Now I'm practically married to her. But the draw was so incredible. We clicked on every conversation we had, we liked most of the same things. She seemed like a sensitive, caring person and apart from the fact that I hadn't had sex in awhile. I really liked her personality and everything else I was learning about her. Still, it's crazy. I should have kept coy about things, but being outspoken, I just blurted it out. Well, I had the night to think about things and I'd see if she actually sent a check. And for the night, I was just going to go to sleep and try to open my mind to the universe and let it guide me.

What else could I do?

* * *

5) A Ticket to Destiny

Syracuse, NY—April 15, 2009

The next day started out on a sour note. I went out to my car and it wouldn't start. I checked the interior lights and found that I had somehow left the parking lights on the evening before.

Terrific I thought. There's not a soul around to give me a jump start. I'm going to have to hook up Les's battery charger and wait for it to put some zip in the battery. Since it was a trickle charger, I knew it would be at least an hour before I could leave the house.

I went in the garage and found the charger and plugged it in. Naturally, when I went to hook up the cables to the battery, one of them broke off. So now I have another thing to fix. Why is it, my entire life, I have to fix things before I can use them. So back in the garage I went with charger in hand. It wasn't a big job putting the connecter back on the cable, just another aggravation in my life. With that done, I went back out and hooked everything up. The charger read "Zero."

"What the fuck?" I said to no one in particular, "I can't believe this bullshit."

I whacked the charger on the top with a screwdriver and the gauge popped up to the charging level that it was supposed to be. "Thank you," I said and walked back into the house.

I did busy work for the next couple of hours. Straightening my files, cleaning up, making sure I had everything in my briefcase for when I finally took off. I went outside and clicked the ignition switch on. "Brroomm." The car started. "Thank you," I said again.

I put everything away, got my briefcase and took off for the library. Just as I was pulling out of the driveway, the mailman came. I decided to check the mail before I left. In the box, I found a letter from R. Patrick of Burkesville, KY. I tore open the envelope and found a postal money order for $ 65.00. No note, no lipstick on the envelope; just the check. I put it in my wallet and headed for the library, my first stop.

"Hey Maggie," I said as I walked in the front door, "now I've got women paying me."

I showed her the check I had just received and she looked at me with a cynical eye and said "Mark, what kind of line of crap did you give her for that?"

I told her that Roxie had offered to pay my bus fare down to visit her. Me, being broke, gladly accepted. "So I'm going to Kentucky for a while to see if we are compatible."

One of the other library girls approached me and said, "Mark, you'd better be careful. We don't want to have to send out the hounds to find you. Weird things happen down in them 'thar woods."

"Yea, yea, yea," I smirked, "I'm just going for a visit. It's not like I'm moving there right away. And if I do decide to do that, I'll bring her up here with me, so I can get your approval."

"Yes, Mark," Maggie said, "if you make it."

I went in the computer room and set up my laptop. The first thing I did was check my email. There were a few jokes from my friends, a few junk mails, but nothing of real interest; nothing from Roxie. So I decided I would call her.

"Hey babe, what are you wearing?" was my opening line.

"I got nothing on but the radio," She replied.

"Ooh baby, I'll be right down. Got your check today and got my reservations all made."

"Oh, Honey, Honey, when are you coming?" She shouted with excitement.

"I leave here on April 22nd and will be there the afternoon of the 23rd. I'm coming into Bowling Green."

"Great. Oh, Honey, I'm so excited," she said, "but I'm nervous too. I've never done this before."

"That sounds like a line from a porno flick."

"Oh, do you watch them?" She asked.

"No, but I'd be a liar if I told you I'd never seen one before. What kind of movies do you like? I can bring some down with me."

"I can't watch anything right now," She said, "my DVD player is broken and I don't have cable."

"No problem," I said "I've got a DVD player I'll give you. I'll pack it with me and we can watch some new videos. I'll bring an assortment of romance, action, comedies and concert videos."

"Mark, you just keep doing things to impress me."

For the next week, AT&T made a lot of money on my cellular phone charges. We talked at least 4 or 5 times a day, deep into the night and with every conversation, I felt myself being pulled closer and closer to Roxie. She always ended her conversations with 'I Love You' and I found myself replying with 'I Love You, Too'. It seemed so natural; like wearing an old shoe. I could hear the anticipation in her voice and she could hear it in mine. In one conversation, she told me that when we meet, I was not to have any contact with her immediately.

"Just what do you mean by no contact immediately," I asked.

"Mark, I just want to gaze at you," She said. "I'm so afraid that if I have any contact with you, I will lose all control and I don't want to do that in public."

"Roxie," I said, "what makes you think I have that much control myself?"

"No, No, No, Mark," she demanded, "I'm serious. No hugs, No kisses; nothing in the way of contact until I feel its right . . . especially not in public."

"Your wish is my command," I said. "You have complete control over me. Think about it. I'm in an alien State, I don't know anybody, including you and I'm broke."

"Well," she said, "I guess when you put it that way; I do have a bit of control."

Now that was something different.

* * *

6) The Long Bus Ride

Syracuse to Kentucky—April 23, 2009

Anticipation churned inside me like a tempest in a teapot. I was so exited to be finally getting to meet my dream lady. Even though this was only to be a short term visit, I thought that I had convinced myself that I was in love already. My friend Michelle took me to the Greyhound terminal and we hugged and kissed goodbye. I bought myself a sandwich at Subway and sat there eating, thinking how great it was going to be to have our first meeting of the blue eyes, our first embrace and possibly, our first lovemaking session.

The bus ride was torture. It was chilly in the bus, even though it was late April. I think it is standard policy to run the air conditioning all year. The seats were definitely not what you would call first class. I sat next to some rough looking Mexican chick with greasy hair and tattoos all over every visible part of her body. The bulk of the other riders were either Amish or Mennonites, dressed out in their wide brim bowler hats and linen bandanas. I tried to sleep, but anticipation and lack of comfort made that a lost cause.

We made stops in Rochester, Buffalo, Cleveland, Cincinnati and finally after 19 hours, we pulled into Bowling Green, KY; at about 3 p.m. My eyes scanned the empty parking lot looking for a redhead. As the bus came around the building, there she was.

She wore a tan skirt, dark green lacy top and sunglasses. I couldn't get a really good glimpse of her face or her body, but the package looked inviting.

"Hi Roxie," I said as I casually strolled off the exit steps.

"Oh my God, you are even more than I imagined," She replied.

Well this gave my ego a tremendous boost. "How was the trip?" She asked.

I was stunned momentarily as she came up and gave me a huge hug and a kiss on the cheek.

"Well, I made it."

The thing about a kiss is, as soon as you get one, you want another. I especially felt on top of the world because Roxie was indeed beautiful. Not that I haven't gone out with beautiful women before . . . or that I'm a troll or something. But it had been a while since I had felt a warm caress. And the press of her 36″ chest up against me didn't hurt either.

I backed up and gazed at her, taking in everything at once. Her breasts defied gravity. Her tummy was as flat and firm as a bar top. Her butt was so tight; I doubted whether I could even get a good bite out of it. She was a natural red head and my mind kept thinking about that patch of pubic hair I might see, that would surely drive me crazy. All in all, I was impressed with the package.

"Hey," I said, "what about all that talk of just looking at each other for a while when we first meet"

"Sorry, I know that's what I said but . . . hmmm . . . never mind. We do have one slight little snag though."

Oh great, I thought. This is where she tells me that she is still married and her husband came home unexpectedly.

"And what would that be?" I queried.

"Well, there's a young kid here that came in on the bus before you. He's been here for about 3 hours and he needs a ride to Glasgow. I told him that I didn't think you would mind. It's right on the way that we will be going."

This came out of nowhere. I've just met this lady and she's got another rider in her car. I certainly hope she doesn't plan on robbing me because I'm broke.

"I'm OK with that," I said, "Where is Glasgow anyway?"

"It's right up the road about twenty miles. We go right by his motel on the road to my house."

"Ok, let's go. How far is it to your house?"

"It's about thirty-eight miles or so, from Glasgow. A straight shot down Route 90. Where is your suitcase?"

"Well, I actually brought everything in a box. I brought a DVD player for you because you said yours had died, and clothes, my laptop and a spare laptop because you said your computer was on the fritz. I'm pretty good with computers so maybe I can get your other one fixed. Over the years, I've acquired a couple of spare units, so you can have this one if you want. I also brought a bunch of other goodies, just to impress you."

"You can quit trying to impress me by being a brainiac too. I was already impressed by our conversations and I'm already impressed with what I'm looking at. The brains are just icing on the cake. We'll just see if you can impress me later. Let's go"

I was immediately struck with three physical sensations at the same time. Her response was a nice compliment but I also caught the subtle undercurrent about impressing her later.

I had a smile on my face, a lump in my throat and a chub in my pants.

We picked up 'Jackie' inside the terminal and after a quick introduction we loaded my box of goodies in her '96 Camry and took off. Jackie, the rider, sat in the back seat and I have to admit that I was a bit nervous in this situation. We chit-chatted about a few things and he disclosed that he had come down from Indiana to meet up with a girl he met on the Internet. Now I'm really feeling strange. I wanted to ask if the girl's name was Roxie but I figured that would possibly get me stranded in Bowling Green with no money.

"So where are you staying Jackie?" I asked.

"I've got a room at a motel in Glasgow. I figured I'd give my girl a call as soon as I got situated."

The conversation went on as we made our trek. Roxie pretty much kept quiet and listened to Jackie and I babble about computers, work ethics and Internet dating. He was actually a likable young guy and I relaxed a bit. We got into Glasgow and Jackie couldn't remember the name of the motel. I felt relieved when we finally pulled into what he thought was familiar and we let him out.

"Enjoy your stay," I said as he walked up the driveway to the Motel Office.

"Yeah you too . . . nice meeting you Mark."

I couldn't help notice that he only addressed me. He didn't say 'nice meeting both of you' or 'thanks for the ride' or anything like that. But alas, it was Roxie and I on our way to her twenty-three acre farm and my beginning of an excellent adventure.

We made our way down Route 90, a two-lane road of hills and gullies. As soon as we were out of the city limits, the landscape stretched out to become a series of farms. There were cows, sheep, horses, goats. I hadn't seen this many animals at one time since the last time I was at the zoo.

"Wow, this is farmland down here. I know Kentucky is called the Bluegrass State but how do they get the color back in the grass with all these animals?"

"Funny man," she said, "you haven't seen anything yet if you think this is farmland. Wait till we get to my place."

"How did you come to live here anyway?" I asked.

"Well, my ex husband and I were tired of Florida and I wanted to start an organic farm. He made good money in our construction company and so we decided that we would move where we could get a little bang for our buck. I did research on the Internet and looked at a lot of places online. So we left Florida and came up here to review the properties that were being offered. As soon as I saw my place, I fell in love with it. It's secluded, no traffic and plenty of room for me to set my garden up."

"So I take it that he is not here anymore?"

"Thank God, no. We got divorced last year and he went back to Canada. He can stay there and rot for all I care."

"Jesus, Roxie, don't hold back. Tell me what you really think."

"Sorry I sound bitter," she said, "but we didn't have the best of married life. But I don't want to talk about him."

It was a definitive statement and I thought better about pursuing it any deeper. I figured that sooner or later I would learn more, but for right now, I wanted her to be relaxed and so I just shut up. On and on we went down Route 90, past towns like Forty-Four, Summer Shade, Beaumont, Dubre and then we came to a place called Marrowbone. Finally I just had to ask.

"I have to say, they have some strange little towns down here. Why would you call a town Marrowbone?"

"These are pretty much dumb old farmers down here. As you can tell, if you blink, you are through the town. And these people tend to take care of their own so I'm sure that there are properties down here where the marrow has drained out of the bone of someone who did them wrong."

"Are you saying people they don't like just disappear?" I said in a shocked tone.

"Well, if you got a good 'ol boy that's maybe had a bit too much of the homebrew, and he gets tangled up with a farmers daughter that's not quite ripe, who knows. There are plenty of people down here that just disappear. What happens in Burkesville stays in Burkesville."

Roxie looked at me and said, "So watch your step buster."

I have to tell you. At this point I wasn't quite sure I liked what I was hearing. I didn't really know whether she meant to watch my step in general, or with her.

"How much further do we have to go?" I asked.

"We are going to turn off the road up here a bit and then it's about six miles to my farm. We'll be there in 15, 20 minutes. Are you ready to eat?"

A little smile crossed my face as I said "It depends on what's on the menu."

"Funny Man."

True to her word we turned off the road on to what looked to be a small highway, almost two cars wide. If you were to pass an oncoming car or truck, both drivers would have to nudge over to the side to get clearance. But at least it was paved. We drove on for about four miles and then the fun began. We turned off on to a gravel road, a little over one-car wide. Farms appeared on the left and right about every half mile or so and low hanging trees brushed the sides of the Camry as we passes. Finally, we went over a half washed-out dirt road, over a rise and there it was; home.

"Honey, we're home." She said.

The farmhouse was a barn board structure with a long front porch. A mother and two baby goats bleated their welcome to us as well as a large Rottweiler with a massive chest and an angry bark.

"That's Riley my dog," She said. "He doesn't take well to strangers, so you better let me introduce you first."

I have always had a good affinity with animals and I wasn't afraid of Riley. I just opened the car door up and greeted him with a "Hey Big Puppy." I cautiously let him sniff me and almost instantly, we were new best friends.

Riley turned out to indeed be a big puppy and he nuzzled up to me like I had been gone forever; much to the chagrin of Roxie. I could tell by the slight scowl on her face that she wasn't real pleased that her guard dog wasn't really guarding; her anyway.

"He never does that." She said. "He won't even let the meter reader on the property."

"What can I say; animals like me. I've always gotten along with them. And besides, he's just a big 'ol puppy, aren't you Riley?"

She opened the trunk and I grabbed the box of goodies that I had brought down. We walked up on to the porch, via a set of broken steps.

"Watch your step," she said, "I have been meaning to fix them but there is always something going on and I just haven't got to it."

"I'll just put that on my project list for you," I said. "I'm here to visit and get to know you and maybe start to set up my online business. That's it. So your wish is my command dear lady"

"You know," she quipped, "I like that in my men."

We stepped into the front room and I thought I was visiting a rummage sale. There was crap all over the house. The table was piled high with candles, antique pumps, canned fruits and boxes from the Post Office and UPS. The walls were lined with an eclectic assortment of litho prints, paintings and wall ornaments. Near the ceiling were two large and long shelves that held brass pots, cowboy hats, glazed cattle antlers and incense burners. A true potpourri of what I would call junk. But I'm no expert. I never really did get into antiques.

I liked to watch "Antiques Road Show" on TV but that's about as close as I ever came to collectibles; except for my records. Those I had. As I said, music was a big part of my life. I started collecting a lot of LP's in '75 and I had a shit load of them. It was mostly rock, but some contemporary and easy listening. At one time I had over 10,000 records in my collection. But carting them around the country with all the moves I made as a contract engineer was a drag and so I pared down the collection to about 2500 or so.

"Please excuse the mess," she said, "but I sell a lot of this on EBay and need to keep them handy so I know what to advertise. I've got a nice dinner planned for us tonight when you get settled. We don't have to eat right now and besides, I want to get something straight between you and me."

"Excuse Me?" I said.

With that, she approached me, put her arms around my neck and proceeded to tenderly kiss my lips. It happened so fast that I was caught off guard but my body took over and I responded the way one would expect. Who am I to complain? It was mid afternoon, the door wasn't locked, and the windows were wide open. I had just met this woman for the first time less than an hour ago and I didn't care. Passion flowed and quite frankly, I wanted her.

Our mouths opened up and we proceed to get into a fantastic game of tonsil hockey. Her hot breath and body rhythms sent me a signal that I could not deny. Nor did I want to. We fell together on the couch and began to sensuously remove each others clothing. It was mid afternoon, the door wasn't locked, and the windows were wide open. I had just met this woman for the first time less than an hour ago and I didn't care. Passion was flowing and quite frankly, I wanted her.

I would be lying if I said that I wasn't nervous. Maybe both of us were. But that didn't stop nature from taking her course. I slipped my hand up under her dark green lacy top while kissing her. The nipple stood erect like a guard at Buckingham Palace. Immediately I went for the gusto by lifting up her bra and enjoying the feel of that supple titty.

It had been so long between lovers for me, that making love to Roxie was the only thing on my mind at the moment. I laid her back against the pillow on the couch, lifted off the shirt and bra in a smooth motion and planted my waiting lips upon her neck, and slowly moved to her breasts. As that happened, I reached down and undid her tan slacks. Slipping my hand inside her panties, I found a wonderful mound that was so fine and soft, that I had to take a closer look.

Down came the pants and panties and I was staring at a beautiful, nicely trimmed red little bush. My mouth went into automatic mode as I leaned closer and kissed her torso. Slowly I moved downward to that crevice between her creamy thighs and kissed, lightly at first and then slid my tongue inside her.

She moaned as I began to explore that heavenly spot. My fingers slid up her leg and joined in the action. First one and then two slid inside her and I felt the awesome wetness as I probed and licked her. Her moaning increased.

By now I was as hard as a rock and somehow mysteriously, my pants came off. I say mysteriously because I don't remember doing it myself. But I do know that I didn't want any distractions or obstacles from man's world or nature to interfere. I deftly slid into her and watched her face. Her eyes were closed but upon my entrance, her mouth opened up and I not only heard, but saw the moan. I began slow rhythmic gyrations, moving slowly in and out of her.

She matched my tempo with the rise and fall of her hips. Together we played a symphony and within thirty or so thrusts, we reached a crescendo. I won't say that it was the best lovemaking session I have ever had, but given the circumstance of the newness and my duration of abstinence, I thought it was extremely satisfying for both of us.

"My God woman, what have you done?" I said breathlessly.

"Was that a better ride than the Greyhound?" She answered.

"I know it was smoother and the accommodations were nicer."

We got dressed and then she said to me, "how about those appetizers now?"

"I thought we already had that course." I said.

"Funny Man." She said.

"I've got crab coquettes, pepperoni and cheese and crackers and Brie; why don't I bring a plate out now for us to nibble on?"

I thought that was a great idea and nodded as I finished dressing. I went over and picked up my suitcase and asked her, "Where do you want me to put this?"

"Just take it upstairs to the bedroom. "She said. "That way it won't be underfoot."

I grabbed the suitcase and went upstairs into the bedroom. I was a large room with a small rug in one corner, an end table and a large bed along one wall and a lamp. When I came downstairs I asked, "I just see a bed up there. Where do you get dressed?"

"I have a dressing room down on this floor. Let me get this served and I'll give you the grand tour."

We nibbled on the appetizer plate and then we took a tour of the house. She showed me the bathroom, the dressing room, her office and a back bedroom with a full picture window.

"You can have this room," She said. "I don't use it and it used to be my ex-husbands room when we were getting divorced."

"You mean I have to sleep in here with no bed?" I asked.

"No silly, this is for those rare times when we are not in bed together."

I smiled and nodded. We went back into the living room and resumed nibbling on the platter and talking. All in all it was a long day, with the bus ride and then the ride from Bowling Green. But my appetite was sated, my horns were clipped and I felt supremely happy for our first day.

We gabbed and gabbed about our likes and dislikes, her past, my past, life in Burkesville and a myriad of non-essential topics. I loved listening to the beautiful tone of her voice; soothing and light like a whisper and tender as a thought. My gut feeling was that here was a caring loving individual that gave more than she took.

She told me about her employment last year at a nursing home and how all the patients loved her. She said that it was a temporary position that she took, just until she could get her organic farm going but that someday she would like to go full time into health care nursing. I admired her dedication and downright 'gumption' to try new things and to be able to keep a level head about her abilities and initiatives. At some point in the conversation, we decided that we weren't really hungry enough for dinner and the best thing that we could do would be to go to bed.

And that we did.

* * *

7) The Morning After

Burkesville, KY—April 24, 2009

The morning sun arrived like a soft pillow in a hazy room. I anticipated another fantastic day. I rose quietly, so as not to disturb my honey and went downstairs to fix coffee. Riley was hot on my ankles begging to be let out.

"Go find a rabbit boy," I said as I opened the front door. He answered with a 'woof' and proceeded to bolt down the porch steps and out into the fields.

I went into the bathroom and shaved my head and face. Even though it would be easier to use an electric razor, I grew up using a blade and still like the feel of lather on my face. I heard the coffee pot gurgle and knew it was time for my wake up potion. I poured a cup for me and one for Roxie. I like my coffee black but she told me that she likes hers with cream and a bit of sugar. As soon as she heard the fridge door open, Cloie, the Siamese cat, twisted and rubbed in and out of my legs. She knew I would take care of her with a bit of fresh milk.

I took our coffee cups upstairs and put them on the end table next to Roxie. She slept softly and her angelic face looked good even without any makeup. I leaned over and gently brushed my lips against her forehead, her nose and then her soft lips. Her eyes fluttered open and she laid there with those beautiful blue eyes peering into mine.

"Good Morning lover," I said, "I brought you coffee."

She put her arms around my neck and pulled me down for another kiss.

"I love the way you wake me up," She said as she kissed me again.

I returned the kiss and then found myself crawling back into the bed with her. My body responded as I put my hand on her left breast and felt the hardness of that pink nipple. She sighed softly as our mouths opened up and the passion flowed between us. She quickly found my reaction to her touch; gripped my hardness, and began a slow stroke.

I rolled over on to my back and pulled her on top of me. It was as natural as homemade butter, the way she straddled me. She mounted me and I knew from her wetness that this session would be a superb daybreak special. With every rise and fall I got harder and went deeper. I reached up with both hands as I gripped and caressed her breasts with my lips. She let out a soft coo and whispered "Yes, Oh Yes."

I responded with "Ride me baby, Ride me." She increased her downward plunges and I knew that I would not be able to control myself for very long.

I said "Baby, I'm going to cum." She answered with another "Oh Yes, cum inside me baby. We're cumming together. Ahhh Yes."

I exploded and I really think I went rib deep inside her. She let out a loud moan; I sensed her orgasm at the same time. There was an ever so slight dampness to her skin as she slowed down and finally collapsed on top of my chest. I kept pumping inside her until every drop of my love juice was expelled. We laid there together in each others arms and let our breathing resume to normal. She lifted up her torso and head, looked at me and said, "Now that's what I call a wake-up call."

"Well, I couldn't find the eggs in the fridge, so I just brought you some sausage."

"Funny Man." She chortled.

"After that appetizer, I'll have to cook you breakfast. What did you want to do today?"

"I'd like to go to Bowling Green and visit the Corvette Museum." I said.

"That's perfect. I need to go shopping anyway, so we can go to Wal-Mart, Aldi's, and wherever else you want to go. Do you know if the museum is open today?"

"Good question, I guess I better call and see . . . .Nah, let's just go to Bowling Green and check it out. If it's closed, we can go another time. We'll just get the shopping done and stop somewhere and have a few drinks. How does that sound?"

She smiled and said, "Sounds good to me. Just spending the day with you sounds good to me."

"Ok, I'm going to start getting my office stuff up," I said.

"I want to get the research done for setting up my new online business, when we aren't doing anything."

"You go do what you have to and I'll get breakfast going. OK?"

"You got it baby," I said as I kissed her one more time. She pushed me down on to the bed and began to kiss my chest.

"Ahem, Honey!"

"Sorry, I just can't get enough of you; that's all. I'll be good."

We got up and went downstairs. I immediately went into my new office space and started setting up my computer and other items. I had my laptop and a backup drive, my briefcase with pens, paper, a stapler and that was pretty much it. Roxie had an office set up across the hallway with every office supply known to man. In looking around, I noticed that she had a laptop on one corner of the desk and a desktop PC on the other corner.

"Hey Hon, do you have a wireless connection to the Internet?" I asked.

"No Babe," she said, "my Internet comes through the phone line into the computer on the desk."

Well there was a snag. There was no phone line into my office space. I'd have to either run an extension cable or get a wireless router. I had to have Internet access. I went out into the kitchen just as Roxie was serving up breakfast.

"Good thing we're going to Wal-Mart today Hon," I said. "I can get a wireless router there and then I won't have to bother you in your office when we're working."

"You're so smart," She said as she kissed my cheek. "Sit down and eat."

I sat at the table and couldn't help notice that she had only 1 egg and a glass of juice. "Aren't you eating?" I asked.

"I can't eat a lot in the morning because I'm just not that hungry," she said, "and this is just fine. Plus, you don't want me to blimp up on you and get fat, do you?"

"I used to skip breakfast altogether," I said, "but my doctor recommended eating 3 times a day is good for you and it would help me to lose weight. I'm not happy at the 221 that I am currently at. I would like to get down to about 180 or so."

"Oh baby, are you going to whither away on me? I like you just the way you are."

"No, I wouldn't call it withering away," I said, "just that I am definitely not happy at this weight and I want to get some of this beer belly gone. I've been lazy lately by not working out and drinking too much and eating junk food. So losing weight isn't just to help me look better. It's better for my health too. You want to keep me around for a while, don't you?"

As she got up from the table she said "Just don't waste away, Honey . . . I'm not done with you yet."

She went over to the cupboard and retrieved a small bottle and came back over to the table. "Here, take this."

The bottle had an eyedropper and she counted out 10 drops of the brown solution into my juice glass.

"What the hell is that?" I asked.

"It's a special herbal tonic that I use," She said. "This will help all of your medicines work better and it's all natural."

"What's in it?"

"It's just a mixture of herbs and vitamins. I order it special from an online supplier. It's got Bloodroot, Garlic, Kava and a bunch of other elements included and it won't hurt you. It's good for you so down the hatch buddy."

I had been taking more than enough medicine from the VA Medical Center for a variety of ailments. Lipitor for my cholesterol, Lopressor for my blood pressure, Niacin for a flushing agent, Naproxine for my prostrate; all of them prescribed and none of them giving me any dramatic results. I had been on a homeopathic regimen of herbs and vitamins years ago and I actually felt better when I was taking them, so herbal medicine wasn't a negative to me and I downed my orange juice without any resistance. We finished breakfast and I picked up the dishes and put them into the sink. I filled the sink with hot water and a bit of soap and prepared to wash them.

"You don't have to do that babe," She said.

"I know." I responded, "but it's just force of habit. I like a nice clean house and one of the easiest ways to keep it that way is to not let dishes stack up. I always clean up after a meal so that there's not a pile of work waiting for me later."

"Well aren't we efficient."

"When do you want to leave today?" I asked.

"Let me get dressed and put my makeup on and then we'll get going. I should be ready by 10:30 or so."

"Ok," I said, "I'm just going to get some more setting up done and when you are ready, come get me. Until then, I'll leave you to your beautification project."

Roxie went into the shower and then went upstairs to ready herself. I proceeded back to the office to get back into my research. After about 45 minutes, she came down, walked into the office and nuzzled my neck. Then she bit my ear, and then she put her tongue in my ear. At that, I had to break from my work.

"Is this a hint that you are ready?" was my question.

"Oh, I'm ready alright, are you?"

"No, I mean ready to get going. You've had appetizers and breakfast, what else could you want."

She swung around in front of me and joined me sitting on the chair, facing me. I lost myself in those beautiful blue eyes and the clean smell of her hair. We kissed passionately and my body reverted to automatic pilot. My hands gravitated to her breasts and I felt them swell under her thin white t-shirt. With one smooth move, she reached down, grabbed the bottom of the shirt and lifted it over her head. With another smooth move, she unsnapped her bra and discarded it in the blink of an eye.

My mouth found the targets that she displayed in front of me and I felt her chin lift upward as she embraced the ecstasy of my soft tongue. I slid my arms underneath her legs and lifted her off the chair as I continued to kiss her. Slowly, I lowered her to the carpeted floor and followed her down. With my free left hand, I undid her pants and slid them and her panties off. This beautiful, naked woman stared up at me with wanton lust in her eyes.

"Take me."

My mouth continued to caress her breasts while my fingers explored her wet lower regions, covered in soft red strands. With deliberate slowness, I moved downward and replaced my fingers with my tongue. She let out a soft hush as I licked her waiting desire. Around and around my velvet tongue went within the moist walls and I could feel her breathing quicken every time my rhythm changed.

"Put them in honey, put them in," She whispered.

I rose up and slid into her slowly. She sighed as I pulled back and forth in a clock-like fashion. Slowly, I let the rhythm of my body increase, along with the force of the inward drives. Even though I was already quite erect,

I felt my manhood getting even harder as I plunged into paradise. Her moaning increased proportionally until she uttered, "Oh, God, Fuck Me. Fuck Me hard Baby."

Her nails bit into the soft tissue of my back. I sensed the air singing around me. A blue mist seemed to cover my eyes; my muscles strained with energy. With a massive push, I exploded inside her as she climaxed. She let out a loud "Yes, Yes, Yes, Oh God, Yes. Oh My God, I Love You."

As my body began to relax, I rolled over on to my back, carefully taking her with me so as not to disturb our positions. She sat atop me and started another series of rhythms that called out to my body to respond again. Even though I am not the viral man I was 30 years ago, there was something about her that forced my body to recover faster than it had in years. Within minutes, I was erect again and Roxie was taking a ride, on my wild baloney pony.

I felt her cum again and I wasn't far behind her. My orgasm was less intense than the first one, but it was equally satisfying. She lay down on my chest as we held each other, drained and happy.

"Now do you think we can go to Bowling Green?" I joked.

"You Bastard; you have a one-track mind." She answered.

"Oh, and you don't?"

She smiled and kissed me and we got up, both fully satisfied. I went into the bathroom to clean up and she went into the bedroom to put her makeup on. She made a brief toilet break and we were ready, smiling at each other, to go to Bowling Green.

It was the beginning of our first great adventure.

* * *

8) Bowling Green Beckons

Bowling Green, KY—April 24, 2009

Our first stop, after the 60 mile trip to Bowling Green, was the International Corvette Museum. As we approached the front entrance, there was a 1966 Corvette on a rotating platform in the front window.

"Les, my roommate had one just like that," I said. "I've got to take some pictures of this place for showing off when I go back to New York."

I hauled out my digital camera and took several pictures of this truly beautiful car. We then went inside the building and were greeted by a smiling hostess at the front desk. Along the center of the building there were 2 lines of nothing but Corvettes, most of them new. There was probably a total of 100 Corvettes in just this section. The walls were enhanced by photographs of different models and settings of the classic car. If this was the entrance, I couldn't wait to see the display.

"Welcome to the Corvette Museum," the hostess said, "are you planning on taking the tour today?"

"Indeed we are," I said. What's the cost?"

"It's 10 dollars per person unless you buy a raffle ticket. Raffle ticket holders get the tour for free." she explained, "and the next raffle drawing is going to be this Saturday at 1 p.m. The odds are very good because we have only sold about 400 tickets so far. Can I put you down for one or two tickets for the drawing?"

"What does the winner get?" I asked.

"The winner receives a brand new 2009 Corvette, straight from the factory. In fact, that's it over there against the wall; the yellow one."

I walked up and took a look at the Grand Prize. It was an absolutely beautiful 2009 Corvette, with all the toys and options.

"And how much are the tickets?"

"Each ticket is $ 450."

As much as I would have liked to pay $ 450 for a brand new Corvette and as good as the odds were, I decided to pass on the offer and just take the tour for $ 10 each.

We wandered through the halls and alleys of the exhibition. Every model was represented, some more than one. Additionally, there were several unique models on display along with story boards and pictures of the history of Corvette, the design team, special editions and just about everything relating to Corvette. The entire tour took us about an hour and I took plenty of photos to show off to my friends.

"Well Honey, what do you think?" I said to Roxie. "Should we buy one?"

"I had a '79 back when I lived in Florida," she said, "a bright yellow one. I really made my mark driving around town in a yellow 'vette with my red hair."

"What happened to it?"

"Oh, I got pregnant and when you are at 8 months of term, you don't fit well behind the wheel."

"I can understand that," I said with a laugh. "Where would you like to go next?"

"Let's go to Wal-Mart first and get that out of the way and then we can go to Aldi's and get the grocery shopping done."

"Done," I said as we exited the building, "I'm glad we came here and I got all these shots. Someday, I'm going to buy another Corvette."

"You had one before?" She asked.

"I had a '64 back in my youngster days. Wish I had that car now because it's worth quite a bit more than I sold it for. Stupid me; I got rid of it because it didn't have Air Conditioning."

We left the museum and made a quick trip to Wal-Mart where she picked up a few things and I got a wireless network for the computer setup. We were in and out in about 10 minutes. I hate Wal-Mart anyway. It's true they have a lot of stuff, but it's very rare that I've been able to walk into the store and get what 'I Need' at that particular time. Maybe it's just me. Maybe my needs are outside the norm. I don't know.

I've never been one of those people who loves to shop; just get in and out; even at Christmas. Correction; especially at Christmas. I really don't know how some people can spend all day, going from store to store; but to each their own. It's just not my cup of tea.

We then found Aldi's and did our grocery shopping. She was receiving public assistance because she had zero income to speak of and she didn't bother to claim any money she made from her online sales. I thought that attitude was a bit shady, but I could understand her motivation. I hadn't known her long enough to get a fix on how much she actually made selling her 'junk', but I assumed it wasn't that much. And I didn't know about how much work she did with the construction company. She was divorced so maybe everything she had a part of was paid at completion.

We stocked up on all the staples and meats we wanted, and with every stop of the cart, she asked, "Is there anything special you want?"

"Hon, I've got that already." I answered.

She smiled and continued going from aisle to aisle with her cart. When we got to the fresh fruit and vegetables section I told Roxie that I thought they were all a bit limp and that 'I don't like limp', especially veggies.

"Funny Man," She answered.

She paid for everything with her Food Stamp card and we were out of there in a matter of 30 minutes or so.

"Ok, what's next?" I asked.

"Well, you promised a few drinks," she said, "and there's a TGI Fridays right around the corner if you like."

"That sounds good."

We loaded our groceries, making sure that the milk, eggs and cold stuff got put on the bottom of trunk to keep it cold, fired up her Toyota, and off we went. It was about 3 p.m. and TGI Friday's was dead quiet. We went into Friday's and sat down. There were a couple of people at the bar that appeared to be part of the regular crowd. We ordered our drinks and the waitress was very efficient in advertising the daily specials. We passed on food and told her we just needed a couple of road brews.

Roxie turned to me and said, "We have to stop at a liquor store while we are up here. You can buy beer and wine here, but not in my county."

"Glad you remembered that. I'm going to get a case of beer for home. And you can get your wine or whatever else you want."

"You look familiar," the waitress said to me. "Do you come in here much?"

"I'm down here on a visit from New York State," I explained. "My lady here lives in Burkesville and I might be moving there."

"Oh, well, welcome to Kentucky. But you look familiar, I swear."

"I've got one of those faces," I said. "You know, like it should belong on a milk carton."

Roxie chirped her familiar line, "Funny Man."

With that, the waitress took off to serve another customer. I turned to Roxie and said "Isn't there any place closer to your house, to go shopping than Bowling Green?"

"Glasgow is 20 miles or so from here. We passed it coming down here. But they are a dry county too and if you want beer or to go shopping other than at an IGA, you have to come here or go to Cookeville, Tennessee."

We stayed for another drink, chatted with a few of the locals and then headed out. By now it was 4:30 and we had a good hour drive to get back home.

"Don't forget, we have to get booze." Roxie reminded me.

We stopped at a sort of liquor mart and went inside. I picked up a case of my favorite, Pabst Blue Ribbon Beer and Roxie picked up a shopping cart.

She strolled around the isles getting boxed wine, rum, vodka, and Kailua. We got up to the checkout counter and naturally she loaded everything right next to my beer. I wasn't really paying that much attention as the cashier rang everything up and put it on my debit card. My case of beer just cost me $ 72.00. Oh, well, we won't need anything for a while I thought.

We headed back home and got there about 6:00 p.m. We unloaded the car and Roxie told me that she was going to cook something really special for me tonight. I knew that would be a treat because I had sampled her gourmet cooking before. She got everything started and joined me on the front porch. We listened to a local classic rock station on the radio while I enjoyed a beer. Roxie had mixed herself a Rum and Coke and we sat on the porch like two old married people. It was very enjoyable and I began to think that I might be able to enjoy the peace and quiet of country life.

"You are not going to like it here." Roxie said, as if she was reading my mind.

"What makes you think that?"

"It's too quiet. And I can tell that you are a social person," She said. "There is just nothing to do down here unless you want to drive to the Sawmill down in Tennessee and hang out at the bar. And even that would probably get old."

"Well, I can deal with a lot. Besides, I wanted to move down in this neck of the woods anyway. I hate New York and it's a pleasure just to be away from it."

Roxie went on to say that when she moved here 3 years ago, she was all excited about the organic farm and the quietude of country living. But now with being divorced and living out here alone, the quiet was sometimes a bit too much.

"I'm a social person too," she said, "and I had been considering a move back to New York to be with my family and friends."

"I don't know if you would like New York now," I said. "For starters, there are no jobs there. Taxes keep going up and more and more people are getting sick of the bullshit politics.

That's why I want out; plus the fact that I hate winter in Central New York. Central New York is like living in a snowstorm, with buildings in it."

"My son lives in South Carolina," She said. "He's graduating from boot camp at Ft. Benning, next month. He likes it there and I had considered checking that area out also."

"I originally thought I would like to live in Tennessee," I added. "I did a lot of research and Knoxville seems like a very modern, but small city. They have a lot of things going on but it's not the hustle-bustle of New York."

"Well, it's something to consider for the future. Hey, dinner is almost ready. We're having Shrimp Alfredo tonight. I hope you like it."

"Lady, you are going to blimp me up with all this fine cooking." I said, "I'm trying to lose weight and you keep doing everything in your power to keep it on. Do you think my name is Hansel?"

"Funny Man," She said as she got up to go into the kitchen. "Come and eat."

We had a fine meal and then once again I picked up the dishes and proceeded to start washing them. I glanced over on to the counter and noticed that the bottle of Rum that she had just bought earlier was about half empty. I thought, no . . . she couldn't have drank that much already. We settled back out on the porch and continued with our small talk. Well, it was small talk on my part and small slur on hers. I could tell that the Rum was having an effect on her because she just wasn't as sharp as usual. Not that I was bothered by someone who got a little tipsy once in a while. Lord knows that I've done my share of it; As long as it wasn't a habit.

The evening was cool and fireflies danced above the front lawn. The evening was tranquil and the air had that musty smell like a combination of damp earth and wood smoke. Yes, it was enjoyable but I could see how it could get boring real quick.

"Want to watch a movie tonight?" I asked.

"That sounds nice," She said. "What did you bring down with you?"

"I've got some comedies, some action, and some drama. Do you like Star Trek?"

"The movies or the series?" She asked.

"Movie's. I've got them all. Star Trek the Movie through Star Trek Nemesis."

"I'd love it. I was always a big fan of the series but I've never seen any of the movies."

We proceeded inside for the evening and put on the video tape. About half way through it though, Roxie decided to get a little frisky and things took an altogether different course.

A course other than movie madness.

* * *

9) Motorhead Mark

Burkesville, KY—April 25, 2009

I got up the next morning and went downstairs to make coffee. I had fully intended to set my office up today but there were a couple of other projects that cut into line. We had taken Roxie's '96 Camry to Bowling Green yesterday and the driver's side window wasn't going down. It was a real pain in the ass, because I like to drive with a bit of fresh air blowing in. Since all the back windows worked fine and they were hardly used, I figured it would be easy to swap out the motor and drive assembly and replace the defective front one, with one from the back window.

The other little job that had snuck in my schedule was that the shower in the bathroom didn't work; But I could hear water running in the wall. That wasn't good. I knew that this was a job that could take a while to get done, and so until then, I would have to take a bath. I can live with that. For the time being, I'm going to concentrate on the priority stuff. Like the car window and my office.

When we were at Wal-Mart, I picked up a Belkin Wireless Network for $ 30 bucks. I figured that was an easy way to solve the problem of dual offices, plus, I wanted one anyway. I'd just hook it up and both computers can go online at the same time; it sounded simple.

I fixed a cup of 'Joe' for myself and Roxie and headed upstairs. She was sleeping peacefully and I put the coffee on the end table next to the bed. I gave her a kiss and watched as her dreamy blue eyes flashed open and looked at me.

"G'morning Honey," I said, "How did you sleep?"

"Better than I have slept in months . . . and let me start the morning off right, by saying that I LOVE YOU."

I just leaned over and kissed her again.

"Mark, I think I loved you already, when we first talked on the phone. Meeting you in person gave me a psychic feeling that you were my soul mate. And now, making love and loving to be with you, I am convinced that I want to be with you the rest of my life. I love you Mark and even if you don't love me, my feelings are set."

"I love you too, Honey, but I've got work to do." was my quick answer.

"What do you have that's so important you can't snuggle up with me?" She asked

"Well for starters," I continued "I want to get that window fixed on your car. And then I want to get the router set up in the office so that we can both get on the Net."

"I thought we could go into town today." She said. "I thought I'd give you a grand tour of our fabulous 'Metro' center so you can see for yourself why they roll the sidewalks up at 5 o'clock."

"We can do that this afternoon," I said, "since I don't know how much time that window job is going to take me. The router should be a piece of cake but I don't have a good working arrangement with cars."

"I can help," she offered, "I know all about cars. I've done tune-ups, oil changes and even pulled a transmission out once. I know cars."

"We'll see," I said, "it should be a fairly easy job if the drive motors are the same. Right now, I'm going to go down and set things up in the office."

"Ok, I'll get up and cook breakfast," She said. "I was going to sleep in and dream more about you but you've got to be 'Mr. Non-Stop' and get me up."

"No, Stay in bed, relax dear . . . I just want to get things set up, that's all."

"No, I'll get up. What do you want for breakfast?" She said as she stepped onto the floor.

"Surprise Me!" I answered as I went down the stairs to the office.

As soon as I got back down to the office space, I pulled the new wireless network out of the box and unraveled the cables. It was a simple setup. Just hook up the power connector to the wall and hook up the USB port to the computer. Plug it into the phone line and the computer should automatically find the signal. Simple right?

NOT!

According to the indicator lights, it was hooked up but there was no signal coming through. I picked up the phone and called the telephone company. After a 5 minute wait listening to the Percy Faith rendition of 'Smoke on the Water', I was connected to technical support. I told them that I had just hooked up a wireless connection but wasn't receiving any signal.

"That's because we have to reset the IP connection to your computer." The tech told me. He went on to explain that I had to shut down the computer and reboot. It would be about ½ hour and when I turned the computer back on, everything should be fine.

"Thank you," I said and hung up. "Well, that was easy."

I could hear Roxie rumbling around in the kitchen as I continued to work in the office. I grabbed a bunch of paper and pens, paperclips, highlighter and other things and brought them over into the new spaces.

"Honey, do you want toast?" Roxie called from the kitchen.

"No, I'm good . . . What are you making?" I asked.

"Bacon and Eggs." was her reply.

I went back to working, when she came into the office and asked

"How many eggs do you want?"

I looked up and said "Two is enough since we have bacon." With that she twirled and went back into the kitchen. I was trying to mount a file holder on the wall and of course the screws I had were too big to fit through the plastic. Roxie came in the office and asked

"Do you want Brown Eggs or White?"

"I don't care," I said, "to me, they taste the same."

Ah. I found the proper size screws, was my thought. Now, what the hell did I do with my screwdriver?

I began the search for the elusive tool.

Not 2 minutes later, Roxie comes back in the office to ask

"How do you like your eggs?"

"Scrambled is fine," I said, "Do you need any help?"

"No, you just get your work done and I'll handle the kitchen." With that she kissed me on the top of the head and left for the kitchen.

I appreciated the fact that she was making breakfast but I hate interruptions when I'm trying to concentrate. I was making real progress. I found the screwdriver and was standing on a chair to mount the file holder when she came back in the office and asked

"Do you want apple or orange juice?"

I give up. Rather than say what was really on my mind, I just got off the chair and put the task away for later and went out to the kitchen with her.

"Here, let me help you." I said.

"No, it's almost done and I don't let anyone else in my kitchen when I'm cooking."

"You forget my dear; I used to own a catering company. I do know what I'm doing."

"Oh yeah . . . Well if you knew what you were doing, you wouldn't argue with me. Now get out and let me finish making breakfast."

"Ok, I can take a hint;" I said, "I'm going to get dressed."

As I went upstairs and dressed, I thought about what she said and I realized that SHE was the one who was interrupting me, not the other way around. Well, maybe she is just grumpy in the morning. I'm not one to make a mountain out of a mole hill, but I did note a bit of pushiness and snotty attitude in her comments. I came back downstairs and breakfast was ready.

We talked about Burkesville over breakfast and she told me not to expect much of a town when we got there. She wanted to go there just to mail a letter and maybe to introduce me to any people who might be out and about.

"I know the entire Sheriff's squad in town," She said. "Pepper Jackson, the head Sheriff, and his Deputy Dex are my buddies."

"That's a good group of buddies to have."

When we finished breakfast and I got up to wash the dishes, Roxie came over to me and told me to hold my mouth open and she dripped 10 drops of her special liquid 'medicine' from the vial into my mouth.

"Ugh," I said, "that tastes like it came straight out of the sewer."

"That's why I always put it in juice or something," she said, "but just think how healthy you are going to be. While I think about it, when are we going into town today?"

"I wanted to fix the window in the car first," I said. "It shouldn't take more than an hour. Are you in a hurry?"

"No, I just wondered what the plan was."

"I'll go out right now and check it out," I said, "and If it's too much of a hassle, I'll put it off for a rainy day. Ok?"

"Ok. I'm going to go get dressed," and up the stairs she went.

I looked at her '96 Camry in the barn. It wasn't a bad looking car except for a small crease on the passenger side where a deer collided with it one night. Actually, it was in pretty good shape except for the driver's window not working. I pulled the inside of the door off and examined the power window workings. I was going to have to remove the entire motor and gear drive, just to take a closer look at what was wrong. I decided that before I got into that, I'd better compare both the front and rear motors to make sure they were interchangeable. I pulled the rear door panel off and looked at that assembly. Ha, Ha I was in luck. They looked identical and the swap should be fairly easy.

I laid out my tools next to the car and proceeded to get to work. I pulled the motor assembly out of the back door and put all the associated hardware in one place on the floor of the barn. I then went to the front door and realized that this part was going to be a bit more complicated. I was going to have to secure the window from falling when I removed the assembly. While I was working on that, Roxie came out of the house and walked into the barn.

"How's it going," She asked.

"Well, I've got the back one out," I said. "Now all I've got to do is get the front out and swap them."

Roxie leaned in close to examine the front door assembly. She grabbed a crescent wrench and began to loosen one of the brackets that held the window frame in.

"No, leave that alone," I said, "just let me do it. I have everything all laid out in proper order."

"Mark, I've done this before," she argued, "and you have to take the whole window frame out to get at the motor."

"No you don't," I fired back. "Just get out of the way and let me do it. Stand there and watch."

Roxie had it in her mind that she was going to show me what an expert she was with cars. My statements went flying into the wind like smoke trailing from an ashtray. She continued to work on the window and in the process, she was kicking hardware here and there, all over the barn floor.

"Get the fuck out of the way, I have it!" I shouted. "All you are doing is screwing up my work area. Go do something."

I could see the red of her hair and her cheeks. She stared at me like I had just told her that I had been having sex with her best girlfriend. There was fire in her eyes. She threw the crescent wrench down onto the ground and stomped out of the barn.

I went back to work on the front motor assembly but I could hear strange noises coming from the house. Noises like drawers being slammed and periodically the word 'asshole' carried across the air. I couldn't figure out why she was so mad. I had asked her twice to let me work on it; I didn't need the help. What was her problem? I decided that it was better to mind my own business and finish the task at hand first, and then deal with my 'upset little princess'.

I shouldn't have yelled at her like I did but when I'm in the middle of a job, any job, I don't like to be interrupted. I've learned over the years that when my concentration is broken, it takes twice as long to get back where I left off.

I got the front motor installed, tested to make sure it worked, and then went about the task of putting everything back together. The entire job, from start to finish took me about 1 ½ hours which I didn't think was too bad for me being a 'non-motorhead'. I picked up my tools and brought them back into the house. One look at Roxie and I knew I was in deep-trouble. She was lying on the couch with her head face down in a pillow.

"Your window is fixed," I announced.

She lifted up her head and I saw the tears still in her eyes.

"Why do you have to be so mean?" she said, "I was only trying to help."

"Honey, I told you," as I walked to the couch, "I knew what I was doing. I didn't need your help and actually you were kicking screws and washers around on the ground. I was afraid some of the hardware was going to get lost."

"You yelled at me," She shouted. "I didn't deserve that."

"Honey, I'm sorry," I said, "but sometimes I fly off the handle. I just wanted to get the job done so that we could get on with what we were going to do, that's all. But you wouldn't listen and I was afraid that some vital part would get lost and then I would be pissed."

"So you're not mad at me?"

"Of course not Hon," I said as I hugged her, "how could I be mad at you?"

She kissed me and put her arms around my neck.

"I missed cuddling with you this morning," She said as she pushed me down to the couch.

My mind whirled at the possibility that maybe she needed some morning stress relief. I reached up and gently pulled her down to meet me face-to-face.

"So what can we do about it?" I asked.

She took the lead and we commenced to make love on the living room couch. It wasn't as comfortable as the king size bed we had been in but I sure wasn't going to complain. I was amazed at what a turn my life had taken with this woman. Even when I was in my 30's with my ex-wife, sex was never so spontaneous or often as it was here with Roxie. After we had exhausted ourselves again, we laid back for a minute on the couch.

"Now, I'm going to have to change my clothes again," Roxie said, "and you've got my hair all messed up and I'm wrinkled."

"I'm sorry madam, but the complaints department is in our Denver office." I said.

"Funny Man," She said as she got up. "Are we still going into town?"

"Yes my dear, as soon as you are ready."

She left and went to 'rearrange' herself. I poured myself a cup of coffee and went out to the front porch. One of the nice things about living out here in the wilds was that it was so quiet. No traffic running up and down the street, nothing but nature in my face. Even though I was sort of a 'City Boy', I did like the solitude that farm life offered; I liked it in small doses.

Fifteen minutes later, Roxie came out and we proceeded to get in the car to go into town. Before we pulled out of the driveway, I had her sit in the driver's seat and check out the power windows.

"Wow," she said, "the windows haven't worked that good since the car was new."

"So I guess Motorhead Mark did alright?"

"Oh, baby, you always do alright. In everything you do."

I assumed by her compliment that our little spat was over and forgotten. I slipped behind the wheel and proceeded to take the 20 minute drive into town. This should be interesting, I thought, because she had told me previously that Burkesville had a population of only about 3,000 people. With me coming from a metropolitan area in New York, I was destined to go through a bit of culture shock, to say the least.

Burkesville was going to be quite a change.

* * *

10) Metropolis

Burkesville, KY—April 25, 2009

We took the Camry out the driveway and headed down the dirt road that leads into town. One of the negatives of living out in the hinterlands like this is that the town never does much in the way of maintenance. Large potholes dotted the road for the first ½ mile, until we reached the paved portion.

"That's my other property," She said as we passed a vacant double-wide trailer.

"You own that too?"

"I bought it at a foreclosure auction after my divorce," She said. "I paid $ 8000 for 5 acres and the trailer."

"No shit!" I said, "It doesn't look that old."

"No, it's only 6 years old," she continued, "but the former owners trashed it. I spent a good month cleaning out all the crap they left. It still needs cabinets and a lot of interior work."

"What do you plan to do with it?" I asked.

"If I stay here, I'd like to live in it," She said. "It has a Jacuzzi tub and a fireplace. The problem with my house is that it doesn't have a heating system; not even a wood burning stove. Sometimes in the winter months it gets a bit chilly. The double-wide is real nice inside. We can look at it later this week if you want."

"Definitely."

Parked alongside the double-wide was a blue sports car. The paint was somewhat faded but the body looked like it was in good condition.

"What's that car there?" I asked.

"Oh, that's my baby," Roxie commented. "It's a 1976 Datsun 280-z. I got that in Florida and I want to restore it because it's fairly rare. It was the first year of that model and it's got an automatic transmission. I drove it up here and it's been sitting there for a couple of years so it most likely needs some TLC, but I know it has real value. The only thing I have to figure out is how to title it in my name instead of my ex-s name.

"Do you have the title to it?" I asked.

"No," she responded, "we got divorced and he left before I could take care of that. But I'll figure out a way to get it because it's my car and I'll be damned if he gets it."

We continued down the dirt road leading to her house and once we hit the main highway, my teeth stopped chattering from the bumpy ride. All along the 18 miles into town, there were billboards advertising 'The Alpine'. I asked Roxie what that place was.

"It's a resort," She told me. "I'm not sure if it's open now but we can take a ride up there. There's a real nice view of the landscape because it overlooks Burkesville."

We came to another billboard advertising 'The Alpine' that proudly stated 'Open All Year'. I turned at the crossroad and headed up the mountain on a road of nothing but hairpin turns and only about 2 cars wide. It was nothing but twisty, turning roads all the way up, until we got to the top of the hill where the road opened up into a large parking lot, but there were no cars there. The place was empty. We parked and got out of the car. The view overlooking town was magnificent. It was a nice clear day and from our vantage point, we could see approximately 50-75 miles out into the horizon. Down the hillside below, lay the town of Burkesville with its churches, small houses and a collection of businesses. I felt like I was peering down at the layout for a Lionel Train set.

"Well, I guess they lied about being Open All Year," I said.

Roxie came over to me and put her arm around my waist.

"I was pretty sure they were closed," She said. "That's what I heard anyway. Something about the owner's son doesn't want to deal with the public or something like that."

"This place is fantastic, "I remarked. "I can see where this would be a real popular place if Burkesville had more tourists, but it must be hell to keep this place up with no business."

We wandered around looking inside at the layouts, the room balconies and then I told Roxie that I wanted to get a picture of us together.

"I don't do pictures," she said, "I'll break the camera lens."

"Bullshit," I answered as I pulled out my digital camera. "I've got to have a shot of us to give to my mother when I go back to New York. She doesn't have any recent pictures of me."

"So why do I have to be in the picture?" she said, "you know I'm camera shy. I don't want my picture taken."

I wasn't about to listen to that sorry excuse because I wanted a picture of Roxie and I; at least for my own collection. I lined up the shot of where we would be standing and set the automatic timer. Then I set the camera down on the hood of the car and stepped into the field of vision.

"I am getting our picture and that's not open for discussion," I said. "Now say Cheese!"

The timer snapped the picture and I went to take a look at what it had captured. It was a nice clear picture that I had lined up perfectly. There we were, standing together, arms around each other and Roxie with her sunglasses on.

"One more Honey," I said, "I want to get one of you without the glasses."

"No, Mark, I'm going to pass. I have sensitive eyes and can't take these off."

I was a bit miffed about this but didn't say anything. Maybe she did have sensitive eyes. It wasn't worth mentioning because I did get a good picture for Mom and that was my goal.

"Ok," I said "Be a baby . . . Where to next?"

"I've got to mail this letter," she said, "and there's not much in town to see. Maybe we can go to the store and get groceries if you want."

"Let's just cruise through and look at stuff. Hey, it's my first visit here and I love taking it in."

We got back in the car and down the hill into town we went. She was right about not being much in Burkesville. Three gas stations, two convenience stores, a hardware store, a couple of groceries, a NAPA, a Pizza Hut and a bunch of small little businesses. That was it.

The only thing that caught my eye was a pawn shop in the middle of town. We decided to go in there and browse a bit. Coming from New York, I had been in pawn shops before. This was something else though. The shop was only two rows of glass cases. That was it. They had a selection of handguns, CD's and mainly junk in the cases. On the wall there were a couple of litho prints, a crossbow and 3 shotguns. Overall, there was nothing that I even wanted to take a closer look at, so we left.

We went down to the local IGA market and did some shopping. After that, we pulled into one of the convenience stores to get gas. Parked there in the parking lot, was a Cumberland County Sheriff. Roxie told me to pull up next to it.

"Hey Dex, how's it going?" She yelled from the passenger side.

"Fine as Frog's Hair," He replied.

"Are you working hard today?" She asked him.

"I'm keeping busy, how about you?" He said.

"Dex, this is my friend Mark from New York," she continued, "I'm showing him the sights."

I nodded politely to Dex the Sheriff and he did the same. Dex was a younger guy, maybe 30 or so, who looked like a linebacker from the New York Jets. In the typical fashion of law enforcement, I could tell that he was checking me out. It's not anything you can put your finger on, just a sense that perhaps you have invaded another dog's territory.

"Well, we've got to get going Dex," Roxie yelled again.

"How long are you here for Mark?" Dex asked.

"Oh, I don't know," I answered, "I'm just visiting for now but I like being out of New York."

"Well, we've got a quiet little town here," He said. "I guess it's not like 'yer used to, I 'spose."

"You've got that right. I'm trying not to fall asleep when I'm driving."

"Ah don't want to have to investigate no personal injury accident," Dex commanded, "and I hope you make sure that I won't have to."

"No problem Dex," I answered, "we'll probably see you from time to time when we're in town."

We drove off and left Burkesville to its quietness. On the way back I told Roxie that I thought Dex was checking me out.

"He probably was," she said, "that's his job. There isn't much goes on around here that everybody doesn't know about. Even I know about happenings here, and I hardly ever come into town. Somehow I always catch the gossip. Dex is a really good guy and I feel safer just knowing he's on duty. He and I have gotten quite close during all my problems with the ex and everything."

We continued on home, talking about how different things were back in New York. She told me that she sometimes missed the hustle-bustle of a bigger town, but especially missed being able to go out and have a drink with friends.

"That's another reason I was thinking of moving out of here," she said, "I miss being able to party. It gets awful boring just sitting at home at night drinking alone."

'Hey, it's good enough for George Thorogood; it should be good enough for you."

"Funny Man," was all she said.

We traveled up the dirt road and pulled into the yard. I backed the car up to the porch to make it easier to unload our cache of groceries. Riley the Rottweiler came up, wagging his tail, like we had been gone for days. I helped Roxie carry the groceries into the house and put them away.

"Maybe next week, we can make a trip to the Sawmill." She said. "That's the little bar I told you about down across the Tennessee line."

"How far is it?" I asked.

"It's only about 15 miles out of Burkesville," she explained, "from the IGA market, it takes 20 minutes."

"Sounds like you've made that trip a few times."

"I've never been inside there myself. I go that way when I go to the liquor store in Celina, but I've never stopped. I don't think it's proper for a lady to go into a bar alone."

"Well it sure sounds like a future trip for us." I answered.

Roxie came up behind me as I put the food away. She put her arms around my waist and whispered in my ear, "How would you like to go on a little trip, right now?"

I turned around and embraced her, "What did you have in mind, my lady?"

She proceeded to pull me tighter and kiss me with those lovely lips. I sensed that this girl was ready for some hot, afternoon lovemaking. Standing in the kitchen and leaning on the counter was not my idea of a perfect situation but Roxie began to fondle me as we stood there and my body responded.

I lifted her off the ground and placed her 'ass first' on the kitchen counter. From there, I proceeded to unbutton her slacks and slide them down and off, kissing her all the while. She helped me by pulling her top and bra off and I was captured by the vision of this beautiful woman, naked in front of me. She looked good enough to eat. From this vantage point, it was easy for me to address all the goodies that her body offered. I caressed her neck, her breasts, her torso and finally, that red fuzzy pit of her passion. I explored her with my tongue and she responded with moans of pleasure. Every once in a while, I would feel her shiver with delight.

"Oh, baby, put them in," she moaned, "put them in now."

Keeping my tongue in place, I reached down and undid my pants. I moved her arms up around my neck and placed my arms underneath her legs to lift her and lower her to my waiting and swollen muscle. As I entered her, she let out a gasp and I felt her arms grip me even tighter. We went into a rhythmic duet with me lifting her up and her pushing herself down. Faster and faster we went until I felt her arms and legs squeeze hard around me and she let out a loud Yes.

"Yes, baby, Yes," she cried, "I love you so much. Harder."

I couldn't control myself anymore and I pushed her against the cabinets and exploded inside her. It wasn't a 55 gallon drums worth, but it sure felt like it. When I was done, we both collapsed on the kitchen floor.

Thankfully, neither one of us hit any chairs.

* * *

11) The Sawmill

Celina, TN—April 28, 2009

The weekend went by with very little getting done on my part. I did finally get the office set up to where I could work and access the Internet. Roxie and I spent a lot of time just hanging out and getting to know each other, mentally and physically. We sat on the porch in the evening and watched the fireflies dance in the front yard, and talk. And Lord did we talk. She told me the story about how she went to the Original Woodstock in 1969 at the age of 15. She had to sneak away from her parents and then her and her girlfriend hitchhiked to Yasgurs's Farm. She also told me that amazingly, she came back a virgin. I told her, that was saying a lot; especially during the New York Summer of Love.

She told me about when she lived in Texas and her next door neighbor was Willie Nelson; that she and Willie used to hang out all the time and smoke dope and drink. In fact, she told me that she saw Willie again at his appearance at Woodstock Reunion at Rome, New York in '99. He still remembered her because he gave her backstage passes to the show. No, we definitely didn't have a communication problem. I loved listening to her tales because they were interesting and I just loved to hear her voice.

On the following Tuesday, we decided (or Roxie did) that we needed to go to the liquor store and stock up. It would be a perfect time to stop by the Sawmill Pub and check it out.

"I've never been there," she said, "but my daughter went last year when she was up for a visit. She said it was a real nice place. The place is huge and at night they have bands playing."

"I'm not sure I want to go there at night," I said. "First of all, I wouldn't know anybody and second, I don't think I want to drink and drive in two different states."

"No, we'll just go this afternoon and check the place out," She said. "We can always go back again if we want to."

"Sounds like a plan to me," I said nodding my head, "Maybe if we decide to go there at night sometime, we can get a designated driver or rent a camper or something."

"Do you like camping?" Roxie asked.

"I don't mind going to a lodge or even a camper, but I don't want anything to do with sleeping on the ground out in the open."

"I love camping." She said. "I used to just take a sleeping bag and go out in the woods by a stream and camp."

"I've got to say that I'm not opposed to it, just inexperienced."

"Maybe someday you and I can go," she said, "I'm an expert."

"I'm sure you are, my love."

About 2 p.m., we took off and went to the 'booze-bin' as Roxie called it. It was a little liquor store down in Celina, Tennessee, just over the state line on Route 61, south of Burkesville. Celina is another small town in the area whose biggest employer is Dollar General. But Tennessee is different from Burkesville because they do have bars. As a matter of fact, there was not much more in Celina other than a couple of bars, a couple of churches and a couple of liquor stores. It lead me to wonder what these people do for entertainment, other than drink and pray.

Roxie picked up her standard allotment of vodka, rum and wine and I grabbed a case of my Pabst Blue Ribbon. Naturally, since I was the one with the money in my pocket, I paid. I looked at it as an investment because it would have cost me more to go out to dinner and hang out in taverns, than the booze cost. We left Celina and headed back towards Burkesville, where our next stop was the infamous Sawmill.

We pulled into the parking lot and there were ½ dozen cars there and a line of cars going through the drive-in window. I thought this was pretty neat because having lived in New York for almost most all my life, I had never seen a drive-in window at a bar. We went in through the front door and I was also amazed at the size of the place. They had a huge bandstand and dance floor at one end, a section of pool tables and dart machines in the middle and the main part was a bar with to-go coolers lined up behind the bar. We sat down on the stools, and a lanky fellow of about 40 came up and said "Howdy, what's ur pleasure?" I ordered my beer and Roxie ordered a rum and coke.

"Sorry Ma'am," he said, "we just have beer and wine here. We don't serve any hard stuff."

"Ok," Roxie came back, "I'll have a Corona please."

The bartender grabbed my can of Pabst and her bottle of Corona.

"Glasses?" he asked.

"No thanks," I said, "we like it nude," as I slid him a ten-spot.

Roxie looked at me with a smile and said, "Funny Man."

The bartender came back with the change and said, "How are you folks doing today?"

We told him we were fine; just stopping in to check the place out; that we lived in Burkesville and had to come down here to get our stash of libations. I remarked to him that he sounded like he was from up north because he didn't seem to have an accent.

"I'm from Rochester, New York," He said.

"Well, I just came down from Syracuse," I replied. "What a small world. I guess we are neighbors"

He introduced himself as Lenny, owner of this fine establishment and we gabbed a bit until he had to go and wait on another customer. All the time we sat there, a bell rang every time a car pulled up to the drive-in window. If I had to listen to that all day while I worked, it would drive me nuts. In between waiting on the window and bar customers, Lenny would come down and chit-chat about New York and his decision to move down here.

When Lenny wasn't there, I tried to strike up a conversation with Roxie, but her normal talkative self had gone for a walk. She seemed like she wasn't interested or she was pre-occupied. I asked her about her experiences with camping and she said that much of her love for it was because of her experience studying with the Onondaga Indians.

"Indians are nature lovers," she said, "and I spent so much time with them back in New York, that I absorbed a lot of their philosophies. I love everything about nature and if you want to piss me off, just throw something out the window of a car."

I vowed that I was not a litterbug; that my attitude was that God gave us this world and man had done a good job of wrecking it. Pollution, strip mining, deforestation; all for the almighty $ BUCK $. We stayed and had another drink and then it was time to move on.

"Lenny, it's been great," I said. "We'll be back again probably next week."

"Ok," he said, "you drive careful and know that you're always welcome here."

"Lenny, I'm such a cautious driver, that I put a condom on every time I get behind the wheel."

Roxie smiled and uttered her standard retort, 'Funny Man'. Lenny laughed and we went out the door. Roxie went over to the passenger side and got in before I could hold the door for her. I got in my side and sat down.

She looked at me with a straight face and said, "Every things a joke to you, isn't it?"

"Roxie," I said, "if can't share my humor, I'm not doing the job God gave me the talent for."

"Who elected you as King of Comedy?" She asked.

"Honey, I've been doing comedy for years. In fact I used to do it on stage."

"Well sometimes it gets to be a bit much . . . You know, I like serious too."

We drove back with very few words between us. I felt uncomfortable because I didn't really know what I had done to piss her off.

"Hon, did I do something wrong?" I asked.

"Not wrong, maybe just inappropriate." She said. "We were in a public place where you don't know a soul and you bring up a joke about condoms."

"Well, shit . . . it wasn't dirty or anything." I snapped back.

"No, but maybe try to show a little class when you're with me. I embarrass easily."

"Ok, sorry," I said, "it won't happen again."

We got home and unloaded our stash. I went into the office to check my email. There was not much there but junk mail and an Irish joke from Maggie. I got a pretty good laugh and sent her my reply. Other than that, I just kept working on my research for a perfect online business. I was getting a bit hungry but Roxie was being a brat and I figured it best to let her chill for a while. I grabbed a beer and sat there 'Googling' for new ideas.

Besides, research was a bit more important than dealing with a pissy attitude.

* * *

12) Evening Shadows

Burkesville, KY—April 28, 2009

"How did you like The Sawmill?" Roxie asked when she walked into the office.

"I had a good time. I mean, it's just a bar and my skin is glowing from exposure to all the rednecks there, but it was fun."

"I had only been there once before," She added. "I went there with my daughter Bonnie when she came down for a visit last year. I had never met Lenny before. He sure liked you."

"What's not to like?" I said.

"Funny Man," She replied.

"You know, you've got to learn to control that ego of yours."

"And what would I have left?" Quick as a whip she came back with "Oh, yeah, I guess you're right."

My mind popped back to a statement she had made earlier about 'never' being at the Sawmill before. Maybe she just misspoke, but I know she said that she had never been there before. It was probably nothing. I didn't know if Roxie was being funny, sarcastic, or just plain rude but I shined on her comments and walked out to the kitchen.

"What would you like for dinner tonight?" I asked, "it's my turn to cook for you."

"I don't know, what are you in the mood for?"

"How about spaghetti?" I offered, "we have sausage and meatballs to go with it and the only thing missing is Italian Bread."

"No, I've got it covered there too," She said. "There's a loaf in the back freezer."

"So spaghetti is good?" I repeated.

"Fine, just don't make too much. Pasta fills me up and I want room for desert."

"Wow, you really agreed on the menu quick," I said. "Usually you ponder this and that and present me with a lot of options."

"All you had to do was mention sausage and I thought that sounded good."

A smile slid across my face because this statement definitely didn't go unnoticed. Damn, is this woman a nympho or what? I've had plenty of willing partners in my life, but my God, Roxie is a machine and she expects me to be one too.

I started by defrosting the bread and bringing the oven up to temperature. Then I cooked and drained the pasta, put the meat in a skillet and opened a jar of Ragu with mushrooms. I always like to spice up my recipes with extra stuff so I added a couple cans of mushrooms, a chopped onion and garlic. When the sausage and meatballs were done cooking, I added about half the grease to the Ragu and let everything simmer. I set the table and pulled out a couple of long stem candles for the setting. The bread was spread with a mixture of garlic powder, onion power and butter then tossed into the oven.

"Hungry baby?" I asked, "it's ready as soon as the bread comes out."

She joined me in the kitchen and wrapped her arms around my waist and said, "How did I get so lucky to find a fox like you that has brains AND can cook?"

"It must be Karma?" I said. "Do you believe that what we do in the past comes back, good or bad?"

"Jesus, I hope not," she remarked, "because I was pretty wild in my younger days."

"What do you mean wild?"

"Not wild-wild but I've always pretty much did what I wanted. Me and my girlfriend took off and went to the original Woodstock," She said. "My parents would have had a cow if they had found out."

"Woodstock must have been a trip." I said "I was still in the Navy when it happened."

"Oh it was a trip alright; Drugs galore. But I'm proud to say that even thought I was 15 at the time, I still came back a virgin."

It seemed to me that the Woodstock experience must have been pretty important to her because she had mentioned the 'virgin' status earlier today. Oh, it was probably nothing. Sometimes I forget what I've told people. Roxie opened the cupboard and took out a glass. She then went over to the box on top of the fridge and poured herself a healthy tumbler full of wine.

"That's saying a lot," I said, "especially in the heady days of sex, drugs and rock and roll"

"I used to do a lot of drugs then, but now I just smoke pot. That's my drug of choice," she said, "and I am so glad I never got caught up in all that Cocaine and Crack bullshit."

"I've done every drug known to man, in my wild and crazy days," I replied, "but I never got hooked on anything. I still take a few tokes every once in a while but nothing like the days when I was known as 'the human chimney'. And I bet I haven't done anything else in 20 or 25 years."

"Do you want wine with dinner, Hon?" She asked.

"Yeah, I'll have a glass since I don't want beer," I said, "I'm not much of a wine drinker but every once in a while I like a glass. We can sit down now because dinner is served."

We dined by candlelight. I looked at her in the dim light and I felt a swell in my heart because she was truly beautiful. I couldn't believe that fate had brought us together and I was thinking to myself that maybe this was the one I was destined to spend the rest of my life with.

"So what do you think about fate?" I asked between mouthfuls.

"I don't know," she paused, "I guess there is a lot to it." When I studied shaman medicine under Chief Shenandoa in Syracuse, I learned a lot about the Indian culture. They believe a lot in fate, but it's more like no matter how good or bad your life is, you have the ability to make changes to it, if that is what you truly desire."

"Shaman Medicine . . . Is that herbs and stuff?" I asked.

"Herbs, spices, chanting, ceremony; all of that. I did 3 years with him and learned a lot about hallucinogenic and trance meditations. Indian medicine is quite powerful you know. There are many rituals that use peyote and other natural ingredients to set the mood for seeing visions; sort of a stupor. I also used to read Tarot cards and Runes, but I threw them all away when I started talking to you."

"Yeah, I remember you said something like that on the phone." I said. "Why did you do that?"

"I get visions very easily," She said. "I got the vision that you didn't really care for that sort of thing and also the vision that we would be together for a long time."

"Well, I've been an astrologer for over 30 years and I believe that talent for reading the planets is God given. My Christian beliefs, as well as what I have learned through studies of occult doctrines indicate to me that Tarot and other forms of fortune telling are at the least a negative influence, and may be Satanic in nature."

"So you believe in God?" She asked.

"Of course . . . I'm not a bible thumping, fire and brimstone kind of guy, but I definitely believe in God."

"I'm not sure I can go that far anymore," She explained. "My visions have always scared me with their accuracy but I've never seen a divine entity or an Angel or anything like that. I used to go to church but I found that most of the people, those who went every single Sunday, were the same ones who were out during the week doing bad things."

"I don't know Roxie. My spirituality came more from listening to my music than anything else. Religion is man-made. God never said that you had to go to one church or subscribe to one religion. He only set forth commandments to follow. I try my level best to follow those, not because I go to church, but because the music I listen to tells me this is the path."

"You are an interesting man, Mr. Mark." she commented, "and I can see that we are going to have some lively discussions."

"Discussions or fights?"

"You don't want to fight with me. I always win."

"In my experience, women usually do."

"Astrology is complicated isn't it?" She asked.

"To a degree it is. I used to cast charts by hand which involved a lot of math calculations. But now, the computer software handles it."

"So where do the interpretations come in?"

I explained that each planet has a specific area of ruler-ship, like opportunity, mentality, emotions, etc. When a chart is cast, there are 12 houses and each one has ruler-ship over an area of your life, like finances, career, relationships, etc.

"But the most important thing is the angles made between the planets. That determines how all the influences manifest. Even though there are computer programs out there that will produce a 'black and white' analysis, the only real way to get accurate information is by having an astrologer do a reading."

"Do you do readings?" She asked.

"I used to do it a lot, but not so much anymore. I've been looking at this new astrology called MAGI Astrology. From what I've been able to determine, knowing the added facets of it can make interpretations very accurate. I've been thinking of having a reading done for myself by a certified MAGI astrologer, just to compare. There is a lady in California,

Magi Helena, who is only one of 4 MAGI astrologer in the United States. I just haven't got around to it."

"How expensive is it to have a reading?"

"Magi Helena charges $ 225 per hour session."

"Yikes!" Roxie said, "I guess she's not eating Ramen noodles for dinner."

"Well, when you compare that to other professionals, it's in the ballpark. Have you checked on how much a lawyer charges per hour?"

"I guess," she said, "but it seems to be awful expensive for something that is not proven."

"Roxie," I continued, "there are good and bad astrologers, just like there are good and bad doctors, lawyers, accountants and just about any so called 'professional'. That's why I thought I might have a reading done some day, so I can gauge for myself."

We finished our meal and chit-chatted about a variety of things. Among the many things that I liked about her was that she could talk about just about anything. I also loved the tremor of her voice. It was soothing and calm, like the cool waters of a lake.

"Let's sit on the porch and listen to the radio," I said.

"OK, I'm just going to get some more wine. Do you want some?" She asked.

"No," I said as I got up, "I'm good. I'm just going to have a soda."

I went over to the fridge and filled a tumbler with Coke and headed out on to the front porch.

"I'll be right out," Roxie said.

The evening was wonderful. The air was fresh, frogs were croaking, crickets chirping and every once in a while, I would see the flash of a firefly. Even though the front yard was a mass of wild hay that really needed to be trimmed, it fit in with the county atmosphere. I clicked the radio on and tuned in a local classic rock station. Most of the music down here was 'wall-to-wall' country tunes but the station north of Burkesville focused on playing rock hits from the 70's and 80's and that was just fine with me.

"You know Roxie, they say that if you listen to country music by spinning the record in reverse, a lot of good things happen. You get your car back, your wife back, your dog back, etc.

"Funny Man," she quipped, "What are we going to do tonight?"

"I don't know," I said. "There's nothing to do in town. I don't really want to go anywhere. This is relaxing; why don't we just hang out here and talk for a while?"

"Well, I was thinking," she continued, "you have that box of movies you brought down. Maybe we could try to watch something again. It's a pain in the ass not having cable but I just couldn't afford it, along with the phone and Internet."

"Yeah, that's cool," I said, "I've got a bunch of concert videos and an assortment of movies too. In fact, why don't I hook up that DVD player I brought down and we can do video madness."

"What videos did you say you had?"

"I've got concert videos from YES, Genesis, Yanni, Pink Floyd and Jethro Tull. I've got some comedies, some crime dramas, some action movies and some stuff that I recorded off the Lifetime Channel."

"I know you love YES. Why don't we watch a YES concert?" She said. "I'd like that. Did I tell you that I have 2 YES songs on my Facebook profile?"

"Really," I replied, "another thing we have in common."

I went in the house to find the DVD player. It was a simple hookup because Roxie had a 40" flat screen monitor but no stereo amp. I just had to connect the single video line and plug it in. It was a drag not having home theatre or even a stereo amp but that's something that could be taken care of later. For now, everything could play through the screen audio section.

"All hooked up," I said as I came back on the porch. "We don't have Hi-Fi but we can live with it."

"Up in Utica," she said, "I have a brand new, still in the box, surround sound system."

"Sorry, babe but I'm not driving to Utica New York to get better movie sound."

"Funny Man." She chuckled. "No I meant that if I ever get my stuff back down here, that's one of the items I want to make sure I have."

"Well for now, we can make do," I said, "besides, just seeing a rock concert in Burkesville should be something new and different for you."

"I sort of miss New York sometimes," She said. "My daughters and my sisters, my mom and my brother, friends all live there. My youngest is graduating from Syracuse University next month and I can't even go."

"Which one?" I asked.

"Barbie. She is graduating from Oswego State on May 16th but I don't have the money to get up there."

"Maybe I can help," I said. "I'm planning on going back about that time. How about if we drive up in your car; I'll pick up the tab for the gas and lodging? Then you'll have your car and when you get done, you can drive back."

Roxie got up out of the chair and literally flew over to mine. She planted herself on my lap, put her arms around my neck and said "You would do that for me?"

"Well of course," I said, "you need to go to your young daughter's graduation. This takes care of it for you, and I don't have to take a bus back."

"Oh Mark, I Lov . . . " She stopped short. "Thank you for being so nice. I really think I totally love you."

I was feeling some very intense feelings about her myself. I had said I loved her on the phone during our conversations but being here and seeing her in the flesh, having good times with her, I really was thinking that this was the real thing.

She kissed me on the neck, the lips, the forehead and said "I have to call my daughter and let her know. She is going to be so happy."

Roxie ran in the house and got the cordless phone. Cell phones just didn't work out here in the hinterlands but Roxie had a 'Magic Jack' connection that routed her calls over the Internet. She told me that her long distance charges were only $ 20 per year. I thought that was a smokin' deal and I may want to invest in one for myself, just for the savings.

Gab, Gab, Gab . . . two old hens babbling on. That was Roxie and her daughter. In the middle of the conversation, Roxie asked "When do you want to go up to New York?"

"I don't know . . . The graduation is the 16th of the month, right? Let's think about it and get back to her early next week."

"Ok, Hon." She said, anxious to get back to her daughter.

More gabbing went on and finally, after 25 minutes, they said their goodbyes. I don't know about her. When I get on the phone with my friends, I get the information out that I want, listen to theirs and get off the phone. I am not one to incessantly chatter. My sisters used to do that when I lived with my parents and it drove me crazy. I guess I'm just not a phone person.

And I guess others are.

"Ready for that concert video?" I asked.

"I'm going to take a quick bath and refill my drink," She said. "Will my honey allow me 15 minutes of quality time for myself?"

"Anything babe; just yell when you want me to come in. I'm going to sit out here and enjoy Mother Nature at her finest."

When Roxie left to draw her bath, I thought about the conversation we had regarding her daughter when it occurred to me she said her daughter was graduating from Syracuse University. SU is not the same as Oswego State. The first being a prestigious 4-year private college and the latter being a state college that let any New York resident attend. Oh well, it was probably just a slight slip. Maybe she told that to people rather than try to explain the difference between the two colleges. Or maybe she just said it because Syracuse University was very well know for it's basketball team and the SU logo imbued an aura of class. At any rate, I noticed the faux pas.

Roxie came out on the porch in her bathrobe and sat down with a full glass of wine. The smell of lavender surrounded her body and it whipped at my senses. My thoughts drifted off and I wondered if my feelings would always be the way they were now, when she said,

"I have a favor to ask if you can do it."

"And what would that be?" I replied.

"Well, if I am going up to New York for a while, I need to pay the electric and water bills before I go. Right now I don't have the money but I am going to be selling one of the trucks and some other things on EBay. Is there any way you could lend me the payments before we go? Then I will pay you back when the truck is sold."

"I don't see that as being a problem," I said, "what kind of money are we talking about?"

"I need $ 117 for the electric bill and $ 83 for water."

"That's it? . . . $ 200 total?"

"I would also like to pay on my double wide mortgage, but I guess that can wait. It's only a month overdue."

"How much is that?"

"I've got a good deal with the mortgage holder. I bought it on a land contract and I only pay $ 75 a month."

I thought about what she had told me and then I said, "How does this sound? I'll pay all of them; the electric, the water and get the mortgage current. That's about $ 400 total right. Then you won't have to worry about it. And you can pay me back later."

"Oh, honey," she said, "I don't know how I missed you all these years but I'm going to make up for it from now on."

With that, she got up, sat on my lap again, and smothered me with one of her very wet, very sensuous kisses. "I think we should go watch a concert now."

"Put your arms around my neck and I'll carry you," I said.

"Don't you da . . ." with that I hefted her up off the chair and carried her into the front room and gently placed her on the couch. I went back, shut the front door, killed the lights, and sat down next to her. Once I pressed the 'play' button, I knew we were going to enjoy the rest of the night.

"I wish I had some pot," Roxie said. "There's nothing like a concert with a little weed to go with it."

"I could go for doing a bowl myself," I said, "but I haven't smoked in so long, I'd probably pass out or something."

"Normally one of my friends turns me on to something but I haven't seen either of my suppliers in a while. I love to smoke and wish I could afford to buy a stash that would hold me for a while. I even thought about growing it here on my 23 acres but the State Police are always checking out the farms with their helicopters."

"Well, babe, "I said, "I guess we're out of luck for now."

I had seen the concert before. It was YES Live from the House of Blues in Las Vegas. But Roxie had never seen a concert on her current setup and had never seen YES live ever. She sat there mesmerized watching the guitarist, Steve Howe, playing riffs at lightning speed. The rest of the band was great also, but it was Howe that kept her eyes riveted to the screen. Halfway through the footage, she asked me to put the concert on pause.

"I can't take much more of this," she said, "that guy has so much energy. He's like a Tasmanian Devil."

Then she leaned over to me and said "Anyway, I'm so pumped up, I was thinking of taking a sex break."

"Well are you sure sex and YES mix?" I asked with a smile.

"I think sex mixes with anything, don't you?" With that, she loosened her robe and out popped my two favorite love pillows. She wrapped her arms around my neck and guided my waiting mouth to hers. The essence of Lavender filled my head and the sweetness of her probing tongue fanned the flames of my desire. I laid her back on the couch and opened her robe all the way.

I alternated between kissing her sweet mouth, then her neck, then her mouth again and then her breasts; back to her mouth and on and on as I worked my way down. I got to just below her navel and she said to me "Are you going to do what I think you are going to do?"

My only answer was 'mmmm' as I kept a steady movement to the red covered 'y' of her pelvis. I slipped my tongue inside and began to probe and even though her thighs were clamped over my ears, I could hear short bursts of pleasure coming from her mouth. I slid my fingers inside her as I licked the clit with an up and down motion and suddenly I felt a warm burst of juice coming from her. That was my signal to go even deeper with my tongue and she let out a cry that the next town could have heard.

"Put them in honey, put them in." She cried.

I slowly rose up and gently slid between the milky thighs, putting my stiff member right where it felt the hottest. She cried out again as we began the steady push-pull of passion. I lightly fondled her breast with one hand and the other with my mouth, as I drove my hardness in as deep as it would go. She wrapped her legs around me and bit my shoulder with her teeth. I felt the exotic pain and pushed even harder.

"My God, Yes, My God, Oh Mark, Yes, Yes, God Yes, Harder, Oh Baby, Yes."

My cock was harder than Chinese Arithmetic, and every ounce of my strength reached towards the goal of making her cum as many times as possible. I knew it was very close for me to burst forth and so I reached down into the depths of my reserve and channeled all of my energy. Our climax was like nothing I've ever experience. Bells, whistles, bright flashes of light, sweat bursting out of our bodies, the whole nine yards. It felt like I came for 10 seconds or more. I just could not stop pumping. Finally, totally spent, I rolled off her and collapsed on the living room floor.

Even though I had just expended a titanic amount of energy and was completely satisfied, I remained hard. I was not about to waste this new experience. I staggered upright and mounted her again. I enjoyed the look of shock in her eyes as she felt the fullness of my manhood, not two minutes after what she thought was the end.

"Oh my God Honey, again?"

"Yes my love, again and again until I can't."

I slammed her hard this time. I wanted to make sure that when I looked at her in the light, that she had that freshly-fucked look on her face. My hard-on obeyed as I pushed deep into her with new force. She cried out again and again and once again my body answered. My head was dizzy and I felt like I was going to pass out if I didn't stop this adolescent insanity. I had cum twice in 10 minutes and this was something that was not the norm; at least, not at my advanced age. I allowed my body to relax quietly on her heaving chest for a few seconds before I rolled off and back onto the floor.

"I'm dead," She said. "I think I died and went to heaven."

"So you're saying that you got off?" was my smart ass reply.

"Got off?" she hissed, "are you kidding? I got off 3 times, before you even got on me. What's wrong with you? How can you go like that?"

"You just affect me that way," I said. Then I asked, "Do you like it when I have oral sex with you?"

"Now that is really a dumb question." she said, "you couldn't tell?"

"I'm so glad," I said, "because that is absolutely one of my favorite things to do."

"About that," she murmured, "I would like to do that to you but, I've got a little problem with doing that. It's not my favorite recreation, Honey."

"I understand . . . I just wanted to make sure that I don't offend you or anything."

"I think," she continued "that it's because I was raped when I was 12 years old and that was the first thing he made me do."

She rolled over and lay on top of me on the floor. "But nothing you can do would offend me. You definitely know how to treat a lady."

"Ok Lady," I said. "I'm never one to press an issue. "I just love being with you and making love with you."

There was something sticking in my head about the conversation but I just couldn't fathom it. It probably wasn't important anyway. I was still on fire from our last encounter and loved just being with this wonderful woman. I wanted to admit that I was falling completely in love with her, but thought better of it; at least for the moment. At this point it was just best to enjoy the moment.

But something still remained stuck in the back of my mind. What was it?

* * *

13) The Decision for Heaven

Burkesville, KY—May 1, 2009

I had been with Roxie for over a week now and it had been pretty much heaven. Sure, we had little snippets of arguments now and then but by and large I thought the relationship clicked. We did something unique every day. We traveled to Cookeville, Tennessee and checked out the town; we went to Dale Hollow Lake to watch the boats from above the marina. And with every event, we looked like a couple of young kids in love.

Even though Roxie was not overtly into public displays of affection, she would still accept me holding her hand or putting my arm around her. Just simply sitting by the streams in the backyard was nice. Every night, we would have a wonderful meal. If she didn't cook, I did. And then there was the sex. Here was a woman who I don't think would ever say no to my request. In fact, many times she was the aggressive party. Neither one of us were into being kinky or doing 'rough' sex. But my God, how she would wail when she climaxed. It truly made me feel like I was the best lover in the world.

On one particular day, after we had gone at it 4 different times, I had to tell her that I was not a machine.

"Jesus, Hon," I said, "I love you and you never fail to satisfy me, but keep in mind that I'm not a spry 25 year old anymore."

"You could have fooled me," She said. "I had never climaxed before I met you. You found my hot button."

"Get out of here," I said, "you've never had an orgasm before?"

"No, it's true. My ex husband always told me that I was a lousy lay." she explained. "I did everything he wanted but he still complained. I thought there was something wrong with me."

"Well, babe," I continued "I knew when I did your astrology chart that you were a good match for me. I'm just glad that it goes both ways." "Oh, and by the way, there is nothing wrong with you."

"I love you, Honey," she mewed, "I don't think I've ever been in love before now."

"Roxie, I love you too. THERE; I've said it." I told her. "I know I said I loved you on the phone in our conversations before I came down here, but now I'm convinced of that statement and you have stolen my heart. I've been feeling this way for the week I had been with you, and I just thought it was too early in our relationship to feel like this. But there is no denying it. I LOVE YOU."

"Oh, Mark," she said, "don't ever change. I want to be with you the rest of my life."

We lay together on the couch and talked. It was very relaxing. She told me that she didn't know what to do about living down here. And she had reservations about me going back up to New York next week.

"I know we are both going back up to New York this month," she said, "but I'm afraid of what happens then. I've got to come back here, but you don't."

"Well, let's see. You have stuff up there in storage don't you?" I asked.

"It's in Utica near my daughter and the rest of my family." She said. "It's been there for over a year. Every month I pay storage on the space."

"How does this sound?" I continued, "we go back up, get a U-Haul, pick up your stuff and my stuff and drive back down here."

She jumped up off the couch and said "You mean you want to come back here and live with ME?"

"Why not?" I exclaimed. "We get along great and I can't think of anyone I'd rather be with. And once we are down here, we can take care of any business we have to here and think about maybe moving next year to a bigger town."

"Oh My God, I love you so much."

She sat down on my lap with her legs wide apart facing me and embroiled me with her kisses. I knew if I let this continue, we were going to be headed for another acrobatic competition on the couch, the floor, the kitchen table or some other location.

"Slow down my love," I said, "let's figure this out before we get distracted."

"Ok, what's the plan?" She asked.

"How's this sound. I just got my back payments for my Social Security," I went on, "I checked my bank account online today and the money finally came through. I have about $13,000 in the bank right now. Les, my old roommate, has a Camaro Z-28 just sitting in his garage that he's making payments on. I'm not in love with the car, but it is pretty nice and it's a collectible. If I bought that, it would be helping him out too. So we go up, I buy the car and get it fitted with a hitch. Then we can leave your car at your daughter's house and tow the U-Haul with the Camaro. Later this fall, before winter sets in, we'll fly back up and visit and pick up your car and drive it back. How does that sound?"

"You're so smart. I don't know how I got so lucky," she said, "and that sounds perfect."

"When is your daughter's graduation?" I asked.

"It's Saturday the 16th of May," She said. "We're still going aren't we?"

"Of course," I said, "I was just thinking that maybe we should go up the week before and get everything all packed. You never know how long it's going to take."

"Where would we stay when we're up there?"

"Well, I can stay with Les," I said, "and I thought you wanted to stay with your daughter and granddaughter. Does that work?"

"I don't think I can stand to be away from you for a week." she said, "and I know I couldn't stand to stay with my daughter that long. Can't I stay with you and Les at his house?"

"Maybe for a night," I said, "but the problem is that I only had a single bed and I don't want you to cramp my style."

"Funny Man."

"It's only for a week," I added, trying to let her see my logic.

"Well, I guess you'll have to figure something out, won't you, because I won't have my style cramped."

"Oh I see," I said, "I'LL have to figure it out."

We had another great dinner, watched a movie from NetFlix and crashed early that night. In the darkness, I listened to Roxie's lightly snoring as I laid there. I felt fulfilled because I had finally made the first major step in my life in years; I was moving out of New York and starting a relationship. I rolled over and put my arms around my lover. She moaned softly as we fell asleep.

The next morning I got up as usual and went down to fix coffee. Today was the day that I was going to make a final decision on my web business. I wanted to get it going as soon as possible because I wanted money coming in the door. I took our cups upstairs, placed them on the end table next to the bed and gave Roxie a good morning kiss. She opened up her eyes and smiled with those beautiful blue orbs of sensuality. I knew that if I let her, she would have me crawling back into bed and that was a distraction I didn't need today.

"You looked like you were dreaming," I said.

"I was dreaming of you Honey," she answered, "are you my husband?"

"Not by any legal standards," I said, "but I guess that's what you would call me since I've made this commitment now."

"I like that." She cooed. "It makes me feel so safe, secure, so needed. But I would like the chance to say 'I DO' again."

"You keep on thinking that way dear, because I will always be here. But I did the marriage thing once and will never do it again. You can have my love, my respect, my body, my assets and everything else, but you can't have my name."

I could tell that Roxie wasn't overjoyed with that statement but she didn't say anything.

"I'm going back downstairs and make the decision on my business. Here's your coffee. You relax and come down when you're ready."

"I thought maybe we could . . ."

"Later." I said as I practically ran for the stairs.

Research is critical to being a success in any business and since I had never done online sales before, I planned to spend as much time as I needed to get it right the first time. I looked at different medical products because I owned a medical domain name and wanted to start a website that offered these products for sale. So I began the process of checking out acne removers, magic crystal body toners, colon cleaners, pre-built medical websites and a whole gamut of health/beauty related products. I knew that I wasn't going to be able to launch the site right now, but I at least wanted to have all the basics done so that when we returned from our trip, I could hit the road running and fine tune everything.

Roxie came downstairs about ½ hour later and began rumbling around in the kitchen. She had told me that she was an early-riser before I showed up; but since I'd been keeping her up late at night, she had the urge to stay in bed longer. I smiled at that thought. She came in the office and asked told me she was making breakfast.

"Do you like Eggs Benedict?" Roxie asked.

"Absolutely . . . It's one of my favorites." I said.

"I have some good Canadian bacon but I'm going to have to make the Hollandaise sauce from a mix." she said, "is that OK?"

"The mix is fine Hon," I answered, "do we have anything to get done today?"

"I thought we could go down to the double-wide and you could check it out." She said from the kitchen.

"Yeah, OK," I yelled back, "I'm just going to keep plugging away in here until then."

Twenty minutes later, Roxie came in the office and kissed me on the neck.

"I have a breakfast fit for a king; for m'Lordship." She said.

"The Lordship requests the presence of his Lady at the table." I answered.

I went out into the kitchen and what a spread she had laid out. Eggs Benedict flowing with Hollandaise sauce, cut slices of cantaloupe and honeydew melon, dainty biscuits, juice and coffee. All presented on platters with fancy napkins and very heavy silverware. I thought I was at the Hilton executive suite.

"Baby, you didn't have to go through all this," I said, "I just like simple."

"Get used to it Buster," She said. "This is how we do things when there's royalty in the house."

"It looks like a royal pain in the ass to me," I said, "I'd be happy with paper plates because your cooking is so good. I don't need any extras."

"Well fine then," She said as she threw a potholder at me. "See if I go out of my way again."

"Jesus Honey, settle down," I said, "I'm sorry. It's just that you didn't HAVE to do all this."

"Well I wanted to," She said. "I'm sorry if I went out of my way for you. It won't happen again."

Now I was getting pissed. I thought my statement was pretty clear that I didn't require all this and here she was taking it the wrong way. I knew Redhead's had fiery tempers, but this was bordering on irrationality.

"Like I said, I'm sorry," I repeated, "Can we just sit down and enjoy this beautiful feast."

She sat across from me at the table and proceeded to take her standard small helping, while I was busy gorging myself on the delicious meal. I didn't really know how to respond to her little hissy-fit so I just ate and uttered a few 'mmms' in the process. Finally I asked her,

"When do you want to go to the trailer?"

"Whenever," she answered, "there's no great rush. You do what you have to get done."

She got up and went to the cupboard and pulled out her special 'medicine' and my pills. She put the pills in a little cup and brought everything over to me as I was eating.

"Do you want this raw or in your juice?" She asked, gesturing towards the bottle of 'medicine.'

"Definitely in my juice," I said. "I Don't think I like it raw, like the other day. But what I really want to know is what the ingredients are? I don't want to be taking something that isn't healthy."

"I told you," She barked. "These are special herbs that I get in town and grind up and put into capsules. That's why there isn't an ingredient list on the bottle. Everything in here comes from the health food store in Glasgow."

I didn't like her tone but I wasn't about to get into an argument. I had just admitted that I was in love with this woman so I had better start trusting her. We finished breakfast and I got up and put the dishes in the sink.

"I'll take care of that honey," She said. "You go get your work done so we can relax."

"OK," I said and proceeded to go back in my office.

At about 1 o'clock, I decided that I was done for the day and went out in the living room. Roxie was lying there on the couch with a book on her chest as she snoozed away. I wondered to myself how she got anything sold on EBay and those other sites, because since I had been here, I hadn't ever seen her do any work listing or shipping items. I came around the front of the couch and knelt down and kissed her soft lips.

She Jumped.

"Oh, my God . . . You scared me." She said.

"Sorry," I said, "do you want to go down to the trailer?"

"Sure, we can go. Let me just freshen up."

When she was done, we took the Camry down the road about ½ mile to the double-wide. Weeds took over the front lawn and the place looked abandoned. The trailer itself looked in very good condition except there was no stairway or porch to get into it. Instead, she had placed a 4 foot stepladder up against the front door.

As we were walking up to the entrance, I took a closer look at the Datsun 280-z that was parked there. It was unlocked and I opened the door to check out the interior. Basically, the car was pretty clean except for weeds that had found their way under the lower seam of the door. The exterior was in good shape, even though it needed a serious buffing and wax job, but all-in-all, the car was in good shape. After my quick inspection, I headed up to the entrance of the house.

"Watch your step," she said, "someday I'm going to get someone to build me some decent steps."

We went inside, and I was amazed how big it was. We went from room to room and Roxie pointed out all the damages that the former owners had done to the place. There were holes knocked into walls in every room. The kitchen cabinets were missing because these fine people had left the water in the kitchen sink running and completely soaked the floors. All-in-all it looked totally trashed. Building supplies including large patio doors, exterior doors, interior doors, sinks and other items filled the living room and back bedroom. An exercise machine sat in the middle of one of the bedrooms next to a wheelbarrow full of some kind of muddy gunk that had been shoveled up; a racing bike and a couple of stacks of full sized ceramic tiles added to the decor.

"What's all this stuff," I asked.

"I brought all that stuff from Florida when we closed down the construction company." She said. "Most of it is brand new and it has a lot of value so I put it in here to store until I could sell it."

That made sense. There had to be over $5,000 worth of supplies here. We looked at the rest of the rooms and she became excited about the prospect of living in the trailer this winter.

"I think this could be a cozy little love nest for us," she said, "since you've decided to stay here with me . . . Besides, the house where I live now doesn't have any heat in the winter. This place has a nice fireplace and a Jacuzzi that I'm sure we could find a use for."

"Oh, yeah," I said. I had noticed that little twinkle in her eye and caught her secret meaning in reference to the Jacuzzi. "With a little work, this place could be very nice."

We finished inspecting the trailer and started driving back to the house. I asked her about the Datsun in the 'would be' driveway.

"What are you going to do with the car? It's not good to let it sit out there in the elements."

"I don't know," She said. "That was my baby in Florida and I really like it. Like I told you, it's kind of rare because it was the first year of that model and it's an automatic."

"Maybe we can put it in your barn," I said, "at least it would be out of the weather."

"That's a great idea. I'd like to put money into getting it refurbished some day. I guess that's just another project for my 'to do' list."

We stopped at a group of mailboxes on the roadside, and Roxie picked up the mail. She pointed out a very large, modern house that looked like some kind of mansion, set back from the road about 100 feet.

"That's my neighbor Walt's house," She said. "He comes over once in awhile and smokes a joint with me."

"He's certainly got a nice house." I said.

"Oh, he's got some bucks," she continued, "he used to work at the Toyota factory but got laid off. Now he just works for various people around town. I think the house is all paid for. It's something his ex-wife didn't get in the divorce."

"That's a rarity," I said nodding. "Do you know how a woman is like a hurricane?"

"No," she replied.

"They scream when they come," I continued, "and when they leave, they take the house."

"Funny Man."

We got back to the house and Roxie asked me if I wanted something to eat. I told her that I was still full from that massive breakfast but would probably be ready for dinner around 6 or so. She came over to me and put her arms around me and gave me a kiss. My hands went around her waist and pulled her ever so tightly. I knew what she had in mind and I had sort of promised her a little action earlier this morning. Now was as good of a time as any to keep that promise. I kissed her passionately and unbuttoned my shirt and she was busy undoing my pants. As she gripped my trusty sword she looked straight in my eyes and said "I'm going to do something that I haven't done in quite some time."

I watched the top of her head slowly caress my chest, my stomach, my beltline and finally my throbbing member. I hadn't asked her to do it, and indeed we had discussed it previously when she told me that she had negative thoughts about 'blowjobs'. Roxie had told me that she had done it before but it was not one of her favorite things to do. I'm a typical man and oral sex to me is never a bad thing. In fact, I think it is one of the most personal things that two people can share. But it is also something that the parties must enjoy themselves; not do it just for the satisfaction of the partner . . . And now here she was, without coaxing, taking me in slowly and driving me out of my mind. She gently kissed and licked the head and slowly opened her mouth to take it in. I was in heaven.

"Am I doing OK, Honey?" She asked.

"Oh Honey, there is no wrong way to do that, baby . . . You are driving me crazy."

She kept alternating between hand and mouth on my shaft and with each change; she got a bit more aggressive. I wanted so much to go down on her but being selfish; I didn't want to interrupt what she was doing. Finally, I pulled her up and rotated so that she was lying on the couch. I pulled down her jogging pants and proceeded to attack that red haired little pussy with my tongue. It was like I wanted to lick the inside of her belly button. Roxie moaned in gasps and between my fingers and my tongue, I brought her to two rapid climaxes. I mounted her and drove into her like a heat seeking missile headed for a target in Afghanistan.

"Yes, Yes, Yes," She repeated. "Oh, baby it's so good, Oh, Yes, Harder, Harder."

Our rhythm was increasing and I couldn't hold back anymore. I exploded inside her with a vengeance. It was almost like a fire hose shooting its angry stream at a burning building. She gripped my neck and thrust her legs around my back, pumping the last of my load into her. Finally, with our hearts racing at a dangerous pace, we swooned into each other, totally and completely spent. When I finally got my breath back, I said "You definitely surprised me with that special treat of yours."

"I just wanted to make you feel the way that I feel when you do that to me. I wasn't sure if I was doing it right because every man in the past has told me I was no good at it. That's why I said that I didn't like doing it. But with you honey, it's different. You make me feel so good and special and I just wanted to return the favor."

"Well you did that alright. As long as you like doing it, I'm good with that. I would never make you do something you didn't want to."

"I believe you are teaching me well, my love," she said, "and maybe you will let me do that again sometime." Just hearing the way she put that statement, I started getting a tinge of excitement in my groin. "Are you threatening me with a good time?" I asked.

"No," she replied, "Just warning you though . . . Sometimes, I bite."

I wondered if Eve ever said that to Adam.

* * *

14) Ready to Roll

Burkesville, KY—May 7, 2009

We spent the better part of the week preparing for our trip up north to New York. The way Roxie was packing clothes, you would have thought we were going on a cruise for a month. She had 2 large suitcases, an overnight bag, a cosmetics bag, a delicate fabric bag, her attaché case, her purse and an assortment of plastic bags filled with snacks, soda and other goodies.

"Christ Honey," I said, "we're only going to be gone for 2 weeks. What do you need all these clothes for?"

"I'm a girl," she said, "and I have to dress like a girl. I like being a girl. And girls wear clothes that match."

"Well, the only reason why I said anything," I continued, "was because I might want to take a bag or two of my stuff."

"We've got plenty of room," she said, "and my stuff will fit in the trunk . . . well, most of my stuff. And you can put yours in the back behind the driver's seat."

I knew better than to argue and I really didn't have all that much of my stuff to take. All I had was my attaché case with my computer and a duffle bag with my clothes. Most of my clothes were in Syracuse and we would be bringing a U-Haul back with us. But still, the Camry was fairly waited down with her 'girly' things.

Roxie had volunteered to map out our route home because she had taken the trip before and we were trying to avoid as many construction areas as we could. I spent some time making sure that the car was road-worthy by checking the oil, air, belts and any other items that could lead to a breakdown on the road. We decided to leave around 7 p.m. at night because it was a 19 hour trip and by driving at night, we could avoid a lot of traffic delays.

"Here's our route Honey," Roxie said as I came in from the porch. "It's the most direct way of getting from here to there."

I looked at the map. We would start on Route 75 in Somerset, Kentucky; about 50 miles east of us, head north through West Virginia and Pennsylvania and hit Route 81 north, right into Syracuse. Since we were always heading either north or east, I figured that we should make pretty good time. I estimated that we should get into Syracuse about 2 p.m. the next day, allowing for gas and pee stops. It looked like it was a good route to go.

"I like it," I said. "It's direct and pretty much avoids all the big city snarls. But I think we are going to be screwed when we get to Pennsylvania."

"Why?"

"Because that state is always under road construction," I said. "I drove Route 81 for 15 years when I was on the road and I don't think I've ever missed road work."

She looked at the atlas and said "We can go up Route 65 to Cincinnati and cut over."

"No," I said. "This is fine. Driving at night and getting through West Virginia by morning will be OK. Once we hit 81, it will be like an old shoe to me."

"What time do you want to leave tonight?" She asked.

"I want to be pulling out of town, GOT IT, out of town no later than 7 p.m."

"Yes, your majesty," She snorted. "We wouldn't want the King to be disappointed."

Everything went as planned throughout the afternoon. We finished packing, loaded up the car, and even had a bite to eat. I told Roxie I wanted to take a little power nap, 'til about 5:30 p.m. because it was going to be a long night.

"You go take your nap Hon," she said, "and I'm going to finish my stuff. Then I'm going to snooze a bit too."

I put the last little items in the car and headed upstairs to the bedroom. I like power naps. Just being able to catch a few winks for 20 or 30 minutes is a great help. I laid down, but my mind kept racing about things I needed to do here, things I needed to do when I got there, and trying to squeeze the maximum amount of scheduling into a 2 week period. Needless to say,

I didn't get much sleep. Roxie came up about ½ hour later and lay down next to me. She curled up next to me and I thought she was just going to take a quick nap also. Then I felt her hands moving over my shoulders and down my side. She rubbed a little bit there before her hands found there way to my leg. I didn't need a PHD to figure up what she was doing. Even though sleep would have been nice . . . sleep was avoiding me . . . and Roxie wasn't. I let her dally with me until she started getting more serious about the placement of her fingers. When they found my crotch, my body said 'Wake up Mark, it's time to go to work.'

I remained motionless while Roxie reached up and undid my belt. I thought about pretending to be asleep and let her have her way with me, but I got a sudden flash in my head, of a zipper coming down and catching skin. No way did I need that, so I rolled over and faced my attacker.

"Did you have something in mind?" I asked.

"Oh nothing . . . Just go back to sleep and let me play."

I didn't go back to sleep; we both played.

* * *

15) Driving Madness

Burkesville to Syracuse—May 7, 2009

Finally, at about 6:30 that night, we pulled out of the driveway and headed east. My many years of working various jobs that put me on the road had conditioned me to long stretches of driving. I didn't mind it because I liked to drive and I had my music with me to make the time go faster. In fact, my music was such a major part of my life, I never went anywhere without it.

Back in the 70's, I began collecting albums. Not like an ordinary person; I collected albums at closeout markets, outlet houses and record stores. Sometimes it was just a really neat album cover that caught my eye; but I spent my hard earned money just the same. I think I set a record for music purchases in 1978 when I bought a total of 1134 albums; mostly bands I knew. As of late, I only bought CD's because the records were old technology and way to heavy to be carting around the country like I used to do. I still owned about 2500 albums, but my CD collection was growing to the point that I had about 500 of them also. And my stereo system was always Top Notch. God knows that I loved my music and couldn't wait to get my current system set up at Roxie's house.

"Why don't you put a tape in Honey?" I asked Roxie.

"What do you want to listen to?"

"Surprise me . . . The case is there in the back seat."

She pulled the tape case out and rummaged through it until she lifted out a cassette and slipped it into the player. The music started and I recognized it as 'Roundabout' by YES.

"You did that on purpose," I said with a smile.

"What? . . . I didn't know you liked YES," She said with an innocent look.

I smiled and thought to myself; what a wonderful woman this was. She knew YES was my favorite band and she specifically picked this tape just for me. What a gal.

On and on we went for what seemed forever until finally, we came to the entrance of Route 75 North. This road would take us north to Lexington, where we would catch Route 64 East to Charleston, WV. Then Route 64, another major highway, would take us through the hills of West Virginia where we would catch Route 77 North. This artery would head north again, through the Appalachians, then Pennsylvania, then home.

We drove on through the night, our way lit by the halogen beams of the Camry and the approaching full moon of May. The countryside was very sparse but every once in a while we would see a farmhouse silhouetted in the trees.

"Do you want me to take over driving?" Roxie asked. "You've been at it for 5 hours."

"We're going to be coming into Charleston shortly," I told her, "I've got to get gas and you can take over for a few hours."

I pulled off the highway on the outskirts of Charleston, WV to get gas. After filling up the tank and emptying my tank, I picked up a few road snacks and went back out to the car. I checked the road atlas to make sure we were fairly close to our schedule.

"How about if you drive for a couple hours," I said. "All you have to do is get on here, and go east here," as I pointed to the map, "Route 64 East to Route 77 North. OK?"

"That should be easy," she said, "I'll wake you up if I have any problems."

"No," I rebutted, "You will wake me up if you have any questions at all. The last thing I want is to get lost in West Virginia; the drive's long enough. Remember; Route 64 East to Route 77 North. It should be an exit about 5 or 6 miles from here."

"Yes, Master," was her sneered reply.

Roxie got behind the wheel and aimed the car for the entranceway of Route 64. I tucked myself into a semi-ball and curled up in the passenger seat trying to relax. I would have normally handled all of the driving myself, but 19 hours is a bit much and I didn't really get my power nap earlier that day. So I was a little tired and figured now was as good a time as any to catch some winks. I knew that Roxie could deal with the wheel; she was a fast driver but still pretty good at handling the car; so I felt safe enough to relax while she drove. Within about 5 minutes, I was dozing quietly; the rumble of the road lulling me off to sleep.

I dreamed. In my head were visions of skyscrapers falling all over the place. Everywhere I looked there was the rubble of decimated buildings. For some reason, I didn't seem to be scared, even though it was dangerous where I was standing. I looked around and there weren't any other people in the vicinity; just me . . . and a clown who was laughing.

A short clown with Red hair.

I woke up with a start and looked at my watch. We had been traveling for about an hour and a half since Roxie took over the driving.

"Where are we?" I asked.

"I'm not sure exactly," she said, "but we're still on Route 64."

"SIXTY FOUR!" I said with alarm, "we should be on Route 77 North. Christ, we were only 5 minutes away from the entrance."

"I took the entrance that said Route 64 and Route 77 just like you told me," She replied. They were the same road."

"No, Dammit," I fumed. "Route 77 breaks off and goes north to Morgantown and Route 64 goes southeast."

"Here smartass," she said as she tossed me the map, "you know so much . . . you find out where we are."

I felt my blood pressure rising with her 'holier than though' attitude. Just then we passed a road marker and the BP jumped another notch. Clearly written on the sign was Route 64 and Route 77. The only problem was that the road was heading south. We were coming close to Beckley,

WV. I checked the atlas and we were roughly 60 miles from where I fell asleep; going in the wrong direction.

"Get off at the next exit," I said, "we're going the wrong way."

"I followed the signs," Roxie said. "I did what you told me to do."

"No you didn't . . . I said if you had any questions to wake me," I hissed. "I thought it was a simple enough request but I guess not because now we've lost a couple of hours!"

We got off the highway at the exit, made a U-turn and got going north on the same road. Roxie asked me if I wanted to drive and I just answered no. I had always been taught that if you can't say anything good about or to a person, that it was better to not say anything at all. That's what I did now. I sat there, pissed and listened to the road roll underneath the wheels. Two hours of additional driving was going to make this trip even more of a drag than it already was. And the last thing I wanted was to spend the time arguing with Roxie. So I didn't say anything . . . Just rode. We got to Charleston (again) and she asked me if I wanted to drive. I told her no again and said that when we got to Morgantown, about 2 ½ hours from now, that I would take over the driving.

"It's a straight shot up Route 77 North," I said. "Just stay on this road and don't turn off."

"Why are you being so mean?" She asked me. "I followed the signs. How was I to know that I was going the wrong way?"

"Roxie, I said if you had any questions, to wake me . . . You didn't." I said. "The fucking sign said 64 and 77 south. Now we've lost 3 hours; making a 19 hour trip 22 hours."

"Well I think it's pretty stupid of them to have confusing signs like that."

I was pissed at losing time and pissed at her for not asking directions. But it didn't make much sense to get into an argument over it. Perhaps if I was unfamiliar with a road, I would have made the same mistake but having been on the road so often before, I was very observant of signs. So I just let it pass.

"Don't worry, it's only time," I said, "we've got all week so it's no big deal."

"Oh Honey," She said. "That's why I love you so much. You are so forgiving."

"What else can I do," I said with a smile. "You've got me trapped in a Camry in 'Deliverance' country. Just make sure you wake me up in Morgantown. By then, I'll want coffee and a pee."

I rolled over and tried to get back to sleep. I was still pissed, but somehow her mistake was washed away in the flood of love that I felt for her. I let the road noise take me again to the valley of dreams. We hadn't driven very long at all when Roxie woke me up.

"You've got to take over," she said, "I can't handle this."

"What can't you handle?" I asked.

"Just look at this fog," She whined. "I'm not good driving in fog anyway, but these hills and curvy roads are killing me."

If I had known what was coming up on the road, I might have turned around then myself. It was hilly, but that wasn't the problem; the problem was the fog. We could only see about 10 feet in front of us. Now and then we would hit a clear patch where we could drive without grinding our fingernails into the wheel. But that was few and far between. Most of this stretch was up and down the hills at 30 miles per hour. Needless to say, I was getting even more pissed. It was bad enough having to make this now 22 hour trip, but this was brutal. We pulled over and switched seats. I thought that if we were going to go over the side of a mountain, I wanted to be driving. Even Roxie was nervous. Periodically she would hiss an intake of breath or try to put her foot down on an imaginary brake pedal when the road would shift and the car would sway as I negotiated the curves.

"Will you slow down?" She yelled.

"Honey," I answered, "it's the road . . . I can only go about 30 and even that's a bit fast for all these damned curves. Who designed this road anyway . . . Stevie Wonder?"

What I thought would be 2 ½ hours to our next stop, turned out to be more like 3 ½ hours because we were going so slowly. Finally at 6:30 a.m., we pulled off the road to get gas in Morgantown. My ass was dragging and we still had another 10 hours to go. This was turning into the trip from hell. God help us if we run into any more unexpected delays. I checked the road atlas again to verify our route.

"We're going to take Route 68 East to Cumberland, WV." I said. "From there we can keep going straight to Hagerstown and hit Route 81

North or bypass that and take Route 70 North. Both of these roads lead to Harrisburg, PA. I like having options, in case we run into construction."

"Oh my honey, you're so smart," She said.

I just smiled at her and headed for the highway. The rest of the trip remained uneventful. We ran into some traffic snarls around Hagerstown, MD., which ate up about an hour, but other than that, everything went fine. The trip was monotonous; I had traveled this road thousands of times when I was doing my consulting business years ago. But I was headed home with my honey. And that was worth all the aggravation of this trip.

We finally pulled into Syracuse at 7:30 p.m.; only 5 hours later than my original estimation. I was dead tired and just wanted to grab a bite to eat and sleep. We stayed at a cheap motel on State Fair Boulevard because it was right off the exit, close to tomorrow's destination and had vacancy. When we got into our room I was pretty disgusted at the condition of it. It was shabby, had exposed pipes in the bathroom and looked like the setting for a 50's horror movie. But it was only $ 65 per night and I figured that tomorrow we could get another place.

Roxie was busy unloading the car. Bag after bag was coming in through the door when I finally asked her why she was unpacking the car.

"I need my things Honey," she said, "you know . . . my girly things."

"I know," I said, "but do you need everything in here? Can't you just grab a bag for tomorrow clothes? We're not moving in here."

"I like to be dressed nice and I need my things," She barked. "I have to match up what I'm going to be wearing tomorrow so leave me alone. You just relax."

Bitch, was the word that floated through my mind. But I kept my mouth shut. I was too tired to fight about anything anyway. She got all her stuff loaded into the room and we called Pizza Hut and had a pie delivered to the room. We already had a cooler of cold beer so I was a happy camper, eating pizza and having a brew. And I was back in Syracuse; this time with my sweetheart. It was a 24 hour trip and Roxie had shown a bit of her 'nasty' side. But we were both tired and the next week was going to be so much fun. I knew we would be meeting friends and family, saying tearful goodbyes for the present and getting ready to start a new chapter in our lives. I felt optimistic about the future.

I allowed the quiet night to wrap itself around me as I drifted off to sleep. In the darkness, I lapsed into another dream. What was up with that? I hardly ever dreamed; at least I hardly ever remembered my dreams. In this one, I was walking across a frozen lake. It was cold and I could feel the wind on my cheeks, but it wasn't uncomfortable. I didn't have any idea where I was going, but for some reason I was out on that lake.

"Plink," I heard. I looked around and couldn't see anything.

"Plink," again.

What the hell was that noise? Again, I looked around and saw nothing. This time I concentrated and then I heard it again.

"Plink."

It was the ice. As I walked, minute cracks formed behind me. Only one word formed in my brain.

RUN!

I saw cracks in the ice behind me; I ran forward and made a large semi-circle on the surface of the lake. I took off full speed for the waiting land. I had to get to the shore before any major cracks materialized. I was about 20 feet from the edge of the water when I heard a large 'whoosh' behind me. As I raced toward the shore, I glanced over my shoulder and saw a large chunk of the frozen surface had collapsed behind me; right where I had been standing 20 seconds earlier. A fissure arose out of the opening and followed me to the shore. With all the strength I had in my reserve, I leaped and landed on the snowy surface of dry land.

I shot straight up out of bed. The room was dark and Roxie was lying next to me lightly snoring. I felt a light sweat on my shoulders as I shook the cobwebs out of my head.

What the hell was that about? I thought. I hadn't had nightmares in a long time and I had a difficult time remembering daydreams. Now in two days, I've had visions that were unnerving. Had I changed medicines lately?

No.

Was I under stress?

Maybe.

I didn't know what the answer was but I didn't want it to become habit. I got up, went to the bathroom, had a drink of water and settled back down into bed. My sleeping beauty was there next to me. I was home for a while and things were going to be great. Even with all the aggravation of the long drive, I was thankful that life was good.

I allowed sleep to once again take me away.

* * *

16) Back Home Again

Syracuse, NY—May 8, 2009

I woke up the next morning with a huge erection. This was sort of a surprise for me, because it had been awhile since I began the day like that, and since I had just driven 24 hours and was exhausted the night before. At my age, I am appreciative of any gift the universe gives me so I rolled over to the beautiful redhead laying next to me and began kissing her ear. At the same time, I began to lightly massage her shoulders, her arms and then running my hand down her side and back up again. I continued my gentle caresses until her eyes fluttered open and she said to me,

"And what do you want?"

"Oh, nothing my dear," I said. "I'm just lying here watching you sleep and wondering when the swelling will go down."

Roxie bolted upward and turned to look at me. She looked at both sides of my head and then reached up and started feeling the top of her head, her face and her shoulders, and then she asked," What swelling?"

I took her hand and guided it to my penis and said "right here dear. See, it's all swollen." She smiled and said "Maybe we can do something about that."

That was the invitation I was hoping for. We began our usual hugging, kissing and general foreplay which led into a full fury lovemaking session. I presumed that the neighbors could hear us because the walls of the room looked paper thin. We laid there in the stillness of the room and held each other. "You know how to wake up a gal Mr. Mark." She said.

"Well I figured I better get something out the $ 65 bucks I spent on this palace."

"Funny Man," was her comeback.

Roxie got up and went into the bathroom. She yelled out the door to tell me that she was starving. I told her there was a Denny's about a mile up the road where we could get breakfast if that was ok.

"That's fine with me," she said, "what's on our agenda today?"

"First stop is to go over to see Les and make arrangements to pick up my stuff this week." I told her, "That way, I can pick up my Buick and have a set of wheels. Then, I thought we would drive down to your daughter's house so I can meet her. I don't know what you plan as far as being there or staying with me or what."

"Bonnie wants me to stay at her house," She said. "I want to see my mother and sisters but I have all week to do that. The only thing I have to do is call Barbie and let her know I'm here and will be at her graduation next Saturday."

"OK," I said, "let me clean up and we'll catch breakfast and get going."

As soon as we were both ready, I helped Roxie reload her 200 fucking bags into the car. It was really more like 5 bags but still, a lot more than she needed. We ate a nice breakfast and then headed over to see Les. I had called him on the cell phone and so I knew he was home. It was a beautiful May morning in Syracuse as we pulled into Les's driveway. He was in the garage working and we both walked up like we owned the place.

"Les," I said, "this is my Kentucky Woman, Roxie."

"Mark," Les said, "does she know about your lurid past?"

Here we go . . . Les starting his shit right off the bat. He couldn't just be like a normal person and be civil. No, Les had a penchant for continually busting balls.

"Of course she does Les," I said, "and that's why I brought her here to show her what she was rescuing me from."

"You asshole," was his response.

"Where are the keys to my car?" I asked.

"Right here hanging up," Les said, lifting them off a key hook. "You're not going back now are you?"

"Hell No," I said emphatically. "Roxie is going to see her family and I'm coming back here. We're here for 2 weeks. I've got a lot to get done."

"OK," Les said, "I'll leave the garage unlocked so you can come and go as you please."

"Thanks man." I said and started up my car.

Les said, "I've been driving your car to work. It gets better gas mileage than mine and since I lost my license, I don't want the cops looking for my car on the road."

"And who is going to pay the towing and storage costs if you get caught?" I asked. For starters, you shouldn't even be driving without a license."

"That's why I was driving your car dickhead," He said. "You think I want them to impound mine? Anyway, it kept your battery charged up. I didn't know how long you would be gone."

"Man, you are a real piece of work."

We hung around for a while talking and making arrangements for getting my stuff out. I told him that I would give him a call later to let him know the schedule. Roxie and I got into our cars and made our way down the road. I got about a mile down the road and I pulled over and went back to her car.

"How the hell can you stand him?" she said, "he is so obnoxious."

"That's Les," I said, "Now you see what I've been putting up with for over a year. Actually, he's not a bad guy. He just doesn't have any social graces and he seems to think that the world owes him a favor. I think he talks, just to hear himself talk."

"Well no wonder his wife left him," She said. "I couldn't stand to be around him more than an hour. He never shuts up. I don't know how you put up with him for so long. He's obnoxious."

"Well Honey, he's part of my past now." I said. "I know that today isn't the last time you'll have to deal with him but once we get my stuff out, it will just be by telephone."

I told her to lead because I didn't know the way to her daughter's house. It took us about an hour to drive to where Bonnie lived. We pulled into the drive and Roxie just walked up and opened the door.

"We're here," she said as she walked inside, "get up and get dressed."

"Mom, I'm dressed and you're late." Bonnie said. "You told me you'd be here by 10 and now it's almost noon."

"Sorry," Roxie said as she smiled at me, "we got sidetracked"

"Where's Brianna?" Roxie asked.

"NANA!" came a shout from the hallway. Standing there was a little 6 year old girl.

"Oh baby, I've missed you," Roxie said.

With that, she turned to me and introduced me.

"Mark," she said, "This is my daughter Bonnie and my granddaughter Brianna."

I shook hands and smiled, being as cordial as I could around strangers. Bonnie didn't seem to be friendly at all. She didn't smile and her handshake more obligatory than anything. I shifted the conversation to the huge stereo system in the living room that I noticed when we came in. "That's quite a sound system you have Bonnie."

"Oscar bought that last year," Bonnie said. "We like it."

I presumed Oscar was Bonnie's husband and Brianna's father. I didn't feel like I should clarify that right this minute, so I filed it away for a future question. We hung around and talked for about an hour and decided that Roxie would stay here for a while and I would go back and stay at Les's house. Roxie didn't like the idea but it was just easier for me to get my stuff done. And her being here with her family, kept her out of my hair. We made arrangements for me to come back down later during the week to pack Roxie's goods and get them loaded in the U-haul. I still had to buy a bumper hitch for the car and rent the trailer. I said goodbye and left to go back to Syracuse.

Roxie and I talked on the phone about 3 times during that day. She complained about how her daughter was pissed because she wasn't spending every waking hour with her. Roxie told me that Bonnie was just a natural born whiner and although she was used to her complaining, she was going to have to get out of there soon.

"I miss you already Honey," she said, "and I want to stay with you."

The rest of the day was pretty much how I planned it. I went and visited some old friends, catching up on news and letting them know my plans to move to Kentucky. After tipping back a drink with each one of them I headed back over to the house. I told Les I had a super deal for him.

"Les, here's what I'll do for you," I said. "You're not driving the Camaro and you haven't had anyone beating your door down for it. What do you need to get out of it?"

"I've had it advertised for $10,000 in the paper," He said.

"And how many calls have you had?"

"None."

"What's your payoff on it?" I asked.

"I still owe $6,800 to the credit union."

"Les, I'll give you $7,000 cash." I told him.

"Hey . . . I'm not making any money," He whined. "As a matter of fact, I'm losing money. I paid $8,900 for it last year."

"Keep it then Les," I said, "I'm not in love with the car, but I thought I'd be doing you a favor by taking it off your hands. I'll just drive the Buick to Kentucky instead."

"You're a thief Mark," Les fumed. "You know I bought that car to make money on. This is a collectible and the value will go up every year."

"And then you got a DWI and can't drive it," I said, "I suppose that's my fault too."

"$7,500 and it's yours." He finally said.

"Les, I'll give you $7,000 and my Buick that you've been driving," I replied. "That's a good deal because the Buick is worth at least $ 500 and it's a nice car to drive. That way you can still hide from the cops."

"Deal," He agreed and we shook hands.

I said, "I'll go to the bank and get the money Monday and we can meet at the DMV and transfer the title and get my plates for the Camaro."

"Deal," He confirmed.

"There's another matter I want to discuss," I continued, "I can stay in motel rooms while I'm here or if it's acceptable to you, I can stay here and sleep downstairs. I'll be out by May 21st."

"Give me a C note and we'll call it even." He said.

I figured he would let me stay for free since I gave him $2,000 back in November for his DWI fund and I was supposed to be paid up through the end of May. But not Les, Mr. Mercenary. Oh well, he needed the money for his legal defense.

I started packing up all my stuff. I had most of it done but there were clothes and small items that needed boxes. I spent the rest of the day packing and then went inside to watch television. Les came down and invited me upstairs to watch TV and to share some Kentucky Fried Chicken. I accepted and we talked about my upcoming trip.

"What if things don't work out between you two?" He asked.

"Fuck it," I said, "I'll be that much closer to Tennessee won't I. What do you think of her?"

"She seems nice. She's definitely good looking," He said. "I don't know how you do it Mark. You always seem to come out smelling like a rose. Look at you, 6 months ago you were homeless and now you've got this little fox eating out of your hand. You must have a 10″ dick or something."

"No, I've only got a 2 inch dick Les," I said, "but the diameter isn't everything." We both laughed.

"Is she a good piece of ass?" Les asked.

"Les, have you ever had a bad piece of ass?"

We both laughed again.

On Monday, I got the money from the bank and met Les to transfer the paperwork. I got insurance and plates, signed the Buick over to him and took the Camaro out for the first time. Les had owned the car for all the time I lived there but he would never let me drive it. So this was a real treat. The car itself was loaded with every option including T-Tops. It had a Corvette LT-1 engine and actually sounded like a Corvette going down the road. Even though I wasn't in love with the car, it was probably the nicest car I had owned in 20 years. I had always been content to drive winter rats. They weren't really shit boxes but they were not pristine either. I'd drive them till something major went on them and then I'd buy a new one . . . It worked for me.

Roxie and I talked several times on the phone throughout that week and I never mentioned the car. I figured I would surprise her when I went down to pack her stuff. We made arrangements for me to go down there on Friday and pack all day. I got all the boxes I needed and finished packing up my stuff. Friday came and I went down to Bonnie's house to pick Roxie up. You should have seen the look on her face when I pulled up in the Camaro.

"What's this Mark?" she asked, "did you win the lottery?"

"No Honey," I said, "I figured you needed to ride in style so I bought it."

"What happened to the Buick?" She asked.

"I traded it to Les; that and $7,100 got me this."

"God, I love it," she said, "and it goes perfectly with my Red hair."

We took off and went over to her storage facility. I thought her house looked like a rummage sale when I first saw it, but her storage facility was ten times worse. She had more crap stacked up than I have ever seen. Boxes and boxes of knick-knacks, old chairs, clothes and every other thing in the world.'

"Honey," I said, "we are never going to fit all this in the U-haul with my stuff. I've got 2500 record albums and all my stereo equipment, computer equipment, clothes and whatever."

"We're not taking all this," she said, "but I have to weed through this and figure out what is going and what is staying. My sisters are getting most of this and my mother has some of her stuff stored in here too. Don't worry."

We spent the day going through everything and by the time we were done, we had arranged the storage bin into 3 nice, neat rows; there was other people's stuff, stuff that's staying and stuff that's going. I estimated that even though space was going to be tight, we would be able to fit everything in the U-haul.

"Well," I said, "That takes care of that nasty little problem. What now?"

"Let's go over and you can meet my mother," She said.

So we got in the Camaro and headed over to her mother's house. It was actually her brother's house but Roxie's mother lived there in a separate section. She was a very attractive woman of about late 60's or early 70's and I could see the resemblance between the two of them; except that Roxie had the Red hair. We chatted for a while and her mother loved me. She told me how Roxie had a lot of bad luck with men and sheshe really was happy that she finally found someone nice. I took the compliment graciously and gave her a hug. Roxie told me later that doing that made her day.

We decided that Roxie would come back to Syracuse with me and spend the night at Les's because she was going crazy at her daughter's house. Then, I could drive her to the graduation tomorrow and she could ride back home with Bonnie. Plus, she also said that she wanted to get her horns clipped.

I knew what that meant.

* * *

17) Attraction Madness

Syracuse, NY—May 16-17, 2009

Saturday morning came and I took Roxie to her daughter's graduation. It was about an hour north to the State University campus and I figured we would have time to talk a bit. We stopped at a diner on the way up and had breakfast because Roxie didn't know when the ceremony would be over and wanted to have a little in her stomach.

"I swear Mark," she said over coffee, "I will never spend another night at Les's again."

It wasn't the fact that we were in his unfinished basement. It wasn't the fact that we both slept on a twin bed. It was the fact that Les kept coming downstairs with some lame excuse to talk. First he wanted to know if we were hungry. Then he came back and wanted me to find an article in the paper for him. The he was back with pictures of his grandson. Naturally, on each visit, he had to get into an elongated story about how he did this or did that or went here or whatever. He just talked, to hear himself talk; and it was all pretty much bullshit, which he was spewing out.

"In a way, I feel sorry for Les, I said. "I think he's always been like that and people tend to dislike that in a person. I know people here who run when they see him coming their way. They know how he is and want to avoid him. It's almost like he has a persecution complex."

"He's just obnoxious." Roxie said. "I know he's your friend but he offends me."

"Well Honey," I said, "You don't have to worry about it. The next time we are there, it will be to pick up the trailer and scoot."

"Thank Christ for that." She said.

"No . . . Thank Mark." I said with a grin.

"Funny Man," she muttered, "but I'll say one thing. I've grown to appreciate my own bed a lot more."

"Yeah, that single bed is brutal," I said, "it's OK for one person, but for two people it's a bit too much."

"How did you like my daughter Bonnie?" She asked.

"She's fine," I commented. "A bit subdued I thought, but she is her mother's daughter."

"She's more of a bitch than I ever thought of being." Roxie said. "I love her and I especially love Brianna; but I have to take Bonnie in small doses."

"Is Oscar her husband?" I asked.

"No," she said, "they have been living together for about 4 years now."

"So Oscar isn't Brianna's father?"

"No," again she explained, "Oscar came into her life when Bonnie's husband died 5 years ago."

"What happened to him?" I inquired.

"Back in 2000, her husband was working for my construction company doing remodeling." She said. "He fell off of a 3 story building and landed on a pile of rocks. He died instantly."

"God, that's awful." I exclaimed.

"Bonnie was pretty shaken up of course," she continued, "but he did leave a $1 million dollar trust fund for his daughter. That's the only thing about him that I liked."

"You didn't like him?" I asked.

"No, he never listened to a damned thing I told him." She said. "My ex-husband and I were living up there at the time and we wanted them to buy a house. He wouldn't. He just wouldn't listen to common sense. He and I didn't ever really get along."

"A million bucks is a lot of money." I said.

"That's another thing he did," Roxie barked, "He put the money in a trust fund for his daughter; not Bonnie. Brianna has to wait until she is 14 years old to get half of it, and then when she is 18 she will get the rest. Bonnie could have used the money after he died but she got screwed on that point."

"She doesn't get anything?" I asked.

"No, not directly," she continued, "but Bonnie and I are co-executors of the will. When Brianna gets her money, we get paid for our help. When she turns 14, both Bonnie and I will get about $ 50 thousand dollars each; then a final amount when Brianna turns 18 years old."

It seemed to me that Roxie was more interested in the trust fund, than the welfare of her daughter, or granddaughter. But I'm not a parent and I don't know anything about the situation. Maybe Bonnie's husband was a jerk. Maybe he slapped her around. I don't know. I just seemed to get an odd feeling about the whole thing. It was almost like she was happy the guy was dead. Maybe his death was somehow Roxie's fault . . . Nah, it's probably just my over active imagination.

I dropped Roxie off at the University Auditorium when I saw her mother and daughter there. I kissed her and told her to call if she had any problems. Then I wheeled the Camaro around and went back home. I didn't really have anything more to do that day, so I spent the time visiting some of my old haunts. I met friends and banged back a couple of beers while watching the games on TV. I was going to miss this part of my life.

Burkesville was no social Mecca in the first place but being able to go to a local bar was one of the things I always enjoyed. Now that was off the table for a while. It just gave me more motivation to straighten up some of the things in Roxie's life and then get to another vibrant location. Plus, I really wanted to get this online business set up, and by staying out of the bars, I might have a chance.

Roxie called later that night at about 8 p.m. and her ass was on fire. I could tell that she had been drinking, but she was pretty much screaming on the phone about her ex-husband and what a moron and blah, blah, blah.

"What the hell is the problem?" I asked her, being as calm as I could be.

"That son of a bitch ex-husband was there at the graduation." she screamed. "Fucking asshole had the balls to show up after what he did."

"What did he do?" I asked.

"He abandoned me. He abandoned us." She said. "He got me pregnant and left 6 months later."

"Doesn't he talk to Bonnie and your son?" I probed.

"NO!" she screamed again, "he has really nothing to do with Bonnie or Bobby, because he is not their father. This was a guy I married after I divorced Bonnie and Bobby's dad. What a mistake that was. But he is Barbie's flesh and blood and he up and left us without any support or anything."

"How did he know that Barbie was graduating?" I asked.

"He and Barbie have been talking for 15 years," she explained, "That's why I'm not as close to Barbie as I am to the other two kids. Barbie thinks the world of him and I found out that he told her that he left because of me."

"Jeez," I said, trying to be funny, "you do put the fun in dysfunctional, don't you?"

"It's not funny," She screamed again. "You don't know what it's like to have to raise four kids, at the same time, all alone." She went on with here rage.

"I had 4 hungry mouths to feed and I was never there to see them, because I had to work 2 jobs." "It was only the fact that I got insurance money from my dead daughter that we were able to survive. I haven't seen that asshole in 20 years and now he shows up at Barbie's graduation." she said, "and I want to stay with you tonight."

"How about tomorrow Honey?" I said. "It's late, you've been drinking, I've been drinking and tomorrow we can get together and spend the day and I'll get a room here . . . OK?"

"I suppose," She said reluctantly, "I just need to see you. I need you."

"I know baby. I'll pick you up at Bonnie's around 10:30 in the morning." I confirmed.

What dead daughter? I thought. That's the first I'd heard about that. I had met Bonnie and Barbie and had heard about her son; but a dead daughter . . . that was a new one. It was something I would have to explore at a later date. Roxie was way too emotional right now to go into it.

"So I'll pick you up tomorrow at around 10:30, OK?"

"Don't be late baby; I can't stand being without you this long. I love you."

"See you tomorrow, Honey. I love you too."

I hung up, thankful that I didn't have to make the trip down to Utica to rescue her tonight.

True to my word, I was at Bonnie's house the next day at 10:30 a.m. And true to Roxie, she had multiple suitcases. The Camaro is not that big and certainly not big enough to carry 3 large bags in the back seat. Besides, it was a nice day and I wanted to leave the T-Tops out and not have to worry about someone stealing her clothes.

"OK, here's the deal," I said, "leave 2 of those bags here. We are not going on a cruise; we are going to spend an overnight in Syracuse."

"But I need my girly things," She whined.

"Leave 2 bags or I will leave . . . Without you."

"You're a royal asshole," She spouted. "Why can't I take this with me?"

"You don't need it for an overnight," I said. "I want to leave the tops out and not have to worry about some light fingered passerby. What part of no don't you understand?"

"Can I at least take a toothbrush and a coat, your highness?" She snapped.

Her attitude was pissing me off. I thought that she, of all people, would be able to understand but it seemed like she wanted to have her way, all the time.

"No," I said, "I've got a mechanic's jacket in the trunk and paper towels to brush your teeth."

"You are not being funny, at all." came another snap.

She took two bags into the house, came out and slammed the door. We got into the car and drove towards Utica, with no place in particular in mind.

"Honey, don't be mad," I said. "I just didn't think you needed your entire wardrobe for a one-night stay, that's all."

She sat there with a sour look on her face and I started thinking, 'why did I even bother coming down here'. I was having a delightful time back home with my friends and now I've got to put up with this shit all day?

"You didn't have to yell at me," she finally said, "I just like to look nice."

"Honey, you would look nice in a grease-rag wrap."

That brought a smile to her face. She turned in her seat and said "I'll bet you say that to all the girls."

"No, just the ones I love."

Whew . . . dodged another bullet.

What was up with that attitude again? Hopefully it wasn't going to continue. It looks like the storm is over; at least for now.

We spent the day running around Utica and then we went to Turning Stone Casino and I dropped a few bucks trying to gamble my way into the lap of luxury. I just couldn't get a run at blackjack and Roxie looked as if she was bored stiff. So we left and headed back to Syracuse.

"I got us a nice room at the Ranch Motel," I said. "We can check in and go down to the restaurant and eat or go into the bar and drink."

"I like that idea." She replied.

We checked in, went down to our room on the lower level and unloaded our bags and then proceeded to go into the bar. There was some kind of party going on there because the place was packed. We ended up getting seats at the bar and settled into a serious night of drinking. I asked Roxie if she wanted to eat and she said that she just wanted some bar munchies. She had a big breakfast and it was still with her and I knew that she ate like a bird anyway. I was happy to save the dinner money for more drinks; drinks and Quick Draw.

Quick Draw is a lottery game that is played in a lot of bars and restaurants in New York. It's basically Keno, but the games come up every 4 minutes. You just fill out your numbers, pay the ticket and then watch, as every number that you didn't pick comes in. There are some winners but it's a tough way to make money. Both Roxie and I filled out cards and submitted them to the cashier.

"You feel lucky tonight?" I asked her. She grabbed my arm and said "I'm already lucky. I've got you."

We sat there for a couple of hours, drinking and playing Quick Draw. Roxie hit a $ 55 winner and we used that money to buy more booze. I drank my Pabst beer and she was on her Rum and Cokes. I wasn't worried because we weren't driving and we just had to walk back to the room. Hence, both of us were getting a bit tipsy.

The crowd thinned out and I happened to catch a glimpse of an old acquaintance of mine, Wanda. She saw me and came right over to us.

"Hi Wanda," I said. "Long time, no see."

"Mark it's good to see you," she responded, "I moved to the east side and don't get over here much. I'm here with my husband's work crew party. Well, he was here but he's passed out."

"Looks like more than a few of these people have been over-served." I said.

"Including my husband," She said. "He's crashed down in our room. I was just going to head back when I saw you two."

I made the introductions and it was like these two girls were long lost friends. Chat, Chat, Chat . . . you really would think they knew each other forever. Chat, Chat, Chat, Chat. We stayed at the bar for another hour and the girls did most of the talking themselves.

Finally I told Roxie, "Hon, they are getting ready to close. We've got to go."

She agreed and we got up to head for the room. Wanda continued to talk as we walked down the hallway. When I got to the door of our room, I told her goodnight and opened the door. Wanda proceeded to follow us into the room and ask if we had anything to drink.

"No babe, sorry," I said, "we didn't bring a stash because we were drinking at the bar."

"Well," she said, "I can run up to my room and grab some beers."

"No, I'll pass," I said, "I think we've had enough tonight and tomorrow is going to be a long day for us."

"Are you kicking me out?" Wanda asked.

"Well, it is late," I followed. "Why?"

"My old man is passed out and I thought maybe you two might like to play," she said, "you know, the three of us," as she glanced at Roxie.

I caught the meaning and looked at Roxie, waiting for her to tell Wanda to get lost. I was a bit taken back when Roxie just looked at me and shrugged her shoulders and said, "Whatever you want dear,"

I was dazed. I never in my life expected this response from her. Men all over the world have fantasies about ménage 'a trios, but maybe I'm too old or too prudish. It just wasn't my thing. I didn't know if Roxie was just trying to make me happy or if this was something that she had experience with before. But I didn't like it.

"No Wanda," I said. "Sorry but I got to pass on that. Like I said, tomorrow's a busy day."

"OK," she said, "it's your loss." And with that, she trotted, or rather staggered out the door.

I didn't really know how to handle this scene that I had just witnessed. I kept thinking to myself that it had to be the alcohol. Roxie wasn't like that. Maybe she was just so drunk that she didn't know what to say. Whatever the reason, I sensed a small crack developing in our relationship. It was nothing major because it could have been a combination of things.

But it was a crack, nonetheless.

* * *

18) Say Goodbye to Syracuse

Syracuse, NY—May 18-21, 2009

We got up in the morning and checked out of the motel. Neither one of us mentioned the 'incident' last night with Wanda. I think either Roxie didn't remember or she wanted to forget. Either way, the topic never came up. We had a nice breakfast at Stella's Diner, a local landmark in Syracuse and then we got on the Thruway and headed back to Utica.

"Are you staying at Bonnie's tonight?" She asked.

"I hadn't planned on it," I said. "I don't really have anything going on tomorrow so I could stay. I'd need to get some toiletries."

"Well, I'd better ask Bonnie first," she said, "she's kind of picky about who is in her house."

Just then, my cell phone rang. I looked at the caller ID and didn't recognize the number but I picked it up anyway. It was Roxie's mother calling for her. I handed her the phone and they gabbed for about 15 minutes. I didn't care because it was the weekend and I had free minutes but if it had been during the week, I would have had an issue. When she hung up, I asked her, "How did your mom get my number?"

"I gave out your number to everybody in my family," She said. "That way I don't have to pay roaming charges and minutes on my phone that has a Kentucky exchange."

"Oh, so it's ok that I pay for you?" I said with a scowl.

"Well, you've got a local number and I don't, "she barked back, "quit being so cheap."

"I am not cheap!" I said, elevating my voice, "but don't you think you should have asked me first?"

"What's the big deal," she said, "it's a couple of stinking phone calls."

That attitude again. There's an old saying to never assume anything because you make an ass out of you and me. But I guess nothing bothered Roxie in this department because she had an attitude that anything you don't have, you take. I didn't like that attitude. Maybe it was because I was brought up to be courteous and to say please and thank you and all that social stuff. It wasn't the end of the world, but I damn sure didn't like it.

"My mother wants us to get together with the family," Roxie said. "I didn't know what the schedule was so I told her I would get back with her."

"I was planning on Wednesday to pick up all your stuff at the storage bin," I said. "I'm getting the U-haul that morning and would like to load your stuff first."

"OK," she said, "that works for me. We can load everything and go over to Bonnie's for the family get-together. My mom, my brother, my sisters and all their families are going to be there."

"Did you decide anything about your car yet?" I asked.

"I don't know." she said, "I hate being without a car in Kentucky but I want to ride back with you. Bonnie already told me I could leave it at her house for a while. What do you think?"

"I was planning on coming back to Syracuse in the fall; maybe Labor Day or so." I said. "Can you go that long without having your own wheels?"

"If I can drive this baby, what do I need my car for?"

I broke into the Beatles song, Baby you can drive my car; Yes, you're gonna be a star.

She laughed and said "Mark, don't give up your day job."

We got to Bonnie's house and went inside. Bonnie and Brianna were sitting at the breakfast nook finishing breakfast and when she saw us, she jumped off the stool and ran to Roxie saying "Nana, Nana."

"There's my little munchkin," Roxie said, "did you miss me?"

It was obvious these two got along really well. Her conversations with Brianna were better than those with Bonnie. Roxie broached the topic of my staying the night at the house and I could tell that it wouldn't have been Bonnie's first choice. She didn't come out and say no but there was an aura about her that told me she didn't know me well enough to trust me.

"You'd have to sleep in the office Mark," She said. "We don't have any other rooms. We have a nice couch in there."

I told her that would be fine. Roxie told me I could use her toothbrush and other toiletries so I didn't have to go shopping. We hung out the rest of the day; Roxie cooked a nice dinner for all of us. By then, Oscar had come home from doing some masonry work and we talked a bit. Later in the evening, we all played Monopoly and ate cake and ice cream.

I got up at 6:30 the next morning when I heard rumbling around in the kitchen. Bonnie and Brianna were at the breakfast nook again where Bonnie got her ready for school.

"What grade are you in Brianna?" I asked.

"Kinnergarten," she replied. "do you go to school?"

"No Honey," I said, "I'm old and have to work."

"Do you work with my daddy?" was the next question.

"No, I live in Syracuse and I work there."

"How do you know Nana?" She asked.

"I met her on the Internet and I went to visit her." I answered.

This question and answer game went on for 5 minutes until Bonnie stepped in and told her to get ready or she was going to miss the bus. I was thankful for that because not having any kids of my own, I found conversations with a 6 year old extremely difficult. Roxie wandered into the kitchen and gave Brianna a hug and kiss. Then she gave me a hug and kiss. She avoided Bonnie. I didn't know if maybe they had an argument last night after everybody retired or what, but I was not about to ask. I went into the bathroom and did my morning routine, came back out in the kitchen and grabbed a to-go cup from the counter and filled it with coffee. Roxie asked me what I had on my agenda for the day.

"Just running around, getting last minute details taken care of," I said. I have to see if the bumper hitch is in at Auto Zone and if it is, I'll install it on the Camaro."

"I'll call you later today Hon," she said, "Bonnie and I are going shopping today."

I kissed her again and left. Today was going to be my first day of the last week in Syracuse and I wanted to make sure I have everything lined up. If I had dead time, I could always go hang out at a bar and visit, but my main objective was to get everything done so I didn't have to worry about it.

The rest of the day went pretty much as planned. I got the bumper hitch from Auto Zone and went home to install it. Once that was done, I set about the task of wiring up the plug for the lights. The next door neighbor came over to 'supervise' what I was doing. Jimmy was a retired electrician and I thought maybe I could get a circuit tester from him.

"Jimmy," I asked, "do you have a continuity tester?"

"Sure I do," he said, "I'll be right back."

He returned ten minutes later after I had everything wired but not taped, so it was easy to test for power. I hooked up the tester and was pleased with the results.

"Shit, everything works the first time." I remarked with a smile.

"That's because I helped you," Jimmy said. So you're moving, huh. Who's going to keep Les in line with you gone?"

"That's your job now buddy. I'm getting out while the getting's good."

We chatted a while and then I told him I had a lot more work to get done. Jimmy left and I went inside to crash for a while. The entire bumper hitch/wiring job took me the better part of the day and wrestling around the floor jack and making sure nothing was going to fall off on the road tired me out. A little power nap would do me good.

Later that night, I talked to Roxie and filled her in on my activities of the day. She said that her and Bonnie went shopping and bought a few items for the trip back.

Great, more crap to carry back with us.

We chatted for about an hour, said our phone hugs and kisses and promised each other that we would talk tomorrow.

I rolled over on the single bed at Les's house and her lavender scent, still lingering on the sheets, greeted me. I couldn't believe how fast everything was happening; and how lucky I was to have this wonderful, beautiful woman in my life. Tonight, I would have good dreams.

Tuesday, I had absolutely nothing to get done. My friend Michelle had been storing my records, CD's and stereo equipment at her house over the winter. I had planned on picking all that stuff up on Thursday but called her to make sure that was good with her.

"When are you and I going to get together?" she asked, "I'm not going to like having no one to party with when you're gone."

Michelle and I had been friends for 5 or 6 years and I always loved going out with her because she was a looker. Guys would just fall in love with her and wonder what I was doing with her. We were just friends and never had any kind of relationship between us other than friendship. For me, it was good having a female 'buddy'.

We spent the afternoon at the Bridge Street Tavern, knocking back Pabst Blue Ribbons and laughing. We always laughed together. And there was never a lack of words between us. To an outside viewer, it looked like two people who were really in love. But there was no touching.

"I'm going to miss you Mark," Michelle said. "I don't know what I'm going to do when I'm down. You always get me out of my bad moods."

"Michelle, you know I love you," I said, "and I'm going to miss you too. But with Roxie coming into my life, it's like winning the lottery. She's beautiful, smart, we have a good time and most of all, going to Kentucky gets me out of New York."

"Am I going to meet her?" She asked.

"Of course you are," I followed, "we will be at your house on Thursday to pick up my stuff. I have to take her by the library too and get Maggie's approval."

"Are you going to marry her?" She asked.

"No . . . Absolutely not!" I said. "I'll give her my love, I'll support her and everything that goes with a marriage but I won't ever get married again."

"So there's still hope for me?" She said with a smile.

"Bullshit artist," I responded, "you've had more than enough chances at me if you were really interested."

"I know," she said, "but it's fun to tease you."

We had a couple more drinks and headed to our respective homes. I didn't want to be driving drunk but hanging around with Michelle, I just lost track of time. Besides, it was late afternoon anyway and unless I made a serious mistake, I figured I was fairly safe behind the wheel. Years of practice, you know. I had dinner with Les again and listened to his incessant chattering. He flapped his jaw like the tail of a kite in the wind. I didn't want to be rude, but I needed some peace and quiet, so I told him I had to finish some last minute tasks downstairs. He seemed to understand and didn't bother me the rest of the night.

At 10 p.m., I talked to Roxie and went over the days activities. She seemed a little miffed that I was out with another woman but I told her she had nothing to worry about because if I wanted Michelle, I would be staying in Syracuse. I'm not sure if she was convinced of my sincerity, but it was the truth.

The next day, I slept in until 10 a.m. because I had told Roxie I'd be there at noon. I got my morning routine done and went down to the U-haul depot to pick up the trailer. I paid for it while the attendant hooked everything up to my car and like a flash, I was on the road. I anticipated a long day because we had to load up her possessions and then we had the family gathering to go to. I made up my mind that I wanted to leave Utica, no later than 8 tonight. When I arrived at the house, Roxie was in the front yard getting stuff out of her Camry.

As soon as I pulled in the driveway, she came over to the car and said, "You've been a bad boy."

"What are you talking about?" I said with a puzzled look, "I'm here on time."

"No, I mean you've been a bad boy. You come with me right now."

I couldn't figure out what she was talking about. I followed her into the house and went directly to the breakfast nook.

"Here," She said, and she handed me my pills. "You haven't been taking your medicine since we have been up here."

"I thought I was on furlough," I said, "and besides, you're the one that's supposed to be in charge; Miss Nancy Nurse."

"Funny Man . . . just take them." I gulped down the pills and took the obligatory 'special' medicine with the sewer taste. She offered me a broad smile and said "That's my healthy, handsome man . . . I want to keep you around for a long, long time."

"I still want to know what's in this shit," I said, "I don't feel super energetic or anything and the VA would have a cow if they knew I was taking something they didn't prescribe."

"I told you . . . they are just natural herbs and vitamins, she informed me. "It's not FDA approved so they don't need an ingredient list."

That sounded illogical because I had taken herbs before and they always had some sort of listing. But I didn't want to get into a pissing match with her so I let it drop.

We headed out the door and went to the storage area and within 2 hours, we had all of her stuff neatly loaded into the trailer. "What time do we have to be at Bonnie's for the party?" I asked.

"Everybody is getting there around five o'clock or so," She said. "It's informal; just people who haven't seen me in a long time. I haven't been back in this area since 2004. Five years is a long time to just talk on the phone with someone."

"So what do you want to do for 3 hours?" I said.

"Normally, I'd have an answer for you, but we are in public," she said, "so how about if I give you a guided tour of my hometown taverns?"

"Sounds good to me," I answered.

We dallied around the afternoon and hit a couple of bars. There was really no one out during the day that she knew but I kept thinking that these bars were beneath her. These were dives; working man taverns. They weren't the type of place I would expect her to frequent. She was the kind of woman that would want to show off her pretty clothes and hot figure. She might stop in one of these places to have a quick cocktail, but I seriously doubted that she 'hung out' here. I passed it off as just a fluke. After all, I've spent plenty of my time in dives too.

We went over to Bonnie's and people were already showing up. I met everybody in her family, including her uncles, aunts, sisters, brother, mother, neighbors, everybody. It was a fun time and I was glad to be part of it. One of her sisters came up and told me that I was the nicest guy she had ever seen Roxie with. It felt like I was accepted by my new 'family' and I was happy about that. I left the party at 9 p.m., about an hour later than I wanted to, but it was still early. Roxie and I had already decided that she would stay and I would pick her up the next day, so she could help me load my stuff and then meet some more of my friends. We kissed goodbye at the door and I took off for my temporary home at Les's.

I got settled into the basement and flipped the TV on. Everything was done except for loading my stuff at Les's and my stereo stuff at Michelle's house. I called my friend Ken in Colorado and we talked for a while. Then I called Corbett in Pennsylvania. I told him what was going on and how I'd like to see him and his wife if their schedule permitted.

"I've got company coming on Saturday Mark," he said, "but you and your lady are welcome to come down Friday if you like."

"That would be great," I said. "Then we can leave there on Saturday and make our way back to Kentucky."

We chatted for a while more and then said our goodbyes. I felt pretty happy that everything had gone so smoothly this week. I set the timer on the TV to turn off automatically and I drifted off to sleep, happily filling my head with visions of the future.

On Thursday morning I unhooked the trailer from the Camaro since I had to go to Utica to pick up Roxie and it didn't seem logical to drag a half loaded trailer down and back. I would pick it up when we got back to Syracuse because I only had to get my stuff loaded and we were done. I noticed that without the weight of the trailer, the Camaro ran smoother and handled better. I went over to my friend Gary Gillfallon's house and had coffee with him and told him about my plans to leave. Gary had been married to my ex-girlfriend Grace years earlier but there were no issues between us. We got along just fine.

"So you're going to do it . . . Move?" He said.

"Yeah, Gary, I'm all set." I told him. "I'm going to pick her up today in Utica, come back here, load my stuff and tomorrow we'll be on our way back to Kentucky."

"It'll be good to get out of this shit hole town," He said. "I wish I could go somewhere but I've got it made here; Cheap rent, plenty of friends."

"Grace," I said.

"Yeah, her too," He agreed. "Really, the only reason why we still see each other is because of our daughter. That's the common link."

"I know," I said. "Grace is lucky to have you to call on when the car breaks down or she runs out of beer or money. And I know you really do still love her . . . So do I."

We talked for a while and then I decided to get going. I told Gary that if we got our loading done early, I'd swing by and introduce him to my new lady. When I picked up Roxie at Bonnie's house, she was ready with a million bags to bring with her. Apparently her shopping expedition was more fruitful than she had disclosed to me on the phone.

"Honey," I said, "I didn't bring the trailer, just the car. How are we going to fit all this inside?"

"Oh, we can make it," she said, "but I just couldn't resist these little decorative lamps I bought and some of this stuff is for Christmas presents later this year."

"You couldn't get this down in Kentucky?" I asked.

"Quit being such a prick," she snarled, "I bought it and it's going back with me . . . got it?"

If a man had spoken to me in that tone of voice, I would have considered it a challenge. I just figured that Roxie was a bit nervous about the move and maybe when she got nervous she shopped; like some people get nervous and they eat. I was irritated with the attitude but it was too late to do much about it now. Perhaps when we got down to Kentucky, we would have a little discussion about it.

We loaded everything into the car, some of it by force and headed out. I called Michelle on the way and told her we were in-transit and we'd be there in an hour or so. We went to Les's, and picked up the trailer and put all of Roxie's new treasures inside, then left for Michelle's house. Michelle came out of the house and the first thing she did was come over and give me a big hug. Out of the corner of my eye, I saw Roxie standing there with a sour look on her face.

"Honey, I'd like you to meet my good friend Michelle," I said, as I introduced them.

"So you're the lady that stole my man," Michelle said with a smile.

Roxie didn't find any humor in that statement and the look on her face showed it.

"I don't know if I stole him?" she said, "he told me that you were just good friends."

"Oh, he's my friend alright," Michelle continued. "This man is one of the best in the world. I hope you appreciate what a good catch you have."

Roxie came up to me and put her arm around my waist, "I know," she said with a smile, "and I think he will make me very happy."

I loaded the stereo equipment, records and CD's into the trailer as the girls stood there watching and talking while. When everything was done Roxie and I said our goodbyes and left Michelle. I promised her that I would keep in touch and she promised the same.

"She's in love with you, you know." Roxie said.

"I know," I answered, "but it's more like brother-sister love."

"No, Mark," she continued, "she's in love with you. I'm psychic . . . I could read her. She's very jealous of me."

"Honey," I said, "I think you are reading a bit too much into it. Michelle and I are just good friends."

"Say whatever you like," she said shaking her head, "a woman can tell."

We stopped in the library and I introduced Roxie to Maggie and the workers there. They were all cordial and behind Roxie's back, a few of them gave me the 'thumbs up' signal; indicating they approved of her. Roxie made a quick bathroom stop and Maggie approached me.

"Mark," she said, "if I hadn't seen it with my own eyes, I would have thought you were bullshitting me about her. She is a keeper."

"Yeah, Maggs," I responded, "I think so too."

Roxie returned and I said my goodbyes to everyone. I promised to stay in touch and we left and headed back to Les's house to drop off the trailer.

"You have some good friends Honey," Roxie said. "Maggie is very impressive."

"Maggie is a smart cookie and we've been friends for a while," I said. "She is sort of like a mother hen with me. She had a lot of concern when I first told her I met you on the Internet."

"Well, perhaps it's good that you're moving then," she said, "because I'd hate to be in competition with all these 'ladies' that love you so much."

"Hey, what's not to love?" I remarked.

"Funny Man." She snickered.

We dropped off the trailer and I offered to take Roxie around to some of my old haunts and have a few cocktails. I called Gary up and he said he was going to the Bridge Street Tavern and would love to meet us.

"Hey Gary" I asked, "Do you have a small bag I could buy?"

Both Gary and I periodically smoked a little reefer and Gary always had the best stash. I hadn't bought any reefer in probably 5 years and I figured if I could get a little stash, it would be a nice way to relax and it would keep Roxie happy. She smoked all the time down in Kentucky but didn't have any of her own. She told me that her friends periodically 'turned her on' but hadn't made a connection lately. I thought this would be a nice surprise for her.

"Yeah, Mark," I can help, with a small bag. "It's not a lot but I'll let you have it for $ 50."

"Great man," I said, "I'll see you there."

Gary showed up and I again made the introductions. We had a couple of drinks and played a few games of Quick Draw at the bar. Gary and I stepped out of sight and made our little 'dope deal'.

"Its good shit Mark," He said. "I think you'll like it."

"Hey, anything is better than nothing."

We went back in and had a few more drinks. A couple of other acquaintances came by our table and said hello and met Roxie. Four hours slipped by quickly and I definitely had a buzz on. I told Gary that we had to go and he agreed that it was good to get home before dark to avoid any legal entanglements. We left and went back to Les's house, prepared for a quiet night before the move. Everything else was done; the trailer was packed; we had a road stash and we were ready to begin our great adventure.

I clicked the TV on hunted for some form of entertainment to kill time. We ate our dinners while watching Discovery Channel and just making light conversation. I reminded her that we were going to visit Corbett and Catherine tomorrow and stay at their house.

"Is that far from here?" She asked.

"No, about 3 hours from Syracuse; down in the Lehigh Valley, Pennsylvania."

"Well, that will be good to break up the traveling," she said, "because I wasn't looking forward to another 24 hour trip with a trailer behind us."

"Me neither," I replied, "but Saturday is going to be a bitch."

"Oh, we can handle it Honey," She said.

And then she put her arms around me and kissed me.

"Would you like to leave Syracuse with a bang?" She asked.

Roxie was feeling particularly frisky and I told her we couldn't do anything because Les was right above us. It wasn't that he didn't know that we slept together but, I am just not a person that advertises my personal life. That argument didn't hold water with her because she proceeded to keep her playing around and moved her head down into my crotch. I thought about it for a minute and then decided 'what the hell'. How much noise can she make with her mouth full? It was the first time, in a long time, that I just let a woman service me without reciprocating.

I'm glad I did.

* * *

19) The Final Leg Home

Syracuse to Kentucky—May 22-24, 2009

We rose on Friday morning, to be greeted by a beautiful May sunrise. I sensed that this glorious day would be made especially glorious by the fact that we were officially starting our life together. I spent the next ten minutes hooking up the U-haul to the Camaro and we left, driving through the city and onto Route 81 south; straight to Pennsylvania.

We were headed south out of Syracuse to make a side trip down to visit my old buddy Corbett and his wife in Easton, Pa. Corbett had been a friend of mine for over 30 years and even though I'd been down to his house a number of times, I figured it might be a while before I saw him again, once I got moved down to Kentucky.

"You'll like Corbett," I told Roxie. "He and I worked together years ago and he has been there for me through a lot of my trials and tribulations."

"Thirty years is a long time. So I guess he knew your ex wife?"

"Oh yeah, he knew Donna, my ex wife and I've known all his ex wives. He has a bit of a roaming eye but I think he has finally settled down with Catherine. He hit on Donna one time, but I don't think he knows that I know."

"He hit on your ex wife? That sounds like a real friend."

"She was married to me at the time and she told me about it the next day. I could have gotten pissed, but what was the use. Like I said, he had a roaming eye, alcohol was involved and I wasn't going to take it seriously because I had known him so long. So, we're still friends."

"Do you think he'll hit on me?" She asked.

"I don't know; probably not. This happened a long time ago and he knew Donna and I were going through some marital problems. Plus, where would the opportunity be to do anything. Catherine is going to be there and we'll be gone tomorrow."

We ambled down Route 81 into Pennsylvania and then cut south to the Lehigh Valley. I gave Corbett a call on the cell phone and we arranged to meet at a local restaurant for a beer.

"He has a great house," I said. "He used to live in New Jersey but he got this house a couple of years ago across the river in Pennsylvania. He told me the exact same house in New Jersey would have cost him $ 200K more than he paid where he is at."

"Are we going to eat there?" Roxie asked, "because I'm starting to get a little hungry."

"The game plan is to meet for drinks and wait for Catherine to come home from work. Then we're going to eat there and go to a ball game."

"Oh, that sounds fun."

We pulled the Camaro and the U-haul into the parking lot and waited. Corbett was right there and we got out, hugged and shook hands. I then made the introductions.

"Buddy, this is my Kentucky Woman, Roxie."

"So you're going to do it," Corbett said, "you really are moving down south. I know you have been talking about this for years. He's a good man Roxie and you two look good together. Take care of him."

"I'll take care of him alright," Roxie replied, "he doesn't know what he has gotten into."

We laughed and Corbett started checking out the Camaro.

"This is a beauty. Matter of fact, I think it's the nicest car you've ever had."

"Yeah, I like it. I bought it from my roommate Les," I explained. "He got that DWI back in November and is probably going to lose his license. He only bought it to pick up chicks anyway. And with him, the car didn't help. So I figured I would help him out and get him out of the payments. I didn't really want it but I figure I can drive it for a while and then get my Corvette."

"Well, it's a nice stepping stone until then," he said, "and being such a collectible, it will probably go up in value too."

Corbett pulled me to the side and quietly said, "That's a real nice looking lady you've got there. Don't fuck it up." With a grin I said, "Buddy, I don't plan on it."

We decided not to go into the bar for drinks because Corbett's wife was coming home from work early. Instead went over to the house and unloaded our overnight bags. It was about 2 in the afternoon and Catherine was not getting home from work until about 4. So we just sat there, the 3 of us, had a couple of beers and shot the shit. It was wonderful sitting on the back deck, on this sunny spring day and relaxing.

Catherine showed up at a little after 4 and the introductions went around again. Catherine was her typical 'reserved' self and she proceeded to busy herself inside the house while Roxie, Corbett and I sat on the deck. Pretty soon Catherine popped her head out the porch door and asked, "What time is the game tonight?"

"It's scheduled to start at 6:30," Corbett answered, "I guess I better get the grill going so we can eat and get there on time."

"Who's playing tonight?" I asked.

"It's the Iron City Hogs against some other team," Corbett said. "Catherine and I usually go when we have the time, because it's the local team and we try to support them."

"Iron City Hogs, huh," I replied, "boy have I got just the thing for tonight. I'll go get it."

I went out to the U-haul and opened one of my boxes of clothes. There on the top was one of my most prized possessions. It was a baseball cap. But it wasn't just an ordinary cap. This one had been a promotional item from a Syracuse restaurant that specialized in Bar-B-Que. I put it on and walked back into the house.

"How do you think this will go over?" I asked.

Everybody laughed as they looked at me standing there with a pink corduroy baseball cap that was shaped like a pig. It had the snout sticking out and two beady eyes staring from the brim.

"That is going to be a big hit down here," Corbett said, "these fans are sort of rabid when it comes to their local team."

We had a nice steak dinner with all of the fixings and then because we still had time before the game, Corbett and I retired back out to the deck to have another beer; Catherine and Roxie proceeded to take care of putting the dishes in the dishwasher and Roxie said that she would be out shortly.

"I brought something else for us to enjoy," I said and I produced a nicely rolled joint.

"Whoa, it's been a while since I had any of that," Corbett remarked. "Where did you get that?"

"Gary hooked me up when I was in Syracuse," I said, "and Gary has always got nothing but the best. I picked up a quarter ounce for 70 bucks. It's expensive, but a quarter will last me 6 months. I'm not the human chimney that I used to be."

As soon as Roxie came out of the house, we lit up the joint and the 3 of us proceeded to indulge while drinking and talking. It was, as Gary said, Primo quality. In less than 5 minutes we all had a real good buzz going on. Catherine came out of the house and made a comment about our maturity level.

"Smoking that shit will make you crazy," She said.

We finished our beers and got ready to go to the game. Corbett said "We'll take the Mercedes tonight because I have to get gas anyway. Besides, Catherine's Jaguar would be a bit cramped for the four of us."

We left for the game and when we got to the stadium, I noticed was that it was a very big crowd for a local farm team and just about everybody was wearing some sort of promotional attire spouting their pride for the team. There were hats, shirts, jackets, beer cups, belt buckles, everything. I was pretty impressed with the fan support.

"Hey man, nice hat," said one of the fans, "where'd you get it? I've got to have one."

"I got this up in New York," I said, "but I may start marketing them down here. Do you think they would be a hit?"

The fan told me that these people were just crazy about their hometown team and that if I ever decided to sell hats like the one I was wearing, he would be first in line to get one. And it was like that through the entire night. I'll bet that no less than 30 people came up to me and wanted to know where I had gotten the hat. I started thinking that maybe this was something I should explore as a possible business venture in the future. Hats and other unique apparel that would appeal to the hometown farm teams. I could go online and get a list of the local teams and then search vendors that made items that bore a likeness to the team logo. Then I could get a local printing company to do the finish work and sell them online, from a single location. I put this thought into the 'future consideration file' of my mind.

When the game ended and we headed back home for the night, Roxie was not her typical "chatty-cathy" self during the evening. When I asked her what was wrong she just shrugged and said, "Oh, I'm just a bit tired from all the running around and I've got a lot on my mind."

"Ok, we'll just get some quality sleep tonight and head out early tomorrow." I said.

She whispered in my ear, "I'm not that tired."

We got back and said our good nights and proceeded to our room. True to her earlier hints in the car, Roxie was not as tired as she had let on. Because it was someone else's house and I didn't want to be rude, we had to keep our vocalizations to a minimal level.

"We have to keep it quiet," I said.

"Maybe if you put something in my mouth, it might help," She replied.

"Baby, I want you to get off too. We just have to keep it quiet."

"Don't you worry about me," she said as she nuzzled closer, "I just want to make you feel the way that you make me feel."

She proceeded to unbuckle my pants and attach her luscious lips to my throbbing hard-on. Even though she told me that she never cared to do that with other men before, I got the distinct feeling that she had more experience at it than she was letting on. I continued to undress while she was working on me and I just couldn't let her have all the fun alone. I stripped off her clothes and proceeded to go into a 69 position, with the lights still on. It was absolute heaven hearing her moan while she had my rock hard cock in her mouth. As my tongue explored her inner depths, I felt Roxie climax. Her body writhed with pleasure and the liquid sunshine of her pussy just flowed into and around my mouth. She came at least 3 times more before I couldn't hold back anymore.

"Honey, you better stop now, I'm starting to lose control." I said with a warning.

The only response I got was 'mmmm' and a more aggressive pumping up and down with her fabulous mouth. I shot my load and she gobbled up every drop and drained me like a flushed toilet.

"God I love you." I said.

The next morning, we got up about 8 o'clock and I went downstairs to brew coffee. I'm usually good for 3 pots of the stuff a day. I set the brewer and went back upstairs to get ready for our road trip. I figured, since we went a bit out of our way to come to Pennsylvania, we had to put about 12 or 13 hours driving in today, in order to make it home tomorrow.

"You want the shower first or me?" I asked.

"Now that's a silly question, I want you dummy. Get your little body over her and take care of the queen."

"Honey, can we cool it until tonight?" I replied, "I mean we are taking advantage of our hosts and we've got a long ride today and I want to make as many miles as possible."

"Sure, deny me," Roxie said. "You'll pay for your transgressions, believe me."

Even though she said this with a smile, experience with her over the last month had told me that this was a woman that was not used to being refused and experience also told me that she was open to sex any time, any where and any how.

"Baby, it's not that I don't want you; believe me. It's just we have other fish to fry and you want to get back home ASAP, right?"

"Yes, dear, you're right. I'll suffer. Go take your shower."

"Coffee should be ready. I'll be quick so you can get in there." I said

"Oh, now you're not even going to bring me my coffee," she said, pouting. "I guess the impressing stage is over, huh."

So we made it through our showers, our dressing and her makeup session. And naturally, I had to take my 'medicine' that she always kept close at hand. It was funny because I never saw her taking any of it; only me. But then, I thought maybe it was special for cardiac patients like myself.

We went downstairs together and were met by Corbett and Catherine at the breakfast nook.

"What's the game plan?" Corbett asked.

"Well, I thought maybe we could buy you guys breakfast somewhere and then come back and pick up the car and get on the road."

"Ok, there's a diner right over the bridge in New Jersey. I have to go to the bank and the post office over there anyway. Let's go there."

"Alright, that was simple," I said, "and hey, thanks you two for putting us up last night. It was really great seeing you again and I really appreciate the hospitality."

"What are friends for man?"

We piled into the Mercedes again and headed over the bridge to Jersey and had a nice breakfast at the Phillipsburg diner. The conversation was light and everybody was just chowing down and making small talk. We headed back to the house and picked up the Camaro and the U-haul and we were ready to rock and roll.

"Well, buddy good luck," Corbett said. "Enjoy your stay down in Kentucky and keep in touch."

"Oh, you know I will. And here, something for last nights rent." I handed Corbett a couple of joints.

"Thanks man, I really think your life is turning around. Like I said, don't fuck it up."

"Thanks again and I'll give you a call . . . Bye Catherine"

"Bye Mark," she responded, "Bye Roxie; enjoy your trip."

With a roar, the Camaro came to life and we were on our way. After a brief stop to get gas, we hit the interstate and headed for Wheeling, WV.

"I want to make it to Wheeling by nightfall and get a motel to stay over," I said. "That way, we can get on the road early tomorrow and get back by about 3 or 4 in the afternoon."

"Sounds like a plan to me," Roxie answered, "just don't fall asleep driving. If you feel tired, pull over and I'll drive."

"Oh, you can drive a 6 speed?" I asked.

"Well, it's been a while but I can handle it. I just have to get used to using a clutch again but I've driven plenty of sticks."

"I'll bet you have my dear." I'm not sure if she caught my double entendre or not.

Even though we stayed on the interstates, the road to West Virginia just seemed to go on forever. Up and down the monotonous mountain passes, twisting and turning all the way. Finally at 7:30 p.m., we found a Holiday Inn just outside of Wheeling. I didn't care if it was a roach motel; I was so tired. We parked the Camaro and while I went in and registered, Roxie pulled out the bags that she needed, leaving mine behind. I guess I didn't need mine, I thought. Fuck it.

"The first thing I want is a drink," She said as we got into the room.

"We can do that," I said, "just jet me just take a quick look at my email and we'll go down to that little bar they have attached."

"I'm going to leave this stuff here," I said as I placed my small baggie of illicit stimulant in the drawer cabinet.

"Where did you get that?" Roxie asked me.

"Oh, my friend Gary came through. I figured it was enough to keep us happy for a while in Kentucky. And then maybe somebody down there might be able to help."

"Is that what we smoked at Corbett's house?"

"Sure is . . . did you like it?

"Yes I did," She said. "I thought he provided that. I caught a good buzz. As far as Kentucky pot goes, I can get all you want Honey. I told you, I've got friends down there."

We went downstairs and into the small bar at the back of the motel where we ordered our drinks; my Pabst Blue Ribbon and Roxie's Rum and Coke. There were only about 3 other people in the bar but the motel was full. I wondered how they could keep a bar and restaurant open with so few clients. At the far end of the barroom there was a door marked "Casey's Casino."

"Hey look honey," I said pointing at the sign, "They knew I was coming."

"She looked at the door and asked the bartender, "Where does that door go?"

"That's our small casino," She said. "We have slot machines in there."

"Gambling is legal in this state?" I asked.

"Just slots and lottery," the bartender answered. "If you want to play cards or dice or any other games, you have to go to a full casino across the state line."

"C'mon hon," I said to Roxie, "let's go press our luck."

We entered the casino and saw about 40 or 50 one-armed bandits. The place was packed with people sitting at the machines smoking and leaving empty glasses everywhere. I gave Roxie a $ 100 bill and told her to have a good time.

"Where are you going?" She said.

"I'll be right here," I answered, "I just wanted to make sure you have play money."

We looked around and finally found a couple of machines that were not in use. I parked my butt down on the stool and proceeded to donate my hard earned money to the state of West Virginia. I had a couple of cheap hits but nothing dramatic. Roxie took up residence down the line at her own machine, throwing more of my hard earned money away. We spent about 4 hours in the casino. At times, both of us would go out to the barroom and get drink refills. I told Roxie to just put her drinks on the room tab and I would pay it when we left. I was starting to get quite drunk by then and was down about $ 300 in the machines. I decided that I would play out my last $ 20 bill and be gone.

Cha-Ching; The lights of the machine burned a red flashing glow as bells and whistles went off. I looked at the machine and had over 4000 credits. I had hit a jackpot.

"Roxie!" I shouted, "check this out."

She came over and looked, and looked again. "You just won $ 400." She said.

"Yeah, just when I was going to quit," I grinned. "I think I will quit because now I'm ahead by $ 100 more than I had. That pays for the room."

"Good Boy," she nodded, "by the way, I have a question to ask you."

"What's that Hon?"

"The bartender would like to get a joint from you." She said.

My mouth must have dropped open because when I looked at her with disbelief, and she only said "What?"

"How did the bartender know I may be in possession of any joints?" I asked.

"Oh, she and I were talking while you were in deep concentration here."

I was pissed. Not only were we in a strange town, full of unknown people, but Roxie somehow figured that it was OK to discuss illegal substances with one of those strangers.

"Absolutely not," I said, "Jesus Roxie, how could you think I would let anybody know my business?"

"I'm sorry," she said, "I just thought I'd be nice and offer some to her because she is taking care of our drinks so good."

"Not at all," I fumed, "how do you know she's not with hotel security or something? How fucking stupid can you be?"

Her face took on a dark expression but before she could say anything to me I told her to grab her drink and that we were leaving. I cashed in my credits at the bar, took my $ 400 payoff and asked for the room tab. The bartender slipped the tab over to me and I took a look at the total.

There were 9 Pabst beers at $ 2.50 each and 14 Rum and Cokes at $ 3.75 each. The total came to $ 75 even. I paid it, tipped the bartender and Roxie and I left. We got back to the room and she let out the anger that had been churning inside her.

"You've got a lot of nerve calling me stupid." She said. "I have a 148 IQ and I am definitely not stupid."

"Offering an illegal substance to a total stranger, in a totally strange town is pretty fucking stupid in my book," I said. "Besides, that stash is for us and no one else unless I say so. I bought it; I deal it out, not you."

Her face flushed red and I knew that Roxie was totally pissed. She didn't say anything but just stormed into the bathroom and slammed the door. I was drunk and I knew that she was too; after 14 Rum and Cokes who wouldn't be?

I decided to just let sleeping dogs lie and I lay down on the bed to wait for her to come out of the bathroom. But the alcohol had other plans for me. I passed out without even putting in a wake up call. The next morning I woke up with my head on fire. I looked at the clock located on the top of the television set and it read 11:18 a.m. I shot up out of the bed. I was pissed because we had a 10 hour drive in front of us and I had intended to get started early. Now we were behind the 8-ball because of last nights festivities.

"Roxie," I said as I gently shook her, "c'mon Honey, get up."

She looked groggily at me and asked what time it was; and I told her 11:30.

"WHAT!" she jumped up, "how could you let me sleep so late?"

"I know . . . we are late," I said, "we have to check out, now."

We made a mad dash to the bathroom for quick cleanups. I told her we would get something to eat on the road; that we were way behind schedule. We finished up, grabbed the luggage and shot out of the door. I left the key on the drawer cabinet so I wouldn't have to go to the front desk. At the first intersection, we stopped and gassed up, got large coffees, a couple of breakfast sandwiches and shot onto the interstate. I had planned to be back in Burkesville by mid afternoon but now we wouldn't get home until late night. I was not pleased; but it was my own damned fault.

"I'll tell you one thing Mark," Roxie finally said. "There are some things that are going to change if you want to keep me around."

"Like what?" I said.

"You seem to think you own me or something. My ex-husband used to be one of those Know-it-All assholes who did things without considering anybody else. I swore that I would never put up with that again."

"Look baby, it's been a long two weeks, I'm sure that both of our nerves are on end and I just want to get home and relax. Can we table this discussion until we are a little fresher?"

She didn't say another word, just sat there looking out the window. Finally, she granted me a two word response to my statement.

"I suppose."

I was a bit taken back by this burst of crankiness coming from her but not totally surprised. I had seen snippets of her attitude before but I figured we would always work things out. Getting up late today was also and inconvenience that added to things. But it wasn't the end of the world. I wondered where this shit was coming from.

The remainder of the long ride flipped from boring to uneventful and back to boring. We barely said 5 words to each other and I knew that she was still pissed at me for my comments the night before. The date was May 23rd and this had been our first real argument since we had been together. I hoped that this little spat wasn't going to be setting precedence for days to come. I made my mind up to be extra cautious about what I said.

Now that, was going to be a task.

* * *

20) Back in Burkesville

Burkesville, KY—May 25, 2009

"Whew, what a trip!" I said the next morning, "I don't want to make that run again for a while."

"Crawl back into bed Mr. Energy," Roxie answered from under the covers. "My body tells me that its way too early to get up."

"But I brought you coffee and a little sweet roll," I replied, "and by the way, it's 12:30 in the afternoon."

Roxie peeked out from under her fortress of blankets and gazed at the alarm clock on the table. For someone who proclaimed to be an early riser and a workaholic, she was definitely not portraying it. As a matter of fact, I had never really seen her do any work at all. There were no packages of 'sale items' going to the Post Office. We never had a UPS or FedEx truck pick anything up. And I never heard her make any comments on the 'supposed' buyers of her items. I wondered just what she did to bring in revenue, and when. She had told me that she was in charge of boarding horses, but I never once saw her feed or groom any. That set me off wondering how she made her money? I never really asked her; had never seen her bank balance and when it came to money, I seemed to be the only one with that resource.

Even though she was usually beautiful in the early morning light, today she looked like she had been shot at and missed and shit at and hit. She propped herself upright in the bed with her bare breasts standing straight out.

"If you are going to get me up, then I want to get you up too." She said with a smile.

It seemed as though the argument we had yesterday about her stupid move in Wheeling was long forgotten. I knew how much she loved sex in the morning and this seemed like the perfect way to mend any fences that were damaged.

"Oh, baby," I said, "I drove a long time yesterday. I don't know for sure if you can get me up, but I'm open to give it a try."

Her unseen hand slipped under the blankets and moved strategically towards my half open bathrobe. I felt her reach in, and gently massage my waiting member. Response time was approximately 5.2 seconds. With her other hand, she reached up and grabbed me around the neck and pulled me down for a kiss. My body melted to meet hers and we proceeded to start the lovemaking process that I was so familiar with.

For some reason, my mind sort of drifted to the last time that we had done something other than oral sex. It was the first night in Syracuse; May 8th to be exact; and today was the 25th. That meant I had 16 days of makeup to attend to.

"Oh Mark, give it to me harder," She gasped.

I complied and drove into her, like a wayward car skidding on a patch of black ice. Thrust, Thrust, Thrust, rest, Thrust, Thrust.

"Oh, God, God, I'm coming again," she said between taking quick breaths, "oh my God Mark its so good baby."

I tried my damnedest to keep control of my own orgasm. I slowed down, withdrew and went down on her. She clamped her legs around my ears and all sound went quiet. I'm sure I did hear at least one instance of Fuck carry across the air, but everything else was muffled. When I felt that I had my control back I went back to re-enter her.

"Oh Baby, take me from behind now," She said as she rolled over. I propped her hips up and began to enter her little muffin, doggie style.

"No," she said, "not there, in the other entrance."

I was never one to be shy about sex, but anal sex was not my idea of fun. I had done it before but it was not my favorite thing. But I figured if she could perform oral sex on me and had not liked it, I could do this for her because she wanted it. I slowly entered the brown cavity and took small short strokes at first because I knew how sensitive this area was. She moaned with delight and uttered just three words: "Deeper Honey, Deeper."

I increased my depth and rhythm as I felt her convulse in another orgasm. Because she was so tight here, I lost all control and released my load deep inside her. This sent her into yet another frenzy, as she felt me fill her and it triggered another orgasm from her. With both of us spent, we lay entangled together on the bed; exhausted from the effort as well as the long drive home. In one respect I was totally satisfied but in another, I couldn't help thinking that she was a lot more sexually experienced than she had told me. I remember her saying that all of her former lovers told her she was a lousy lay. I just couldn't believe any man would be that cruel in the first place and in the second, it just wasn't true. She was a fantastic lover; Even though I didn't particularly care for our last act.

Eventually we got up and went downstairs to the kitchen. I didn't feel like a big breakfast so I just had cereal. Of course I had to take her required 'medicine' with my VA prescriptions.

"After that performance this morning, I want to keep you around and healthy." Roxie said. "You never know when I'm going to need to use you again."

"Oh, so now I'm a power tool?" I questioned.

"Funny Man," She said as she offered me my morning pills and 'special' tonic.

We spent the rest of the day unloading our possessions from the U-haul so that I could drop it off in town. I was a good boy because I hung up all my clothes in my closet and put my boxes of 'junk' in the pole barn. That was really no problem because I wanted to go through everything and sort through it. Some of it, like the records, I intended to sell on EBay because I had CD copies. Some of it was going to be filed appropriately. And some of it was just going to be pitched because it had been a while since I had totally gone through everything and you know how junk accumulates.

Roxie made a nice meatloaf for dinner and we sat on the porch listening to the radio and talking. It was nice to sit and relax after our grueling trip.

"If you could move anywhere," she asked, "where would you go?"

"I've been drawn to Tennessee for a long time," I said. "I thought Knoxville would be a nice area, but I haven't really given it a lot of thought. Basically, I need to be somewhere there is a VA hospital so I can get my medicine and treatments."

"I think Knoxville would be nice," She said. "I've never been there but I want to move from here. As a matter of fact, I've never been anywhere but on the East Coast, but I need to get away from here eventually. There are just too many bad memories here and I want change."

"Memories of the divorce?" I asked.

"The divorce is only part of it," She continued. "I told you about the man that lived here last year?"

"I don't know, maybe you did. Not your husband?" I asked.

"No, his name was Terry Jacoby," She said. "He was a 78 year old patient of mine when I worked at the nursing home. He moved in with me and had lived here for about 6 months. One day, I came home from work and he called me into the house. I was sitting on the porch and just wanted to relax for a minute. I told him I would be right in and I went about having a drink and finishing my cigarette. Then I heard the shotgun go off. I thought he had been cleaning it and it went off accidentally. I went in his room and found him with his face blown off. He committed suicide."

"You've got to be shitting me," I said, "he blew his brains out, just like that?"

"Yes," she said mournfully, "I really think he was in love with me and he was going to kill me at the same time. If you look on the ceiling, you can still see the blood stains."

"Didn't the police come out?"

"Of course they did," She answered. "My Sheriff buddy Dex and the State Police did a full investigation and ruled his death a suicide. I was so shook up, I had to get away. So I left here and went to Detroit for a while. I was there until March of this year."

"Jesus Honey," I said, "that's pretty traumatic. No wonder you want to move."

"It's not just the trauma," she added, "the people around here kind of look at me funny; like I had something to do with Terry dying; another reason I want to get away."

"Well babe," I said, "let's get settled and get our stuff taken care of here first. Then we can start to look for another place that is a little more social. Burkesville is really too quiet for me also."

We went to bed early that night and I had a bit of problem falling asleep. It upset me that my beautiful lady had been put through the horror of having someone kill themselves in her own house. But as I thought about it, I wondered how that scenario fit into what she had formerly told me about herself. If she ran this organic farm and also had to handle construction contracts in Florida, when did she have time to work in a nursing home? I was starting to think that maybe I should casually ask some questions that might shed some light on things.

I finally fell asleep, and again I had sort of a nightmare. In the dream I was sitting in a small room with bars on a steel door. Through the bars I couldn't see anything but I could periodically hear the patter of quiet footsteps. I kept looking and every once in a while, I would make out a flash of movement down the hall leading to the room. I yelled help but there was no reply. Again, my tomb was silent except for those footsteps that I heard. There was no pattern to it, nothing that I could time accurately. I kept peering out between the bars intently and it paid off. I caught a quick glimpse of red; not enough to identify what it was, but just a flash. I yelled help again and I could swear I heard a quiet giggle. What the hell was going on? I stood there at the bars staring out and naturally nothing happened. It was only when I sat back down on the cold stone floor that those footsteps would begin again. I decided that I was going to catch, or at least identify, whoever had me caged like this. I slowly crawled over the floor and lay there watching. Finally, my vigilance paid off. THERE . . . just a brief flash but I saw red again. I kept my eyes peeled and THERE . . . again, that flash of red. This time it was a little clearer and I knew that it was a person. THERE . . . There was no mistaking it now; I realized that I now knew what I saw. Running back and forth across the hallway at random intervals, was a clown.

A short clown with Red hair.

* * *

21) Memorial Day

Burkesville, KY—May 30, 2009

The following Saturday, brought big doings to Burkesville. When I say big doings, I mean big for Burkesville; it was the annual Memorial Day outing and car show. From all around the local area including Tennessee, motor heads brought their classic cars into town to show off. It gave the public the opportunity to see some really nice machines of all different makes and models. This was one of the few outings in town that wasn't 'church related'.

We finished breakfast, including my medicine routine, and headed into town. There were a lot of 67-69 Camaro's, Corvettes, Corvairs, Desoto's, Ford's and every other type of vehicle imaginable. Three-Wheel Harley Trikes, Drag Go-Carts and a 1932 Cadillac Hearse were some of more exotic models. One guy even brought a wheelchair powered with a Briggs and Stratton engine. I parked my red '97 Camaro right in front of the local Subway shop in a space where I could see it from every angle of the town square; and it could be seen by everyone else at the show.

"Pepper is going to love your car," Roxie told me, "he collects Camaro's."

"Who's Pepper?"

"Pepper is the local Sheriff," she said, "and he's the head of the whole department. He lives over the bridge off Route 61 and he must have 3 or 4 classic Camaro's in his garage."

"Hmmm," I said, "maybe he'd like to buy it?"

"Oh no you don't! You are not selling that car until we get a Corvette to replace it."

"Yes, ma'am," I said. "He probably wouldn't want to pay what its worth anyway."

The activities stretched across downtown—food vendors, a sign-up booth for the Cumberland River Rats Car club, and the local high school band. All the participants showed off their local talent. I walked around and viewed all the cars while holding Roxie's hand. I wanted people to know who I was, since I was new to the town and she had lived there for over 3 years. Other than the cars, there wasn't much going on. We bought some raffle tickets and hung around for the drawings, but after 3 hours of all this 'high-level excitement', I had seen enough.

"Let's get out of here babe," I said.

"Where do you want to go?" She asked.

"Let's go back down to the Sawmill, get some beer and chat with Lenny if he is there."

"I'm there with that," she said, "I think I've seen enough classic cars for one afternoon. Besides, I like your Camaro the best of all."

"So I guess you would like to drive?" I asked.

"You don't have to ask me twice," she said, "bear with me though because I haven't driven a stick in a few years."

We got in the car and she fired it up. I told her to wait a second; I was going to pull the roof panels out because it was such a beautiful day. She loved that. After a bit of getting used to the clutch, Roxie was like an old pro behind the wheel. She did tend to slip clutch a bit more than I liked but I wrote it off as just a need for practice. We left the town square with her red hair flowing in the breeze, in a hot red car and headed for the Sawmill. I figured we would have a few drinks, pick up a 12 pack and maybe do some sightseeing at Dale Hollow Lake.

"I need to go to the liquor store," Roxie told me.

"I thought you had that Rum and Vodka from when we went to Bowling Green," I asked.

"Ha . . . that was gone before we left for Syracuse," she said, "and I forgot to pick anything up when we were traveling so I need to go now."

"OK, no problem," I said, "do you want to go there first?"

"No I can wait," she said, "just don't forget."

We pulled into the Sawmill and Lenny's SUV was there. I had met Lenny a few weeks ago and liked talking to him, so this should be an enjoyable afternoon. We walked in and sat at the bar with 6 or 7 others—all having their afternoon cocktails.

"Mark and . . . .uh," Larry stuttered,

"Roxie," I said.

"Roxie . . . that's right. How could I forget? What can I get you folks on this fine Saturday afternoon?"

"I'm going to have my usual, Pabst and Roxie . . . ," I looked at her.

"Rum and Coke please."

"Sorry, no hard stuff here, remember?" was Lenny's response.

"That's right, I forgot. I'll just have a Corona." She uttered.

Lenny brought our drinks and we chatted for a while. I told him that we had just returned to Burkesville from New York. He was scooting around talking to everybody and Roxie and I just sort of starred at the TV screen mounted on the wall. I tried to engage her in some small talk but she was somewhat unresponsive. All of her answers were pretty much 'one syllable'. It was almost like she was doing me a favor having a drink here and couldn't wait to leave. I asked her if she wanted to go sightseeing at Dale Hollow Lake and she said we could take a drive down there because it was right on the way to the liquor store. She told me that there was not much there to see except a bunch of houseboats in a marina.

""Honey, I just like looking around down here," I said. "This is my new life and I want to get to know where things are so if I like them, I can go back."

We finished our drinks, grabbed a 12 pack to go and left. I let her drive again because we had only had 2 drinks and it was the middle of the afternoon; and she loved the car.

"I love this baby, Mark," She said as she broke the tires loose coming out of the drive. "How fast do you think it will go?"

"It's got a Corvette, LT-1 motor in it," I said. "Probably 150 or 160 I'd say. But let's not try it here."

"Of course not idiot," she said, "I just wanted to know."

I damned well did not like her 'idiot' reference; kidding or not. Maybe she was still pissed off about our conversation in Wheeling but I thought she was over that by now. Her tone indicated a total lack of respect for me, even though she could be so nice at times. I thought better of saying anything though because she was driving and I didn't need a pissed off driver in a speed demon's dream of a car. I let it ride.

We pulled into the liquor store and she turned and asked me "Do you have a $ 20 I can borrow?"

"Sure," I said and reached into my wallet,

"Make that $ 50 if you have it" She followed.

"What are you buying?" I asked.

"I decided to get us a nice bottle of wine too," She said.

I gave her the money and watched her wiggle into the store. Dammit she has a great looking ass. She came out with a carry basket, and less $ 50 dollars for booze I didn't even drink. She knew I was not a wine aficionado. And I wondered what happened to all her money. I had given her $ 100 at the casino and I don't think she blew it all; maybe she did. Oh well, anything to keep her happy. That was my job.

"Pop the trunk," She commanded.

I opened up the trunk and she unloaded the carry basket. There were two bottles of Rum, a liter of Vodka and two bottles of wine. She was either stocking up or we were going to have a party; I didn't know which.

"Are we inviting guests?" I asked.

"Well, it's good to have something on hand in case people come over," she said, "besides, it's not like it's going to go to waste."

I accepted that answer and we got on the road. We went up to the Dale Hollow Lake Marina and looked at the sailboats and houseboats out in the cove.

"That's it," she said, "and now do you see what I was talking about? . . . There's nothing else here to see."

We decided to go back home and relax. I was still a bit tired from the trip and it seemed that relaxing was one thing that living in Burkesville was good for; maybe to a fault. It was getting on toward dinner time anyway and I thought it would be nice to just sit and chat again. I cooked dinner tonight for a change. I made Spanish rice with plenty of spicy chilies, onions and ground round. It was quick and easy and tasted great. Cleanup was a snap too, because everything was made in one large pan and poured over the rice. That kept the rice from getting soggy. Roxie told me that she had never had it that way but she liked it better than her own. I took that as a compliment.

"Hey," she said, "that reminds me. Where's that pot you bought?"

"I'll go roll us a joint." I said.

I got up and went into the other room in search of my stash. I went through my overnight bag, my suitcase and then it dawned on me. We were in such a rush to leave the motel room in Wheeling that I completely forgot about putting the stash in the lower drawer at the motel. Of course the slight hangover I had hadn't helped either.

"Shit!" I said as I returned to the porch, "guess where the stash is?"

"Don't tell me you left it in the motel room?"

"You got it," I said, "We were in such a rush to get out that I forgot to check the drawers; Looks like the maid is going to have a good time."

"You stupid fuck!" Roxie yelled. "When the lord passed out brains, you must have thought he said trains and asked for a slow one."

"Bite me bitch. Where do you get off with that remark?"

"I wanted to have a nice relaxing night and catch a little buzz," she said, "and now I find out that Mr. Moron had his head up his ass and ruined it for me."

If I hadn't had problems with my blood pressure before, I damned sure would have now. I was hot enough to fuck. I'm not a violent man but her berating of me was more than I wanted or needed right now. It was a little bag of pot; Not a big deal. But Roxie was going off on me like it was a major catastrophe. I can see where some men get so strung out that they would turn to hitting their mate. I've never been one to subscribe to that answer and I wasn't going to start now. I got up, picked up my beer and went into the house. I thought about going back into my office and doing some work but I was too pissed, so I sat down on the couch and started going through my CD's, looking for some music to play.

"Don't you walk away from me prick," a voice echoed from the porch, "get your ass out here and finish this discussion."

I yelled from the living room, "Roxie, I'm not going to discuss this anymore. What's done is done and I can't change things. I am sorry for being so lax but we were rushed and I didn't do my normal reconnaissance before we left. I'm Sorry for ruining your night."

Roxie came in the living room and sat down on the opposite side of the couch. "You're Right." She said. "There is no sense in fighting about it. I know you didn't do it on purpose."

I was relieved that she understood that I had made a mistake and that maybe we could get back to the 'heaven' we had once enjoyed. The only thing that stuck in my brain at the time was the fact that she hadn't really apologized to me for the nasty barrage that she had unleashed.

Rather than get into that, I just passed it by and asked her, "What do you think about setting up a list of priorities for us?"

"I think that is an excellent plan, my love," was her response, "Maybe it's just that this town that is pissing me off more than anything."

"I can see that, Honey," I replied. "We are both social people and we are kind of like 'in jail' out here in this barren wasteland."

"The first thing that has to be done is the double-wide," She said. "I was planning to live in it but if we move, I can rent it out if we just put a little money into it."

"I remember when I looked at it and seemed to me it just needed some drywall and a set of lower kitchen cupboards." I said.

"That's it . . . Easy fix up," she told me, "The cabinets are going to be the expensive things but I'm looking on the swap sheets for used ones."

"Tomorrow, I'll go down there and measure everything we need," I said. "Then we can hunt around and get the ball rolling on that. Do you want to set a moving goal?"

"Well, I don't really want to spend another winter here," She said. "I'd like to be out of here no later than October if we can."

"That sounds like a good time frame," I followed, "By then, I can have my Internet business set up and get the trailer fixed and ready to rent. You need time to sell some of this stuff on EBay that you have here too, don't you?"

"Are you kidding?" she said wryly, "I've got so much to sell its not funny. Just look at all those vehicles out there. The two pick-ups, a sailboat, these antiques; all this stuff has to go."

Just looking around the room and thinking about all of the stuff that was in the pole barn, I got a sense of how much there was to actually get rid of. Even without having to do any work on the double-wide, just inspecting, photographing and listing the antiques and other items on EBay would take 2 months. Then there was tracking the sales, packing and shipping the items. October was only 4 months away and it seemed like trying to complete everything by then would be really pushing it.

"Are all those vehicles yours?" I asked.

"They are now," she countered, "they used to belong to my ex, but he abandoned them. All I have to do is get titles for them in my name. Or I could forge his name; he'll never know."

"That's a dirty trick Roxie," I said, "I think you should go about it the legal way and get them signed over to you. If I ever lost my vehicles like that, I'd feel like a raped ape."

"What would you know about rape?" she stared at me, "I was raped before and it's not a fun thing."

"I didn't mean it like that," I said, "I merely meant that losing vehicles in that manner would get me so pissed off I'd probably do something stupid . . . like hunt that person down. I would have to hurt someone who did that to me."

"Well, I'm just telling you," she continued, "even the word rape brings chills to me."

"When did this happen?"

"When I was 12 years old," she answered, "I was petrified of men for a long time afterward."

"Did they ever catch the guy?"

"I don't want to talk about it. It brings back bad memories." she said, "besides; we were talking about my ex-husband anyway. That shit head will never be back here," she remarked, "because I had him deported because he was a Canadian National."

"Wait a minute," I interrupted, "You had your husband deported back to Canada?"

"Mark, he beat me up one night when he was drunk," She told me. "The police came and they had to Taser him because he was so belligerent.

My deputy friend Dex and I had a good laugh about that when hubby was in jail and the Sheriff came back out here because he needed some forms filled out. I filed for divorce right after that and because of the incident, the court deported him."

"What happened when he got out of jail?" I asked.

"The Sheriff's deputy escorted him out here so he could pick up some clothes and one of his cars and then he was gone; never to return. The last thing I heard about him was that he was back living with his mother in Canada."

"How did he get the rest of his stuff?"

"Fuck that!" she exclaimed, "I figured what he left here was mine, to pay for the abuse I put up with. It was bad enough that I had to fork over $10,000 to him to get him off the deed to the house."

"How did he accomplish all that, if he was in jail?" I asked.

"He hired Phil Stevens, a local attorney. Phil arranged all this. All I had to do was sign the papers and pick up the check."

"I can't believe it," I told her, "He just up and left all this stuff, his vehicles, his construction equipment and everything for $10,000?"

"It was that asshole Stevens did it," she countered, "he made it sound like I would have to take him back and put up with more of his shit. When he finally got arrested, it wasn't the first time that he had assaulted me. I was just fed up, but I was pissed I had to pay him. At least I got to be friends with the Sheriff's deputy out of it."

I'm no lawyer and I didn't know much about the laws; especially in Kentucky. But I got the feeling that there was more to this story than Roxie was telling me. Just like that bombshell she dropped on me earlier in the week about the guy who killed himself. Something just didn't fit but I couldn't put my finger on it. And then there was something about the rape that she mentioned. She had told me past events before, but one thing I remembered was that she had said that she went to Woodstock when she was 15 and came back a virgin. What was up with that? Either she misspoke or lied about something. I was hoping that maybe it was just the booze caused her to have memory lapses as opposed to her being a pathological liar.

I also knew how she got when she was drinking and I decided not to press the issue. Add that to the fact that both of us were pretty wound up from the past 2 weeks. One of these days I would find a proper time to fill in the blanks. Until then, I was just going to have to be happy with the solitude of country living and my beautiful red haired princess.

Even though I was seeing a few dents in her crown.

* * *

22) Affairs of the Past

Burkesville, KY—June 5, 2009

We spent the next week doing our respective tasks. I put a lot of time into organizing the possessions that I brought from New York. I sorted through boxes and boxes of assorted items, some of them just heaped together in picturesque disorder. Roxie spent her days getting items such as clocks, canning kits and lightweight photos ready for sale on EBay. But life began to take on a routine. Every morning, I would get up, make coffee and bring a cup to her. Sometimes we would make love and sometimes not. She would get up and make breakfast, we would eat and I would take my 'special' medicine and then go about whatever had to be done for the day.

In the evening, we would have dinner; taking turns doing the preparation and then we would sit on the porch and talk—always learning more about each other. I soon discovered that she was an avid pothead; that one of her 'friends' whom she ran into in town, had given her a little stash and because of that, she was 'little miss happy-go-lucky'. If I didn't mention smoking a bowl or something, she would bring it up. When she got this stash, she gave it to me for safe-keeping, claiming that if she kept it, it would be gone in 2 days. I asked her where she got it and she only would tell me 'I have friends'. I wondered if they were invisible friends because nobody had ever been to the house since I had lived here.

One night as we were sitting on the porch, she asked me if I wanted to do a bowl. I like to smoke every so often but it's not every day; all the time. I told her that I was good but if she wanted to, she could have at it. Like a flash she was in the house and she came out with a little hash pipe.

"OK, I've got a pipe" she said. "what do I put in it?"

I went inside and took half of her/our stash out and put it in a little baggie. I brought that out to the porch and said "Now you've got your own little bag . . . how's that for service?"

"Oh Baby, you're so good to me."

She loaded up the pipe and started smoking. When she handed it to me and I declined. So she went right on back to smoking alone. We started talking about our families and I told her that I was the oldest of 4 kids. I have 2 younger sisters that live in Syracuse and that my younger brother died back in 1991. She asked me why I didn't have any kids of my own and I said that basically my wife and I decided that we were both too selfish to bring a child into this world and never had any.

"My son is graduating from boot camp next weekend." she said, "and I would like to go down there if we could."

"I don't see why not," I told her. "Is that where he lives?"

"He and his wife live in South Carolina, across the state line from the army base." she told me. "They are going to stay there for a while, but he may get shipped out after graduation."

"We can go down early Friday morning and go to the graduation," I said. "Then we can stay overnight and come back the next day if that's ok."

"Ok," she said, "I'll give him a call tomorrow and let him know we're coming."

She went into the kitchen and got herself another drink and then came back outside and loaded up another bowl. I realized that at this rate, it was no wonder we had to continually restock the liquor cabinet. Even though I wasn't really counting, I could tell by her swagger that Roxie was starting to get boxed again.

"You mentioned something about the guy who shot himself the other night." I asked. "How did he end up here?"

"Terry." She mused. "Terry was a great old man that I met in the nursing home when I worked there. He loved me and used to get me presents all the time. He hated the nursing home because he was pretty independent and he had to give up his double-wide trailer when he got so bad that he couldn't take care of himself."

"Was he bedridden?" I asked.

"No, as a matter of fact he was quite mobile. I finally asked him if he would like to live with me at this house. It was a lot cheaper than the money he was paying the home, and I could take better care of him. He jumped at the chance and moved in about a week afterward. Between the money I made at the nursing home, and the money he paid me for living here, I was doing alright."

"He must have had a few bucks himself." I commented.

"Oh yes, he had quite a little nest egg. He felt sorry for me having to pay the mortgage on the house after my divorce, so he went out, got qualified and bought this house from me."

"Wait a minute. I thought you owned this house."

"Technically I do," She said. "He gave me this house on a quit-claim deed before he died. He said that if anything ever happened to him, he wanted to make sure I had a place to live."

"How long did he last?"

"He died about a week later. He blew his brains out with a shotgun. I told you that story."

"Well, I'm confused," I said, "why would a man get a mortgage on a house, and then kill himself."

"A lot can happen with thread." She remarked.

"What do you mean?"

"Oh, forget it. You know how I sometimes ramble; especially when I drink. Let's talk about something else. How long were you married Mark?"

"We were married for 4 years but the relationship was a lot longer," I said. "We dated on and off for 10 years then she got married. I moved out to Washington State for work and when I came back a year later, she was going through a divorce. We hooked up again and lived together for 3 years before getting married."

"Why did you get divorced?" Roxie asked.

"When I got married, my wife was a manager in Kmart." I said. "Shortly afterward, she quit her job and was taking a series of low paying jobs that put her on the road a lot. She was doing inventory control jobs. Meanwhile,

I was busting my ass trying to manage 2 appliance stores. We had sold our house and we were living in an apartment complex. She started having an affair with the guy that lived below us. Plus, both of us were pretty good hitting the bottle, so the combination spelt disaster."

"Did you ever cheat on her?" She asked.

"Never," I said. "I had plenty of opportunity and one time she came into a local bar and I was talking with some barfly. She went ballistic. But truth was, I never cheated."

"I cheated twice when I was married." she told me, "my ex was out of town a lot and I just got lonely living here all alone."

"Were they just a sexual fling or a regular affair?" I asked.

"One was just a fling but the other was going on until I moved back here in the spring." She admitted. "He's a public official and he's married, so we had to be pretty careful."

"Well, that's one way to keep the law off your back," I said, "unless, of course, you liked him on your back."

"You are one sick son of a bitch." she said, "why does everything have to be a joke to you?"

"What?" I questioned. "You're bitching because I'm witty?"

"No, Mark," she continued. "I'm bitching because you think you have to be a comedian all the time. I get sick of it."

"Sorry," I said.

I really didn't think I should have to put up with this kind of verbal abuse, just because I was quick with a comeback. As a matter of fact, she had frequently said that I was the funniest guy she had ever dated and now I'm finding out that she is sick of my wit. I couldn't help wonder what else she was sick of.

"Look," I said, "I'm sorry if I offended you in some way. My wit has always been sharp and sometimes it's faster than my brain works. But it was just a snappy comeback and I didn't mean anything personal. But you're the one that had the affair, not me."

"Fuck you asshole." She shouted.

She got up and bolted into the house. I sat there in amazement and wondered whether or not I had made a mistake about Roxie's mental state. She flipped from hot to cold in a heartbeat and at this particular moment she was in hot mode. There is no way that anyone should have taken offense to a truthful statement like I made. Like the old story goes; sometimes the truth hurts, But damn it, it wasn't my fault . . . I guess there won't be any sugar cookies for Mark tonight.

And I was still bothered by our earlier conversation about her ex-roommate Terry. Something just did not add up and she was way too quick to get off the subject. Had Terry been her lover also? It seemed hard to believe that she would tie up with a 78-year-old man but for all I knew, he belonged to the Viagra club. Stranger things have happened.

That night I slept on the couch to avoid provoking more confrontation with Roxie. Maybe it was the alcohol or maybe she had a degree of bi-polarity. Either way, I wasn't going to do anything to accelerate her obvious mood swings.

I got up the next morning, went into the kitchen and made coffee. Maybe if I took her flowers, she might forget about her anger. Yes, that was a good idea. While the coffee was brewing, I got into my car and drove down the road to town. There were groups of wildflowers growing all over and I made stops at every patch to get a nice variety. I came back and found a vase under the sink and put my arrangement together.

I poured our coffee cups and took everything upstairs to the bedroom. Roxie was lying there, naked under the covers and snoring softly. I awoke her with a kiss on the forehead. Her eyes fluttered open and I saw a peaceful calm in them.

"Good Morning Love," I said, "I brought you coffee but I couldn't find a donut or anything else sweet for you."

"You can be my sweet roll honey," she said as she put her arms around my neck. I gave her a quick kiss upon the lips and she pulled me back for more. I kissed her cheeks, her nose, and her lips again, both sides of her neck and then her lips again.

"Well don't stop there," She hollered with a smile.

"I brought you something else, too" as I brought forth the vase with the flowers.

"Why you little lover boy," she said, "I can't remember the last time a man gave me flowers."

"Honey, you were pretty upset last night," I said. "I just wanted to sort of apologize for saying anything that got you there."

"I know, sometimes I over-react." She said. "It's just that I was being serious and you made a joke out of it like you always do."

"I guess I have to learn to watch my mouth." I told her.

"No, let me watch it for you." as she pulled me down for another kiss. Of course I knew what was on her mind and of course, I didn't mind either.

We made early morning love, got up and went downstairs for breakfast. I told her that I was just going to have cereal again because I wanted to get busy on all the chores.

"You're still going to take your medicine." She said as she brought over my pills and tonic.

I made a mental note that somehow, I was going to find out what the ingredients were in this tonic. It wasn't so much of a lack of trust, but more a curiosity of what was going in my body and the knowledge that is was safe for me. But there was also the trust issue too. We spent the day on separate tasks. She was in her office on the computer most of the day and I assumed that it was listing items for EBay. At about 2 in the afternoon, I asked her if it was time for a break.

"Break Hell," she said, "I'm done for the day; How about you?"

"I agree," I said. "I think I've done enough for one day and think I'll knock off early."

We went into the living room and put on some music. She handed me a beer and poured herself a tall Rum and Coke. We sat on the couch and talked a bit about music and then she said, "What are the plans for going down to see my son, Bobby? It's this weekend."

"You called him . . . is Friday morning good with him?"

"He graduates at 11 a.m.," She said. "We would have to leave really early to get there on time. It's a 6 hour drive."

"No big deal," I answered. "We leave here about 3 a.m., get there by 9, have breakfast and go to the base."

"OK, it sounds fine to me as long as you can get up that early."

I got up to put another CD on. "Any requests?" I asked.

"Do you have any Styx?" She asked.

"Coming right up; any particular album?"

"No," she said, "I love all their music. I saw them when I lived in St. Augustine, Florida."

"Why did you move from there if you had a going business?" I asked.

"Our double-wide trailer exploded." She said.

"Get out of here!" I said with a questioning look, "exploded?"

"Yes, exploded."

She told me the story of how her and her ex-husband lived in a double-wide and one day when she was outside in the parking lot talking on the phone, the damn thing just exploded.

"Was anybody hurt?" I asked.

"Well, my ex-husband escaped with slight burns but other than that, we were OK."

"Do you know what the cause was?" I continued.

"The fire inspector said that we had a faulty electrical socket" she said, "LP gas from the stove must have leaked out and the spark from the outlet ignited it. At least, that's what they thought."

"Christ you were lucky," I said. "LP gas is really flammable. How is it that you weren't inside too?"

"I had just received a phone call and my ex had the music on." She said. "So I stepped out into the parking lot to take the call. That's when it happened. I turned around to just in time to see the flash of ignition."

"Did you have insurance?" I asked.

"We had insurance on the property but not on my personal stuff." she said. "I lost everything like pictures, antiques and such. We used the insurance money to buy this place here."

"That's a hell of a story baby," I said. "I don't think even Les could top that one with his bullshit."

"It's not bullshit," she barked, "I know; I lived through it."

"No," I said. "I didn't mean your story was bullshit. I meant that Les, who is full of bullshit, probably couldn't make up a better story."

The afternoon went drifting by. Roxie sat there drinking and smoking bowl after bowl and I just listened to her talk about everything under the sun. When I asked if she got a lot posted on EBay she said that she had to get to that eventually but she was working on something else.

"I have decided that I want to go back to home healthcare," She said. "I have applied to Kaplan University Online for a grant. If I get it, I can go to nursing school online and they will pay me a stipend to live on."

"Wow," I said. "That's great. There may come a time when I need a nurse."

"Baby," she said, "you know that I'll take care of you. You can count on it."

My mind was whirling and it wasn't from the alcohol. It was from all the information that I had absorbed this afternoon. First, she tells me this story about her trailer exploding and how conveniently she was outside at the time. But I couldn't help wondering why, even after having an event like that happen, why would you pack up and leave the state where your business was located? Secondly there was my belief that all the time I thought Roxie was listing stuff on EBay to sell, she was applying for grant money to go into nursing. What about her alleged construction company involvement and her desire to leave Kentucky? And third, I still had questions about Terry, her former housemate. That story about the quit claim deed to regain this house just didn't sound plausible; especially when she made that comment about 'thread' and wouldn't give me an explanation. I was beginning to have the feeling that all was not as it seemed. There just seemed to be more questions than answers and I didn't like it.

The rest of the day and the evening were spent relaxing, nibbling on leftovers and talking; Oh, and drinking and smoking too. At about 11 p.m., I decided that I was tired and was going to hit the sack. She asked me if I would like some company and of course I accepted.

I think I got to sleep around 2 the next morning.

* * *

23) Breakup and Makeup

Burkesville, KY—June 11, 2009

On Thursday morning, the day before the graduation, I wanted to get an early start and finish early so that I could catch some sleep before we took off for South Carolina. We had planned to leave at 3 a.m. so that we could get to the graduation by 11 a.m. I never like to plan anything right down to the minute so I figured 2 hours of slop time should be more than enough. It was a pretty direct route and I figured I could get us there without getting lost.

My friend Michelle in Syracuse told me that she had sent a government check to me and I had forgot to check the mailbox yesterday. So I went down today to pick up anything that came in for me. I needed the money because I had asked Roxie about opening up a local bank account so that I didn't have to constantly go to the ATM to access my New York bank account. I needed to put money the account anyway so the check was perfect timing.

The mailbox yielded the usual junk mail but my check was there along with some items that Roxie had bought on EBay. And of course the usual bills—water, electric, insurance and something from her doctor. I took everything back to the house and walked in just as Roxie was coming down the stairs from the bedroom.

"Where were you," She asked.

"I went to get the mail," I answered. "I knew I had this check coming and we forgot to get the mail yesterday." I opened the check up and showed it to her.

"Fifty-Eight Hundred dollars?" she said in shock, "what's that for?"

"This is a special Navy dispensation check," I told her. "I got this because I was eligible as a veteran of Vietnam War era. I didn't know I had it coming until someone told me I had to apply for it. I applied last November and they finally sent it."

I put the check on the kitchen counter and sat down for breakfast. Roxie cooked up some sausage and eggs and I wolfed everything down like a starving man. She brought over my daily dose of pills and tonic and then we both went to our respective offices to do our daily chores. Even though I wanted to get the online business set up, it seemed that organizing my New York items took priority.

"I got a bank account all set up for you Honey," Roxie said as she came into my office. "All you have to do is go down to the bank, give them your SSI number, sign and make the initial deposit."

"How did you do that?" I asked.

"I can do everything online," She answered. "I just figured that since you wanted a local bank account, it was easiest to set it up at the same bank where I have my account."

"Great," I said, "we'll go down there this afternoon. When do they close?"

"They're open till 6 tonight." She answered.

I spent the rest of the morning setting up the office, eating lunch, and more work. I still wanted to do the measurements at the double-wide and build a set of entrance steps. Getting in and out of the trailer with just a stepladder is both inconvenient and dangerous.

At 3 p.m. I said, "Let's go into town and get to the bank, do our shopping and get back here."

"I need 15 minutes to get ready," she said, "I'm a mess."

I wondered how she could be a mess, just sitting at a computer desk all day. The 15 minutes that she asked for turned into 45 minutes. When I went into her office, she reached up and quickly turned her monitor off before I could see what she was working on.

"Are you just about ready?" I asked.

"Five minutes more . . . Promise," She affirmed.

"OK," I said, "Five minutes . . . then I leave, with or without you."

I left her office and she got up and closed her door. I wondered what the hell she was doing that she didn't want me to see. Being a naturally trusting person I figured maybe she had some private bank info or a private email or something that was none of my business. I let the thought go and went out to the porch. Roxie soon came out on the porch and told me she was ready. We got into the car and headed down the road when I suddenly stopped.

"What's wrong?" She asked.

"I forgot the check for the bank . . . Shit."

I turned the car around and headed back to the house. I went into the kitchen to the counter where I had left the check and to my surprise, it was not there. I looked in the cupboards, under the sink, on the table, in the living room, in both offices; all over, and no check. I went back out to the car.

"Did you put that check somewhere?" I asked.

"No, where did you put it?" She questioned.

"I left it right on the counter at breakfast this morning." I said.

"I didn't see it other than when you showed it to me."

I went back in the house and hunted again. Now I started to get pissed off. I opened up the closet and pulled out the garbage bag and emptied it on the floor. I sifted through coffee grounds, papers, food and the rest of the magical assortment one would find in a garbage bag. Still there was no check. My pissed off attitude elevated to livid. She had to have taken it.

"C'mon Hon," I said, "This isn't a joke."

"I don't have your fucking check," she shrieked, "what the fuck would I do with it?

That attitude again. Instead of doing what a normal person would do; help me find it, she copped an attitude; an attitude that I did not like one bit. I knew where I put that check and I also knew that I should have shoved it in my wallet. But of course hindsight is 20-20. I was now missing a Six thousand dollar check and had absolutely no idea where it was. And the only other person in the house was my loving partner, Roxie; who had an attitude.

I went back out to the car. "Well that settles it," I said, "without that check, we're not going anywhere."

"What do you mean?" She said.

"I wanted to open the bank account before we went and I can't without that check." I told her. "I need to take some cash with me." How can I do that when I have a grand total of approximately $ 30 dollars in my pocket now?"

"You must have lost it," she said, "how could you be so stupid?"

"Then I suggest you go in the house and find it," I said, "since I'm so stupid."

"Screw you!" she answered. "You lost it, you find it. The only thing I know is that we are supposed to be in South Carolina in 17 hours."

"I left that check on the counter," I explained, "I went into my office and worked all morning and half the afternoon. You brought my lunch into me so I wasn't even in the kitchen. Now when I go to get it, it's gone. I was not in the kitchen, you were. If you want to go to South Carolina, you find that check; and fast."

"You're an asshole," she sniped as she got out of the car and slammed the door. She stormed up the porch, went in the house and slammed the front door. I didn't know if she was going to look for the check, getting away from me or just doing her act for dramatic purpose. What I did know was that I was so hot I couldn't breathe. Not only was I pissed about the check, but also her attitude. This was a side of her that I had never seen until we got back here; and I damned well did not like it. I got out of the car and went up to go into the house. I grabbed the door knob and found the door locked.

"Son of a bitch Roxie," I yelled, "open the door."

No answer. I looked into the front window and couldn't see her. I went to her office window and she wasn't in there either. I went around the back of the house and the back door was locked too.

This was ridiculous.

"Roxie, open the door," I shouted, "and I mean now."

Still nothing.

I listened and didn't hear a sound. My tool kit sat on the porch and I grabbed a screwdriver to take off the storm window, thinking the main window would open. Wrong. That one was locked also. Well nothing left to do but . . . .

CRASH!

The blade of the screwdriver went through the pane as it shattered, leaving shards of glass all over the living room floor. I reached in and unlocked the window and crawled into the living room.

"Well I hope you are good at replacing glass, asshole."

"Fuck the glass," I said, "I want my check."

"I don't have your check," she argued. "You must have misplaced it or lost it."

"It's more than that Roxie," I said. "It's your attitude. I don't like it and I'm not going to put up with it."

"Well then why don't you get the fuck out of here?"

I was shocked at her response. I knew she was mad but this was more than that. This was a person that couldn't keep her hands off me, always complimented me and kept me feeling happy; right up until we went up north and got her stuff transported down here to her house. Then, after that, it was like someone threw a switch on the wall and she went from 'Angel' to 'Devil'. Ever since our return we did nothing but fight. And now she is telling me to get out of the house. I had been with a lot of woman in my life and had never had an altercation like this one. Even when I was going through my divorce, my ex-wife and I were civil to each other. What was it that was so different about this relationship?

"So, when are you leaving asshole?" She said.

"You want that, you got it," I said. "I'll pack everything up and be out by Monday."

"You'll be out tonight," She demanded.

"Like hell," I said as I went into my office.

She followed me into the office and continued her bantering. I tried to ignore her but she just kept chattering like a squirrel whose nest was being invaded. Finally I turned around and pushed her out of the office and locked the door. She stood outside the door ranting on and on and on. This verbal assault went on for at least 10 minutes. All this time I just sat at my desk trying to figure out what went wrong? Was it her fault, my fault, both of our faults? I was confused; I could not think straight to save my ass.

It was a while before I realized that her vocal assault had ended. It was quiet; too quiet. I figured that maybe she went out to the porch but when I opened the door, I saw her sitting at her office desk with the phone in her hand.

"I'm just calling the police, Mark," she said, "and I want you out of here tonight."

"You forget something my love," I said. "My mail comes here too, so this is my address and I don't have to leave."

She threw the phone at me, got up and slammed the office door shut. I went into the living room and put a CD on. At least I could listen to some music while I tried to figure out what I was going to do. After about 15 minutes, she came out of her office and plunked down on the other end of the couch.

"When are you leaving asshole?" She asked.

"Tomorrow I'll go into town, get boxes, pack my stuff, rent a trailer and I'll be gone by Monday," I told her.

"Then you just keep your distance from me," She said. "I don't want anything to do with you and I damn sure don't need to listen to you."

She got up and rushed upstairs to the bedroom. I made a couple of toasted cheese sandwiches and had many, many beers. About 10:30 or so, I passed out.

I spent the next day, Friday, the day we were supposed to be in South Carolina, in Burkesville; hunting the grocery stores for boxes to pack up all my stuff. I went to the local depot for a U-haul and arranged for a trailer to be picked up on the following Monday. The next biggest thing I had to do was find a place to stay for a couple of days while I decided where to go. All this caught me by surprise. One minute I was in relative bliss and the next, a world of shit.

I had about $1,800 in my New York bank account that I could tap. The missing check really pissed me off and now I was going to have to put a stop payment on it and have another one reissued. I would have to wait until July 3rd before my regular SSI payment came in and I would have any more money. That meant I was going to have to be very frugal with my funds.

Renting trailers and storage bins and paying motel bills was not really what I wanted to be doing. I killed 3 or 4 hours in town to arrange things and also because I really did not want to go home. I could feel my heart pounding every time I thought back to the fight the day before.

Actually, I was sick over it.

I finally bit the bullet and went home. What I saw when I got to the porch just put me into orbit. All my CD's were thrown out into the front yard. I went into the house with my boxes and found that she had taken my laptop off the desk and tossed it across the room. It hit the floor so hard that it broke out the bottom cover, spilling out the memory chips.

If there was the slightest doubt about whether or not I needed to move, this was the last straw. I was so mad, I was afraid that if we had any conversation at all, it would turn violent. I'm not a violent man. I've never hit a woman before. The closest I've ever come was with my ex-wife when we were going through a divorce. I grabbed her by the throat and pushed out of the apartment. That was it. I thought it best to just avoid Roxie and do what I knew I had to do.

I proceeded to go outside and pick up all my CD's and put them back into the boxes the had been stored in. I didn't bother to put them in alphabetical order like before, because all I wanted to do was pack my stuff and get out. I went inside and cleaned up the mess in the office as best as I could. Fortunately, the laptop damage was minor and I was able to put the memory chip cover back on and make sure it was still working.

Roxie and I avoided each other like the Black Plague all the rest of Friday and Saturday. I spent all day packing up my records, video tapes, CD's, computer equipment, clothes and every other thing that I had just unpacked. With every new box, I could feel my heart rate jump another notch. This was something I did not want to do, but had to.

Sunday was even worse. I could not control my emotions as I arranged everything for transport. I found myself having to sit down and cry every 5 minutes or so. I was an emotional wreck. I was thankful that most everything was done before I started having these breakdowns. Roxie must have heard me crying because late in the afternoon she wandered into my office and stood behind me as I was sitting in the chair. Suddenly I felt her put her arms around me and kiss my neck.

"I don't want to do this Honey," I sobbed.

"I know," she said, "and I don't really want you to go Mark. I love you."

"Then what is with this attitude?" I asked.

"It's my medication," she answered, "I'm sorry, but I haven't been taking it and I know I should be."

"What medication?" I questioned.

"I'm supposed to be taking pills for my menopause symptoms," She said. "I haven't been because they are expensive and I've been trying to save money for fixing up the trailer."

"Don't you think your health is a bit more important?" I asked

"Probably," she said, "but before you, there was no one to see my mood swings. I realize now that these affect you too. I promise if you stay, I will get more pills and everything will be alright."

"That's it?" I said, "Simple medication?"

"That's it," she affirmed, "I've been on them before and they definitely work. I just thought I could do without them and save the expense. I know now that I can't."

It seemed logical to me. I did know that menopause affects women differently and if I could have my beautiful red haired princess back, I would pay for the pills myself. Roxie swung around to the front of the chair and sat on my lap. We kissed gently at first and then more fiercely. I knew where this would probably lead and I didn't want it to go there. Not right now at least. I pulled back and gazed into her soft blue eyes. She was truly beautiful.

"Honey," I said, "let's call a truce and give it time to settle into place."

"That sounds fair enough to me," she said, "but would it be too much to ask if I could cook you a nice dinner tonight?"

"I suppose I could handle that. Cheese sandwiches only go so far."

We kissed again and she got up and went into the kitchen to make dinner. I looked around at everything I had packed and wondered if I dare start unpacking. After all, she wasn't on the medication yet.

We finished dinner, complete with small talk and sat on the couch to watch a movie. Roxie was particularly attentive to me. Not in a sexual way but more cuddling and acting happy. Every time she would get up to fix a drink she would ask me if I needed anything. This was more the way it was when we first got together and I loved it. By the end of the movie, I had my arm around her neck as we sat there and each of us planting spontaneous kisses on each other.

I debated on whether or not to sleep in the same bed. I wanted to, but again, the lack of medication reared its ugly head. I decided to test the waters.

"I'm not sure if we should sleep together yet." I said.

"You don't want to sleep with me?" She questioned.

"No, that will never happen," I continued, "but what I'm saying is that we just got through a major fight. I want to make sure that we are on firm ground before intimacy takes over."

With every word I spoke, I felt Roxie sliding her hand up and down my leg. At first, the movement was subtle but it gradually increased until the movement interfered with what I wanted to say to her. I was becoming aroused and I'm sure that she knew it.

"Well Honey," she said, "we don't have to do anything. I'm just happy that you made the right decision and are going to stay. I'd be happy just holding you close."

For some reason, that sounded rational. Maybe it was the stress of the last couple days or maybe it was the emotional relief that I was not moving. But her logic rang true in my head. All the while, the steady movement of her hand on my thigh rang true on the other head. She laid her head on my shoulder and we continued to talk. Slowly, in a subtle manner, she allowed her body to slip down to where she placed her head on my lap. Every time she would talk, the reverberation of her voice would vibrate through my pants. I was getting erect and by now, she knew it.

As predicted, her subtle movements became more obvious. Not outrageous but more obvious. More and more, the hand would 'accidentally' glide over that sensitive spot I had. As much as I wanted to put up resistance to what she was planning to do, my mouth couldn't find the words to say no to her. I couldn't escape the emotional grip she had.

I couldn't escape that grip; for who can escape what they desire?

* * *

24) The Bank Bungle

Burkesville, KY—June 15, 2009

We ended up sleeping together that night after all. When I awoke, it was like nothing had changed in our relationship. Roxie dozed quietly on her side of the bed and I looked at that face and body with an essence of true love. I didn't know if I had made the right decision to stay with her but I was sure going to give it a try. I got up and went downstairs and made our coffee. I went into my office, checked my email and the balance at my

New York Bank. Fortunately, I had not written any checks and I still had about $1,800 in the account. I wouldn't have to be wasting my money on trailers and motels.

I started writing a list of projects that had to be done. One thing that was for sure was getting the online business going. I was convinced that the best way to go about that was to buy one of those pre-packaged offers that I kept getting emails about. Another thing on the agenda was getting some work done on the double-wide trailer. Whether we ended up moving into it or moving out of state and renting it, the work had to be done. The coffee was done and I took our cups upstairs. I started my lover's day off with a gentle kiss on the forehead. She woke up and smiled at me and said,

"Let me start the day off by saying I Love You."

"I love you too Honey," I said. "Here . . . fresh hot coffee to get you going."

"What's the plan for today?" She asked.

"I'm just putting a project sheet together right now," I told her. "I've got work on the double-wide included. And I'd like to make the final decision on my business plans this week. Plus, I've got a shitload of calls to make to cancel the trailer and put a stop payment on the missing check."

We went down to the kitchen and Roxie commenced making our breakfast. We were just talking about things that had to be done when suddenly I remembered something.

"We have to go back up to New York next month," I said. "I have to appear at Les's trial as a witness."

"A witness for what?" She asked.

"He got a DWI back in November last year," I said. "I was living there at the time and told him I would be a witness for the defense. I have to tell the court that I didn't see him drinking. It's bullshit, because that night we were out to celebrate my birthday. He was supposed to be designated driver but he was right there pounding down the drinks in a strip club. He was trying to pick up some whore in this bar and there was a blinding snowstorm going on outside. I told him I wanted to go home before it got too bad but he was bound and determined to get laid that night."

"Oh, he found someone who would actually sleep with him?" She asked.

"I know, I know," I chuckled, "but he was going to try anyway."

"He took me back to his house and then he and his whore went out drinking. I guess he found out she was a hooker and he didn't want to pay for it, so he went back to the strip club and had more to drink. He never came home that night because he got stopped on the way because he forgot to turn his headlights on."

"So you are going to lie for him?" She asked.

"Well, he is an alright guy, even thought most of the time he acts like an asshole." I said. "If I can do anything to help, I will."

"I think he's an obnoxious asshole," Roxie said, "I wouldn't help him out. How are we going to get there? I'm not ready for another 24 hour ride."

"Let's fly up and pick up your car at Bonnies's house," I said. "That way we'll get that back here and you'll have a set of wheels; I'll take care of what I have to and everybody is happy."

"We would have to go to Nashville to catch a flight you know," she told me. "That's the closest Airport; unless you want to drive to Louisville or Cincinnati."

"Let me think about that," I said, "I think I also want to try to make an appointment at the VA hospital and have a checkup while we are there. Then I can hold off any medical issues until we decide where we are going to live."

"You really are organized, aren't you?" She remarked.

"I certainly try to be." I answered.

We finished breakfast and I went back into my office and started working on a list of supplies and tools needed for the double-wide. I opened up the desk drawer and right on the top of all my papers was, guess what? . . . The missing check. I was immediately filled with mixed emotions. I was happy to find the check but pissed because I knew that I had not put it there. Roxie had to have done it and didn't have the nerve to tell me. I went back out into the kitchen.

"I found the check," I announced, "Thank you."

"Don't thank me," she replied, "I didn't have anything to do with it. You must have put it there yourself and blamed me."

I wasn't about to get into another argument with her so I just went back into my office. Two things that I can't stand in this world is a liar or a thief. I knew I had not put it there and I knew that she did. That made her both of the things that I hated.

How could I handle this? I couldn't just accept it because it was wrong, but Roxie's hold on me was so strong that even though in the back of my mind I knew I should leave, my love for her and my sometimes overly generous nature wanted to give her a second chance. After all, she had promised to get medication.

I worked until about noon and then told Roxie that we had to go into town to get the banking set up. She agreed and said she wanted to pay some bills and get food for the house. We finished up our house tasks and took the Camaro into town. The first place we went was Citizen's Bank, where she had her accounts. She told me that she had set an account up for me online and all I had to do was show them my SSI card and sign the papers. We went in and she spoke to one of the tellers and in a few minutes the teller came back with all the paperwork.

I was so happy that I had my check back, that I wasn't paying close attention. I just signed on the dotted line when the teller asked me to and then she handed the papers to Roxie who also signed. I handed over my check for the initial deposit and it was done. The teller told us that the ATM cards would be issued in about a week but we could write checks and make deposits now. Because my check was a government issued item, I took out $ 500 immediately, for day to day expenses and put the balance of the $6,000 in the bank. It wasn't until we got in the car and I started looking at the paperwork that I realized I had just signed on a joint account with Roxie. This was not what I wanted.

"I didn't want a joint account," I said, "I just wanted a simple checking account for local transactions. I still want to keep the bulk of my money in my New York account."

"Well," Roxie said, "I'm sorry, I didn't know. Do you want to go back in and start over? At least now you have a local account."

I thought about it and she was right. I had money in my pocket and there was no great rush to change right now. So we agreed that sometime in the future, I would open up my own account and transfer the money into it. It seemed like a logical plan. I mean, I was living with her and I supposedly trusted her . . . didn't I?

Roxie said she had to go see the estate lawyer. She was the executrix of Terry's estate and had to handle a lot of things since his death. I told her I was going to hang out and visit some of the little shops in the town square.

She was only in the lawyer's office about 10 minutes when she came out and found me in the pawn shop across the street.

"I knew I'd find you here," she said. "What are you going to buy with that money that is burning a hole in your pocket?"

"I was just looking to see what kind of assortment of tools they had, but there's nothing here that I see I can use."

I browsed around a couple of minutes or so and then we decided to go shopping and take care of her chores. We needed to pick up some staples, go to the post office and get gas. We got our shopping done, Roxie wrote out checks for the electric and water bills, which we mailed and then went back home. Again, not being as sharp as I usually was, I failed to notice that she wrote the checks out on the temporary checks from 'our' new account.

The rest of the day was pretty much our usual routine. We had dinner and sat on the porch watching the fireflies and talking. She told me that she was still irritated at me, because she had missed her son's graduation from boot camp.

"That's my only son and I really wanted to be there for him," She said.

"I'm sorry baby," I said, "but the situation was out of control. I'm glad we got back on track. We can go down and see him when we get back from New York if you'd like."

I knew her daughter Barbie had just graduated from college and I had already met Bonnie. I asked her if Bobby was the oldest.

"He is now," she said, "he had an older sister Brenda, but she was murdered."

"Your daughter was murdered?" I said with an element of shock. Then I remembered that she had mentioned a dead daughter once before.

"Yes, back in 1991," she said solemnly, "she was 16 years old at the time."

"What happened?" I asked.

"She was running with a wild bunch and I didn't like it," She answered. "She was doing drugs and hanging with a bunch of hippies. She and I had an argument and she ran away to Rochester. I was frantic. She called me and told me that she was going to lead her life the way she wanted to and I could lead my life the way I wanted to."

"That sounds like a teenager," I said.

"I went to Rochester to try to talk some sense into her but she wouldn't listen. A day later, the State Police called me and told me that they had found her body."

"My God Roxie," I said, "That is terrible. What did you do?"

Roxie started to cry now. It was the first time that I had ever seen her cry. She told me that she couldn't talk about it because she was still sensitive. I understood and attempted to change the conversation.

"I'm going to build a set of steps and a deck for the double-wide," I said. "It's too hard getting in and out of the front door on that ladder. You have plenty of wood in the back behind the pole barn so I just need to cut everything to size and put it together."

"That will be nice," she replied, still sniffling. "I've wanted a deck on there since I bought it but just never got around to having it done."

There was suddenly a chill in the air and we decided to go inside and watch a movie. Needless to say, the atmosphere between us was rather somber. I was almost afraid to bring anything up in conversation because I could tell that depression had taken over my Roxie. We watched the movie in silence and then went to bed.

I had another bad dream that night; so bad that I woke up sweating in the middle of the night. I sat upright and tried to remember the particulars. In the dream I stood in an open field surrounded by 5 or 6 helicopters. The air churned as the rotors spun in the twilight of the night. I didn't know where I was but I wanted to get out of there. I also wanted to find out who was in the choppers to try to make some sense of where I was and how I got there. I approached the cabin of the first chopper and the pilot just shook his head as he slowly took off and rose into the air. I couldn't recognize a face because the pilot was occluded by a helmet with a smoked faceplate. As I approached a second helicopter, the same thing happened; and the same with the third machine. Some unknown fear captured me and I ran blindly towards the last aircraft on the ground just as it was lifting off. When it was gone, I would be all alone and lost. As the helicopter took flight, I caught glimpse of the pilot. Whoever it was dressed in a clown suit and flashing a broad grin. And there was something else . . .

The clown had a tinge of Red hair.

* * *

25) The Fabulous RV

Burkesville, KY—June 17, 2009

A couple of days later, we sat at the breakfast table enjoying our first meal of the day, listening to the local radio station and the Swap Shop program. It was a program where people would advertise items they were looking for or wanted to sell. One of the items that a caller had was an RV being advertised for sale for $2,200.

"That thing must be a piece of shit," I said between mouthfuls.

"I don't know Mark," Roxie countered, "I've bought some awful good stuff, dirt cheap down here through the Swap Shop. Are you interested in an RV?"

"I might be," I said. "I've always wanted to own one and you like to go camping. Should I give them a call? I don't know Jack Shit about them."

"It can't hurt." she said, "it doesn't cost anything to look, and I know RV's. Let's just find out what it is."

I called the number that was advertised and spoke to the owner. It turns out that it was a 1985 Fleetwood Arrow in good condition. The people were moving and didn't want to take it with them. Roxie and I decided to drive out and take a look at it. The location was about 60 miles from home, way out in the backwoods of Kentucky. We finally found the place and took a look at it. Roxie told me that she had a lot of experience with RV's before and would inspect it. She knew what to look for.

When we finally got there, the RV was parked in the front yard. From the outside you could see obvious wear and tear but it wasn't too bad. The inside was in very good condition. It had sleeping bunks for 6 people, a small kitchen with a sink, microwave, a couple of folding tables for eating, a little portable store and good lighting throughout. Roxie took her time inspecting every facet of the vehicle and told the owner's that she would like to take it for a test drive. We scrounged up a license plate and she took off while I commenced in some small talk with the owner. When she came back she pulled me aside and told me that it was in great shape.

"I can't pay your asking price for it, but what would you take?" I asked Marlene, the owner.

"What would you offer?" She asked.

I pulled $ 500 cash out of my wallet and told her I would give her $ 500 now and another $1,000 in check form. We could come and pick it up as soon as the check cleared.

"I'll go $1,750 cash only," she said, "since we are moving this weekend and I don't want to hassle with checks or anything. You guys are the first ones to look at it and I've had a lot of calls so I'm not worried about selling it."

I looked at Roxie and she nodded that it was worth it. I told the owner I would be back later that day to pick it up. I had to go to a bank and withdraw the money. I gave her the $ 500 deposit and got a receipt. Roxie and I took off and drove into Glasgow, about 25 miles away and I used my ATM card to withdraw the balance. It was a hassle because you can only take a maximum of $ 600 out of the bank per day, so I had to withdraw $ 600 from my local account and $ 600 from my New York account. Roxie had about $ 100 in her purse so we were covered on the money. We went back and finalized the deal with the owner.

In the state of Kentucky, a notarized title is required in order to transfer a vehicle. The owner told me that she would be happy to follow me to her local bank where they had a notary public. Roxie drove the Camaro, I hopped into the RV and we went down to the bank. We got the title and the bill of sale all done at the same time and then we left to go back home. Since I was driving with an illegal plate and no insurance, I was being especially careful. I thought the RV handled pretty good for such a big vehicle and I smiled at the fabulous deal I had negotiated. About midway to our destination, I pulled over to talk to Roxie, who was following me in the Camaro.

"Let's just take this baby down to the mechanic and have it checked out," I said. "I don't want to go on a road trip and get stranded."

We drove straight to the mechanic shop in Burkesville, dropped off the RV, and asked him to go through it with a fine tooth comb including a tune it up, oil change and make sure their were no bad belts or hoses. I wanted to make sure it was roadworthy in case we took it to New York or some other place. I then stopped at my insurance agent and paid them to insure it and went to the clerk's office to register it in my name.

The next day the mechanic called me and told me what great condition the RV was in. It had new brakes all the way around and after the tune-up it ran great. The bill was $ 238 which I thought was quite reasonable. We picked up the RV and brought it home.

"Let's go on a road trip next weekend to break it in Honey."

"Where do you want to go?" She asked.

"I don't know . . . somewhere close like Bowling Green or Nashville."

"Let's just go down to Dollywood in Tennessee," She said. "They have a KOA there, where we can stay for about $ 40 a night. This will give you an idea of how it handles on the road and what kind of gas mileage it gets."

"Sounds like a plan to me," I answered.

We then continued with our home tasks. I cut lumber for the deck of the trailer while Roxie, I assumed, was back to putting items for sale on EBay. Since I was out in the pole barn doing my carpentry work, we had little contact with each other all day. The only time that we got to see each other was at supper time. That was our routine for the next week.

The following Friday arrived and we prepared to go on our maiden voyage in the RV. Roxie had packed food, blankets, a radio and anything else we needed for our trip. We got into the RV and no matter how hard I tried, the damned thing would not start.

"This is not good Honey," I said. "Our first trip has hit a road block."

"I'll call my AAA account and get a jumpstart." She replied.

The AAA driver came out and within 5 minutes he had us up and running. We drove into town and went directly to the mechanic who did the work on the vehicle. I wanted him to check it out because we were going to be out of town and I didn't need a dead RV on my hands. He did a few checks and told me that the battery needed replacement. It just wasn't putting out enough juice to start this big 350 engine. I didn't argue, even though I also didn't think the battery would do that. I paid another $ 135 for a supercharge battery and we were on our way.

During the trip down to Dollywood, we stopped for gas a number of times and the RV never gave us a hint of trouble. We just would get in and fire it up. We finally got down to the KOA Park and settled in for the night. Roxie handled all the electrical and water hookups and I handled all the financial transactions with the park. We were both excited because it was our first trip together in the RV and everything worked like a dream. The lighting was sufficient, the AC worked great and we had a nice dinner; cooked in our little RV stove. We played cards the rest of the night.

The next morning, after breaking in the RV with our body fluids, we decided to go into town and see the sights. The RV had other plans.

It would not start. No matter what I tried, this behemoth sat there cranking, but not firing. Needless to say, I was a bit upset? What was more upsetting was the fact that all mechanic businesses seemed to be closed on the weekend. I hunted high and low for someone to come out and take a look at the RV and tell me what was wrong. The only answer I got was 'call again on Monday'. So that put a real damper on our plans.

We ended up taking a bus into town and doing a little shopping in the souvenir shops. What a waste of time. Roxie and I settled in for the night, played cards, made love and went to sleep. On Monday, bright and early, I contacted a local garage and they sent a mechanic over to the KOA park. He did all the normal tests I would expect him to do, and finally determined that the float in the carburetor was stuck. I would need a rebuilt carburetor, if I expected the RV to run.

"How much is that?" I asked him

"Oh, you're probably looking at $ 350 to $ 400 for a new one," He chirped. "I may have a rebuilt one over at my shop I could let you have for $ 150 plus installation."

I agreed on the price and he headed back to his shop to get the 'rebuilt' carb. He was back in about an hour, and in another hour he had it installed and the RV running. By the time I got the final tally, with parts, labor and service charges, the bill had escalated to $ 578 dollars.

I went ballistic.

"I thought you told me $ 150 for the carb," I said angrily.

"Yeah, for the carb" he replied, "Then you've got 2 hours labor at $ 150 per hour, the gasket kit at $ 50 and $ 25 for the initial service call . . . Plus Tax."

I put the charges on my Visa card, pissed as I was, and dismissed the mechanic. At least the RV was back up and running. Because the delays had taken over the noon mark at KOA, I was forced to pay for another day of space rental at $ 40 a day; another local screwing.

Roxie took care of unhooking everything from the park. We loaded up and literally dashed out of there. We had traveled maybe a half mile when this horrendous screeching came from the engine compartment. All of a sudden, the screeching stopped. I looked down and saw my engine temperature indicator going through the roof. I knew I had broken a fan belt.

I pulled into yet another service station and asked if they could work on the RV. They told me to just park it and they would take care of it. The mechanic found the broken belt, called NAPA and ordered another one. It took NAPA 3 trips to get the correct belt. Replacement cost was a measly $ 96 total.

Time wasted, another 3 hours.

By now it was 5 p.m. and we were still in the Dollywood area. Based on how long it took us to get here, I estimated that we would not get home before 10 p.m. that night. The drive home was quiet. Roxie didn't have very much to say because she knew that I was fuming. I could feel the blood pulsing through my veins. We rode in silence and finally arrived in our driveway at 10:45 p.m. I keep good records, and the amount of money I had spent for this maiden voyage shoved my blood pressure up another 5 notches.

Battery Cost	- $ 135
Fuel Cost	- $ 118
Mechanic 1	- $ 578
Mechanic 2	- $ 96
Food	- $ 55
Souvenirs	- $ 32
TOTAL Cost	- $ 1014
TOTAL Fun	- ZERO

The RV wasn't looking too fabulous that night.

* * *

26) The Sorrows of Summer

Burkesville, KY—July 1, 2009

After our trip to Tennessee, things just weren't the same between Roxie and me. Every day, I could look forward to some form of verbal abuse; either a snippy comment or an outright slam about something I allegedly did. I was beginning to feel like ET, lost in an alien world. I had nobody down here that I could talk to and the romance of my life had gone on vacation. We hadn't made love since that little trip to Tennessee and I was reluctant to make an approach or even bring the topic up for fear of getting another tongue lashing; and not the good kind. The long and short of it was that I was tired of putting up with the fights, the attitude, and Roxie's general temperament. Plus, there were so many stories that she had told that did not add up. I didn't know if she was just bullshitting me or if there was a grain of truth in what she said or if she was a flat-out liar. But I did know that I didn't like it and that more than likely, I should cut and run. I really should have done it when we had our last blowout; before I was shackled with the RV. But hindsight is always 20-20.

One day while I was looking under the stairs for a plastic bag to put clothes in, I ran across a Mossberg shotgun. It was a short stock 20 gauge model that would not be used for hunting; more like something a gang member would carry. I decided that I definitely didn't want this within her reach and I snuck out the front door with it and put it in the trunk of my Camaro under a blanket. The first opportunity I got, I was going to take it down to the police station and tell them I didn't want it in the house.

I went back into my office and got online with the travel site Priceline. I was looking at airfares for our trip up to Syracuse. Our trip was twofold in that I had to testify in court for Les on the 21st of the month and I wanted to pick up Roxie's car at her daughters house. Then we could drive back down home, I could pack up my stuff and possibly leave her. I didn't really want to, but I felt that this may be the best course of action, under the circumstances. I had to really think about throwing away this beautiful lady and starting over. Lord knows I had invested emotion, time and money in the relationship.

I was sure I didn't want to leave the Camaro in some parking garage while we were traveling so I booked 2 one-way tickets out of Nashville and separately, I also booked a rental car out of Nashville because there were no local car rental outlets that offered one-way vehicles. My plan was simple. We would drive the Camaro down to Nashville on Wednesday the 15th of July. I'd drive the rental back, while she could drive the Camaro. On Friday the 17th of July, the day of our departure, we would get up early and drive to Nashville. It was only about 2 ½ hours and we were going to be flying the rest of the day. We could drop the car off at the airport and be gone.

I got all that taken care of and finished up some work around the office. Most of my office stuff was still in boxes so packing would be a snap. I went out on the porch and found Roxie nursing a Rum and Coke. Roxie's drinking had increased dramatically over the last month. She would start on the Rum as early as 2 p.m. and by dinnertime, she would be stumbling around the kitchen. I made the mistake of commenting on her conditions that day.

"Honey," I said, "do you think you paid enough into the Bacardi retirement fund?"

"What are you talking about?" She responded.

"You have been going through Rum like a chainsaw would go through butter," I said.

"Fuck you Mark," she mumbled, "you have your beer so leave me the fuck alone."

This was not the woman I met back in April. This was a raw and totally obnoxious drunken bitch. It was bad enough I had to put up with this attitude in the first place but the other factor was that she wasn't paying for the booze . . . I was. Every time we went to the liquor store, it was my account the checks were written on, not hers. Maybe that's why she so deftly made sure that we had a joint account.

"Fine," I said, "drink yourself into a coma . . . but do it on your own dime. If you are going to act this way, I'll be damned if I pay to get you there. From now on, you buy your own booze."

Roxie didn't respond. She just got up out of the chair, sidestepped a bit and went into the house. There was no drama and no discussion. She just left. It was another night that I spent on the couch.

I had been weighing the decision of staying with her or leaving and with this latest interchange, I finally decided that since we were going back to New York later this month, we would pick her car up, drive back down here and I would pack my stuff and leave. I loved this girl so much, but my heart could not take the daily up and down roller coaster ride that she was putting me through. Maybe I should have said something earlier but I didn't. She could tell me all day long about the menopause related mood swings but it still didn't do anything to alleviate the depression that I was feeling. I made the decision that from now until we went back, I would keep our conversations light. I didn't want to do anything that would provoke her.

One evening when we were sitting on the porch after dinner, I brought up the topic of living up north and how different it was down here.

"I'm not sure anybody down here could handle living up north," I said. "The pace would probably kill them."

"It is a lot different down here," she said, "and I think northern people are smarter. I've lived in New York and Michigan and had a much better rapport with people up there, than I do here."

"Where did you live in Michigan?" I asked.

"When Terry killed himself last year," she explained "his son came down here to help me with the estate. He knew I was in a bad state and so I moved to Detroit and lived with him until I finally came back in March of this year. Besides, there were financial issues up there that I didn't want to deal with."

"Why would you move up north in the dead of winter anyway?" I inquired.

"They had gone through the investigation of Terry's death and it was ruled a suicide and I was cleared," She said. "I was depressed and I didn't see any purpose of staying here. Besides, Terry's son was so warm and compassionate to me that I thought I owed him."

"Owed him for what?" I asked.

"I don't know," she continued, "just owed him."

So it was looking like Roxie not only was Terry's lover, but also Terry's son. Hmmm . . .

Just then I spotted a truck coming up our driveway. Who would be visiting us? Nobody ever visited us. It turned out to be the neighbors Ritchie and Rachel. They got out of their truck and came up on the porch.

"Hey guys, how is everything?" Ritchie asked.

"Fine," Roxie answered, "what brings you out tonight?"

"We heard that this house was going into foreclosure," Ritchie said. "I had some business at the clerk's office today and that was the rumor going around."

"That's bullshit Ritchie," Roxie stated, "the lawyer thinks that the loan company where Terry got the mortgage is playing games. I just had a meeting with him the other day."

"I'm just telling you what I heard," Ritchie continued, "You know how these people are down here."

Ritchie and his wife stayed for a few minutes more and then left. Before they went, they invited us to come down some night and have dinner. Roxie told them that she would get back to them. I was very confused because it was my impression that this house belonged to Roxie. After they left Roxie made the statement "Thank God they're gone."

"I thought you got along with your neighbors," I said.

"I get along with everybody, but those two are just weird," She said. "They raise chickens and sell them for cockfights. I don't like that. And more than once they have mentioned that they are into group sex."

"I'm not trying to change the subject," I said "but what was all that about the house in foreclosure business. I thought you owned it on a quit-claim deed."

"I do," She said. "What happened was that when Terry moved in here, I was pretty broke because I had just gone through the divorce. Terry decided to buy this house to help me out. He got the mortgage and then he filed a quit claim deed saying that if anything ever happened to him, I was to get the house. When he died, the house became mine again."

In my mind, that sounded like bullshit. I couldn't figure out what she had meant by her statement and I spent another sleepless night thinking about everything that had happened in the last 5 weeks; since I had moved down here. A lot of things were just not adding up.

First, Roxie was not the owner of the house like she said. She basically had it on a land contract until she could get a mortgage. Even in the best of circumstances, the estate would have to go through probate for her to own it on just a quit claim deed. And why didn't Terry's son get the house instead? And what about Terry's son? Was Roxie the *cause* of his financial problems?

And then there was the issue of so much misfortune happening in Roxie's life. Her son in law was killed in an accident, her daughter murdered, the explosion of the double-wide in Florida, the deportation of her ex-husband, The death of Terry at the house that was ruled 'suicide', her affairs while she was married and the possibility of her being into group sex, based on things that happened during our Syracuse trip. (How convenient to have neighbors that were supposedly into that too). All these things didn't mean much alone; but when you put them together, it seemed like some sort of pattern was emerging.

And then finally, there was the lying. Roxie had said that she was raped when she was 12. But in another story, she had told me that she went to the original Woodstock concert when she was 15 and had come back a virgin. She told me that she was neighbors with Willie Nelson but then she said she had always lived on the East Coast. It was looking more and more like Roxie was either a pathological liar or a calculating Black Widow. Either way, I didn't feel comfortable and this analysis proved that I should let the relationship fade. As much as I hated my decision, I knew in my heart that I had to get out while the getting was good.

Saturday was the 4th of July and Burkesville was slated to have a big fireworks display. I had asked Roxie if she wanted to go and she said no, that she would rather just sit at home and get drunk. We had gone down to the liquor store and the Sawmill earlier during the day, to pick up our drinking supplies so that seemed like a fairly good idea. I didn't want to drive after drinking anyway.

We finished up dinner and took our chairs out on the porch. The radio was playing some great classic rock tonight and it was so very comfortable relaxing and enjoying the cool breezes on a hot summer night. I had a can of beer and Roxie elected to drink wine tonight.

"Got any pot?" Roxie asked

"What happened to that bag I gave you?" I said.

"Oh, that's been gone for a while," She answered.

I got up and went into the house. I still had a little bit of my original stash left after giving her half of it. I couldn't believe that she went through all that alone. Again I started thinking of my decision to leave when we came back. This was one more patch of the quilt that made me think that this woman was not for me. It seemed the more I gave, the more she took. I rolled a joint and brought it out to the porch and handed it to her. She promptly lit it up.

"I can't believe you went through that bag already," I said to her.

"Already?" she answered "You gave that to me 2 weeks ago."

"But still dear, it was enough to last me for 6 months." I said. "That bag wasn't cheap."

"Well excuse me dickhead," she said, "I guess I'm just not you."

I let that last remark slide because we had the whole weekend to go and I was not in the mood for another fight. We sat there in silence, me with my Pabst Blue Ribbon and her with Wine tonight; and of course reefer. I sat back in the chair, closed my eyes and just listened to the music.

While I sat there, Roxie got up twice to freshen up her wine goblet. When she said she was going to get drunk tonight, she really meant it. Since she normally drank Rum and Coke, I knew that the wine was going to hit her very quickly. I yelled to her when she was in the kitchen to please bring me another beer; while she was up.

She came back out on the porch, tripped over the leg of the chair and crashed into a support beam. She giggled nervously, handed me the beer and flopped down into her chair. All around us, we could hear the crackle of fireworks going off and occasionally someone would chime in with a shotgun blast.

"I want fireworks," She suddenly said.

"I asked you if you wanted to go to the fireworks," I said.

"I want fireworks," She repeated.

"Well I'm not driving now after I've had a few drinks." I said.

"I want fireworks," she repeated.

It sounded like a little kid who kept repeating the word 'NO'. I ignored her and closed my eyes again to listen to the music. Now and again I heard the blast of a shotgun in the distance.

"Where's my shotgun?" She asked.

"Why?" I said.

"If I can't have fireworks I want my shotgun so I can celebrate like these other people."

"Roxie," I said, "the last thing I'm going to do is let you have a loaded shotgun when you have been drinking."

"It's mine and I want it," She demanded.

"Absolutely not," I replied, "End of conversation."

She didn't say anything but just got up out of the chair and went in the house. I knew she wasn't going to get her shotgun because it was still in the trunk of my car and I had the only set of keys. A few minutes later, she staggered out of the house. This time she tripped over the leg of the table and crashed into her chair.

"Where's my fucking shotgun?" She screamed.

"Son of a bitch," I said, "I told you not to ask . . . you are not getting it. Now sit there before you fall down, again."

She proceeded to re-light the joint she had been smoking; then she said "Fuck you asshole."

I just ignored her. Somehow, we made it through the weekend without killing each other. She did her thing and I did mine; always apart. At dinner time she would cook and take a plate either into her office or upstairs to the bedroom. She would leave everything else on the stove for me to fetch for myself. I tried to engage her in conversation but she would just say that she didn't want to talk about it and then she would leave the room. Finally, I cornered her after dinner and explained the real world to her.

"I booked our tickets to Syracuse," I said, "We are going to drive down to Nashville, pick up a rental car, come back here and pack and then drive the rental back to the airport on the 17th. We'll fly up to Syracuse and I can take care of my court shit with Les, we'll pick up your car at Bonnie's house and then come back down here."

I looked at the calendar and silently counted off the days until we could fly up to Syracuse and effectively end this bullshit.

"How long are we staying up there?" She asked.

"Just long enough to get stuff done."

Now came the hard part. I knew I shouldn't have discussed the situation with her in her drunken condition but I wanted to get it over with.

"This relationship between us just isn't working out; so when we get back here, I'm going to pack up my stuff and move on. You will have your car so you can get around and I will have my sanity back."

Roxie didn't say a word about it. I had expected some sort of screaming match or at least a tantrum but she just got up and went into the kitchen and refilled her drink. The rest of the night she busied herself sorting through her EBay stuff, her spices and anything else that allowed her to avoid me. I was pretty happy about that.

The following Monday, I went into town and stopped off at the Sheriff's department. After our last little spat about the fireworks, the last thing I wanted was to have her get her hands on a loaded shotgun. I went into the Sheriff's office after taking the shotgun out of my trunk and Pepper, the lead Sheriff was at the desk. I had met him previously when we came into town for the Memorial Day festivities.

"Hi Pepper," I said, "Remember me?"

"Sure I do," he said, "you live with Roxie."

"I wanted to know what I have to do to turn in this shotgun for safekeeping," I asked. "It actually belongs to Roxie."

"What's the matter," he said, "little lady going a little bonkers again?"

"You could say that," I answered, "I just don't feel comfortable with this around the house."

"Can't you hide it somewhere?" he asked, "We're really not set up for that sort of thing."

"I guess I could," I replied, "I just was in town and thought I'd ask. Talk to you later."

With that I left with shotgun in hand and went back out to the car. His attitude bothered me and I especially did not like his comment about 'Bonkers Again'; like the Sheriff's department had been graced with a dose of her mood swings too.

My next stop was at the bank where my account had been set up; the joint account with Roxie that I didn't want in the first place. I inquired as to the balance on the account I had recently opened up. When the teller gave me the amount, I nearly passed out. I knew that the trip to Tennessee had cost me over $1,000 but the account had been seriously reduced down from $6,000 that I opened the account with.

I asked for a printout of transactions and found that a majority of the withdrawals had been by her. There were checks for electric, water, taxes, two from the liquor store, a check for payment on her double-wide and checks that she had written the same day I put the money into the account; before we even got the printed checks. This bitch was totally raping my bank account and I let her do it.

Now I was bonkers. Of the $5,860 that I had put into the account, the balance was $2,610. Out of all the money I put in, I had spent a total of $1,000 on the trip and about $ 100 on gas for the Camaro. Somehow, Roxie had managed to blow over $2,100 in about 20 days.

I wrote a check for $1,900 and cashed it. I didn't want to close the account until I had another one open; one that probably wasn't going to be in Burkesville. Plus, sooner or later, I was going to need funds to pay for U-haul rentals and such. I took my $1,900 and left the bank. I didn't know what I was going to do or say about it but I did know that this woman was pushing me into a corner that I did not want to stand in.

I got home and slipped into the house. Roxie was in her office with the door closed. I closed the door of my office and took out the money I had withdrawn from the bank. I put $ 200 in my wallet. I took another $1,700 and put that in an envelope also. This envelope I taped to the inside leaf of a table in my office. Now I had money out of her control but where I could easily access it.

I went out into the kitchen and rustled up some leftovers, popped them into the microwave and took it out to the porch. I really hated this but it would soon be over. I sat on the porch until about 8 p.m. and then decided that I was tired and going to crash. Roxie was upstairs in the bedroom so I took the couch and avoided her.

The next day went pretty much the same. I woke up and made coffee, brought her a cup and went back down to my little office to continue packing stuff up. I spent the whole day in the office and not once did Roxie bother to come in and say anything to me. She didn't even gravitate to the kitchen to make lunch. I don't know what she was doing but she was out of sight and out of my mind. That evening, she never came down from the bedroom for dinner, even though I called her twice. All I heard was a muted "Leave me alone."

I put a movie on and watched it and then decided to call it a day. I was getting tired of sleeping on the couch but I sure as hell didn't want to invade her privacy. I went into the bathroom, stripped and stepped into the shower. I was just getting the water adjusted to the perfect temperature when Roxie slowly slid open the curtain. It totally caught me by surprise.

She was fully dressed but she stepped into the shower with me. This was very unusual because I had never taken a shower with her and it wasn't like her to get her nice clothes all wet; she always acted so prim and proper. She didn't say anything but just stood in front of me and reached out to touch me between the legs. My reaction was almost immediate. That seemed to bring a smile to her face. I only saw that for a moment because the next thing she did was kneel down and put her mouth on my throbbing hard-on. The sensation was so great that I almost came right there and then. She moved with deliberate slowness and the only other sound besides the running water, was that of two people moaning in unison.

I don't know if it was the uniqueness of the situation or the fact that we had not had anything other than hall sex for a while. Hall sex is when you pass each other in the hall and yell "Fuck You." But anyway my orgasm was extreme. I grabbed her by the back of her neck and pulled her until I could hear her gagging. Waves of incredible pleasure rushed over me from the shower and from cumming so deep in her throat. When it was over, I felt more tired than when I stepped into the shower.

I just looked at Roxie as she disengaged herself from me. She had a broad smile on her face like a girl who had just gotten roses for her birthday. She looked up from me, while still on her knees and said, "I think I owed you that."

I must have had a puzzled look on my face because she got up and stood facing me when she said, "I've been a real bitch lately and I'm sorry."

"Honey," I said, "we have to talk."

"Later . . . We'll talk later."

We got out of the shower and she stripped down naked. She got back into the shower and bathed herself while I dried myself. I left the bathroom and went upstairs to get my robe. My head was still swimming at how she could go from hot to cold and vice-versa in a heartbeat. There was also the question of motive there too. Was she being honest about realizing what a bitch she had been lately? Or was this just another one of her mind games?

Either way, it was absolutely the best blowjob I had ever had.

* * *

27) Bowling Green, Again

Bowling Green, KY—July 8, 2009

Wednesday morning began the same as any normal morning since I had arrived. I woke up first, went down and made coffee, checked my email and did my morning routine. I was actually feeling a little guilty about telling Roxie my plans to dump her in New York when we got there. But I just could not take these mood swings and her vile attitude lately. Medication or not, this was not what I signed on for and even though I loved her, I thought it better to cut and run.

The coffee was ready and I fixed a cup for her and myself. I went upstairs and placed her cup on the nightstand and sat down on the bed watching her sleep. God, what am I doing? Here is this beautiful woman that I fell so hard for; and I'm just going to walk away?

I put my coffee on the night stand and crawled into bed next to her. Sure, I was just thinking of myself but *'shit, its right here, why not enjoy it'* was all that both my heads were saying. What a bastard I am. Last night after dinner, and after we had smoked a joint and had a few drinks, I disclosed to her my plans to leave her again, just to make sure she was crystal-clear. She didn't seem too affected by it because she casually just went to the kitchen and poured another drink. I really expected some sort of argument but there was none.

And then she gave me an Oscar winning surprise while I was in the shower. Whew!

I began to caress and fondle her and soon enough she was responding with an increased breathing pattern and moving closer to me in the bed. I think she was still asleep when I slowly mounted her and slid inside. I held myself up by my arms so as not to put my weight totally on her and I began my gyrations. I felt that she was wet; even though she looked like she was still sleeping. As I gradually increased the pace, her mouth came alive and she started to breath more heavily.

"Oh, Mark, Yes, Fuck Me, Fuck Me Hard, Yes baby." Her arms came up and wrapped around my back and she pulled her head up close to my neck. "Oh baby, take me from behind this time" She said.

I pulled out of her and slid my mouth down between her legs and proceeded to give her a tongue bath. She spread her legs and grabbed the back of my head as if she wanted to pull my entire head inside her. As I was eating her, I lifted her up by the thighs and rolled her over on her stomach. Lordy, Lordy, what a beautiful little ass she had. I had to just take a little bite.

This position was enjoyable and I hoped that she would not request me do go 'in the out door' again. Since we were not going to last together that much longer, I wanted to put in an Olympian effort just to give her something to remember. I glided my hard essence back inside her, positioned my hands on both breasts and began to pump her like a steam locomotive.

"Ah, Ah, More, Ah, Harder, Fuck Me, Fuck Me, Yes, Oh God you're cock is so hard, Oh Yes, Yes, Yes"

She was so vocal in her expressions that I found it hard to control myself. I slowed my rhythm down and almost immediately she said, "No, harder; fuck me harder."

"Is that how you like it baby; you like my cock inside you?" I whispered.

"Oh, fuck me Daddy, fuck your little girl, Yes, Yes, Yes, I'm cumming, Oh God, Yes, Yes, YES"

Her reference to 'Daddy' went over my head at first. A man being called 'daddy' by his lover is not that unusual; at least not in my experience. I kept up my rhythm, alternating between fast and slow; slamming her hard and then backing off.

"Yes daddy, do it, teach me daddy, I love you, fuck me, yes, fuck me hard, yes Daddy, yes, yes, I'm cumming Daddy, harder, harder, yes, Oh, yes, yes., aaahhhh . . . . "

All of a sudden it made perfect sense. Her sexuality, her aggressiveness, her mood swings, everything that we had done since the day I arrived. This girl was molested when she was young and the psychological scars were still with her. Maybe I was seeing visions or maybe I was imagining things but somehow I knew that the man who raped her when she was 12 years old was her father. And it wasn't just once. I believed that she may have had an ongoing affair with him. It was the only logical reason for the way she behaved. It explained why she was prone to any kind of sex, with any man or woman, why she abused drugs and alcohol and why everything she had told me about her owning the farm, the businesses and the horses; virtually everything. It was all fantasy. This woman had serious mental problems brought on by her past.

Even though I was fully excited and deep inside her, I suddenly felt my member starting to lose its temper. Not wanting to waste all the work I had put into motion so far, I turned up the speed and intensity of my strokes and let out a load moan as I emptied inside her.

"Oh, Daddy, it's so good, fuck me Daddy, Oh please, harder."

I couldn't go on anymore and so I just rolled off her, thinking that we would just relax and let our bodies cool down. With almost immediate reaction, she moved her head down between my legs and began to suck on my semi-rigid hard-on. Her head bobbed up and down like a yo-yo and as much as I would have liked to continue, I knew that this session was over.

"Stop honey, I think the cow is dry," I said.

"Oh, Baby," she said, "That was the best ever. How can you think of leaving me after that?"

I really didn't know what to say. It was the kind of statement a guy would get after having sex with a girl and then her asking him if he would call her. I swear if it hadn't been for the mood swings and everything else, the thought of leaving would never have crossed my mind.

"I don't want to baby, you know I don't," I said. "But I just can't take this bi-polar attitude. You promised you would get back on your medicine but you run hot and cold so often, I can't keep up."

"*Well Fuck You,*" She said. "I don't know why I am the one who has to change. You're no prince to live with either."

I knew that she was itching for another fight and not wanting to exacerbate the situation; I got up and went downstairs.

I left her to yell 'Bastard, Bastard, Bastard' at the walls.

We had previously discussed going into Bowling Green for one more shopping trip before we left for New York. She came downstairs and went right into her office and slammed the door. She was in there about 10 minutes when she came out holding the phone to one ear, as she asked me if we were still going shopping today before our trip to New York.

"If you want to go, we can do that," I said, "as long as we get an early enough start."

"When do you want to leave," Roxie asked, still on the phone.

"Whenever you are ready," I answered.

"No," she said, "I want to know an exact time dammit."

"Eleven o'clock, OK?" I answered.

She ducked back into her office for another 5 minutes with the door closed and then she came out and went upstairs to the bedroom. I figured that this would be an excellent time to get the shotgun out of my car and hide it in the house, since I didn't want to carry it around in the car. I took my keys, dashed out to the car, grabbed the gun and ran back into the house. I went in the bathroom and stashed the gun under a pile of bath towels and linens. It was well out of site on the bottom of the pile and not even Roxie would think of looking for it there.

Finally about eleven o'clock, she came down all dressed and went into her changing room to put on her makeup. I was sitting at the computer putting the final touches on my new website when she came in the office and gave me a kiss on the neck.

"Are we ready to go?" She asked.

"Ready when you are," I answered.

We got up and left for Bowling Green. The 38 mile drive was, to say the least, subdued. Periodically she made a comment but I felt coolness to her manner. A number of times I tried to start up a conversation but she seemed as though she was preoccupied with something. We got into Bowling Green and headed for Aldi's to do the shopping. I went and picked up a shopping cart while she walked on ahead of me into the store. On this particular trip, she didn't ask me once what I cared to buy or wanted for dinner or any of her regular comments.

Finally I said to her, "Roxie. I'm sorry that you are pissed off but this is just part of my decision. I love you more than I love myself, but I cannot take this. I don't know how you can put this blame on me."

"I'm not the one who is cutting and running," she said, "I'm willing to stick it out."

"I got news for you. You're not the one on the receiving end. You're not the one on this emotional roller coaster. You're not the one walking around on eggshells all day."

"See," she said, "there you go again; blaming me. And what's this shit about you taking all the money out of the bank?"

Ah, that was it. She had been online and checked the joint account. I had forgotten the fact that she was very computer literate and could do that. It was my account actually but I couldn't access it online because I had never taken the time to set up a user name and password.

"First of all," I said, "I didn't take all the money out. I left enough in there to cover any checks you wrote; I hope. And secondly, that was supposed to be my account. It damned sure was my money."

"Oh," she countered, "you can eat the food I cook, use the water, electricity and internet services and I'm supposed to pay for it all?"

I didn't relish another fight inside Aldi's so I told her that I would meet her in the car. I walked out and tried to figure out just how I was going to make it until we left on the July 17th. I had nine fucking days of putting up with this crap and I was not happy about it. I resolved that as soon as we got home, I would go online and try to move the date up. For now at the very least, I was going to try to placate her as best as I could. She always liked going to TGI-Fridays when we were here, so maybe that peace offering would work.

Roxie came out of the store with a full basket of groceries and we loaded them into the Camaro. I went around to her side of the car and opened the door for her and put my arms around her neck.

"Honey, I love you. I hate fighting." Then I asked, "What can I do to make things better?"

"You can quit being such an asshole," She said. "I cook for you, do laundry, fuck your brains out and it's still not good enough."

"Honey, everything you do is good enough," I said. "It's just the moodiness that gets me. Get that under control and we will be OK."

"You sure?" She whimpered.

"Of course I am. Let's go have a drink and talk about it."

I hated lying to her like that about not leaving her after we got back from New York, but at least I avoided any more confrontation with her. We took off and went to our favorite Bowling Green watering hole. It was a standard, mid-week slow crowd day but the waitress was familiar and gave a cheery 'Hi Guys; the usual?' We ordered and talked about what projects we had to do during the rest of the week.

Roxie had applied for a grant for nursing school and had to take some kind of online test tomorrow. I wanted to tweak my web pages and try to get some more products added. It was a casual Wednesday afternoon and even though the conversation was light, there was no venom in the air.

We had a couple of more drinks and I said that we had better start heading back. I paid the bill, walked out to the parking lot and got in the car. It was at that point that Roxie told me that there was another bar in Bowling Green that she wanted to check out.

"Honey, I've had three drinks, its Five o'clock and we need to get back."

"Sure," she said, "anytime you want to do something it's OK. But if I ask a simple request, you have a million excuses not to."

"Ok, where's this bar of yours," I said, "we can go for one but then we got to go."

She gave me directions and I found 'The Cave,' a rather dingy looking dive just off the expressway. I don't mind dingy looking dives but I wondered how Roxie had come to find this one. I had never been in it before. We sat down at the bar and ordered. This was definitely the place that roughnecks would love. Wood plank floor, spittoons located here and there and as dark and dingy inside as it was outside.

"How did you come to pick this place?" I asked.

"A friend recommended it to me," She said. "Dex said to check it out when I was in Bowling Green but never had the chance until today."

"Dex said to check it out?" I said, "As in Dex, the Cumberland County deputy?"

"Yeah, what of it" she countered, "I know more people down here than you."

Christ, here we go again. I refuse to get baited into this; so much for the makeup talk. We finished out drinks and I told her I wanted to get going.

"Cmon," she slurred, "we geust got here."

The alcohol caught up with her fast. I thought that the bill at the last place was a little higher than it normally was but I wasn't counting drinks. Perhaps when I went to the bathroom she downed a couple of shots or something. But it was hitting her now. Even though I had four drinks in me, I decided, rather than make a scene, to buy one more.

"Ok, one more," I said, "Then we have to go. I don't want to be all liquored up and out late driving."

"Your generrrosssity ovrwelms me." She slurred. It sounded like she was talking in a language that would be familiar to a German shepherd. She was milking her drink and finally I had to prod her to finish. She looked at me like I had just told her that she was the ugliest bitch in the world. It almost seemed like she was deliberately trying to delay me from getting home.

"I'll finish when I'm ready. Don't rush me." She slurred again.

"Come on, it's getting late and we still have these groceries."

"Oh, shit, I forgot about the groceries." she said with a look of shock, "ok, let's get going."

By now it was 6:30 p.m. We had ½ hour to drive to Glasgow and another 45 minutes from there to home. Oh well, it will still be light out by the time we get home. We left 'The Cave' and went outside.

"I wanna drive," Roxie announced.

"Nah, I don't think so. I'd like to get home alive."

"You're drunk too. I wanna drive," She insisted.

"No. I'm driving and that's the end of the story," I said. "You can drive all day tomorrow."

"Fuckin' right I will."

I wish I would have questioned her about the meaning of that last statement, but I wanted to get back and thought better about opening up another can of worms. Drunks are bad enough, but an arrogant drunk tops the pile.

We made it to Marrowbone and I got the tank of the Camaro filled up. We left and made the boring, bumpy ride over the back roads to the house. I really didn't like this drive, from the first day I arrived and now, with the upcoming move back to New York, those nine days were grinding on me.

"Why you always heveta be sush a dickhead?" Roxie slurred.

"Hey, I'm not the one that had to sit there and pound down the booze," I said, "when we have plenty at home. When we get there, you can drink yourself into a coma if you want."

"We're on the back roads now. I wanna drive."

"What part of no don't you understand? You can't wait one more day?"

That was all I needed; to have her crash the Camaro, right before our trip to New York. I started to say more but she stopped me with "Shut the fuck up . . . you're an asshole."

We pulled into the yard and I backed the Camaro up to the steps. I popped the trunk, grabbed my smokes and keys and proceeded to get the groceries out and into the house. I laid my keys and cigarettes on the kitchen table and put the grocery bags on the counter.

"Doan juss put them anywhere," she said, "I've got order in m'life, even if you doan."

It was bad enough to have to put up with her bad attitude when she was sober, but having to deal with her in a drunken stupor was beyond torture. I decided to continue ignoring her comments, event though I was getting very pissed; and the booze probably didn't help.

"Roxie, where are those sunglasses I bought the other day," I asked, "I didn't even get a chance to wear them today."

"If they were up your ass, you'd know." She replied.

I went out and got another couple of bags. One was a bag of glass candle holders and the other was filled with paper towels and toilet paper. When I came back in I was greeted with another barrage of shit.

"That's glass, idiot," she yelled, "put it on the floor before you drop it . . . . fucking drunk."

Hmmm . . . she said that quite clear. No slur at all. And then ferocity of it hit home. I snapped. I dropped the bag with the glass and threw a roll of paper towels at her. I stormed around the table and stood right in front of her and slapped her in the face . . . Hard.

"Don't you dare talk to me in that tone of voice," I screamed, "I've been putting up with your bi-polar bullshit for way to long and it is going to stop."

With that, I stormed out of the house and went to look for my sunglasses in the car. They were not to be located so I figured I must have left them in my office. I bounded up the steps and found myself locked out of the house. This was the second time she had pulled this shit.

Why didn't I bother to get my keys off the table? I couldn't have unlocked the door because I never got a key, but at least I could have got in my car and gone somewhere. Here I was, stuck outside on the porch. Eight o'clock on a Wednesday night. No keys to get in; Pissed off at the world. And I had this drunken hussy on the other side of the door.

A hussy with a bad attitude that had killed my dream.

* * *

Part Two

Welcome to My Nightmare

"Everything is determined,
the beginning as well as the end,
by forces over which we have
no control."

Albert Einstein (German Theorist)

28) Kentucky Justice

Columbia, KY—July 8, 2009

I assumed, incorrectly of course, that if I got arrested, I would be put in the Burkesville jail at the Justice Center. When I asked about it, the transport driver told me that even though it was a brand new building, they did not house prisoners there. They only built it because the Federal Government gave them a boatload of money and they had to have a reason to spend it. Now everybody arrested spends their time at the county jail in Columbia, about thirty miles away. I could see by the way that everything had gone the entire day that this was going to be a very long night. Well, with any amount of luck, I'll be able to convince them that this is a terrible mistake, that there needs to be more investigation to get to the bottom of it, that Roxie will come to her senses and maybe even tell them that she fell or something. I mean, how bad could her injuries be? I slapped her . . . that was it.

And, truth be told, I was sorry for that.

Adair County Jail sits in the quiet town of Columbia, KY. Of all the surrounding counties in South Central Kentucky, Adair seems to be the richest. The jail is located right in the center of town and it takes prisoners from all the area justice centers.

The transport officers escorted me from the van into the secure building. There at the desk was a young man and female who looked official in their Adair County Jail t-shirts and jeans. They went through the processing routine, took off my handcuffs, took pictures of me, took all my possessions, logged everything and then had me take an orange jumpsuit and change in the bathroom. It was tight fitting and it reminded me of the outfits I used to wear back in the disco days.

They handed me a completed yellow processing form and escorted me down the hall to room where they outfitted me with a towel, a sheet, and a bag of toiletries. From there we went around a corner and I was asked to select a mattress from a pile lying on the floor. Their idea of a mattress was a beat up old and cracked piece of foam rubber, 30 inches wide by 5' long. We walked down the hall until we came to a cell marked 142.

"Here's your new home," the jail deputy said.

"Don't I get a phone call?" I asked.

"Sure you do," he said, "Can I see your phone card?"

"What's a phone card?" I inquired.

"It's what you need to make a phone call . . . No card, No call."

The guard went on to explain that the pre-trial representative would be available in the morning and maybe she would let me make a phone call. Until then, I was officially in the 'poky', as they called it here. He pointed the way into the cell and then slammed and locked the door behind me. I shared the cell with 6 other inmates. I think I was the only one that didn't have any tattoos. I flopped my so-called mattress down on the floor in the corner and did my best to avoid eye contact with my new roomies.

"New meat," said one of the inmates. "What are you in for?"

I opened up the processing form and read:

1) Domestic Violence 4th Class
2) Possession of Marijuana
3) Use/Possess Paraphernalia
4) Trafficking Marijuana (Felony)

"I guess they got me for dope," I said, "its dope and domestic violence."

Well, that statement just put me in the 'golden circle' of inmates. I found out later that I was surrounded by two meth chemists, a murderer, a rapist and two more that got behind on child support. Being arrested for any kind of dope was like a Silver Star award in their eyes.

I read through the paperwork with a fine tooth comb. When I got to the officer statement of the complaint, my mouth fell open. Roxie had called the police and told them that I had beaten her with a baseball bat and made the statement "oh and by the way, there is a large amount of marijuana in the house."

I couldn't believe it. My lover, my girlfriend had set me up. I knew the stash wasn't mine and I sure as hell had never seen it lying around the house. Where did it come from? Could that have been placed in the house when we were in Bowling Green? And if so, who did it?

But the bigger question in my mind was "Why?" Why would someone who was allegedly in love with another person do something like this? I just couldn't believe my eyes.

My mind drifted back over the events of the last week. Even with the argument and the slap on the face earlier, I thought that none of it warranted filing this kind of complaint.

A baseball bat?

There wasn't even a ball bat in the house to my knowledge; but then again, to my knowledge there wasn't a pound of pot either. Where was my brain? How could this be happening? I guess the only thing I could do was wait until tomorrow when I got to talk to the pre-trial representative. I hoped that they came early enough that I could maybe get out of jail and get back to the house. That's if they haven't issued a restraining order or some other bullshit. I was bound and determined to get to the bottom of this whole mess. I settled in for some sleep, with the blare of the TV tuned to the cartoon network in the background. This was going to be a pain in the ass. I never really watched a lot of cartoons as a kid.

At 7 a.m. the next morning, another guard came in and called me. "Pre-trial is here." He said.

I followed him up the corridor into a small room and sat down on a metal chair. The pre-trial representative was an attractive young lady of about 25, who sat with a laptop computer in front of her. She asked all the appropriate questions like Date of Birth, Home Address, etc.

"Your bail is set at $ 10, 000," She said. "Do you have an attorney?"

"No I don't," I answered "I don't know one. Can you arrange that?"

"You will have to wait until you go to court," She answered. "If you can't afford one, they will appoint one for you."

"When is court?"

"Cumberland County Court will be held next Wednesday, the 15th," She said.

"WHAT!" I shrieked, "I have to wait until next Wednesday to see the judge or a lawyer?"

"That's right," she replied, "the court meets once a week and since you were arrested on the day that they already had held court, you will have to wait until they convene again."

I was sick. I would spend a week of sitting here in this scum hole, before I even got to see anyone? And what was going on at the house? Did Roxie get out of the hospital? Had she been arrested also? Who was going to feed the animals? All these questions flooded my mind and I could see that this was going to be a real nightmare.

They led me back to my cell and I just sat there dumbfounded. What kind of a justice system had court once a week? Mayberry RFD did, that's who. And that was the category I put Burkesville, Kentucky in.

Breakfast came shortly afterward and what a taste treat it was. One burnt sausage patty, two small biscuits, a glob of congealed sausage gravy and a cup of black coffee. Yuck! Oh well . . . Since I missed dinner last night because of getting arrested, even the glop of sausage gravy looked appealing.

And that's how it went for the next six days. It was breakfast at 7:30, lunch at 11:30 and dinner at 4:30. After eating Roxie's gourmet meals, this crap was gruel. Lunch was usually two slices of bread, a slice of baloney and a cup of Kool-Aid. For dinner, they went all out, by giving us red beans and rice, some sort of salad dish and maybe, just maybe, a cookie. It was all that, and Kool-Aid too. I found out that Kool-Aid was a staple. Meals weren't always the same. There was some variation. But by and large it was pretty scant and I found myself hungry all the time; hungry and cold.

They ran the air conditioner at about forty-five degrees, day and night. Someone told them that the cold temperature keeps the riots down in the jail. As far as I could tell, the only thing the cold temperature was effective at, was making people bitch about the cold. Covering up in a sheet, in forty-five degree cold, does not make it. I thought about setting my mattress on fire just to get warm. But alas, they had taken my lighter. So they were safe from my evil thoughts until I could find two sticks to rub together.

The week passed slowly and finally on the following Wednesday, I was transported the 30 miles back to the courthouse in Burkesville where I sat in a holding cell until it was my turn to face the judge. I stood waiting as the judge read the charges.

"Do you have a lawyer?" the judge asked.

"No Your Honor, I don't," I replied.

"Does the defendant qualify for a Public Defender?" the judge asked the clerk.

"Yes he does," she said, "he has filled out the paperwork and we deem that he is indigent."

"Very well," he said, "you will be back here next Wednesday and at that time you will be assigned a public defender."

"Next case."

That was it. They had wasted a week of my time, fed me nineteen rotten meals and burned God knows how many gallons of gas, transporting me back and forth to jail. And I still wasn't any further ahead than I was when I was admitted to the 'Bad Boy' club last week. What kind of asinine system was this?

Oh, Mayberry RFD, that's right.

* * *

29) A Visit to the Jail

Columbia, KY—July 15, 2009

Being in jail positively sucks.

I think anyone who has ever been there would agree. The food is lousy and the portions are small, your bunkmates are usually punks and the guards are usually surly. I had been in here since the night of July 8th and was doing my best to have limited contact with the other inmates. I didn't even go outside for recreation time because I was more predisposed to keep to myself.

I awoke when they brought the morning chow. Today we were having a ladleful of oatmeal, a small sausage patty and a biscuit. Add that to the 6 oz. cup of black coffee and you get the picture. The only bright spot was that I was going to court today. Maybe they would realize the mistake they made by arresting me instead of Roxie. After all, the drugs were found in her house, where she had lived for over 3 years. I had only been in Kentucky for 6 weeks, didn't know a soul except for her and never had any contact with the law down here before.

They loaded all the inmates in the transport van and headed down the road to Cumberland County courthouse. It was a 30 mile trip and everybody in the van had some issue with that particular county. One guy was being charged with statutory rape. He had done his little 16 year old cousin and got caught because she said it was forced. He told me that he had been doing her for 3 months and the only reason she filed charges is because he wouldn't give her any money.

Another guy was in for owing 6 months of back child support. He expected to get out because his father was going to loan him the money to pay it current. I was the only doper in the mix. I told them the tale of how I got arrested and everyone agreed that it was a serious charge and I should consider killing Roxie. That way there would be no witnesses. I thought that was a bit outrageous.

The transport driver was a very considerate guy. He asked everybody if they wanted cigarettes before we took off. I smoked and so did the other 2 inmates and he gave us each 2 cigarettes and lit them for us. His only request was that we use the ashtray instead of the floor mats. We arrived at the courthouse and were herded into a holding cell to wait to be called. At promptly 9:05, the guard came and brought me into the courtroom. I stood in front of Justice Howard Shule while he read the charges.

"You are charged with 4th degree Domestic Abuse, 1st Degree Possession of a Controlled Substance, 1st Degree Possession of Drug Paraphernalia and 2nd Degree Drug Trafficking. The trafficking charges are enhanced because there was a weapon involved; namely a shotgun."

"How do you plead, Mr. Casey?" the judge asked.

"Not guilty your honor," I said.

"Do you have a lawyer?" He asked.

"No, your honor."

"I see that your bail has been set at $10,000 cash bond." he continued, "are you prepared to pay that bond at this time?"

"No, your honor."

"I am going to assign Ms. Darlene Sorenson to you as a public defender." he said, "she will handle your legal representation from this point or until you obtain your own council."

"Next Case."

And that was it; my day in front of the judge. I was escorted back to the holding cell and in about 15 minutes, this homely, bulk of a woman appeared at the bullet-proof glass window in the room.

"Mr. Casey, I am Darlene Sorenson, your attorney." She announced. I nodded since I couldn't really shake her hand.

"I talked to the local DA on the case. Her name is Carolyn Anthony and I think we've got a pretty good offer from them." She said.

"If you plead guilty to the Trafficking charge and the Domestic Violence charge, forfeit the shotgun and the $1,700 that was taken at your arrest and leave Cumberland County for a minimum period of 2 years, this case will end. During that time, you will be on unsupervised probation."

I didn't know what any of this meant. But I did know that I was not going to plead guilty to a crime I didn't commit; either one of them. And

I sure as hell wasn't going to forfeit my hard earned money; event though the police had it at the time. It took me a microsecond to give my answer to her.

"Absolutely not," I said, "I didn't do anything and I'm not going to plea guilty."

"Very well Mr. Casey," she told me through the glass. "I will relay that to the court. But I have to tell you that with all the scheduling, a trial probably won't be until March or April next year."

I didn't really care because I knew that they had to do discovery and investigation and besides, I had friends who could bail me out. I figured I'd borrow the money, arrange to get over to the house and pack my things and take off until the court date for trial. Perhaps by then they would come to their senses and drop everything; realizing they had no evidence.

As far as my impression of Darlene Sorenson went, I thought she was a very cold, mercenary person who, was only interested in numbers; not people. As my attorney, I would have expected some sort of counseling on her part, but I got none; just a lame offer with no offer for a rebuttal of any kind. And she looked like a bull dyke. Perhaps she and the local DA, another dyke look-a-like, had something going on, and that is why the offer came so fast. I didn't know any of the answers, but I was glad about my decision. One way or the other, this thing would work out.

The guard came in and put me back in restraints and loaded me into the transport van. Once again he offered 2 cigarettes for the journey back. We got back to the jail and as I looked out the window of the van, I saw my beautiful red 97 Camaro parked across the street. This car had a unique hood scoop and I immediately knew it was mine.

All the inmates were shuffled into the jail and the guard told me that I had a visitor. I was taken to the visitor room and on the other side of the glass was none other that Roxie. I picked up the phone receiver and she did the same.

"I'll bet you never expected to see me again," She said.

I immediately broke down and started crying. Just the sight of her and the memory of that last day together came rushing at me like a hot fist. As mad as I was at her, that emotion was replaced by overwhelming love.

"Mark, my face is almost healed . . . look," She said, pointing to her face. I couldn't see anything and if there was anything there, it wasn't because of me.

"You did all this yourself Mark," she continued "and I'm trying to raise bail money, but everybody is pretty disgusted with you. I've called just about everyone on your cell phone list but nobody has committed."

"Roxie please," I pleaded, "do what you have to do to get me out. I can't stand it here."

"I'm working on it," She said. "I've listed the RV on EBay. Maybe we can get some money, but I don't think we can cover the $10,000 bail that they have set. The auction ends July 30th."

We talked for a few minutes more and it was like talking to a stranger. She never once smiled and everything she said was more like an indictment of me. It was like I was this woman-beating, drug dealing asshole that came down from New York to take advantage of everyone.

"You made quite a splash in the papers," she told me, "Front page all the way. I can't go anywhere in public because of this."

"Roxie, we can get through this," I said. "I love you so much, please trust me. But I don't have any money or anything. I can't even call you because I don't have a phone card."

"I've put $ 40 dollars in your account and bought you a couple of $ 20 dollar phone cards," She told me.

Visiting time was over and the guard was telling me to end the conversation. I asked Roxie when she would be back and she told me next Wednesday; the next day for visits. I blew her a kiss and left to go back to my cell. It took all the energy I had to keep from having another emotional breakdown right there on the spot. Despite all the issues between Roxie and myself, I came to realize how much I really loved her, and if I could get out of this, I would probably give our relationship one more try. But not seeing her smile or give me any real hope during the visit; that bothered me.

I questioned whether or not she still loved me?

* * *

30) M.I.A.

Burkesville, KY—July 22-29, 2009

Another week went by, of good grub and fast times . . . Right!

I think it was the most boring time of my life. I never watched a lot of TV myself. I was always more into music. Periodically I would tune into

History Channel or maybe watch a movie. For the most part though, the music and my computer where the things that kept me occupied. But here I watched a constant battle over cartoons or MTV. There was rarely a time when someone wanted to watch something that didn't rot their brain. I never spoke up because I did my best to avoid any contact with the other inmates. The last thing I needed to compound my problems was to get into an altercation.

I called Roxie a couple of times with my phone card. What a rip off that thing was. I paid a fee of $ 20 to make collect calls; no card, no calls. It was a very nice little scam for the jailer, who probably pays $.15 cents a piece for the phone card and sells them for $ 20 bucks. I guess that must be part of the Kentucky jailer retirement plan.

But now, every time Roxie and I talked, we would get into an argument. She became pissy on the phone and I did my best to keep from blowing up at her. That would do no good at all. I asked her if she was coming to visit on Wednesday and she said yes. At least that made me feel a little better.

That Wednesday came and went and I was never called to come up to the visitor booth. I found out that the jail had a visitor day on Fridays also, but she didn't show up then either. I was pissed because I wanted to talk to her but I was out of my time allotment on the phone cards. I knew that she could not call into the jail and talk to me, and I wondered what was so damned important in her life that she would miss having contact. She knew I was like a sitting duck in here.

This particular week, I went to court on a Thursday, the 23rd instead of on Wednesday, which had been scheduled. When I questioned why the change of the day the jailer told me that my case was bumped up to Circuit Court and wasn't in the District Court anymore. We climbed into the van and once again, my favorite driver broke out with the free pair of cigarettes for the ride; that long 35 minute ride from Columbia to Burkesville. And once again we were all herded into the holding cell of the courthouse. I was finally called to stand in front of the judge. This was a different one than I had seen before. His name was Lanier Everett and I could tell that he was a hard ass.

"Mr. Casey," he said, "you are here to hear charges against you, as a result of the findings of the Grand Jury. The Grand Jury has indicted you on 4th Degree Domestic Violence, 1st Degree Possession of a Controlled Substance, 1st Degree Possession of Drug Paraphernalia and 2nd Degree Drug Trafficking, a felony. I understand that Ms. Darlene Sorenson is your attorney, is that correct?"

"Yes, your honor." I answered.

"Very well," he said, "I will put this into the file for a future hearing after you have had an opportunity to speak to her. Until then, you will be remanded to the Adair County Jail, until and if you decide to post bail. I am lowering the bail amount in this case from $10,000 to $5,000 cash bond."

"Next Case."

And that was it. No discussion with my 'attorney'; no questions; no plea offer; nothing. They could have called me on the phone at the jail and told me that. The court would not meet for another 30 days. When they say time moves slow in Kentucky, they mean it. But this wasn't slow; this was grinding. How the fuck did anything ever get done down here?

I was transported back to my jail cell and sat there for yet another week of fun and games. Finally on the 29th of July, I got a call that I had a visitor. Since the only person I knew was Roxie, I figured it was her.

"The bids are moving slowly on the RV Honey," She said.

She had the same somber facial expression that she had the last time; No smile; no attempt to humor me or be kind; she was just all business in a matter-of-fact style.

"We're at $3,100 right now and the auction closes tomorrow," She told me. "I put a reserve amount of $3,600 on it so I think we have a shot of getting it sold."

"That's great news," I said. "They lowered my bail to $5,000 so if $3,600 or more comes in, I won't have that much to borrow. By the way, where have you been; I've missed you."

"I went to South Carolina to see my son," She said. "While I was down there, I put a deposit down on a house for rent. It's perfect. When you get out we will have a nice life down there."

"Wait a minute," I said with surprise, "I thought we were going to wait and check out Tennessee and other places before we made a decision."

"I wanted to be near my son," she snapped back, "besides, you're not in a position to be calling the shots."

It wasn't the fact that she hadn't conferred with me about the house because she was still assuming that we would be together; it wasn't the fact that she wanted to be near her son; it wasn't even the fact that she just up and took off to South Carolina. It was that damned attitude again. Let's just go and do whatever WE want to do and the hell with everybody else. I was pissed and I'm sure my facial expression told her that. It was almost like she was just doing things to push my buttons. I didn't tell her to sell the RV, even though I would have, had I been able to discuss things with her. So I didn't mention that fact, even though it bothered me as much as her snippy attitude towards me.

"What did your son think of my car?" I asked.

"Oh he loved it," she replied, "he said I looked good in it. I let him drive it and he couldn't believe how much power it had."

Part of me had a level of pride that my car was indeed an attractive vehicle. And part of me wanted to jump through the window and throttle her lovely neck. She was acting like it was her car; not mine. First of all, she took it without my consent and put miles on it I didn't want and then she rents a place in South Carolina even checking with me. If we had gone to New York like I had planned to do, she would have known that I was not going to be living with her. I still loved her but what else was she doing without my consent?

It was time for me to go and I asked her if she would come back on Friday for another visit. She said that she would 'try' but she had a lot of things she had to take care of getting ready to move. She bought me another $ 20 dollar phone card and said goodbye without even looking back. My heart sunk as I went back to my cell. I had the distinct feeling that things were going on that I would not like if I knew about them.

Days went by slowly in the cell. I usually spent my day just reading. Once a week they would bring the book cart around and I would go through it to try to find something I could get into. I did get to read some sci-fi and mystery novels, but for some reason, most of the selections were those sappy romance novels. I got lucky when I met an inmate who had a membership in a book club. He hooked me up with a few Dean Koontz and John Grisham novels and I tore through them as fast as I could get my hands on them.

The first of August came along and I decided to call Roxie to find out the status of the sale of the RV. I called 4 separate times before I she answered at about 8 p.m. She said that she was outside and did not hear the phone. Why was I suspicious?

"Oh Honey, it's sold," She said with a bit of excitement. "We got $ 3650 out of it."

That was definitely good news to me. Even with the commission for EBay, I figured that I would get a little over $3,500 towards my release. Plus I had my Social Security coming in the bank on the 3rd of the month. Since I had nothing better to spend it on, I might as well use it for bail. I was pretty sure I could borrow any other money that I needed from somewhere.

"What happens now?" I asked.

"The buyer is going to send a deposit first," she said. "and that money should be my PayPal account by Wednesday. Then he is going to bring a certified check for the balance. Everything should be done within a week if we're lucky."

"Thank you, Thank you, and Thank you." I said. "I'm going to get on the phone tonight and try to round up the rest of the money, just in case I need it."

We stayed on the phone another 5 minutes and then said goodbye. I told her I loved her but she did not reply to that; she just said goodbye. I called my friend Corbett, to see about a loan. He owned a computer company and several rental properties and had sent me a letter saying how shocked he was to find me in this predicament.

"I'm not sure if I can make a loan to you right now Mark," He said. "What's to keep you from getting out and taking off to Mexico?"

I couldn't believe my ears. My friend was questioning my scruples and our relationship. He said that Roxie had called him and she told him that I attacked her with a baseball bat. Again, I couldn't believe my ears. This was nothing more than a flat out lie. She told him that I was drunk and even though she had injuries, she still loved me and was trying to raise money for my bail. She wanted him to send her $10,000.

"Corbett, how long have you known me?" I asked, "Does this sound like something I would do? First of all, the drugs were not even mine. I don't know where they came from. And I DID NOT put a hand on Roxie, other than a little slap."

"Well old buddy," he said, "I think you are both a couple of bullshit artists, but I'll tell you what I'll do. You get bailed out and I'll loan you some money to pay day-to-day expenses. But you have to get out of jail first."

I told him I was limited on my phone time and we ended the call. I thought about it and it seemed to me that Roxie was deliberately trying to undermine any efforts I made to get out of jail. And what was this shit about a baseball bat. My ass. I don't think she would be alive if I hit her with a Louisville Slugger.

The next call I made was to my buddy Ken in Colorado. I had planned to go out and visit him on Labor Day but getting arrested certainly put the kibosh on that plan.

"Mark, Man, What the fuck?" He said, "How did you get into this fix?"

"Ken I was set up, plain and simple," I told him. "Roxie told the police that I beat her up and that there was a large quantity of Marijuana in the house. Its right in the police report that I have. And then I hear from one of the guards that she told the cops I was planning to take it to New York and sell it because I could get more money up there. Ken, I never saw the shit. I knew she smoked and always had a little baggie around but I never saw a pound of it."

"Well buddy," he said, "I'm strapped for cash. I might be able to send you a C note, but not much more than that." He also told me that Roxie had called him.

"Mark, she said that you attacked her with a tire chain."

"Jesus Ken," I said, "The stories keep getting better and better. Let me tell you something. I've never owned tire chains in my life but if I get out, I'm going to be looking for some; just for that very purpose. I'm sick of all the bullshit lies she is spewing out. She told my friend Corbett that I beat her with a ball bat. I just got off the phone with her today and she didn't say anything about calling you or my friend Corbett."

"I don't know man," he said, "she sounded so sweet on the phone. She said that you just went off and started wailing on her. She said she was hurt and needed medical attention which is the only reason why she called 911."

"Ken, I didn't do any of it," I said, "including the pot. I am being set up and this is really scary. I'm here in the middle of nowhere, with no friends around, and I've got Roxie running around all over God's green earth doing God knows what and telling stories about me that aren't true. I don't know a soul down here except Roxie."

I told him my situation with the phone card and that I had put Maggie at the library in charge of being point person. Any news he needed he could get from her. He wished me luck and we hung up.

One by one, I made calls to my friends. Greg, Mike, Paul, my sisters Mary and Marge, my friend Michelle; they all had the same sad story about not having the money. I was running out of numbers. I tried to call Les but nobody answered. I figured he was at an AA meeting or something. I finally gave up trying at 9 o'clock because in Syracuse, it was 10 p.m. Eastern Time and out of courtesy, I don't like calling after that.

This whole situation was getting uglier by the minute.

* * *

31) Cops and Robbers

Columbia, KY—August 3, 2009

The next day, I put in a call to Phil Stevens, the attorney. I had chosen him specifically, because Roxie had told me once how much she hated him because he was her ex-husband's lawyer in their divorce. I never questioned her about it but somehow she ended up having to pay her ex $10,000 for the divorce settlement. I figured if she hated Phil for that issue, she was really going to hate him for representing me. I was convinced that she was working behind my back at some plan or scam of hers. Phil came to the jail that night and I hired him on the spot. I gave him my Visa account number and he drafted $1,000 out of my bank account for his retainer.

The next night I called Roxie. She sounded all cheery and happy that I called which was a radical swing from the way she had been sounding lately when I talked to her.

"Oh baby, I'm so glad you called," she said, "The guy paid the deposit on the RV and he is coming next week to pick it up. Since you are the owner, I need you to sign the title over so I can transfer it to him."

I decided not to relay to her any of the stories I had been hearing. There was enough time for that when I got out.

"Well, babe," I said, "you have to take the title down to Phil Stevens in Burkesville. He is my lawyer now and he has power of attorney. The title has to be signed and notarized before ownership can be transferred. You remember the crap we had to go through when I bought it last month?"

"WHAT!" she screamed, "You hired that asshole!"

"Baby, I have to get out of here," I said, "he was at the jail visiting another inmate and I grabbed him and explained my situation. I gave him a deposit and he claims he can get me off all the charges."

"Fuck you! I will not deal with that asshole, ever. He cost me so much money in the past and I don't ever want to see him again."

"But Baby, he's my lawyer! . . . What am I supposed to do? . . . Days go by and I don't see you or even hear from you. I'm stuck in this shit hole and when I saw him, I thought this might be the answer to my prayers. Maybe you don't understand it but I want the fuck out of here now."

She slammed down the phone and that was the last time that I ever spoke to her. I guess I must have really struck a nerve. I had seen her fly off the handle before but this was something else. But now, I was back to square one; I couldn't count on the proceeds from the RV to cover my bail and there was still the problem with my car that Roxie was driving., I also had concerns about my possessions that were at the house; my computer; CD's and records. I needed to find a way to secure everything. I was hoping that the lawyer was going to be able to get me out somehow. Since I didn't have any ready cash, and who knows how much from my bank account Roxie had spent, I thought that maybe I could put my Camaro up as the bond. That would at least get it out of her hands.

I knew I would probably never talk to Roxie again after our last conversation, especially in light of the fact that she had told me that she put a deposit down on a house in South Carolina, I had visions of her jumping in my Camaro and moving down there and I would never see or hear from her again. I wanted to put a stop to that. This whole situation continued to worsen. The Camaro was the key to my release.

I had to get out of jail and the Camaro was the only real asset I had, besides the RV; and who knows what that situation was. I decided to try my friend Les in Syracuse again. I bailed him out by taking the Camaro off his hands so maybe he could do the same thing for me. He had good credit and I intended to give him a smoking deal on the car. The phone rang about 7 times before he picked it up.

"Les, its Mark," I shouted, "what's happening?"

"I should ask you the same thing. I heard you were in jail."

"Yes, you heard right, my friend," I admitted, "I had a spat with Roxie and got picked up for domestic violence. But I never hit her. When the cops came into the house, they found a bunch of pot and so here I am, and I need a HUGE favor."

"I'm not sending bail money,' Les said in his typical mercenary fashion.

"No," I said, "I need you to buy back the Camaro. It's the only security I have and my bail is set for 5 grand. Even though I paid you over $7,000 for it, I'll sell it back to you for $5,000, just to get out of here."

"Nah, not interested, "Les said, "I'm on a mission to pay off all my credit cards and I still owe my lawyer for the rest of his bill; for the case you never showed up for."

"Les, I got arrested," I pleaded. "Even if you don't want the car, put the money up, buy the car cheap and make yourself a quick profit. You know it's a great deal. Please, Les, I am begging you."

"I'm sorry Mark, I just can't do it," Les continued. "You got yourself into this, get yourself out. I can't help you."

Here's a guy who I thought was my friend telling me to go fuck myself. I couldn't understand why because we had always gotten along before and I had even given him money for his DWI defense. It just didn't make any sense. Les had always been one to take 'free money' and for him to turn down such a lucrative deal was alien to his very nature. I knew he had bills to pay and this deal would have given him an avenue to help out in that department. Why was he being so hard nosed about it?

The next day, I received a letter from my friend Maggie in Syracuse. I had given her the passwords for my bank account and email accounts and asked her to field any questions from my friends. I also had relied on her to withdraw money from my New York bank account and send it to me as I needed it. In her letter she said that I had received a bank statement and it showed 2 transfers from my New York Bank account. Both of them were dated a week after I went to jail.

Being incarcerated, there was no way I could have made any transactions. The first was a $ 590 withdrawal from my checking account. The second was a $ 50 withdrawal from my savings account. In addition to that, a $ 200 paper check had been written by Roxie and apparently cashed through our joint account in Burkesville.

Elton John wrote a song a few years ago entitled 'Rocket Man'. That was me, when I found this out. I positively went into orbit. $ 840 was missing from my bank account; an account, that was for me only. I never gave Roxie any authorization or privileges to access it. I was distraught to say the least. Here I am, sitting in the poky on charges that weren't mine, while my ex-lover was out there free, driving my car and taking money that was also mine. The worst part was that I couldn't do a damned thing about it.

I kept thinking about Roxie driving around in my car and the insurance coverage that was about to lapse. I wanted to do something to keep her from leaving town with it. New York titles can be easily forged because they don't need to be notarized. Even though my title was with my friend Michelle, it wouldn't stop Roxie from getting a duplicate, if she really wanted to. She told me that she had already done that with the Datsun 280-z that was titled in her ex-husbands name in Florida.

I called the Kentucky State Police and explained that I was in Adair County Jail but wanted to report a stolen car. The sent an officer down to talk to me.

"What kind of car is it sir?" He asked.

"It's a 1997 Chevy Camaro Z-28," I said, "It's very distinctive because it's bright red and has a special sculptured hood scoop. I don't think you would have any problems identifying it."

"And why do you think it was stolen?" He asked.

I told him the story of how I was incarcerated and how Roxie told me she was moving to South Carolina; in fact, had already been down there once. I told him that the insurance had run out on the car and the New York plates would be invalid next month.

"Well sir," he said, "There is nothing we can do about it. It's considered community property because you were living with her."

"Officer," I said, "I don't know where you went to law school, but she has no authorization to drive that car; especially with no insurance. If she were to get into an accident, who's ass would be in a sling? . . . MINE. And for your information, the car is not community property. She has taken the car without my OK and she has essentially robbed me of my vehicle."

"I'm sorry sir," he continued, "but there is just nothing we can do. I will check with Burkesville Police to see what they say about it, but I'm sure they will say the same thing."

Well, isn't that lovely. I've got a potentially stolen car and nobody will do anything about it. I knew the officer would not follow up on it because he didn't even bother to write anything down. I got hold of my lawyer Phil and told him to check on the balance of the joint account I had with Roxie. I had taken all my money out of there except about $ 100 dollars. Maybe that was still there. I wanted him to close the account and withdraw any funds. I also directed him to get over to the house and get my car, my laptop and my business records. These were the only items I was worried about right now. The RV was really too big for someone to steal or hide and the clothes and rest of my stuff was probably not something that was high demand. The laptop, on the other hand, held all my personal records, business connections and passwords. Roxie had already accessed it to get my bank information and there was stuff on the laptop that I just couldn't replace. I needed to make sure that it was secure.

"Phil," I said, "There is a very good chance that she is planning to steal that car. She knows the value of it and she has already taken money from my bank account. I need you to get my laptop and car. Everything else can wait.

There are 3 neighbors on my road that will be happy to store the car for me. Walt who lives directly across the road, Rachel and Richie who live about ¼ mile up the road on the same side and Pastor Rogers who lives about ½ mile up the road. Do you know any of them?"

"I know Walt and Pastor Rogers," he said, "but I'm not sure about Rachel and Richie."

"They're right up the road. Richie raises exotic chickens."

"Oh, sure," he said, "now I know who you mean."

Phil told me that he would take care of it. He requested me to get bank statements and he would try to recover that money too. That same day, I wrote Maggie and told her to send copies of my bank statements to Phil. I told her I was going to have Phil file charges against Roxie on my behalf. It sounded like a reasonable plan to me, but once again, laxity stepped in and changed the rules.

Maggie got sick and didn't address the bank statement very rapidly. Phil closed the bank account but never did anything about going out to the house. Roxie still had my car and the rest of my possessions. On the plus side, there was $ 192 in the bank account when it was closed so I knew that Roxie had been using it and must have made a deposit or two. By closing it, I'm sure more than one of her checks bounced and at least I got my $ 100 back.

When I finally saw Phil again, 2 weeks later, I asked him about the car and my possessions. He told me that he hadn't had a chance to get out to the house yet, but he was going to take care of it. That pissed me off. Apparently he never heard the term 'time is of the essence' since he was taking such a lax attitude towards it. I told him that she had been to visit me here at the jail and informed me that she had put a deposit down on a house, out of state and that she was going to move. I was not very nice when I told him to get his ass over there and take care of it; that's what he was being paid for. I reminded him that I had given him power of attorney, just so that he could act as my representative in these matters.

In the long run, hiring Phil was not a good investment on my part.

* * *

32) The Cost of Law

Columbia, KY—August 19, 2009

I hadn't heard anything from anybody. No letters, no calls from my lawyer, silence. Just sitting in the cell going day-to-day, wondering what was going on in the real world. I put another call for Phil, my attorney, to call me. I had no more phone card time and I need him to buy one for me. It was a very, very depressing day. I have a court date next week to discuss a bail reduction that Phil was trying to secure, but other than that, I am not making any kind of progress at all.

Yesterday was Roxie's birthday. How much I would have enjoyed being with her; even though she trampled all over me and is probably long gone from this area. I was so nervous about losing the car and RV it makes me sick. These are the only two possessions I have in this world that have a monetary value. Sure, I've got computer equipment, stereo equipment, CD's and records and a fairly large assortment of clothes. But the car and the RV could be instant cash if or when I needed it. Thank God the title for the Camaro is still in New York.

The guards here treat me OK. I don't give them any shit and they don't do anything to me. Some of these guys are better than others. Sonny, Eddie, and Artie are probably the best ones; at least they are the most considerate. Curt and Alan are pretty inconsiderate and act like guarding the inmates is an imposition.

The following week, I was once again transported to Cumberland County courthouse; this time for the bail reduction hearing. My attorney Phil met with me outside the holding cell and brought up the topic about payment of his fee.

"To get you out of this," he said, "I will need $5,000 dollars."

"Phil," I said, "You are assuming that this will go to trial. I don't think it will. They do not have any evidence against me except whatever testimony Roxie may decide to manufacture."

"Well, Mark," he said, "you have only given me the $1,000 retainer fee. I will need more in order to defend you."

"Ok, how about this?" I replied, "How about billing me per hour, or a per diem rate?"

"I can't do that," He said. "If I did that for all my clients, it would be an accounting nightmare."

"Let me ponder that and get back to you. What's the deal on my car? I've been waiting 3 weeks to hear from you about it. Is she under arrest?"

"The car was picked up yesterday," he told me, "we went out with a flatbed truck and got it. She had all kinds of boxes inside and we had to wait for her to unload it before we could take it."

"What about my computer?" I asked.

"I couldn't get the computer because I didn't have a Sheriff with me," he said, "and she told me that if I ever showed up on her property again, that she would have me arrested."

"What the fuck Phil!" I said emphatically, "You are my attorney; you have power of attorney in my affairs. Why would you let this little bitch push you around? And why didn't you take a deputy?"

"None of the deputies wanted to get involved," he said, "they just don't want to deal with her."

"DAMMIT!" I yelled, "That is their job. They are supposed to be protecting the public. I'd like to know who is protecting my assets."

"Hey," Phil yelled back, "just settle down. You know this is a small town and their resources are strapped. I'm sure they had better things to do than to 'guard' me."

"So where did you end up storing the car?" I asked.

"Don't worry," he said, "it's safe and sound in a warehouse in Burkesville. The owner is only going to charge you $ 15.00 per day to store it."

"Phil," I said with a slightly elevated voice, "I had 3 neighbors on the same road that would accept the car. That's why I told you about them. Why the hell should I pay storage on my car when I could have gotten it for free?"

"Well Mark, I thought it would be best to have it where Roxie couldn't get at it and vandalize it. I was looking to protect your interests."

I was pissed off. I didn't need a storage bill on top of everything else. But since he had gotten the judge to accept the car as collateral, I figured it would be in custody of the county very shortly and I wouldn't be paying much of a bill anyway. I told him that I would need him to get me another phone card because I only had 18 minutes left on the one I had and I was going to have to make calls to arrange bail, even though it was lowered. He told me that he would take care of it and put the $ 20 charge on my bill. Just then we got called into the courtroom. We stood in front of the judge and my attorney put in his request for a bail reduction due to hardship.

I had never seen such a thing before in my life. It was a verbal request; not a formal motion. Phil just simply asked for consideration of a bond hearing. The judge set it on the calendar for the following Thursday as the day he would hear arguments. Great; now I had another week of waiting. I was starting to understand why nothing ever got done down here.

If I thought time moved slowly up to this point, the following week was at a standstill. I went through the same routine every day but it seemed like the days were 48 hours long. Finally, September 3rd rolled around and I was transported back to court.

My lawyer and I stood in front of the judge and the lawyer presented his argument that I had no money and my only asset was the car. He asked the judge to accept my car as collateral for my bond and then he added that even though I was putting the car up for security, I needed to be able to drive the car. His reasoning was that if I posted the car as bail and they kept it, I would have no way to get around. My residence was 13 miles outside of town and there was no public transportation of any kind.

The judge flatly turned that part of the motion down. He did rule that he would accept the car as collateral for my bond, but I had to relinquish it. He further told me that he would accept the car as bond, but only after he saw the title to insure that it was free and clear. I told him that I would have to redeem the title from New York and the judge said that would be acceptable.

Phil, the consummate brave lawyer, then announced to the judge that he would no longer be my representative in court. This caught me by surprise, and I wanted to talk to him after we left court about the phone card and other things. I never got the opportunity because I was put back in my holding cell and eventually transported back to jail. I couldn't believe that I had paid this guy his deposit of $1,000, just to show up twice to court for a grand total of 15 minutes each time; and then to quit on me.

I should have been a lawyer. Now I was going to have to go through the hassle of finding another defense attorney to represent me. I wasn't about to let any public defender handle this case.

What the hell was I going to do?

The only saving grace was that my lawyer owed me the proceeds from the joint bank account. That was $ 192 total. Plus I had another $1,100 from my September Social Security check and whatever else was in my New York bank account. My net worth right now was approximately $1,500 where 90 days ago it had been $16,000 if you count the value of the RV and the Camaro. Other than that, I was dead nuts broke. I needed a new attorney, I never got my phone card that Phil had promised to get for me and I was not really any further ahead than when I was first locked up. So I committed myself to being extremely frugal with the 18 minutes of time I had left, while trying to come up with some ingenious plan of making something out of nothing.

And people think that Hell is some fiery pit . . . Ha!

* * *

33) . . . . Lost—Columbia, KY

September 3, 2009

I got back to my cell that afternoon and started assessing my situation. If I could just find some bright spot to focus on, perhaps I could do something that would stop this endless downward spiral of my life.

1) I was in jail for something I did not do.
2) My heart was broken because even with everything that had happened, I had to admit that I was still madly in love with Roxie. I just could not believe that someone who had been so loving could do this to another human being.
3) My lawyer had just quit me, which meant that I was probably going to be assigned another public defender until I could hire another attorney. I didn't like that because a PD, by and large just does not go into court to aggressively defend; they have too many cases to deal with. They're basically dealmakers.

4) My Camaro was in some impound lot and my RV was in limbo; meaning that I did not know where it was. Roxie did not have her own car here in Kentucky, so the logical thing was that she would use the RV to transport her stuff when she moved.
5) I had nobody I could call down here because I didn't know anyone locally.
6) None of my friends could give me any money for bail.
7) I didn't have any money to buy a phone card to even call someone for help.

Everything and anything related to my life came crashing through to me like the hot kiss at the end of a wet fist. Events, conversations, faces of people I had met, everything was a blur. I thought of the night of my arrest and how Roxie had come out of the house with a shotgun. She had somehow found where I had hid it when the Sheriff wouldn't take and store it. That led me to think about poor Terry Jacoby, putting a shotgun under his chin and blowing his brains out.

That led to the conversation where Roxie had mentioned thread.

A lot can happen with thread, she had said.

What did that mean?

Then it hit me. It was almost like a vision in my head. I saw Terry, subdued by some sort of 'special' medicine; possibly the same 'special' medicine that Roxie was giving me. I saw Roxie putting the shotgun under his chin as he sat semi-comatose in the chair, and wrapping a thread around the trigger. I saw her draw the thread down underneath the seat of the chair; away from the back blast of the gun. I saw her pull the thread and in a flash, brain matter splattered on the ceiling. And I saw Roxie examine her hands to make sure that there was no gun shot residue on them. But even the most careful people, especially someone emotional like Roxie, is bound to make mistakes; mistakes that a trained investigator would find.

Roxie had said she was having an affair with a public official who was married. Could that public official be a member of a police force? Now my thoughts were coming to me rapid fire. What if it was Dex, from the Cumberland County Sheriff's department? Dex; the same guy who arrested me and tasered her ex husband? It was becoming crystal clear now. When I reflected on the clarity of my thinking, it dawned on me that it had been over 2 months since I had taken any of Roxie's 'special' medicine. What if that was some sort of drug potion or hallucigenic substance? She did say that she had learned medicine from her experiences with the Onondaga Indian tribe. And that would explain a lot about my complacency when she did something that I would ordinarily have a fit about.

Now I was on a roll. Roxie was a lot closer to the Sheriff's deputy than I imagined. They had met when he first arrested her ex husband and I now believed that she had been, or still was, having an affair with him. He could have easily used his influence to shield her from the investigation of Terry's death as well as placing all of the blame for the drugs found in her house on me. Maybe he was even responsible for putting the drugs in the house. I remember how it seemed that Roxie was doing everything in her power to delay our return that day.

I thought and thought and thought for a word to describe my situation. I wanted a word that would have to have positive attributes because I am, by nature, an optimist. I have been in tight spots before and somehow I had always been able to flash upon a working idea that might have a chance. But even in meditation, all I kept seeing was a floating figure that looked like the letter 'F'. I drilled down deeper, trying to think of anything without using the "F" word. I heard a loud clanging in my head. The letter in my head wasn't an 'F'; it was a 'P'. What is the significance of the letter 'P'? Deeper and deeper I drove into myself. Even though my eyes were closed, flashes of colors kept swirling around my head. Ever present was that letter 'P'.

PINNED! That's it . . . I was PINNED.

All my options were cut off. Like a wrestler being put into a submission hold, I was PINNED. Maybe Roxie hadn't planned it this way or maybe she had. But one way or the other, I was in a cage with no obvious way out. The depression filtered in and I snapped. I broke down into an uncontrollable bout of sobbing. Waves of tears flowed as I buried my head into my plastic mattress. I got up and punched the wall. It hurt and bruised the skin but I didn't care. I swept my arm over the shelf and sent shampoos and other toiletries flying in every direction. A full roll of bathroom tissue fell into the toilet. I fished it out and threw it at the wall. I grabbed the single sheet off my bed and tied it around my neck. The other inmates in my cell watched me implode and probably feared for their own lives; or at least for their rolls of toilet paper.

Somebody called a guard and within a minute, 3 hefty individuals had wrestled me to the floor and held me down. The uncontrollable sobs continued to rage out of me.

"Casey, Casey," someone shouted, "Casey, what's wrong."

I couldn't answer. All I could do was sob. I didn't care. All vanity was lost. I was lost. The guard pulled me out of the cell and escorted me down the hall and put me in another cell across from the security station. This cell was used for inmates that were on suicide watch because the security station had ½" thick glass and the guards could see everything going on in the cell.

About 5 minutes later, a guard entered the cell and sat down on the corner of the bunk. He asked me what was wrong and I muttered something that he couldn't understand.

"Casey," he said, "you have to tell me what's up or I can't help you. You do want to be helped don't you?"

"I hate my life," I said, "I just want to die."

"Look man," he continued, "you've been a pretty good guy here. We've never had any problems with you. Why all of a sudden this outbreak. You scared the shit out of the other inmates."

That made me chuckle. Imagine that; me, all 5'5", 60 years old, scaring the shit out of someone probably ½ my age and twice as large.

"C'mon man," the guard said, "level with me. I don't want to have to write up a bad report on you or put you on suicide watch. Just tell me what is going on. Maybe I can help."

I recognized that he was being sincere with me. Actually I felt he was more sincere than anyone had been to me in a long time. I told him about the false charges, Roxie moving, the jerking around at court, the lawyer quitting, everything. I told him that I was in a box and couldn't get out and no one could help me.

"Man, you are in a rough situation" he said, "and the only thing I can tell you is that I have a lawyer who is known as a Pit Bull around here. He's not cheap, but he is very good. If you like, I can give him a call and tell him to contact you."

"What's your name?" I asked

"My name is Artie," he answered, "I'm the head jailer here."

"Artie" I said, "If I thought he could do any good, I would hire him on the spot. But the truth is I have another court date coming up and I'm going to just plead guilty and be done with all this."

"You do that," he said, "and you are going to be spending a lot of time in here. Any kind of trafficking is serious in this state and Judge Everett hates dopers. His grandson died of an overdose and he generally throws the book at any drug related defendant."

"I don't care, Artie," I replied. "They originally offered me a plea of probation and forfeiture of my money. Maybe I can get that back on the table. At any rate it's doing something other than going to court every month and being disappointed. I have to feel like I'm doing something."

"Are you going to kill yourself?" Artie asked. "I really don't want to have to put you in a jacket."

"No," I said, "I just lost it. Morally, I'm too strong to ever commit suicide. It's just everything ganging up on me, and having to sit there and watch cartoons all day long, and listening to all those bullshit tales of crime from those punks. Then all the shit that happened with my lawyer in court. That's really what pushed me over the edge."

"I can leave you in here if you like," He said. "You don't have to go back into the population."

"I would like that. I don't miss the fact that there is no TV here. As long as I can read, I'm fine."

"Don't make me look like an asshole," he told me, "I'll do you this favor once. You fuck up and you're back in the population or a straitjacket."

"I promise, Artie," I said, "and thanks."

I spent the next two weeks in solitary confinement, but at least it wasn't a suicide watch. I didn't mind not having TV and I certainly didn't mind not having to deal with a bunch of other assholes. The biggest adjustment was not having a shower stall. I had to ask a guard to take me to the showers every other day. I wasn't allowed to shave either. No razors for suicide watch people. Other than that it was peaceful. I read, ate, and slept. Read, ate and slept. Read, ate and slept, and grew my beard. Two or three times a week a guard would escort me down to the community room where I could watch TV for a couple of hours. I got to watch what I wanted to watch. And because of the good rapport I had with the most of the guards, they would periodically slip me an extra tray of food or more than one cup of coffee at breakfast. All in all, it was much better than being in the other cell.

September 24th finally came. I had planned, like I told Artie, to plead guilty and get this bullshit behind me. The transport driver picked me up, gave me my 2 free cigarettes and we were on our way to the courthouse. I choked both those cigarettes down in about 10 minutes. My mind kept trying to think ahead at what I was going to say to the judge. About one half of the way to the courthouse, I started feeling queasy. Not really sick to my stomach, but just off. At first, I thought it was because I chain smoked my 2 freebie cigarettes, but I could feel my heart rate increasing and that is when I started to get alarmed. These were some of the same signs I had before my last 11 heart attacks. Yes, 11 over the last 19 years. So I damned well knew the signs. And these mercenary assholes would not let me have my regular medication, including my nitro-glycerin for emergencies.

By the time we were within 5 miles of Burkesville, my heart felt like it was ready to explode out of my chest. I tried to calm myself but the more I thought about it, the more pain I felt. We pulled into the courthouse garage and I asked the driver if they had any Nitro-glycerin there.

"What do you want that for?" He asked.

"Because I feel like I'm having a heart problem," I said, "and Nitro will usually fix it."

"Forget it Mr. Casey," he said as he put me back in the van, "we're going to the hospital."

It was a short trip to the Cumberland Hospital and we pulled into the emergency room entrance. He took me inside and found a nurse while I waited in one of the rooms. She came in and did the standard tests; blood pressure, pulse rate, temperature, etc. I told her that all I wanted was a Nitro tablet but she continued to treat me like I was a STAT. They hooked oxygen up to me and made me lie on a gurney. I stayed that way for an hour while the transport driver stood guard. I guess they had to make sure I wasn't going to escape. The nurse came back in and asked me how I felt. I told her that I was fine now and wanted to get back to court. That's when the shocker came.

"Court's over with Mr. Casey," the transport driver told me, "but you'll have another shot at it next month."

"What do you mean, next month?" I asked.

"Court's over with," He said. "The court meets once a month. You'll be scheduled to go back then."

Now I was pissed. I really wanted to get all this over with and here I was, strapped to a gurney and being told that it would be at least another month before I could make my plea. If I was ever going to really have a heart attack, it would have been then.

"We're going to keep you overnight," the nurse said, "We want to watch your vitals."

"I get all my primary care at the VA hospital." I told her.

"Not this time," She stated. "But don't worry; the county is paying for this trip."

They wheeled me up into a private room with a nice view of the outside. It was the first time I had seen the outside, except during transport, since I had been arrested. I even had a phone that I could use to make local calls. Now if I just knew someone to call.

There was a guard stationed inside the room, just to make sure I didn't try to drown myself in the water pitcher. And GOD, a real shower. The first thing I did was to call my old lawyer Phil, to update him and see if we could work out a deal. He wasn't in but his secretary told me that she had just received the title to my car from New York. I thought about it for a minute and then asked her if she would have the lawyer take it over to the courthouse to post my bail.

This might actually turn out to be a good thing. She told me that he was out of town until Monday but she would give him the message. Now I felt a lot better. I was suddenly filled with the idea that it was the hand of God who put me in pain, to send me to the courthouse, to miss out on pleading guilty so that I could put my car up to get bailed out and fight this damned case.

They brought the dinner tray in and it was a treat to eat real food. That night's special was Chicken breast, potatoes, corn, a biscuit, a salad and chocolate pudding. I was living large. I asked the guard how long he had to stay and he told me overnight. He was a likeable chap named Bart Dennis; one of the Sheriff's deputies. We hit it off immediately. We talked about everything including computers, old cars, music and what pains in the ass politics were. I told him the story of my arrest, the setup and everything. He had gone through a similar situation with a woman several years earlier and it ended up costing him about $30,000. His attitude was to just take your lumps and let it go.

I finally decided to crash about 1:30 a.m. I thanked Bart for being so understanding and he said if I ever needed someone to talk to, or any help at all, to give him a call. He gave me his home number and I faded off to sleep. The next morning, I had a nice breakfast, got a final checkup by the doctor and then they shipped me back to the jail. I decided that I would take Artie up on his offer to use this pit bull attorney of his.

"Artie," I said, "I've changed my mind about the attorney. What's his name?"

"Brian Dickerson," He said. "His office is in Greensburg."

"Can you give him a call and have him get in touch with me?"

"I'll do it after lunch," he told me, "He's usually in court until mid afternoon anyway."

I thanked Artie and applauded him for being so considerate and accommodating to me. It wasn't often that someone would go out of their way to help an inmate; even if they understood that the situation I was in was not the norm that they encountered in a jail. But the truth was, unfortunately, I wasn't as accommodating as he was.

I had a big ax to grind.

* * *

34) . . . . FOUND

Columbia, KY—October 6, 2009

I've always been a Christian, but in the last few years I had fallen away from my beliefs. I didn't pray, seldom attended church, and even though I didn't flagrantly violate all I learned in Sunday school, I wasn't a model parishioner either. In fact, I had a problem with organized religion. I believed in God but I didn't believe that God made the Church. Church was man-made.

That night, I found the Lord again. I knelt in fervent prayer and called out with my heart. I confessed my sins and asked for forgiveness. I asked the Lord to get me out of jail. I didn't go to the point of promising to be good forever and start preaching, but I did ask for the end of my incarceration. I truly believed that God would be merciful because I did not belong here.

The next day, shortly after lunch, they called me and said I had a phone call. It was Brian Dickerson; the lawyer that Artie had told me about. Brian said that he would come to see me that night around 7 p.m. and we would talk about the case.

Brian showed up around 7:15 and I told him what I was in there for. I gave him the background of how I had moved here to fall in love and all I had accomplished was that I fell. I told him about hiring Phil Stevens and then having him quit on me. I told him about my assets that were in jeopardy and my limited finances.

"I believe you Mark," he said, "and I will take your case and get you out of the charges; but the cost is $5,000 and I run my own show alone. I don't need any help from my client."

"Deal," was all I said. I liked his 'no bullshit' attitude immediately.

"The first thing we've got to do is to get you out of here," He said. "You say that the judge will accept your Camaro in lieu of a cash bond?"

"That's what he told Stevens and me in court."

"Judge Everett is a friend of mine," He told me. "Get me the title and I'll talk to him."

I told him that it had been sent to Steven's office and he had it. He said he would contact him and take care of my release. I was already feeling better about my decision when he said, "Let's get you off these charges and then we'll kick some ass. Can you put a retainer deposit down?"

I said that I had about $1,400 in the bank and could give him my Visa card to withdraw the money form my New York bank. He said that was fine and we walked up to the processing table to get my wallet. I handed him the wallet and he wrote down the card number and security code and handed the card back. The guard took the card, put it in my wallet and stowed everything back in the secure lockup area. We shook hands and he told me he would get back to me if there was any problem. He left the jail and I decided that I liked Brian Dickerson.

The next day he called me at the jail and told me that Stevens had sent the title to Darlene Sorenson, the public defender because he was off the case. She also sent my $ 192 dollar check from the joint bank account, to the jail. Brian told me that Darlene was going to send one of her representatives over to the jail to have me sign the title over as bond. As soon as I signed it and she returned it to him, he would present it to the court.

I had hoped I did not have to sign the car over because I didn't like the idea of me being in jail and a signed title for my car being outside the walls. Also, there were too many people in Burkesville who wanted that car. The Sheriff of Burkesville was a collector of cars, mainly classic Camaro's. I knew he would love to get his hands on mine. But what choice did I have? I had to trust that Brian was doing the right thing. The following day, at 9:30 a.m., the representative from the public defender's office came to the jail with my title. I signed on the dotted line and she was gone. The only thing I was left with was a photo copy of my signed title. I didn't get a receipt because the bond had not been approved by the Circuit Court Judge yet. I was antsy, but I looked forward to getting out of jail by the end of the week.

A week went by. What could be taking so long? I put a call into Brian's office and was told that he was out of town on a murder trial. I left a message for him to get back to me. In the meantime, I received another letter from my friend Maggie in Syracuse. She basically just updated me on things that were happening in her life but ¾ of the way through the letter, she handed me a bomb.

"I don't know if I should tell you this Mark," she wrote, "but you will probably find out when you finally get back to Syracuse."

What was it that I shouldn't know?

"Roxie is living at your friend Les's house," She announced. "She apparently had a garage sale this weekend and your friend Michelle saw her. Michelle had stopped by the house and they would not let her in but they did confirm that Roxie was living there."

You could have pushed me over with a feather. In fact, I almost did faint. Roxie, living in Syracuse, with my ex-roommate, a man she told me that she despised and called 'the most obnoxious' man she ever met. This story was getting more and more crushing. I always knew that Les was mercenary and I now found out how mercenary Roxie was. But this was nothing less than salt in the wound. No wonder Les refused to take my car when I asked him. Like I said, it was alien for Les to pass up free money. Apparently, Roxie and him had been in contact since my arrest.

I think I cried myself to sleep that night. My heart was pounding so hard, I couldn't hear anything except the gush of blood forcing its way through my veins. I was sure that the little tidbit of information I had just received was going to give me a heart attack and at that point in time, I really wished for it. This cut me deeper than I have ever been cut before.

Another week went by and still no word from Brian's office. I was going out of my mind. It was almost like life had decided to see how much stress I could put up with. Now, along with all my other problems, I had signed the title to my car away and I had no idea what was going on. Had this all been a scam to get my car?

I put another call into Brian's office and begged the receptionist to please have him call me. My mind was replaying all the events over the last 3 months; the arrest, the court dates, the delays, the lawyer quitting, the signing over of my title.

I felt that everybody was in the 'good 'ol boy' club and everybody wanted me dead so they could divvy up my assets. I went through another major breakdown in my cell. I began looking up at the ceiling, trying to figure out how to attach something to hang myself. Even though I always believed that suicide was wrong, I now had convinced myself that it was the only way I would find my way out of this Hell-hole. I actually went into a sort of stupor where I turned down my food and didn't even bother to shower. I just sat in my cell and starred at the wall; all my waking hours, 7 days a week.

Three weeks had dragged by and I still hadn't heard anything about my release. I never in my wildest dreams thought I would be spending my 61st birthday, in jail but my birthday was 3 weeks away and I probably wouldn't even get a piece of cake. One of the guards came down and pulled me out of my cell. When I asked where I was going, he told me I had a phone call.

"Where are you living now Mark?" the voice asked. It was none other than Brian Dickerson, my new attorney.

"I'm still in this stinking jail," I said, "I thought you were going to get me out."

"Why are you still there?" he asked, "I turned the title over to the court 3 weeks ago."

"I don't know Brian," I told him, "You are the highly paid expert in all this. You are the one who wanted to run the show. Just shove me in a fucking cell and forget about me."

Now calm down Mark," he said, "I'll get to the bottom of this. I'll find out what's up and call you back today or tomorrow."

I didn't know if I should feel true optimism or the fullness of taking a bite from another dangling carrot. Because of everything that had happened, namely all the delays and false stories, I decided that I would just file this in the 'tales for the crypt' folder. I was definitely more depressed now than before I talked to him. I went back to me cell again, almost in the same stupor I had been in for 3 weeks. The only difference was that I was pissed that the system was doing this to me. I felt like a caged lion at some sort of zoo; one that people constantly threw stones at and generally teased.

The next morning was no better. I picked at my lame breakfast and curled under the sheet to doze off. At lunchtime they announced that lunch was here and I didn't even move. Apparently, my lack of movement must have alarmed them because Artie himself opened up the cell and came in. I thought he was going to give me another 'pep' talk but he told me to pick up all my belongings. I figured I was going to be transferred to the psycho ward or something.

"Where am I going now Artie?" I inquired.

"Home I hope," he said, "you are being released."

I heard the words but they didn't register. I just blindly picked up all my sheets, my mattress, my books and toiletries and followed Artie down the hall.

"Put the mattress on that stack and the sheets here." He directed.

I did that and we went out to the processing table. He went in the back room and pulled out a storage bag and handed it to me.

"What is this?" I asked.

"It's you street clothes dummy," He said. "Make sure everything is there that you had when you came in."

My mouth must have been standing wide open because Artie got this little smile on his face and opened the storage bag for me. There on the table were my shorts, my orange shirt, my sneakers, my wallet, copies of the signed title and the $ 192 check that Stevens had sent me; everything I was wearing back in July when I was arrested.

"Do you want to take a shower before you leave?" Artie asked.

"I'll pass," I said, "I just want to get the fuck out of here. Can I get a ride to Burkesville?"

"This is a jail Casey," he said with a smile, "not a taxi service."

"C'mon man," I said, "it's 30 miles to Burkesville."

"Would you rather stay here?" was his only reply.

I went in the locker room and changed clothes. I stuffed my books and toiletries in a Dollar General bag they gave me and I came back out. I handed them my orange jumpsuit and flip flops. It was 12:10 p.m. on October 30, 2009. I had been in this jail for almost 4 months. I didn't want to spend any more time here. I picked up my treasures and walked out the front door.

Freedom tasted like the best meal I had ever had.

* * *

35) The Living RV

Burkesville, KY—October 30, 2009

I walked out that front door and vowed to myself to never see the inside again. I had the check for $ 192 in my pocket and figured I could use that money to jumpstart my new life. I still had the court issues to go through but it would be so much easier to face them now, rather than as a prisoner.

My first order of business was to get back to Burkesville, go out to the house and face whatever I would find there. It was a 30 mile trip and calling a cab would cost me about $ 100. That was would not be my first choice. Anyway, I had to get this check cashed first.

I walked into the Farmers and Traders Savings bank and stepped up to the window. I told the teller that I would like to cash this check. She looked at it and asked me if I had an account.

"No, I don't," I said, "I have an account in Burkesville but not here."

"I'm sorry then," She said. "We are not affiliated with the Burkesville location, even though it is the same bank. They are an independent branch and not on our system."

Great! I thought. One more screwed up situation in Kentucky. I was starting to learn that was the reason why Kentucky abbreviated their state with the letters K-Y; just like in the jelly. I turned to go and saw one of the guards from the jail standing behind me in line.

"Hi Mr. Casey," He said.

"Hello Elmer," I replied. I started to walk out and I thought 'what the hell' and went back inside.

"Elmer," I asked, "you wouldn't be going anywhere near Burkesville would you?"

"I'm going ½ ways there," he answered, "why?"

"I've got to get back to Burkesville," I told him. "I just got released today and thought I could cash this check and take a cab but this is a different branch and they won't cash it."

"I'm not doing anything right now," he said, "I'll take you to Burkesville."

I knew now that God had answered my prayers. Not only was I released but now one of my guards was giving me a ride home. I got in his truck and we headed down the road. I told him that when we got into town, I would go to the bank, cash this check and give him gas money. He seemed to appreciate that. We talked about my case a bit. He had heard all about it when he was at work but now he was hearing my side of it. He told me how stupid Roxie was for planting a pound of pot when she could have got the same results by planting only 4-1oz bags. The charges would be the same. He said it was a real idiot move on her part to forge my name on a check.

"That's a felony in Kentucky," he said, "even if it was only $ 200 dollars."

We got to Burkesville and went to my bank. I went inside and cashed the check and gave Elmer $ 30 dollars for the ride. He thanked me and dropped me off at my next stop; the office of Mr. Phil Stevens, my original lawyer.

"Is Phil in?" I asked the receptionist.

"May I tell him who is calling?" She asked.

"Mark Casey," I answered.

"Oh Hi," she said with a smile, "How are you today?"

"I'm a lot better now that I'm out of jail," I said. She buzzed Phil and he came right out of his office.

"Hey, you're out," he exclaimed, "Come on in to my office."

We had a bit of cordial conversation and then I got to the point of my business.

"I need the files you had on me," I said. "I've hired another lawyer and I want to give him everything that you had in my file, for my defense."

"Who's representing you?"

"Brian Dickerson from Greensburg" I said.

"Ooh, how much is he charging you?" he said, "He's not cheap."

"He quoted me the same price that you did, and he promised not to quit me."

I had to throw that last little dig in there because it bugged me that Phil just left me hanging and wouldn't even submit my title to the court for my release.

"Mark," he said, "you told me you wouldn't pay me. What was I to do?"

"Phil," I commented, "I never said I wouldn't pay you. I said I didn't think it would go to trial. I still don't. I got the discovery package when I was in jail. They have her statement, her shotgun, my money and somebody's pot. That's it. No testimony from anybody I sold to. No history of me ever being arrested for anything other than DWI. Plus, it all happened on her property. She's skipped the state now and I doubt she will be back, because she forged checks of mine and I intend to press charges."

Stevens pulled out my file and handed it to me. "That's all I have on you." He said.

We chatted a while longer, mainly about my car. He told me that the guy who picked it up at the house wondered whether Roxie had some kind of 'golden pussy'. He said that I was the 4th guy that he knew of that got screwed over by her.

"She's good," I admitted, "and she is a good actress too. She had me convinced she really cared."

I left his office with the file and headed to a convenience store where they had a pay phone; the only pay phone in Burkesville. In my file, Roxie had listed our neighbor as a contact when she was taken to the hospital the night I got arrested. The phone number was also there.

I wondered if Ritchie and Rachel could get me out to the house where my RV was. I gave Ritchie a call and he answered. I explained that I was in Burkesville and wondered if he would come down and take me back to the house. Ritchie was very cordial and said he would be there in 20 minutes. I ordered a cup of coffee and read the paper. Ritchie walked in and we shook hands. I hadn't seen him since before I got 'sent up' as he called it.

"Before we go," he said, "you owe me an apology."

I had no clue what I was apologizing for, but I told him whatever it was, I was sorry.

"You owe me an apology for not taking Roxie to jail with you," He told me.

I laughed at that and told him that I thought she would be there soon enough. He took me back to the house and waited to make sure I could get into the RV. This was going to be my living quarters and transportation for a while so I needed to make sure it ran and the heater worked. By some strange stroke of luck, the keys were in the ignition and none of the doors were locked. The battery was dead so it wouldn't start but Richie had a set of jumper cables and we got it fired up on the first try. I thanked Ritchie for the ride and told him I would keep in touch.

It was too dark to do anything that night so I settled in for my first night of freedom in almost 4 months. The RV ran as smooth as I remembered it and the heater would blast you out if you wanted it too. It was still fairly warm in Kentucky, even though it was late October, so I didn't need to run it. I lay down on the back double bed and thought how lucky I was to be out and how lucky I was to still have this vehicle. Tomorrow I had to face the demonic mess that I knew Roxie had left for me. Tomorrow was Halloween, usually my favorite holiday of the year. In the past, I normally had house parties to go to but this year I was all alone, in a foreign land and feeling very, very down.

Well, at least I wasn't in jail.

* * *

36) Mr. "Nice" Guy

Burkesville, KY—October 31, 2009

On Saturday morning; October 31, 2009 I awoke after spending a well-deserved and restful night in the RV. I knew I had a lot of work ahead of me to reorganize my life, but the freedom made it all worthwhile. I climbed out of the RV and bounded up on the porch. It was a mess. There were boxes all over, most of it belonging to me. It looked as though Roxie had just shoved all my possessions into whatever container she could. Why didn't she just leave them in the house?

I turned the knob and the amazingly, the door was unlocked. I went inside and it was an even bigger mess. There were empty boxes strewn here and there and the awful smell of raw garbage coming from the kitchen. The first place I went was my office space. It was stripped of anything that slightly resembled organization. There were half-opened boxes on the floor filled with bits of computer hardware, books, papers and other items that really had no value. The only reason I kept them, was in the event I had to fix something. My filing cabinet lay on the floor with papers pulled helter-skelter out of the files. Someone had taken the time to go through everything. The first file I wanted to find was my important papers file. That file held my Social Security card, my Navy discharge papers and my birth certificate.

I wasn't prepared to find that the file was missing. Missing also was my laptop computer, the power supply, an external hard drive, my cell phones and various other items that I knew where they should be. The only thing left there was my printer; minus the power supply.

For two days, I stayed in the RV and meticulously went through all this junk to find out what was left of my possessions. Every evening, I would leave and drive over to the Marrowbone Market about 5 miles away, and get sandwiches, sodas, cigarettes, snacks and whatever else I needed. The RV was rough on gas and so I didn't want to be running all over the place. Then I would return and keep plugging at sorting the remains. I have to say, there wasn't much. All my clothes were gone except for a few summer shirts that had been stuffed into one large garbage can. All of my socks, shoes, underwear, jewelry, winter coats and gloves were gone.

Winter was on the way; what was I going to do?

I sat down on the porch and cried. The missing items were bad enough, but it was the memory of what 'could have been' with Roxie that drove me into this depression. Roxie had originally been my ideal woman. Even though we had issues between us, I was sure that they could have been worked out. And if they couldn't, fine. I could accept that. But to strip me of everything that I had worked my entire life for was just plain evil. I theorized that Roxie just didn't have a soul. She had probably done this before and with every man in her life, and she was becoming more expert at it with each new target.

Finally, I found the stamina to keep going. I spent the weekend sorting though every item that was still there. My record collection was in the pole barn but every box had been gone through. My antiques were gone as well as some collectible artwork. I figured that Roxie had gone through everything and only took what she figured she could make a quick buck on. She left the records because they were too heavy to transport and probably took up too much room.

But the worst thing was the fact that my entire collection of CD's, DVD's and Video tapes were gone. The rest of the music I had was on the computer and hard drive which were gone. Roxie had taken my music; my children. That was a sin that I could not forgive her for.

On Monday, the 2nd of November, I went out to the mailbox along the road to the house. Inside, there was so much mail forced into the box by the carrier, that it was difficult to even get it out. There had to be at least 15 pounds of accumulated letters, flyers and junk mail. At least half of the mail was for the estate of Terry Jacoby. I knew that Roxie was the executrix of his estate and figured that the lawyer might want these pieces of mail in his possession.

I decided to be a 'nice guy' and take it down to him. I went through everything, separating Roxie's, Terry's and my mail into bundles. I had a lot of things to get accomplished today and so I bundled up the estate mail and went to the lawyer's office in Burkesville. I told the receptionist that I had all this mail in the mailbox and I wanted to know how to get in touch with Roxie because I had her mail too. The receptionist told me that they had not heard anything from Roxie but if I wanted to, I could leave the estate mail. According to her, that was all they were interested in. She told me that Roxie had just up and left and didn't leave a phone number or a forwarding address. I gave the estate mail to her and left, feeling confident that I had done my good deed.

I drove the RV 30 miles to Columbia, Kentucky; the same town as the Adair County Jail where I had been housed. It had the closest Wal-Mart in the area and I needed to get a cell phone. For about $ 40 dollars and change, I got a nice Samsung phone, both chargers, 300 minutes of airtime and a case. While at Wal-Mart I picked up 3 gift cards. They were for my next stop. I went to the County Jail; I pressed the intercom button and asked for Artie.

"Hey old man," he said as he came to the door, "I thought we got rid of you."

"I'm a bad penny," I said. "I wanted to give you this." and handed him the gift card.

"What's this for?" He asked.

"You helped me out when I was in here," I said "and you hooked me up with a lawyer."

"You don't have to do this, man."

"No," I told him, "I want to. It's my way of saying thank you for your kindness; Thank you for your humanity; and thank you for caring about me. There is one there for Eddie and Sonny also."

"I'll make sure they get them." He said.

I left the jail feeling good that I could get in my vehicle and drive away. I also felt good because Artie, Eddie and Sonny had really been good to me and I liked being good back. My next stop was to the barracks of the Kentucky State Police. I asked to see a trooper for the purpose of filing a report.

"How can I help you?" the trooper asked.

"I want to report a theft. I also have information regarding the death of Mr. Terry Jacoby that was investigated last year and dismissed." I told him. "I have new information that may cause you to reopen the investigation."

"And what would that be?" He asked.

I told him the story of living with Roxie and the many conversations that we had while I lived there. I told him about one in particular that involved her statement 'You can do a lot with thread'. I told him that she had a history of violence in her life and also a history of running from it to out of state locations. I told him about all the possessions of mine she had taken. He listened while I told him everything I knew about her.

"I really don't see what I can do Mr. Casey," He said. "You two were living together and if she took your possessions, then it's a civil matter. Because the check was drawn on a New York bank, you will have to file any charges against her up there. As far as the situation with Mr. Jacoby, that case has been ruled a suicide and it is closed."

"Officer, that is my point," I said, "When they investigated it, they had no witnesses. I would be willing to tell my story as States' witness if you reopened the investigation."

"I'll look into it and get back to you." He said.

With that, the discussion ended. The trooper would not take a formal report until he had time to look into my allegations. I just had to accept that. I got into the RV and headed back to Burkesville. It bothered me that the police would just sort of blow me off as they did, but I figured the trooper would, at least take a closer look at the case. For now, that's the only thing I could hope for.

With my new cell phone, I called Corbett in Pennsylvania. I told him that I was finally out because I put my Camaro up for bond. He didn't have much to say to me and I thought that I had just caught him at a bad time. I told him I was living in my RV and I would get back to him when I got settled.

The next call I made was to Ken in Colorado. He was happy that I was finally out and he told me that he had an interesting call earlier that day.

"Guess who called me today?" He said.

"No clue man," I said.

"Roxie called about an hour ago."

That was a shocker. Why would she be calling Ken unless, unless . . .

"What did she have to say Ken?" I asked.

"She said that she knew you were out because she received a call from her lawyer," he said, "I guess you were in his office today trying to find her."

So much for trying to be a nice guy and take the mail to him; that was a stunt that backfired on me, because the last thing I wanted was for Roxie to know that I was out. Now it was too late.

"That fucking son of a bitch!" I said. "I went to take the Terry Jacoby estate mail to him. I did ask if they had a forwarding address but that was it. I guess that was stupid because I didn't want her to know I was out."

"Well, she knows now," he said, "she only said that she hopes you aren't planning anything stupid. She is not going to testify against you as long as you leave her alone."

"Ken, I don't believe anything that woman says," I told him. "Everything that comes out of her mouth is turning into a lie."

"But Mark," he said, "she sounded so nice and sincere on the phone."

"Ken" I said, "All I can say is that she is a good actress. She had me fooled all this time."

We talked for a while and I told him I would get back to him. I parked the RV in a convenience store parking lot and spent the night there. I had to find a permanent place to live because the RV was definitely something that would attract attention. I went inside the store and made sure that it was OK to park there overnight. I got myself a sandwich, dessert and a soda and sat in the RV to eat my luxurious dinner. I decided to call my ex-roommate Les, just to see what he had to say. What the hell, he already had to know I was out.

"Hey Les," I said when he answered, "It's Mark."

Les must have been lost for words because there was a definite delay before he said, "What's going on?"

"I just got out last week and thought I'd give you a call," I said, "I hadn't talked to you since July and I wanted to explain why I didn't make it up to Syracuse to help you with your DWI case."

"That's all over and done with Mark."

"I figured it was," I said, "How did you make out?"

"I got convicted and lost my license," He answered. "They didn't send me to jail but I got 5 years of probation."

I knew from my experience in the past that the sentence sounded about right. I really was surprised that he didn't do some jail time because he was a repeat offender.

"Les, I'm sorry," I apologized, "I really had it all planned to come up there. I even had the plane tickets bought and paid for."

"It's OK Mark," he said, "I'm not sure that your testimony would have helped anyway."

"Les," I asked, "I was wondering if Roxie has called you."

"No," He said. "I haven't heard from her. Why?"

I thought to myself what a lying son-of-bitch he was. Here's a guy that I did nothing but good things for; buying the Camaro, giving him money for his legal defense and paying my own way to try to help him at his trial. And this bastard is lying right to my face on the phone. I knew he had talked to her because Maggie wrote me about her being there. I knew that she found Les the most 'obnoxious' man she had ever met. The most logical thing was that maybe she was in Utica with her family and was trying to pick up more of my stuff from Les or something. Who knows? Maybe the fact that a garage sale was going on at his house was just happenstance. Who knows? Maybe it was just a simple case of mistaken identity.

"Well she has called just about everybody else in my phone book," I said, "She stole my phone and the only reason why I was able to call you is because I remembered your number."

"No," he continued, "I haven't heard a word from her. Where is she?"

"I have no idea," I told him, "I'm sure she went to South Carolina to be close to her son because she wrote a check out for the deposit."

"Are you trying to find her?" Les asked.

"Not right now," I said, "I just made bail and I can't leave the state until this shit comes to trial."

"So what are you going to do?" he said, "Where are you living?"

"I'm living at her house. I can't do anything until probably next year. It depends on what the court says. For now, I've just got to try to make a life down here."

"You mean she left and didn't turn the utilities off?" He asked.

"No, everything is off in the house, but my RV was parked in her driveway. It's very secluded and nobody is going to give me a second look about being there."

"Well I've got to go," He said. I could tell that he couldn't wait to get off the phone with me.

"Alright man, take care," I told him, "and I'll try to call again when I have more news."

I hung up and started to cry. This used to be my friend. And my friends I hold dear. How could he do this to me? How could she do this to me? I had lied when I told Les that I thought Roxie was in South Carolina because I didn't want anyone him to know that Maggie had tipped me off to the fact that she had been seen at his house. By flashlight, I read my bible and then crashed for the night. The RV offered comfort and security that I hadn't felt in quite some time.

But my mind didn't.

* * *

37) Investigations 1

Burkesville, KY—November 2009

The next week or so was pretty much routine. I spent a lot of time in the town of Burkesville for two reasons. My cell phone would work there and it wouldn't work at the house. I burned up countless minutes talking to friends and family. It was my only link with the real world because I didn't know anyone locally. But more importantly I stayed in town because emotionally, being at the house was just too hard on me. Not a night went by when I was at the house that I didn't break down and start crying. My feelings ran from heartache and missing Roxie, to intense rage and hate.

I forced myself to drive out there and pack what few items I had left. My heart wasn't in it and I kept thinking how I had done this once before; before I went to jail. If only I had left when I was going to originally, I could have avoided all of this hurt and loss. I also kept wondering why all this had happened to me. The closest I could come up with, was that the events brought me back closer to God. I found God again while I was in jail and I did spend a lot of time reading bible passages in attempt to understand.

I also thought that maybe the reason was to give the powers that be, ie: the authorities, another bite at the apple, in regards to Roxie and her various misconducts.

Because there were no witnesses to when Terry blew his brains out, they pretty much took her word for it. They ruled the incident suicide and in my heart, I knew that that wasn't true; not after hearing all her ramblings when she was drunk and her 'off the cuff' statements. So perhaps some good would come from this odyssey. Only time would tell.

One of the first things that I did was to go to the library and access my email account, so I could change the password on my personal accounts. It was a royal pain not having my laptop but I could usually find an open computer to use, to get done what I had to do. Once I opened my email account, I could tell from the dates in the mailbox that Roxie had accessed all of my mail and read it. The most interesting thing was that she went to the "Roxie" file that I kept and erased all the emails and pictures that I had of her. I guess she didn't want any evidence of our involvement. Maybe that is why she was so reluctant to let me take her picture and maybe that is why nobody else had ever filed charges against her. With no pictures available, it would be pretty hard to identify her; even on America's Most Wanted.

Next, I went to the bank where we had our joint account. I had them pull all the bank statements for the time that I was in jail. Boy, did Roxie have a good time. Not only did she forge my signature on a $ 200 check from my New York bank account and cash it locally, but she also accessed the account and drained all the money out of it via, wire transfer to our joint account. She did the same thing with my New York savings account. Once the money was in the joint account, she had legal access to all my funds.

She had gone on a little trip in July to see her son in South Carolina and had written a check from our joint account for a security deposit on a house; another $ 600 of my money gone. Plus she made multiple purchases using the ATM card and charged everything from gas to food. Naturally, there were several entries for purchases at a liquor store. In the end, the result was that she had grabbed me for $ 840 from my New York account and another $1,200 from our joint account. I had this severe throbbing going on and it wasn't coming from my dick.

Being in town allowed me to have contact with some of the locals and that was important to me because the local papers had painted me as some crazed Yankee who came down to their little town to deal drugs. I wanted them to get to meet the 'real' me. One person I saw regularly was the mechanic who had worked on my RV and my Camaro. His name was Marty Jerald. One day, I stopped into his station to get gas and got talking to him about Roxie. He knew, from the rumor mill, that I had been arrested and now I was out asking questions about Roxie.

"Did you get any more information on your girlfriend?" He asked.

"I don't know Marty," I said, "she wrote a check for a deposit on a house in South Carolina. I found it when I pulled the balance sheet from our account. I think she might have moved there to be closer to her son."

"I know the boy that dun moved her." He said.

"Moved her where?" I asked.

"Ah have no idea. His name is Carl Jessup and he works for the Chevy dealer in town." he continued, "but ah didn't tell you nuthin."

Now I was really confused. Maggie had told me that she was living at Les's house. But she wrote a check out for a house in South Carolina. A little more conversation revealed that she had hired this guy named Carl, by putting a call into the Swap Shop on the local radio station. I decided that I was going to investigate this matter further. I had to find out what part of South Carolina she went to, if that's where she ended up. I assumed that it was near where her son lived but maybe she just said that to throw everybody off. I just couldn't believe she was actually living with Les, because she found him so obnoxious. This might just be a ploy to throw everybody looking for her, off the trail. I got back in the RV and pulled out my "Camillus Police' shirt. I was going to make this whole investigation of mine look like it was official. I pulled out of the gas station and headed for the Chevy dealer.

I found Carl working in a back annex where he was detailing cars. I approached him and introduced myself. I made sure he could see the 'Police' logo on my shirt and I had a clipboard with me.

"Carl," I said, "I understand that you recently had contact with Ms. Roxie Patrick."

"Yeah I moved her stuff from her house," he said, "is there a problem?"

"Well, she is being investigated for a number of things," I said, "least of which is a case of forging names on bank checks."

"Man, all I did was answer her ad for a mover," He said. Carl was nervous and I could tell he thought that he was in trouble.

"Where did you meet her?" I questioned.

"Just from the ad on the radio," he said, "she gave me the address and I drove out to her house with 2 other guys. We loaded up the truck she had rented and I drove."

"That must have been what . . . a 7 or 8 hour trip?" I said, thinking that was how long it took to get to South Carolina.

"No," he said, "It was more like 15 or 16 hours and that was just with gas stops."

"Fifteen hours?" was my response. "Where did you drive to?"

"We went to New York." He answered.

New York, her home state, my home state' and it was turning out that she wrote the check out in South Carolina, to throw everybody off her trail. My first assumption was that she moved back to Utica where her family was. So maybe she was just using Les to dump the possessions she stole from me. If she had the garage sale in Syracuse and lived in Utica, nobody would be any wiser. I was sure that Carl wouldn't remember the address but he may know the city.

"Was it Utica, New York?" I queried.

"No, it was a town called Syracuse."

"You don't happen to remember the address do you?" I asked him.

"I didn't know the address," he said, "I just remember that we drove through the city. It was somewhere on the west side."

"Carl," I continued, "Did you put the stuff in a storage bin?"

"No," he said, "we delivered it to a house."

"Was this house a short distance off the expressway; a small white house; with an upper and a lower driveway?"

"That's the one," He confirmed. Carl had just perfectly described Les's house in Syracuse. It was a confirmation of what Maggie had written in her letter that I received in jail. That crazy bitch was living with Les.

"Am I in trouble?" Carl asked.

"No," I said, "she is but you aren't. You don't happen to have her number do you?"

"I have it at home," He said. "I don't have my cell phone with me but if you want to stop back tomorrow, or you can give me your number, I'll get it for you."

Carl and I talked for a while and I explained to him why she was being investigated. I asked him about the stuff they loaded into the truck. He said that she was very specific that everything except the stuff on the porch had to go. She had rented a trailer to tow behind the truck to carry her precious Datsun 280-z. She rented a car and she drove that while he and his helpers drove the truck.

"Did you see her put anything in the RV or take anything out?" I asked.

"No," he said, "the RV was just sitting there beside the house."

Carl went on to explain that they unloaded everything into Les's garage. He said that there was some squirrelly little guy there, supervising everything. That would have to be Les. I thanked Carl for his help and told him I would let him know what happens. I left and didn't know what to think of the whole thing. Here was my girlfriend, who stole all my stuff, now living with my ex-roommate; my ex-friend.

I needed a drink.

Carl called my cell phone about 20 minutes later and gave me Roxie's cell number. It was the same one that she had used when we went to New York. I kept a notebook and wrote down every piece of information that I received. I had no idea what I would do with it, but I had it just in case. I found other little tidbits of information. She had failed to pay her water and electric bill; she had put a note on her file at the phone company that they were not to discuss her whereabouts. The post office would not verify a change of address or not.

A number of people that I talked to told me that they had seen her in town in the RV. Still others told me that in August; she was seen all over town in my Camaro. The local minister that lived down the road from us said that he had seen her making 3 and 4 trips a day in the Camaro. I assumed that she was storing stuff locally but could never verify it.

Another little bit of information I found out was when I was packing up my stuff at the house. In her office space I found several pieces of papers with hand written notes. There were several phone numbers written down. I called one and was connected with a U-haul company in Tennessee. I wrote down their address and made a point of paying them a visit.

Another number was a number in South Carolina. In my rush, I called the number and received a voice mail to leave a message. Without thinking, I told them I was investigating Roxanne Patrick and I left my cell phone number.

I took a drive down across the Tennessee state line to the U-haul depot I had called. They verified that Roxie had rented a truck and trailer there in August. I couldn't believe it. That little snake deliberately rented out of state, just so that there would not be a local paper trail. I continued to amass information on Roxie. I found a picture of her on 'My Space' and copied it onto a disk. I didn't have any pictures of her and this one was not very good; but at least it was a start.

My call to the mystery number in South Carolina backfired on me. I got a call the next day from Ken out in Colorado. He told me that he got another call from Roxie.

"She said if you don't leave her family alone, she will testify against you." He said.

Apparently the number that I called was her son's cell phone. I was in such a rush for information that I failed to even try to verify the owner. Now I was screwed. I had left my cell phone number on his answering machine. That was not a good move on my part.

"Ken," I said, "I didn't know it was her son's phone or I wouldn't have called. I fucked up."

"You're right about that buddy," he said, "she sounded pissed."

"Well" I continued, "at least now I know who that number belongs to. I won't be calling that one again."

I found other things out too. She had sold her Toyota Tacoma to a bunch of Mexicans who loaded it on a flatbed and took it to Mexico. It had a blown motor so she probably didn't get as much out of it as she wanted. She sold the red Ford F-150 to a guy in Tennessee. I found the guy who notarized the sale. When I told him that the title was forged by her he almost shit. She sold the Avion trailer to someone else. She sold the sailboat on EBay. She sold the lumber in the back of the pole barn on the Swap Sheet. All of these things went into my file.

And the file was getting fatter.

* * *

38) The Landlady's Computer

Burkesville, KY—November 12, 2009

It was starting to get chilly at night in the RV. It was also inconvenient not being able to shower on a regular basis. I was worried about what I was going to do when the weather really changed and knew I had to find a permanent place to live. As fate would happen, I talked again to my ex-neighbor Ritchie. He told me that his sister-in-law Wendy was running a boarding house and looking for tenants. I had met Wendy once before and she seemed to be a very nice lady. I remember thinking that if I wasn't with Roxie, Wendy would be someone I'd be interested in.

I gave her a call and talked about her house. It was a large house that she was renting rooms out from. She gave me a figure of $ 175 month plus utilities. She had a computer and a phone I could use when she wasn't and I thought that this would be an ideal situation.

I met her at the house, reviewed the living space and made the deal on the spot. I met the other 'boarder' there at the same time. His name was Nick and he seemed like he was eyeing me up and down. I passed it off as just his concern for another person in the house.

Great! I thought. Now I have a place to live. I moved my stuff into the house that night, parking the RV in her expansive front yard. I spent the majority of my time just hanging out in my room. I had a TV that I could catch up on the local news and some 'entertainment' type shows. Wendy had a computer that I could use for the Internet and do research and the house phone had voice mail, so I could get messages.

Things were looking up. The computer was the real bonus in my life. It allowed me to search for information on Roxie. I 'Googled' her name and came up with a lot of information. She had been on blogs and she had a profile on My Space, Facebook, and My Life. I accessed each of these sites and signed up to look at her profiles. The Facebook profile yielded the most amount of information. She had friends and family members listed as contacts. The only way I could directly see her profile was to become a friend and I didn't want to do that. I didn't want her to know that I had computer access; at least not yet.

But I could access her profile through her contacts; kind of a back-door approach. Between that, and the other Google info searches, I found out that Roxie had no less than 10 aliases that she had been using. She would change small details like her middle initial or she would hyphenate her last name. But it was still her. My file on her grew until I had data going back 10 years. If she had known that I was getting all this information on her, she probably would have considered it 'stalking' and had me re-arrested. But I was smart enough to not do anything that would set off alarms. Whenever I was required to put in an email address or something, I would create a phony one in a different city, and use that.

There were pictures of her too and I download them. I put together a 'wanted' poster with the some of the information that I had gathered. The poster asked for information regarding her moving or storing items in the Burkesville area. I had 3 color pictures on the poster and I made reprints at the library so I could hang them up in public. I listed my cell phone number and placed the posters in a variety of stores, vending machines and bulletin boards around town;

I also put my own profile up on Facebook and did a search for any of her ex-husbands. I found two of them and I wrote them a message asking for any information on her. Both of them responded to me and told me that they had nothing but disdain for the woman. One of her ex's even told me that Roxie had threatened his life.

Through all of this information, I developed quite an evidence file on Roxanne Patrick. It was 4 pages of deeds that she had done, her drivers license number, her social security number, a list of people whom she had either worked for, screwed or been married to' or all of the above. My goal in all this was to get her arrested for the forgery which had been verified by the bank where we had the joint account, as well as filing charges for the theft of my property. I intended to make a trip to Syracuse and talk to the New York State Police because that is where she was living now.

Nick, the other tenant at the house turned out to be the landlady's boyfriend. He was an odd person and I determined that he was extremely jealous. He was always asking me personal questions that were none of his business. He told me that he had a laptop for sale if I was interested and I looked at it and agreed that it was worth the $ 50 dollars that he wanted for it. It was missing a couple of keys but I knew I could get that fixed. It was almost a clone of the one that Roxie had stolen from me. I bought the laptop and now realized that I could get a wireless connection and stay in my room all the time. I didn't need to come down to Wendy's space to use her computer.

With all that in place, and my portfolio on Roxie completed, I decided to make a trip to Syracuse and file the charges with the New York State Police. Even though I was free on bond, there were no restrictions on me, which meant that I was free to come and go as I pleased; as long as I made all my court dates. I called Enterprise and booked a car for the week of November 22nd. I never in my life thought I'd be driving to New York from Kentucky on my 61st birthday.

What a tangled web we weave.

* * *

39) Verifications Hurt

Syracuse, NY—November 22, 2009

I picked up the rental car at Enterprise in Glasgow on Sunday morning. Today I celebrated my birthday and above everything else, I wanted to be happy. I was fairly happy; at least not unhappy. I had money in my pocket, a place to live, a nice landlady, and I was going back home to Syracuse for a quick break. I wanted to visit some old friends and verify with my own eyes that Roxie was indeed living with Les. This was going to require a high level of 'stealth' on my part.

I had rented the car for the week and my time was my own. Wendy, my landlady, took me to the rental place and I told her I would be back for Thanksgiving dinner later this week. I wasn't sure how long a drive it was, but I estimated that I would get into Syracuse early on Monday morning.

I left Glasgow, Kentucky at 8:30 a.m. and got to the New York State Thruway by 9 p.m. that night. The Ford Focus had satellite radio so I was in my glory with the internet music and that I was making good time. I got off the Thruway at 11:45 p.m. on Sunday night. The trip had taken roughly 15 hours straight. The only thing I stopped for was gas and bathrooms. I couldn't believe what a difference it was from my last horrendous drive with Roxie, way back in May.

When I arrived, I went directly to Les's house to check and see if anything of mine was being stored in his garage. I parked the car on a side street and walked quietly up to the garage door window. All the lights in the house were off as I peered into the garage window. There inside sat the Datsun 280-z that Roxie had brought up on a trailer. But I saw no familiar boxes of any kind. I snuck around the outside of the house and looked into the cellar window. Again, there were no boxes. That told me that if she was living there, all of her and my goods were being stored elsewhere.

There were two cars in the upper driveway. One was Roxie's 96 Camry; complete with New York plates instead of Kentucky plates. The other was a 95 Honda. When I had left last year, Les owned 2 white Buicks. He must have sold them and bought a Honda, but I wondered why would he do that if he didn't have a driver's license?

I wrote down the plate numbers and left to go back to my car. The shit would hit the fan if someone saw me skulking around the house. Now I just had to figure out how I was going to truly verify that she was there. I went to the local Wal-Mart and bought a set of cheap binoculars. I didn't know what Les's work schedule was but figured that he would leave around 6 in the morning like he always had before. I set the alarm on my cell phone for 5 a.m. and curled up for a bit of sleep.

I woke at a little before 5 and drove to a Hess station to get coffee. I was tired from the long drive but exhilarated by being back. I finished my coffee and returned to Les's neighborhood and parked the car 2 blocks away from the house where I could watch for lights. At 5:15 the bathroom light came on and I knew it was probably Les, getting ready for work. I left the car where it was parked, took my new specs and walked down the street towards his house. Across from his driveway, a copse of evergreen trees offered excellent cover. I buried myself deep inside where I was not visible.

And I waited.

Even though it was still dark in the early morning dawn, I could see the front door where Les would be making his exit. At 6:15, the porch light came on and I knew it was . . . show time. Les came out of the house and with his signature trademark, his stogie; he got into his Honda and started it up. After letting it warm up for about 10 minutes, he proceeded to back out of the drive and go down the road. The porch light stayed on and I had no indication as to whether Roxie was in the house or not. I guess I was just going to have to do some serious surveillance. I killed time by going to the Target store and just sitting in the parking lot. I decided to periodically drive by the house, and I made sure that my Kentucky plate was not seen, by smearing mud on it to obscure the letters.

After several unsuccessful hours of half-assed surveillance, I cleaned off my plate and left for the State Police office to file my report with them.

"How can I help you?" the trooper asked me.

I told him the story of the theft and the forgery and that I was there because there were no branches for my New York bank in Kentucky. He looked at the file I had brought and went back to confer with his sergeant.

"I'm sorry Mr. Casey," the trooper told me, "We can't do anything here because the actual forgery and theft occurred in Kentucky. You have to file these charges there."

"I tried that but they told me that the bad check was drawn against a New York bank and I had to file here," I said. "I would have saved myself a trip if I could have filed down there."

"Well, I'll check with our District Attorney, but I think you need to file there, because that is where the crime occurred."

He returned shortly to tell me that, indeed, they could not help me. I was not pleased but couldn't do anything about it and would just have to press the issue when I got back. I thanked him for his time and asked him if I could leave my file of information for the record. He agreed to put it in their 'tip' file and I left.

About 12 noon, I took a ride back into the neighborhood. I now parked 6 blocks away at the end of the street. I had my Wal-Mart binoculars and I just sat there waiting for something to happen. I didn't have to wait long. Roxie came out of the house and let the dog out. She went over to her car and got something out and then went back in the house. About 15 minutes later, she came back out and took the dog in. It was the verification of Roxie's presence that I needed. But it wasn't good enough. I wanted a close view. I decided to repeat my surveillance one more day from my hiding place in the evergreens. I went through the same routine on Wednesday morning and decided that I would try to draw Roxie out of the house.

I went to the house again, this time earlier. I let the air out of one of the tires on the Honda and then once again planted myself safely hidden in the evergreens. At the same time that morning, Les came out of the house carrying the trash, which he placed in a refuse bin. Today was garbage pickup day in the neighborhood so he brought the bin to the roadside. He went to his car and started it, letting it warm up again and while that was happening, none other than Roxie brought more trash out. She was dressed in her bathrobe.

"Have you got your lunch sack Honey?" she asked Les.

When I heard that, I almost puked. This was a man that she despised, but to hear her patter, you would think that they were long time lovers. I knew that this was her next target, just as if Les had a bull's eye tattooed on his forehead.

Les acknowledged that he had his lunch and proceeded to drive down the road like before. He got about a half block away when he stopped and backed up.

"What's wrong?" Roxie asked him.

"I've got a flat tire."

"You're kidding," she uttered, "do you want me to take you to work?"

"I guess you better," he said, "I don't want to be late."

Roxie went into the house and came out with the keys to her Camry. She still had her bathrobe and a pair of flip-flops on. They got in her car and left, leaving the disabled Honda in the driveway. I knew that they would be gone at least 20 minutes and so I dashed across the street to try to see if any of the doors or windows of the house were unlocked. It was still dark so I didn't worry about anyone seeing me.

I tried the garage door and it was locked. That was a new wrinkle because when I lived there, the door opener was broken and you just had to lift the door to get in. Les must have had that fixed when Roxie moved in.

Next I tried the front door and that also was locked. Finally, I crawled up above the garage to try to gain access through the bedroom window. That entrance was buttoned down also. After about 10 minutes of trying various portals, I gave up. I went back to my car and got out of the neighborhood. I took up a vantage point 2 streets away so that I could judge how long a round trip ride to Les's worksite would take. Thirty four minutes later, Roxie came back and parked the car in the drive.

The next couple of days I had the opportunity get the keys replaced on my newly purchased laptop replaced, to visit my mother in the nursing home, my friends Maggie and Michelle, my friends Greg and Gary and finally, my ex-girlfriend Grace. That was the most difficult of all because we had a rift between us and I wanted to mend it. But Grace is one bull-headed lady. I finally talked her into meeting me for a drink.

"You look good," I said as she came in the door, "I like the blond hair."

Grace and I had been partners and lovers in the past but it sort of fell apart. When we were together, she knew of my penchant for red hair and one day, she just dyed it. Just for me.

"You look like you have lost weight," She said.

"Jail will do that to you," I said, "but that's not a bad thing. I was starting to bulk up last year. I guess I could have chosen a bit less radical method though."

We had an emotional conversation and I apologized for putting her through hell, even though she put me through hell also. I didn't mention that because I had gotten her to this point and didn't want to go wrecking a chance at re-establishing our once, good friendship. I brought my Roxie file with me and gave it to Grace to read. It was important for her to understand some of what I had gone through. When she finished she just sat there and looked at through sympathetic eyes.

"I'm sorry," she said, "I had no idea that you had gone through all this. I only heard that you were arrested for dealing drugs."

"As you can see," I said, "it was nothing like that. Besides, you know me; when have I ever dealt drugs?"

"That's what was so weird about it," she said, "it just didn't sound like you."

We had another couple of drinks and talked about some of our mutual friends, her family and my plans for the future.

"I have this court deal to go through," I said, "and when it's all over with, I am getting the hell out of Kentucky."

"Where are you going?" She asked.

"It will be anywhere but New York," I told her. "I'm close to Tennessee and you know I've always wanted to live there and try it. It's going to be rough after losing everything. I have to rebuild my life and my lifestyle."

When we left, I gave her a very passionate kiss; just like in the old days. Grace didn't resist.

I stayed in town another night and went back to Kentucky the next day; Thanksgiving Day. One of my contacts called to tell me that both license plate numbers were registered to Les. I had accomplished what I had set out to do. I verified that Roxie was living there. I verified the 280-Z was in the garage. I verified that my possessions were nowhere in sight. I got Roxie's dossier in the hands of the police, even if they would not take an official report. And I got to see my friends. The $ 250 I spent for the rental car and expenses was well worth it.

* * *

40) The Psycho Boy

Burkesville, KY—November 30, 2009

I got back to Kentucky about 10:30 on Thanksgiving night. It was a good trip. Wendy and Nick were both home when I got there. Wendy offered me a plate of turkey and fixings which I devoured. Nick, once again started with the questions. He had a deep Virginia accent and he was hard to understand if you didn't really listen.

"Hoz Neeyok," He asked.

"It was fine," I said, "for this time of year, it was quite warm."

"Ya'll dint stay va long," He remarked.

"No Nick," I said, "I just made a quick trip to get some things done."

"Wad ya'll hafta do?"

"Just tying up loose ends," I said starting to get annoyed, "I hadn't been there since last May."

I had been living at the rooming house since early November and had put up with this type of interrogation all the time from him. His jealousy annoyed me; He watched my every move, questioned everyone who called for me, and was a general pain in the ass. I told Wendy about his antics but because they were involved romantically, she didn't really do anything about it. I wanted a wireless Internet connection. So I just didn't have to ask Nick's permission to use the computer.

"You've got to give him a little latitude Mark," Wendy told me in private, "He is bi-polar and I don't think he has been taking his meds. He has his good and bad days."

"Wendy," I said, "If I would have known that I was sharing a house with your boyfriend, I never would have committed to moving in. Another tenant I can handle; but he is so jealous."

"I know, I know," she said, "I've told him that jealousy doesn't work with me and I'm trying to wean him of that habit."

"Wendy, you are much too nice of a person," I said, "I'm sorry but if this crap keeps up, I'm going to have to find another place to live. I don't want to, but I can't deal with him."

Another one of Nick's talents was to take my personal stash of food. I had a 12 pack of beer in the refrigerator and suddenly it was all gone. When I asked him about it, he said he took 2 but that was it. Here was a supposedly reformed alcoholic, and here he was sneaking beers when Wendy wasn't there. He also helped go through a large can of coffee I bought, that was in the kitchen. It was just little things like that, that caused me to take a dim view of Nick. I just didn't like him; and I like most people.

I got out of the kitchen after finishing my meal and went to my room to unpack, update my journal and finally, sleep. The next day, I ran errands and I was in and out all day. After a busy day I went home and tried to get on the computer, assuming Nick didn't have the door locked. It was and I had to wait until Wendy got home from work, to let me into 'their' space and get online. I couldn't use the laptop I had purchased from him because I didn't have a wireless card in the computer. One of my high priority goals was to go to Wal-Mart and get one, the next time I was in Glasgow.

During the next two days, Nick and I had a number of minor 'confrontations.' I grew angrier with his attempts to be a 'control freak'. If he wanted to control Wendy, that was her business. But that shit didn't fly with me; and I told him so. Nick stood about 6'3″, which was towering, when compared to my 5'5″ frame. But his height didn't bother me. I never ran away from a fight in my life and I wasn't going to start now; even though it had been at least 20 years since the last time I got into a fisticuffs match.

"Nick," I said, "I'm going to tell you one last time. Leave my food alone and keep out of my personal life."

"All ya damn Yankis is the same," he said, "Ya'll come down here thinking yoose betta then us sothen folk."

I refused to answer; just walked away and went upstairs away from the potential fray. On Saturday, Wendy had promised to take me back to return the rental car in Glasgow. Nick asked if he could go and Wendy told him that she was just going to run me up there and she would be right back.

"Nick," she said, "I'll be back in half an hour. He's just dropping of the car and I'm giving him a ride back. I'm not even going shopping."

One look at Nick's face said it all. He felt like I was taking his rightful place in the passenger seat of her truck.

Wendy and I took off and went up to Glasgow with Wendy following me in the truck. I turned in the keys, got my deposit back and came out to go back. The entire procedure took all of 5 minutes.

"You should call Nick and tell him that I didn't rob or rape you." I said.

"Oh, he'll be alright," she said, "We have an appointment with the psychiatrist next week. I didn't realize he wasn't taking his medicine; and getting into your beer didn't help either."

We got back to the house and I wanted to set up the wireless connection for my computer. I had already installed the router on her system so I just needed to plug in my wireless card and put the settings in my laptop for access. I went up to my room and turned on the laptop.

Nothing.

The computer just sat there. It would light up for 2 or 3 seconds and then shut off. The laptop had been working perfectly since I had bought it from Nick. Why all of a sudden was it not working now? I looked it over carefully and couldn't be sure, but I thought it looked like some kind of stain was on the keyboard. I knew it was nothing that I had done. I decided to have a professional look at it.

"I'm going into Burkesville," I announced to Wendy and Nick. "Does anybody need anything?"

They both said no and I took the laptop and crawled into my RV. While in Burkesville I wanted to pick up my mail and stop at the computer shop. I walked into the shop and spoke to Charlie Thompson, the owner. I explained to him that I had bought this laptop and it had been working perfectly; even as late as this morning. But when I turned it on now, it just sits there. Charlie checked it out and pulled out the memory chips.

"Here's your problem," he said, "it will never work with this gouge in the contact board."

I looked at the memory chip boards and both of them had a gash running the entire length of the contact strip. It looked as if something, or some one, had taken a knife and sliced the board so that it would not make contact.

"Somebody sabotaged this, my man," Charlie told me. "Who did you piss off?"

"Charlie, I know exactly who did it," I said, "and I've had enough of this crap."

I explained to him my situation in the boarding house and this psycho who lived there. I told him that I would like to get the laptop fixed but right now I had to save my money because I was going to have to move.

"We have a nice place here for rent," he said, "would you be interested?"

"I'd have to know more about it," I said, "but it's very possible."

We discussed it and I liked the idea. First of all, my cell phone would work here, where it didn't work where I was living. Second, I would be close to town for shopping, picking up my mail and any court dates that I might have and third, I would have a place all to myself; nobody else including psycho boy. I told him that I would let him know on Monday. I gave him $ 20 for his time and I left. I knew that somebody's ass was going to be grass and I was going to be a lawnmower. This case of sabotage was no accident. I know that it must have happened when I went to Glasgow with Wendy. That meant that Nick had been upstairs in my room. I wondered what else he had done in my absence.

I stopped at a convenience store and picked up a sandwich for dinner. Then I headed straight out to the house and took my laptop in with me. Wendy was sitting alone at the kitchen table.

"The gloves are coming off Wendy," I said, "I've had my fill of you boyfriend."

"What's the matter Mark?" She asked.

"That asshole sabotaged my computer," I replied. "He cut the contacts on the memory boards so that it won't work now. I'm trying to get my work done and the laptop would have meant that I didn't have to bother you to use your system. Now, I'm screwed. Not only did I pay him for it already, but now I have to put more money into it to get it fixed."

"I don't think Nick would do that," She said.

"Bull, Wendy," I retorted, "it was working fine this morning before we went to return the car. I turned it on when we got back and now it doesn't work. And the sabotage obvious—it's not like some kind of accident happened to it. This was deliberate. You tell that clown to steer clear of me or I will light him up like the 4th of July."

I stormed out of the kitchen and returned to my room. I hadn't talked to Charlie about rental prices but I had decided that I was going to move as long as rent was in my budget. Monday, I would go back down and try to work out a deal. For now, I just laid on they bed and watched television. It was all I could do, because the broken computer was putting a kink in my work routine and I would be damned if I would ask to use Wendy's. At about 7 p.m., I ventured downstairs to fix my sandwich and grab a soda out of the fridge.

From the other room I could hear Wendy say "Nick, don't."

I heard the door open and Nick came barging into the kitchen.

"I didn't' touch ya fucking computer, boy!" he ranted. "Ya gonna take that back or I gonna whip ya ass."

"Where are you going to get 10 men in a hurry?" I asked Nick, "because you sure as fuck are going to need them."

Wendy came out in the kitchen and tried to act as a barrier between the two of us.

"Now everybody, cool down," she said, "I don't want any fighting going on in my house."

"They ain't gonna be no fightin'," Nick said, "Ah'm jus gonna kick his ass a bit."

"Nick," I said, "if you attack me, seeing your shrink is going to be the least of you problems."

"Fuck you Yankee boy," he screamed.

With that statement, he charged me. Wendy stepped in between and pushed Nick back. I just stood there, waiting. I did not want to get into a fight because I knew the police would show up and it could possibly result in my arrest. If I got arrested, it was a certainty that they would pull my bond and I'd be sitting back in jail; whether I was wrong or right.

"If ah had my shotgun," Nick said, "ah'd blow ya brains out righcheer."

I didn't know if Wendy had any firearms in the house, but I was not about to take the chance. I walked over to the side door and exited the kitchen. This was not a good situation because this nutcase was probably serious. I walked around him and Wendy and slipped inside the living room. There on the table was the portable phone. I grabbed it and went outside. I called the Kentucky State Police. If there were going to be any problems, I wanted them to be there, before the shit hit the fan.

I reported that Nick was a mental patient who wasn't taking his medication and he had threatened my life. The dispatcher took down the address and told me it would be about 20 minutes, because the closest car was on another call. Twenty minutes later, two KSP patrol cars showed up. I walked out to meet them and told them that I was the one who called.

"Are you the owner of the residence?" one of them asked.

"No Sir, I'm a boarder here," I said, "and the other guy is also a boarder."

Wendy came out and talked to the troopers. She told them that Nick was a boarder and he was bi-polar and hadn't been taking his medication. She let them know that I claimed Nick had wrecked my computer but she could not attest to that, because she didn't see him do anything. Two troopers went inside to interview Nick and two stayed on the front porch with me. They asked me for identification which I gave them, and then one of them asked me if I had ever been in trouble with the law in Kentucky.

"I've had nothing but trouble since I've been in Kentucky." I answered.

I told them the whole story of Roxie and the drug bust and jail and being bailed out.

"I thought you looked familiar," one of the troopers said. "I was at the house the night of your arrest."

"Then you know what I've been going through," I said, "and I've just moved in here after getting out of jail on October 30th."

"Are there any drugs in this house?" He asked.

"Officer," I said "Whatever drugs you found where I used to live before, were planted there by my ex . . . and NO, there are no drugs here . . . I don't do drugs."

The other two troopers came out of the house and went over to talk to Wendy. It seemed that since there was no actual fight, they weren't going to do anything. But they recommended that the two of us keep a wide distance between us, because if they had to come back tonight, everybody was going to jail. And that was it. I considered this just another extraordinary example of the superb law enforcement by the KSP.

What ever happened to 'protect and serve?'

* * *

41) There's a Trial Coming

Burkesville, KY—December 10, 2009

After that near scare over the weekend, I was more determined than ever to get moved out of the boarding house, to somewhere in Burkesville. On Monday, I went to see Charlie at the computer shop again. I told him that I was interested in the place he had to offer.

"It's a one bedroom house Mark," He said. "You pay the utilities yourself in addition to the rent. I can give you the place for $ 175 per month but you will have to set up accounts with the electric and water companies."

He told me that I couldn't move in right away because it had been vacant for over 6 years and he had to repair a few things first. We walked up and took a look at it. It was small and compact but I liked it. I definitely wasn't the Ritz Hotel but for what I needed and for the price, it would serve me well. I wondered when I would be able to move in, since I wanted to get away from Psycho Boy.

"How much time do you need to get it ready?"

"Give me a week and a half to finish everything," he said, "I need to check out the piping, sewers, and the electrical to make the repairs that I know it needs. You should be able to move in by December 10th or 11th I think."

I told Charlie that was perfect for me. That would close out 1 month exactly at Wendy's house and I wouldn't have to pay her again. Plus, I had a court date scheduled for December 10th and I didn't know what was going to happen then. They could dismiss my case, set a trial date or find new charges and throw me back in jail. Saturday December 12th, seemed to be a perfect day to move. While I was there, I discussed buying a computer from him. I already had a monitor and a keyboard. All I needed was the PC itself and a mouse; but it had to be Internet ready.

"I've got one that's Internet ready I can let you have for $ 100. If you're strapped for cash, I would be willing to take payments for it. I can also give you the network key for our wireless router so you won't have to pay for an Internet connection."

Having free Internet was a bonus. Paying for access was an expense that I didn't want, but I needed to be able to get on the net in order to sell items on EBay and to continue to do my research. With the offer for free wireless, things were suddenly heading in the right direction again. I had a new place, a computer, and my cell phone would work here. In the blink of an eye, it looked like I was back in contact with the world again. I could feel the hand of God moving in the background; putting me in touch with the right people. Now all I had to do was keep my nose clean and ride out the legal hassles.

For the next week or so, I was like a mouse hiding in my room. Each day I went to the convenience store and got my sandwich and a cup of coffee. I sat there and jawed with the locals and sometimes told them my tales about Roxie, jail, or the lawsuit. They seemed to take my side in the matter and were friendly to me. This was one of the locations where I put up one of my 'wanted posters' in an effort to get a lead on any place she may have used to store items. If anyone knew anything, they weren't telling. Afterwards, I would return home to the boarding house and either watch TV or read.

In talking with the people, one of the clerks at the convenience store remembered Roxie coming in the store in the past. She told me that most of the locals shied away from her because they thought she was 'weird'.

"She came in one day and wanted someone to bale up her hay," the girl told me. "Nobody would do it because they thought she would accuse them of rape or sumthin."

"How did they get that idea?" I asked.

"I gess she had dealins with one of the local boys," she continued, "and came on to him. He was a married man and he told her no. She said that iffen he didn't' screw her, she would holler rape."

"That sounds like something she would do," I told her, "What happened?"

"I gess he went to his truck and brung out his daddy's shotgun," She said. "He tole her if she tole any lies about him, that rape was the last thin she would be sayin. Then he left. He neva herd no more bout it."

I filed that story away in my memory and continued to prod her for any more information she might have. She told me that everybody thought the 'suicide' was suspicious because they knew Terry and he didn't seem crazy; unless you counted living with her. I went home that night and approached Wendy in the kitchen. I gave her my notice that I would be leaving on December 12th and she understood my decision. I was glad that there were no hard feelings between us.

December 9th, the day before I had to go to court, I went out to the RV and it would not start. No matter what I did, it just whirred but would not catch. I was frantic. How the hell was I going to get to court by 9 a.m. the next morning with no vehicle? I was at least 14 miles from town. As fortune would have it, Wendy had a doctor's appointment the next morning and her and Nick were going into town at 8 a.m. The only snag was that I would have to ride in the back of her pickup truck because I wasn't about to squeeze in the cab with Nick. I must have looked like a real moron the next morning, dressed in a suit with my coat over my head, riding in 25 degree weather in the back of the pickup. But desperate people do desperate things. I made it to court on time and met my lawyer, Brian, in the entranceway. I asked him what he thought was going to happen today.

"I believe they are going to set a trial date," he said, "but don't worry. You just stand there and I'll do the talking."

Sure enough, the judge asked the Commonwealth Attorney what his intentions were.

"We are prepared to go to trial, your honor." He answered.

The judge addressed my attorney and asked, "Does defense have any objections?"

"No your honor," my lawyer answered.

"Then I will set trial in the case of Commonwealth of Kentucky vs. Mark Casey, for March 2, 2010 at 9 a.m."

Five minutes; that's all it took. Five minutes; and another turning point in my life is marked on a calendar. I always thought from day one that this case would be dismissed by now because Roxie was no longer here and they really didn't have any hard evidence against me. But in five minutes, the decision was made to put me in front of a jury of my peers and make me prove my innocence.

No longer was it 'innocent until proven guilty'. This Commonwealth Attorney wanted my head. We left and I told Brian that I had rented a new place in town. As soon as I got settled, I would give him the contact information. I let him know that I still had my cell phone if he needed me. He told me that I may have to come to his office before the trial starts to go through his defense strategy but he also added "unless they decide to dismiss the case."

Either way, I had approximately 90 days to hurry up and wait.

* * *

42) Moving Day

Burkesville, KY—December 12, 2009

I walked to the computer shop after court that day, to find out when I could move in. Charlie was still working on the plumbing and he complained that because the place had been vacant for so long, he practically had to rebuild everything.

"The pipes were a mess," he said, "I've been replacing everything and it's taken me 3 days to get to this point. But I'm almost done. You should be able to move in on Saturday."

I thought that was great because I was getting pretty sick of spending all my money on gas for the RV. At 7 miles per gallon, it didn't take me long to drain my wallet. I still had to figure out why it wouldn't start. I called my friend Bart, the Sheriff I met when I was in the hospital. He had told me that he worked on RV's in the past and maybe he could help me. He said the problem sounded like a starter and he could come out in the afternoon to check it out.

I told him I was in town and asked if he could also give me a ride. He agreed to pick me up at 1 p.m. at the local convenience store. So I just walked there, dressed in my suit, and drank coffee for 2 hours. Bart showed up and came in for coffee.

"What happened?" he asked, "it was running fine the last time I saw you."

"I don't know," I said. "I got in yesterday and it just wouldn't start. I think you're right about the starter being bad. I was thinking we'd pick one up here and then we won't have to come back."

"Well," he said, "it could be the solenoid or anything electrical."

"If it's not the starter," I said, "I can always bring it back."

"OK, let's pick one up and see what we can do."

I went to NAPA and got a starter and we headed out to the boarding house. I told him about my near miss at getting to court and how lucky I was to catch a ride with Wendy. When we got there, Bart poked around and found it was the starter indeed. It took him all of a half hour to replace it and get the RV running.

"What's the damage, doctor?" I asked him.

"Why don't we make it $ 30," He said.

"How about $ 40," I told him as I handed him 2 twenties, "I appreciate the help."

We talked for a while and he told me that he had quit the Sheriff's department. He said that they kept cutting his hours and he had decided to go back on the road as a trucker.

"I can make $ 600 a week driving," he estimated, "and so why would I work for $ 8.25 an hour at the Sheriffs Department?"

I couldn't believe that $ 8.25 an hour was all that the deputies made. Granted, some of them weren't worth much more than that but really, that was nothing for putting you life on the line. Bart picked up his tools and told me to give him a call if I needed anything else. When he left, I went into the house and went upstairs to my room to pack. I grabbed all my meager possessions and loaded them into the RV. Since it was late in the afternoon, I decided to stay at the boarding house one more day and leave tomorrow. But at least I was locked and loaded.

The next day, I picked up my remaining clothes, dropped off the keys and drove into Burkesville to shop for a few items, then I stopped by the computer shop and picked up the keys from Charlie.

"You're all set Mark," he said, "I checked everything out and you're in good shape."

"What about my computer?" I asked.

"Its right here," as he handed me the PC. "I installed the network and logged into the wireless signal and you're ready to go."

"Fantastic," I said, "now I can finally get some work done."

I took the keys and the computer out to the RV and drove up to the house. I lived about 100 feet behind the computer shop and off the main road. It was nice and quiet here and I just knew I was going to enjoy this. I unloaded everything into the house and the first thing I did was to set the computer system up. The PC came on with the familiar Microsoft logo and a few minutes later, the signal bar for the wireless came on. I clicked the Explorer shortcut and just like that, I was on the Internet. FREE. I liked that.

As a matter of fact, free is my second favorite 4 letter "F" word.

* * *

43) Investigations 2

Burkesville, KY—December 2009

Being in my own residence was a boon to doing research. I had the Internet available 24/7; and any time I wanted. I could just point and click. There was no asking for permission; no having to write down a list of topics to look up and no waiting. If I woke up in the middle of the night with some wild idea, the answer was as close as my computer in the living room. I also kept doing research on Roxie by using the computer. Since she had been selling items on EBay when I met her, it seemed that would be a natural place to start. I pulled up her user name and looked for recent transactions. There was nothing since early August. Either she had changed profile names or she was not doing any selling through the auction site.

The next place I visited was the Syracuse.com website. The only listing here was for the garage sale that she had back in October. This listing had expired and I could not read anything but the header for it. I really wanted to see if she had listed any of my things but the expired listing was basically worthless.

Then I went to Craigs List in Syracuse. In the search box, I typed her cell phone number. There were no listings. Then I tried Les's address; again no listing. Finally I put in Les's home telephone number.

BINGO.

I found two listings under 'resume', one under 'items wanted' and two in the community section. I looked at each. She had a resume for a Certified Nursing Assistant. I laughed when I read how she had 10 years of giving 'tender care' especially to the aged. The other resume was for a part time position as a cook. Now that's a stretch; either a cook or a nurse. Knowing her as I did, I wouldn't want her for either one.

Under the 'items wanted' she was looking for a portable dishwasher. I knew Les didn't have a dishwasher at his house and it also confirmed my suspicions that Les had been bullshitting me about selling his house, which he told me the last time I talked to him.

I spent some time working on my profile at Facebook. I made sure that only friends were able to access the full site. Anyone else only got what I wanted them to get. The side benefit of all this was that I made contact with many people whom I hadn't talked to in years. Old friends from high school, old lovers, and people I had worked with. One of those people was my friend Donny "Eel" Tassone, a friend of mine that I hadn't talked to or seen in over 10 years.

I had always liked Donny and being of Italian decent I knew that he had connections with people of questionable nature. Donnie was a great guy but he wasn't one to pass up a chance to make a buck or get involved in something shady. That didn't bother me because we had been friends, but never what you would call 'boozing buddies.' I sent Donnie an email message telling him that I was now living in Kentucky. I was pretty sure he would respond if he accessed Facebook on a regular basis.

I did more research using Google, Public Records Search, Craigs List, Local Sales Network and anything else I could think of. Using my 'back door' approach, I found blogs and other listings that Roxie had put up in the past. Many of them she probably had forgotten about. I found that she was listed as a realtor at a local real estate office. I knew she had her

New York license but never realized that she would actually have the nerve to list herself where the world could find her, including me. But here she was, complete with picture supposedly working only a half mile from Les's house. How convenient.

I also searched anything relative to Les. I found property records for his house, his not-so-ex-wife to whom he was still married, newspaper articles about a couple of his DWI arrests, but nothing about his house being listed or anything else of importance.

While I was sitting doing research, the messenger popped up on my screen. It was an email from my friend Donnie. He said he couldn't believe he heard from me after all these years.

He gave me his phone number and told me to call him. I did that immediately.

"Donnie," I said, "long time bud, what's up?"

"Mark you old dog," He said. I could visualize the smile on his face.

"Where the hell have you been man?" he continued, "I thought you fell of the face of the earth. Nobody has heard anything about you since the old days."

"I fell in love with a Kentucky woman, Donnie," I said. "I moved down here with her in May and it was only then, that I found out I was in the middle of a Black Widow's nest."

"A Black Widow?" he remarked, "You mean like the spider?"

"Yeah," I said, "you know they kill and eat their mates."

"What happened?"

I explained in morbid detail the whole situation, including the jail time, putting my car up for bond and the upcoming court thing. Donnie was genuinely concerned because he knew that I was a pretty straight shooter and the only trouble I had ever had with the law was the DWI arrests years ago.

"Anything I can do man?" He asked, "I have people who can help you if you need it."

"Thanks for the offer Dono," I said, "but right now, I'm taking a wait-and-see attitude. I'm trying to get the bitch arrested for the forgery and grand theft. But if that doesn't work, I may be calling you."

"You know I'm there for you man," he said, "don't hesitate. I love doing things for my friends."

We talked a bit more and promised to keep in touch. I told him I liked his Facebook profile and it was quite a change from when he was managing a strip club. We said our goodbyes and I hung up. I thought about it for a while and decided that I may need to call Donnie in the future for some help. The only problem I had would be the cost and it put me a bit closer to that 'subversive' element than I really wanted to be.

I had amassed a very large file of data on Roxie. Since the New York State police would not do anything, I decided that I would have to go at her by pushing the Kentucky buttons. I knew that dealing with the locals was out of the question. For starters, I presumed that she had been having an affair with 'at least' one Sheriff and possible more, based on what she told me and what I surmised. Everybody down here seemed to be part of some sort of good 'ol boy club, where they cover each other's assess. My best chance of success seemed to be to push it with the Kentucky State Police. If they were anything like New York, they had a very professional and 'no bullshit' attitude. The only problem with that idea was that the last few times I called them, once when I was in jail trying to recover my car, once when I tried to give them information about the alleged 'suicide' of Terry and the time when I got into the altercation with Psycho Boy, they didn't do shit.

I put together a summary of the file I had developed for the New York State Police. I had all the pertinent events concerning Roxie, going back over 10 years. I listed the mysterious death of her daughter and son-in-law, the mysterious explosion of her trailer, the deportation of her ex-husband, the death of Terry Jacoby and how she was conveniently the executrix of his estate, the forgery of her ex-husbands vehicle titles, the forgery of my checks and the theft of my goods.

I noted that after each incident, she had left the locale and relocated; just like she did with me. I sent an inventory of my missing possessions, copies of the banks records concerning the forgery and anything else that I thought would be of use. I even retold the story of how she made mention that 'a lot can happen with thread'.

On the last page, I listed all the people whom I had spoken to about Roxie. I had their name, phone number address and what information they had given me. I put this together in a letter and mailed copies to the County Attorney and to the Kentucky State Police. My goal was to get her arrested for the forgery but a secondary reason was to possibly re-open the suicide case in which she was involved. Unbelievably, nothing happened. Everyone I approached with the file and my story looked at me like I was making this entire thing up.

The County Attorney told me that because we were living together, all of the property that I lost was community property, and therefore no crime was committed. As far as the forged check; I would have to take that up with the bank that it was drawn on. She just wouldn't do anything including return my phone calls after a while. She just ignored me like I was a piece of litter by the side of the road.

The Kentucky State Police told me that they thought my complaint was 'retaliatory'.

"We believe Mr. Casey," the trooper said "that you are just filing this complaint because your ex-girlfriend filed charges against you. We will not invest any time in this."

This was the Fourth time that the Kentucky State Police, in my estimation, had been derelict in their duty. They had more valid information in my letter than they ever had in the original investigation of the suicide. And they did absolutely nothing. It looked like I was going to have to take charge and change the rules of the game.

I sent a letter to the Commonwealth Attorney; the very man that prosecuted me. He at least sent me back a letter saying that even if he believed my story, because of the cost of extraditing Roxie from New York, it was not anything they would be interested in pursuing.

When I wrote to the Attorney General of Kentucky and complained that nothing was being done, he sent back a letter saying that it was a local matter and I had to resolve it here. I had to find some lever to force them to do something. All of these public officials took an oath that they would uphold the law, but it was like my first attorney had stated when he asked if Roxie had a 'golden pussy.' Was it possible that she had sexual relations with a multitude of these public officials? Or was it the fact that these people were just so lazy that they didn't want to do any more work than they had to.

After thinking about it, I came to the conclusion that they just didn't want her back in Kentucky again and would do anything to help me get her here. I needed some lever and I needed it fast.

But Kentucky didn't seem to have any 'Levers R Us' stores.

* * *

44) A Surprise Court Date

Burkesville, KY—January 28, 2010

The gas mileage on the RV was killing me, even though I lived close to everything in town. I decided that I would do a little TLC on the RV and sell it. I advertised it locally and also on EBay. I was looking to get about $4,000 out of it but any reasonable offer would do.

I must have driven to meet 10 or 15 people to show them the RV because the bids on EBay were moving slow. Everybody seemed to like the RV but nobody really made me any kind of offer. One guy told me that he had just bought a similar unit at a local auction for $1,000. That didn't set well with me because I had paid $1,750 for it and put another $1,000 into it when I went on my trip to Tennessee.

There was one day left on the auction and the highest bid I had was only $2,800. I hadn't put a reserve on my price so it was looking like I was going to get less than my target price. My landlord was looking to buy a truck and he offered me his Oldsmobile for $1,000. I thought about it and it would be an acceptable deal, because the Olds was a great car and I knew that the gas mileage had to be better than 6 or 7 mpg. I had already made one trip up to my lawyer's office in Greensburg which was 60 miles away and that alone took about $ 75 in gas, so I was motivated.

The auction closed and the final bid was $2875. It was purchase by a guy in Oregon. He paid the money in full and sent me an email asking what I would charge to deliver it to him. I knew I couldn't do that because of my time and legal restraints so he said that if I would send him the title, he would take care of getting it transported.

I went down to the county offices and had the vehicle inspected, signed over the title and mailed it off to him. With the $2875 that was in my bank, minus the selling fees for EBay, I had enough to buy the Oldsmobile and put a little cash in my pocket. I was a happy ex-camper.

The next day, as I was sitting at my computer in my new home, I looked down at my cell phone and noticed that I had a voice mail waiting. I didn't ever hear the phone ring so I looked to see when the call came in. It was from my ex-landlady Wendy and she had called about a half an hour ago. Right at the time, I was busy putting together a list of items that I wanted to sell and get out of my storage bin. So I put off calling her for another 15 minutes. It was the first time she had called me since I moved out and I figured that she just wanted to say 'Hi'. I got done with my project and returned her call. No one answered her home phone so I dialed her cell number.

"Hello," her lovely voice answered.

"Hi Wendy, its Mark," I said.

"Hi Mark," she answered, "I got a message on my house answering machine for you. Did you know that you have to be in court tomorrow?"

"No," I said, "that's news to me. Who was it that called?"

"I don't know if it was your lawyer or the court." she said, "but whoever called just left the message that you are supposed be in court tomorrow at 9 a.m."

I thanked her for the message and asked her how everything was going. She told me that Psycho Boy had moved out and she was trying to find another boarder. We chatted for a while and then I decided to call my lawyer. Brian's receptionist told me that he was unavailable until I told her who I was.

"Oh," she said, "let me get him on the line."

"Mr. Casey," Brian's voice boomed, "we have to be in Cumberland County court tomorrow morning. Is that going to be a problem?"

"No, Brian," I answered, "what is this for . . . . dismissal?"

"No," he said, "it's some kind of motion the prosecutor wants to present. It shouldn't take us too long. They want to look at your medical records."

"What the hell for?" I asked him.

"I have no idea," He told me. "Do you have any objection?"

"No, I don't' care," I said "but I really was hoping for a dismissal."

The next morning, I met Brian at the courtroom. We waited for about 5 minutes for the judge to call us to the podium and the prosecutor presented his request for medical records; not mine, but Roxies'. Brian told them there was no objection and the clerk noted it.

And we were done.

Brian told me to wait outside for him, which I did. He came out of the courtroom after talking to the prosecutor. I asked him why they needed my OK to get her medical records.

"Apparently," he said, "they tried to find Roxie and they can't. They want her medical records to see what treatment she got the night of your arrest. The already got your records. They were looking to see if you have a history of mental illness or drug and alcohol use."

"It looks like they are going to get another flat tire," I told Brian. "My records are clean."

"Well," he said, "if they can't find her to testify and your records are clean . . . . they're going to have to dismiss the charges."

"Brian," I said, "I figured that was what would happen anyway. They have nothing and I know that she won't be coming down here to testify because she thinks there are warrants out for her."

"Well," he said, "that's a good thing. They will have to drop everything against you."

"Are they going to wait until the last minute to do that?" I asked.

"No," he answered, "They will probably do it between the 15th of February and the end of the month."

Even though I knew exactly where Roxie was living, I wasn't going to tell anyone because I didn't want them to think I was stalking her. I also believed that if there was no accuser, they would have to drop all the charges. We talked for a while and I gave him my new contact information at the house. I told him that I was selling the RV and would give him some more money the next time I saw him. He took off and went back to his office and I went about my business in town. A dismissal would be nice but I wouldn't mind having Roxie show up either. I'm sure if she was in still in Kentucky, there would be charges placed against her. I was also sure that it was for that very reason, they couldn't find her.

She didn't want to be found; but I sure knew where to look.

* * *

45) The Cat Burglar

Somewhere in Time—February 22, 2010

I continued doing research on Roxie, handling my day-to-day routine and generally staying out of trouble. My Internet access was not bound by time constraints and I would sometimes wake up in the middle of the night with an idea or a place to search for information or another resource. If I was shackled with having to wait until the library opened in order to follow up, there is a very good chance that I would forget all the details that I wanted.

But now, I had my PC in the next room. I could just get up and go look up what I wanted while the idea was still fresh in my mind. Needless to say, there were nights when I didn't get any sleep at all because I sat at the computer pounding keys. I would sometimes stay up until the wee hours or until I couldn't keep my eyes open. I remember one such night, where I fell asleep at the computer. I woke up and I was not at home, but back in Syracuse, dressed in an all Black outfit and hidden in my lookout within the trees, across from Les's house.

At the same time up in Syracuse, different things were going on. Within a small copse of trees on a quiet street, the Cat Burglar had donned his winter coat and a pullover cap. Both would serve as a shield from the icy blasts of Syracuse weather. He checked the pouch that I carried, to make sure he had everything with him that he needed.

"Let's see," his mind said as he took inventory. "Glass cutter, duct tape, clear tape, pliers, sap, a small can of black spray paint, a Pepper spray canister, rope, steel wool on a wooden stick, a pint of Jack Daniels liquor, pills and a hand made electrical hookup. "Yep, got everything."

He checked his watch and it read 4:45 a.m. There were no lights on in the bathroom window but he knew from the past that his first target would soon be getting up for work. He slipped out of his hiding place and scurried across the roadway to the vehicles parked in the driveway. The first thing he did, under cover of darkness, was to insert a valve stem puller into one of the vehicles parked in the driveway. The air rushed out and soon the tire was as flat as the surface of a frozen lake. He replaced the valve stem and the cap, and to an outside observer, the flat tire was barely noticeable in the early morning darkness.

Now it was time to hide again, back within the copse of evergreens across from the house. Even if a car were to drive by, he couldn't be seen, because he was dressed all in black and blended in with the dark branches of the trees. The only thing that could have perceived him would be a dog, with an acute sense of smell. Very soon, the house came alive with lights in the kitchen and bathroom areas. It looked like Target # 1 was getting ready to go to work.

It was now 5:40 a.m. Syracuse time, and everyone was still inside the house. He felt a slight tinge of nervousness as he watched the house, waiting for something to happen. Snow that had fallen off the trees where he was hiding could betray this location. But then again, he knew that his primary target wasn't the most observant person in the world.

The front porch light came on which signaled that it was show time again. His first Target came out of the house and went directly to his Jeep. He had his trademark stogie in his mouth and it was hard to tell whether the cloud coming out of his mouth was from the cigar or because of the coldness of the air. He started the Jeep and sat while it warmed up. The Cat Burglar checked his watch and it read 5:52 a.m. He mused to himself that everything was running perfectly on schedule.

Five minutes later and the Jeep was nice and warm. The first Target backed out of the driveway and proceeded down the street on his way to work. Any minute now, he should be stopping to inspect his tires. As the Cat Burglar watched, he thought to himself,

I never imagined myself as a cat burglar; But then again, he wasn't really here to burgle.

The Jeep stopped in the middle of the block. The target got out and looked at his tire and then got back into his vehicle. Slowly he backed up and into his driveway. The only sound heard, as he returned to his house, was the distinct utterance "Son of a bitch."

The Cat Burglar watched as Target #1 entered the house. He remained inside for 5 minutes. Soon afterward, the porch light came back on and both Target #1 and Target #2 emerged from the house. Target #1 had his standard work clothes on and Target #2 had a sweatshirt and pants. They headed straight for a Toyota Camry, parked alongside the disabled Jeep. Target #1 paused briefly while getting into the car, to take a look around and re-light his cigar. In another 5 minutes, the car was warm and they left the driveway; presumably on the way to the first target's employer. Now was the time for the self proclaimed 'Cat Burglar' to make his move.

He sprung across the street in the darkness of the morning towards the house. His point of entry was easy to get to by standing on the roof of the garage. He made his way up to the window that he wanted to open and pulled out the glass cutter. Lifting the unlatched screen, he scribed a small semi-circle in the glass, just outside the window latch.

With the back side of the cutter, He gently tapped where he had cut and the glass broke, right along the line. He reached in with 2 fingers and moved the window latch to the open position, then removed the clear tape from his pouch. Placing it on the edge of the window, he ran a piece of tape across to the other edge in order to seal the hole in the window that he had just made. Gripping the edge, he lifted the window high enough to gain entrance.

He had made it into the house. He was in the bedroom of the house to be exact, and now he had to patch his entry point. With the same precision, he closed the window tight, secured the latch and ran another clear piece of tape from edge to edge on the inside. He wasn't worried about anyone seeing it immediately because the blinds would hide the tape from view. The reason for the tape was to seal out winter drafts that would be a dead giveaway someone had been in the house.

The first item on the agenda was a thorough search. In the bedroom closet he found mainly men's clothing and a few dresses. Behind the dresses was a safe with an electronic combination lock. Shoes scattered the floor of the closet and on a rack, 2 pair of ladies shoes. He opened the dresser, one drawer at a time and assessed the contents. What he found was T-shirts, underwear, socks, a bottle of English Leather, 2 pair of panties, lipstick and a vibrator.

That figures, he thought as I closed the last drawer. "I wouldn't expect anything less."

In the living room there was a 42″ flat screen TV, couch, end tables and a comfy chair. Everything looked familiar to this location except the 42″ TV. That item looked familiar from another location; a location in Kentucky. He stopped in the dining room and peered at the portable phone on the wall. He removed the receiver and pulled the back cover off to remove the battery and then replaced the assembled phone back in its hanger and pocketed the battery.

In the kitchen, mounted on the wall, was a key holder with several sets of keys hanging there. Every set went into the pouch hanging at his waist. Opening the kitchen drawers, he found an assortment of new silverware and cutting utensils.

These are new, he thought. I wonder where they came from.

He went downstairs to the cellar through a door in the bathroom. It too looked familiar. He searched around and found nothing out of the ordinary, so he opened the door leading to the garage; and there it was; parked, filthy and having a flat tire. This was part of the reason that he was here. This was a fairly rare Datsun sports car; a 280-z in fact, with an automatic transmission. Now, all he had to do was find the title. He went over and made sure that the overhead door of the garage was unlocked.

He came back in from the garage and began to make preparations for his plan. There was a tall file cabinet standing there in the cellar. He removed the portable telephone from its cradle on top of the cabinet and placed it in the bottom drawer. Then he opened up the top drawer and began to look through the folders. With a bit of luck, the title to the Datsun would be located in here and his job would be that much easier. After going through every drawer, he finally surmised that he would have no such luck.

There was a steel support pole in the cellar that would be perfect for what he had planned. He placed a chair next to it and then went to the cellar window. With a can of black spray paint, he completely covered the glass to make the window opaque from the outside. He then went back upstairs to the kitchen. On the counter was a stack of papers lined up in a rack like soldiers. He found the water bill, the phone bill, a bank statement and a title; not the title to the Datsun, but to the Jeep that was parked outside; the one with the flat tire.

This will be a good bargaining chip, he thought, as he pocketed the title in his pouch.

He went back downstairs and found an electrical socket near the chair that he had placed next to the steel pole. From his pouch, he pulled out a hand made connection. It had a line plug on one end, a regular 100 watt bulb and socket on one of the lines with an alligator clip and another alligator clip on the other end of the line. One of the alligator clips would connect to a probe with steel wool on the end of it.

Now it's time to test it.

He plugged it into the wall and touched the 2 alligator clips together. The light bulb lit. He unplugged his little invention and replaced it in the pouch. He didn't know if he was going to have to use it, but knowing that it was in working condition was important to the plan.

He decided that the best place to wait would be in the upstairs shower, with the curtain drawn. The bathroom was bounded on one side by the kitchen and a door on the other side that led down to the cellar. The plan was that when his target, Target # 2 returned to the house, she would probably come through the bathroom to go downstairs. At most, I would only have to wait 30 minutes before that happened. The bathroom is where he would confront her. No need to worry about Target # 1 because he would be at work. The Cat Burglar slipped into the tub and pulled the shower curtain closed.

"Well," he thought, "I'm all set. Now it's just, hurry up and wait."

* * *

46) Mr. "Not So Nice" Guy

Somewhere in Time—February 22, 2009

A car pulled into the driveway outside the bathroom window. It was time. There was a jingle as the key was inserted into the lock and the kitchen door opened, then the slam of the door. Movements in the kitchen and it sounded like the target was moving in the opposite direction from the Cat Burglar. She was going into the bedroom or the living room.

At last, there was movement across the kitchen floor. Someone had come into the bathroom and opened up the door leading to the cellar. Down the steps they went and the Cat Burglar knew then that things were going to get complicated. Up the stairs came footsteps as well as the sound of paws. She was letting the dogs out for their morning duty. Since a confrontation with the dogs wasn't in the plan, the Cat Burglar was going to have to wait for them to be put back downstairs again; and hope they didn't pick up any unfamiliar scent. Ten minutes later, the dogs were back in the house and the footsteps were headed down to the cellar again. This was where exact timing was required. One misstep would spell disaster.

He pulled the canister of Pepper spray from his pocket and pulled down the woolen ski mask. He stepped out of his hiding place behind the shower curtain and stood silently behind the partially open door to the cellar. Now the steps were coming back up the stairs. The cellar door swung wide open and immediately he discharged the Pepper spray into his target's eyes.

"Ahhh," She said as she threw her hands up in defense.

He grabbed her by a handful of red hair and slammed her down to the floor of the bathroom. With his knee on her back, he reached into my pouch and pulled out the duct tape and wrapped a generous portion around her mouth and head. Another single layer was wrapped around her wrists which were pulled behind her back.

"I'll bet you never expected to see me again," He said.

She fought back kicking; trying to free herself. He grabbed her by the red hair again and dragged her down the stairs, where he slammed her back up against the steel pole and wrapped duct tape around her throat and one leg. Then he stood back and viewed my quarry.

"I hope you marked your calendar because today is the end of your evil reign."

Terror reflected in her eyes. It must have been intimidating to be facing someone in the house that you lived in, wearing a dark ski mask that covered their face.

"I have a list of questions for you," he said, "and if you answer them without any bullshit or lies, this will go a lot easier. If not, I will still get the answers, but you will be seriously worse for wear. I have a small chore to do now but I'll be back. You think about which way you want to do this."

He bounded up the stairs and into the kitchen. He found her purse lying on the counter and emptied the contents. He took the keys to the Toyota and went out in the driveway and started it up, moving it around the corner and backing it into the lower driveway. It was just becoming dawn as the sun crept over the horizon. A wall on each side of the driveway obscured the view slightly. He ducked down to avoid being seen by any casual viewers, exited the car and crept over to the overhead door that he had unlocked earlier. He lifted it about 15 inches and slipped inside. Now, nobody would be any wiser as to what was going on inside the house. To them, it would appear that a car was parked in the lower drive. That's all. He went back into the cellar. The terror was still in her eyes.

"I want to know where my stuff is; my laptop, my music; my clothes, every last thing that you stole from me."

By now, the target Roxie had figured out who her captor was; but I kept the mask on for effect. She stood there, bound to the steel support pole, wearing a sweatshirt and a pair of baggy jogging pants. I went over to her and pulled a knife out. I then cut the duct tape and peeled it away from her mouth so that she could speak.

"I didn't take your stuff," she said, "I left everything inside the RV."

"You are a lying bitch," I said, "You can tell me that until the cows come home, but its bullshit and I you know it. You went through my box of collectibles and took out anything of value and put the box back. Now you are trying to tell me you left everything in the RV."

Roxie turned silent now. She just stared at me with those pretty blue eyes.

"The fucking RV was locked when I got to it and the keys were in the ignition. I had to break a window to get in. There was nothing there. Now I want to know where my stuff is. I know it was delivered here because Carl told me so. You remember Carl; the guy that drove the rental truck up here."

My statement about the RV being locked was a lie, but I wanted to eliminate her telling me that someone took all the stuff out of the RV when nobody was there. I knew that nobody had been to the property after she left Kentucky, because of all my 'junk' that was on the porch and inside the house.

"I'm telling you I didn't take it," Roxie said. "If it wasn't at the house, somebody stole it."

"Even if that was true," I calmly stated, "it's your fault. You did absolutely nothing to protect my assets. You could have locked everything up and given the key to my lawyer but you didn't. I don't believe a word you say because I know how mercenary you have been."

I reached in my pocket and pulled out the bottle of Jack Daniels. I opened up the pill bottle and shook 2 capsules into my hand.

"Let's have a drink Honey," I said, "for old time sake."

I went over to her and she proceeded to try to resist the bottle. I gripped her jaw with one hand and shoved the two capsules in her mouth, followed by the spout of the whiskey bottle. She fought and fought, but I crammed the bottle deeper into her throat so that she had to swallow to get air. I probably wasted a good shot or two, but was successful in getting at least one down her throat; along with the pills.

"You're FUCKING CRAZY," She shrieked.

"That's right Honey," I said, "I'm crazy because you made me this way. Now I want to know where my stuff is stored or I'm going to get really nasty."

"For God's sake Mark," she said, "I don't have it."

"OK," I nodded, "That's the way you want to play it, fine."

I put the tape back over her mouth, undid her pants and slid them down and off one leg. I wrapped a towel around the bare leg and then I took the rope out of my pocket and tied it around her free leg and towel. I pulled on it until her legs were slightly spread. The towel kept any telltale rope marks from being visible. I tied the other end of the rope to the leg of the cellar sink. She stood there, neck taped to the pole and her legs apart in a 'y'. I took a knife out of my pocket and cut her panties off. There was that beautiful red little bush of hers. I reached in my pocket and pulled out my electrical hook-up. She eyed me with intense curiosity because she knew that this meant trouble.

"Do you remember one of the last movies we watched?" I asked. "The name of the movie was 'Taken'. It was about some teen girls who were abducted. Do you remember the interrogation scene where the guy was hooked up and electrocuted?"

She mumbled something that I couldn't quite understand, so I removed the tape from her mouth.

"No Mark," she begged, "you've got to believe me."

I plugged in the device and touched the two alligator clips together. The light came on.

"I made this especially for you, baby," I told her. "When you see light, you will be getting about 110 volts, surging through your body. You can avoid all this unpleasantness by simply disclosing where you are keeping my stuff and how much of it you sold. If you don't want to do that, you'll be in for a . . . 'ahem' . . . shocking time."

"For the last time Mark," she said, "I don't have your shit."

I reached up and clipped one of the alligator clips to her right ear. I clipped the other to the steel-wool probe that I had.

"Last Chance," I said.

"Please, don't," She begged.

I pushed the steel wool to the crevice between her legs, holding the wooden rod so I didn't get electrocuted myself. The light bulb came on and Roxie went into an immediate upright stance. I pulled the probe away and asked her again. She sobbed as she looked at me but I had hardened my heart in preparation for this.

"Please Mark," she cried, "I don't have anything."

"Fuck You Bitch," I said, "you have no idea how many times I said please. That's all I ever tried to do was to please you. Now it's your turn. I will keep doing this, until the electric company comes and cuts the power off for non payment of the bill. Now tell me where my shit is."

"Les is . . . . Les will," She stuttered.

"Les isn't going to do a fucking thing," I said. "His time is going to come later and believe me; I've got a very special treat for him."

I hit her again with the probe. This time her eyes rolled back into her head.

"Wow," I said, "all this excitement is making me thirsty. Let's have another drink."

I pulled out the whiskey bottle again and once more I had to force the neck down her throat. If there is one thing I can say, Roxie definitely was an obstinate bitch. She ended up choking down about a shot and a half before I pulled the bottle away.

"Why are you doing this to me?" she moaned, "I left you alone. I said I wouldn't testify against you and I won't."

"Honey," I told her, "you set me up from the get-go. I have done extensive investigation and you have had one hell of a past. I'm not the first one you did this to but I'm damned sure I will be the last. And as far as testifying, that's not an issue because they are probably going to drop all the charges against me. They want your ass and would probably add my charges to the forgery and grand theft that is against you now. So fuck you. Where's my stuff?"

"Why won't you believe . . . . ," She started to say.

ZAP, ZAP, ZAP. I hit her with 3 jolts in a row. She let out a scream and I had to stuff the leg of her pants into her mouth to keep things a bit more quiet.

"Keep it up, bitch," I said, "enough electricity will melt you and before long, you won't have any pussy left at all." I pulled the pant leg out of her mouth.

"It's at Roy's," she finally said, "It's up in Roy's garage."

"Now you see," I said, "that wasn't so bad was it. What's there? Are my clothes there? Is my music there? What about my personal papers and my ID?"

"No," she said, "I gave the music to my son. He has the box in South Carolina."

"Good Honey," I complimented her. "You're doing very well. How much of my stuff did you sell on EBay?"

"I sold your computer equipment, that's all."

"Oh, that's all, huh? So it didn't matter that all my passwords, bank information, personal address lists and confidential business stuff is in someone else's hands? I should shove this probe up your ass and leave but I've got a game plan and you are not going to like it."

Roy was a friend of Les' who lived about 6 miles from here. I had met Roy before and had even been to his house once or twice. I made a mental note of the fact that she was using his garage for storage. I'm sure Les never told Roy that some of the stuff he was storing was stolen from me. I pulled out a list that I had made up, of questions that I wanted answers to. One by one I asked them and she told me most of what I wanted to know. When I got to the questions about her bank account pin numbers and passwords, she would not answer. I had to give her a bit more incentive and finally got everything I needed.

"How did you hook up with Les?" I asked, "I know you made numerous calls back and forth. Was this your idea or his for you to move in here?"

"He made the offer," she said, "I was going to move to South Carolina but he said that you would probably find me there."

"Roxie," I said shaking my head, "you have got to be one of the stupidest creatures on earth. I never would have found you down there. I know you made the deposit on the house because I have the cancelled check. But I could only guess your location."

"Mark, pleeeease," She said.

"But when you moved here, my friends saw you back in October when you had your little garage sale here. It's amazing what you can find out on the computer. I know about you working at the realtor's office, you losing your cat, your advertisement for the dishwasher, everything."

"Please," she said, "I've told you everything."

"I want the combination to your safe too."

"I don't have the safe anymore," She replied.

"You must think I was born yesterday," I said. "I found it upstairs in the bedroom. Now give me the combination."

"Mark, you can't take my stuff," She begged.

"Why not?" I said. "You took mine. Give me the combination."

She was continuing to put up resistance and I once again hit her with 110 volts. She started to scream and I had to shove her panties in her mouth to keep her quiet. After the first jolt, I removed the clip from her ear and placed it between her nostrils.

"The next jolt will go directly into whatever brain cells you have left." I said, "And If Les survives his meeting with me, he will find nothing but a blubbering idiot; although you might give a better blowjob that way, because your head will shake uncontrollably. Now I'm going to ask you again . . . What is the combination?"

With the panties still in her mouth, she shook her head.

ZAP once again. This time, her head slammed back against the steel pole.

I brought out the whiskey bottle, removed the panties that gagged her and shoved the neck down her throat. I pinched her nostrils together and forced her to take a long pull off the bottle. This one had to be about 2 shots worth. Her eyes wandered around and it looked like she was having difficulty in focusing. I took the panties out of her mouth and asked again for the combination.

"Five One Two Oh Seven," She said.

"You wouldn't lie to me would you?" I queried "I'd hate to have to give you any larger voltage, but if you lie, I'll hook this fucker up to the dryer outlet. That's 220 volts.

"Four Two Seven One Seven," She came back with.

That made more sense. That was the zip code for Burkesville. I put down my electrical hook-up, replaced her gag and went upstairs to the bedroom where the safe sat in the closet and I punched in the code. POP . . . the door opened. I looked at what it contained. There was $2,700 dollars in cash, her checkbook, the title for the Datsun 280-z, the title for the Toyota, which was now registered in Les's name and a variety of business papers. Just the money alone would have been a good find but the rest was a bonus. I grabbed everything out of the safe and stuffed it all into my pockets.

I went back out into the kitchen and began to go through her purse. I found my cell phone that she had stolen, her cell phone and another cell phone. There was another checkbook in there with her wallet. She had another $ 75 in the wallet. The only other thing in the purse of interest was an address book. I took that, the phones, the money and left the rest.

I did add one item though. I opened up my pouch and placed a small baggie with 5 of my pills inside her purse. The pills were Temazapam, a narcotic sleeping pill that the VA had given me years ago. That was what I had given her when I first encountered her today and by now, she should be pretty close to passing out because you don't mix this stuff with alcohol. At least if you want to stay awake.

I went back downstairs and found Roxie in a haze. Obviously the drugs and alcohol were having an effect but she was a good actress and I wanted to make sure that she had plenty of booze in her. I removed her gag and slapped her in the face. Her eyes instantly flashed open.

"I hope that wasn't as hard as that baseball bat that I hit you with the night I got arrested," I said, "How did you dream that one up when there wasn't even one in the house, you lying puke. One last question; were you planning to steal my Camaro and bring it up here to give to Les?"

"No," she mumbled, "Les said he didn't want that piece of shit back."

"Yeah, sure," I said, "I'll bet you were just going to leave it parked in the front yard when you moved. Even though your son loved the car, he probably wouldn't want that 'piece of shit' either. You are damned lucky the State Police wouldn't do anything about it or you'd more than likely be in jail."

"You'll never get away with this Mark." She slurred.

"Oh, don't worry about it Roxie," I said, "you're future is going to be in the bright lights from now on."

"What do you mean?" She asked.

"Well Honey," I told her, "I had to recover the money that you cost me, so now you are going to be a star. You are going to have the lead in your own movie. I figured that you were such a good actress with me, maybe this was where you should be. So Honey, I got you a part in a movie. You're the star actually. Unfortunately it's in a Snuff film, but what the hell; you always wanted to go out in a blaze of glory."

A look of dismay crossed her face. I know she believed that what I was telling her was true. Between the drugs, alcohol and electricity, Roxie had been altered.

"I really wanted to kill you when I was in jail," I said. "How could you do that to me? I never hurt you and I had only love for you. What are your plans for Les? Were you going to marry him and then be the sad widow when he had an 'accident'?"

She stood there in a daze. I continued my verbal assault on her because I had so much pent up anger that I had never released.

"Roxie, you are despicable and I am happy to be the instrument of your demise. Don't worry if you didn't have sex with Les last night. You are going to get more cock tonight than you have ever had, before the final curtain falls."

"Please Mark," she said, "my family has money. I can pay you. Don't do this."

"Your money is no good," I said, "and your family will be gone also. As soon as I get my music from your son, he is destined to be alligator bait. And your daughter and granddaughter; they are going to make nice bedmates for some sultan in Iran. You see Honey; I don't need your money."

Roxie started belching and then poured out with a flow of the contents of her stomach. It drooled out of her mouth and down the front of her, covering her sweatshirt. I smiled at her and told her that I believed that called for another drink. I held the bottle up to her and her head just dropped. I wasn't going to take any chances. I forced another pill down her throat and pushed the neck of the bottle all the way into her gullet as far as it would go. She gagged but I just held it there until at least 2 shots went down.

"Oh c'mon baby," I said, "you've had more than that down your throat before. Remember the day before my arrest . . . in the shower?"

By now it was almost 11 a.m. I had more to do before I finalized my dealings with Roxie. I picked up all the items that I had brought with me, including the cut panties. I went upstairs and made sure that the safe was closed and locked. I replaced the batteries I had taken out of the phones. I took the keys I needed off the rings and replaced the rest.

I took the list of items I was missing, folded it and placed it between 2 plates in the kitchen cupboard. I pulled a towel out of the closet and cleaned up any mud traces I had left and threw the towel in the hamper. I grabbed Roxie's purse and checked to make sure I had everything that I needed out of it. I picked up her coat and went back downstairs.

"Man," I said, "you were always a decent lay honey, but this is the best fuck I have ever had."

"Mork pliss," she slurred, "don't doooit."

"Oh, Honey," I continued, "don't worry. I wouldn't just throw you into the movies. You're going down and meet my Hell's Angels friends. They are going to break you in before your big debut. I think we should have another drink to celebrate."

I took the Jack Daniel's bottle and approached her. She threw herself left and right to avoid the neck. I grabbed her by the hair and pulled back until she opened her mouth to scream. The scream was silenced by the neck of the bottle. Two more ounces of whiskey went down her throat. Even though she had vomited, the smell was overpowering and I know most of it ended up in her system.

I untied Roxie and cut the duct tape from her leg and neck. I put a single strand around her wrists behind her back after I had redressed her and put her coat on. Roxie was lethargic but I still didn't trust her. We walked out into the garage and I opened the overhead door. I popped the trunk and threw her inside. For the first time since July of 2009, I felt safe.

I made one more pass through the house to make sure I hadn't left anything behind that would identify me. I closed the garage door and turned the handle to lock it. It had been snowing lightly and I took the extra precaution of scattering my boot prints on the driveway. I got behind the wheel and took off down the road. I didn't like doing this in broad daylight, but I made sure that I shielded my face so that no one could pick me out of a lineup if some nosy neighbor noticed.

I drove her car to a bar called Rosey's on the west side of Syracuse. I thought this was appropriate because it was her namesake; with a slightly different spelling. This was a popular lunch spot and indeed there were at least 15 cars in the parking lot by shortly after 11 a.m. The parking area itself was ringed with large boulders to block people from parking too close to the building. On the very end of a row, there was an open space. This was the most dangerous part of my plan. Rosie was completely passed out by now but I was afraid of unintended witnesses.

I pulled directly in front of one of the large boulders and backed away about 25 feet. I got out the Camry and popped the trunk, pulled Roxie out and placed her in the driver's seat, locking her in. I sat on the passenger side. I removed the duct tape and made sure that there was no residue on her skin. I set her purse on the floor along with the remains of the Jack Daniels she had been drinking. I put her foot on the gas pedal and shifted her weight, so that the car was running at a fairly high idle. I slapped the car into drive, opened my door and slammed and locked it as I jumped out.

The car picked up a bit a speed and then rammed straight into the large boulder. I heard the radiator fan clanging as I walked away. Roxie was motionless behind the wheel. I crossed the main street and went into a Denny's restaurant that was located there. I picked up the pay phone and dialed 911.

"Hi," I said, "this is Frank Rogers at Rosey's in Syracuse. We need an ambulance here."

"What is your emergency?" the dispatcher asked.

"Someone drove into our barrier here at the restaurant," I told her. "I think the driver may have a concussion or something because she isn't moving."

"Dispatch is on the way," She told me.

I hung up the phone and walked out the front door. Denny's was right on a bus line and I was lucky enough to catch one right away. I would have liked to hang around and catch the action that was going to unfold but I had to get my ass out of Syracuse . . . pronto.

The bus pulled up and I stepped up to get in. Because of the snow, the roads and my boots were slippery. My foot folded underneath me and I went crashing down into the entranceway of the bus.

CRASH!

My eyes opened and I was lying on the floor of my apartment. I must have dozed off and fell out of the chair as I sat at the computer. I had a lump on the right side of my head that told me I must have hit the desk on the way down. I looked at the clock through one eye and it read 4:45. Was that a.m. or p.m.? It was still dark outside so I assumed that it was 4:45 in the morning. I didn't know how long I had been sleeping in my chair before I fell, but I knew it was definitely time to go and get some rest. I still remembered most of my recent dream.

And it scared the hell out of me.

* * *

47) The Good 'ol Boy Club

Burkesville, KY—February 23, 2009

I staggered into the bedroom and fell upon the bed. If I was so tired that I fell out of my chair, it must mean that I needed sleep. I don't remember falling asleep but it couldn't have been more than a total of 30 seconds before I was dozing. The next time I woke up, the clock read 11:23. Looking out the window again, I verified that it was indeed morning.

Whew, I must have been wiped out, I thought.

I got up and went to the computer to verify that I hadn't lost any more that a few hours during my excursion into dreamland. No, today was still the 23rd, which meant that my date with the court system was 1 week away. I hadn't heard from my lawyer in a while so I decided to track him down and find out what was going on. I called his office, and the receptionist told me that Brian was still in court but she would have him call me when he returned. Brian rarely returned my phone calls unless it was something critical. But true to her word, his receptionist called me about 2 p.m. and said to hold for Brian.

"Mr. Casey," his resonant voice spoke. "I have good news for you."

"Ok, I'm all ears." I was anticipating that the prosecutor decided to drop the case and I wouldn't have to go through all this hassle.

"I've worked out a deal with the prosecutor," He said. "The deal is that you plead guilty to the charges but you will be given a 1 year suspended sentence."

"What does that mean Brian?"

"It simply means that they get a conviction on paper, but you don't have to do anything. No jail time, no probation, no rehab, nothing."

"Brian, I don't like the idea of pleading guilty," I said, "I'm not guilty and so why should they get anything out of the deal. I don't have my car, they've kept my money and I spent over 4 months in jail."

"Well son," Brian said with his Kentucky drawl, "I think it's a great deal. You know you'll get your car back because they won't need security anymore, and as far as the money, perhaps I can work some more magic."

"And you're sure that the prosecutor will agree to this," I asked, "I have to tell you that I don't like the idea of putting in a guilty plea. I want all this in writing before I accept their 'deal'."

"All I've got to do is pick up the phone and call him." he said, "and he will draft up the papers and fax them over to me and you can come up and sign them. As soon as I return them and he signs, it's a done deal."

"OK," I reluctantly said, "I still don't think they have a case against me but like the old adage, a bird in the hand . . . ."

"I think you are making the right choice, Mr. Casey. You'll see that these good 'ol boys aren't too difficult to work with. I'll take care of it and call you when the papers get here."

I hung up the phone and thought about it. Well, this was one way to get out of doing any jail time, if I was convicted. I was doubtful that Brian, the miracle worker, would be able to get my money back either because the county was broke. But the truth of the matter was that I was so disgusted with Kentucky that the $1,700 was a small payment to get out of the state. I decided that if I signed the deal, I would get my car back and get the fuck out of Dodge City.

Thursday afternoon, Brian called and told me to be in his office the next day at 1 p.m. He had received the papers and I would sign them, he would witness my signature, they would get faxed to the Commonwealth Attorney who would sign them and this would be over. I would still have to go to court on Tuesday but it was just a formality. The plea deal would be entered into record and I would basically be a free man. When I say free, I mean that the technical term would be unsupervised parole. I would still have a conviction on record but I didn't care because I would never be back here again.

I drove the 60 miles to Brian's office in my newly purchase car. The only other time I had been up here in Greensburg was when I was driving the RV. That was an expensive trip. I showed up at 1 p.m. as promised and signed the papers. Brian and I talked a bit and he mentioned the balance of his fee. I asked him if there would be a reduction of his $5,000 fee, because we did not have to go to court and he laughed.

"Mr. Casey," he said, "I just worked out a wonderful deal for you and on Tuesday of next week, I will be working to getting your money back. I think I have earned my fee. But I understand that you are a little strapped for cash so I would be happy to make a payment arrangement with you."

"Brian, I agree," I said, "But you never know until you ask. By my calculations, I owe you the balance of $3,000, right?"

Brian agreed with those figures.

"So what I'll do is give you the $1,700 I get back from court and for the next 2 months, on the 3rd of the month when I get my check, I will give you $ 600. Is that fair?"

"Mr. Casey," he said, "I believe you are a man of your word and I accept that arrangement."

With that, I got up, shook hands and left his office. Even though I wanted my day in court, I felt that this deal was more expedient in the long run and relegated myself to accept it. But Christ, this whole thing cost me a lot of money; probably $3,000 to $4,000 cash to Roxie, plus all my possessions, $5000 in legal fees and a shitload of aggravation.

I guess I won't be finding a date on Craigs List in the near future.

I turned the Olds around in an open parking lot and began the hour long trip back to Burkesville. At least I had the rent paid, a good vehicle and food in the house. Six Hundred dollars out of my Social Security check was a big chunk but at least it was only for 2 months. I could do it; had to do it. I got about half-way home and my cell phone rang. I looked at the number and it was my lawyer calling. I picked it up and the first thing out of his mouth came the words, "You have to come back."

"Why," I asked, "what happened? Can't they read my signature?"

"No," he said, "the deal is off the table."

"What! I screamed, "what did you say?"

He told me that he faxed my agreement to the prosecutor, who called him back and told him that after thinking about it, I had to do probation and rehab. I still didn't have to go to jail but I had to go into a program where they can monitor me whenever they like."

"OK," I hissed, "The fucking assholes want to play that game, you tell that prick I'll see him in court on Tuesday."

"Well Mr. Casey, you still have to come back into my office because we have to go over trial strategy. I'm on another case on Monday so today is the only day we can do it."

Even though I was livid, I agreed that I would be back to his office in about 45 minutes and we were going to strategize the major fucking we were going to give to the prosecutor. I also said that I want him to start thinking of a civil suit after we win this criminal action."

I was so pissed.

I hung up and threw the phone to the back seat of the car. Here these assholes were, trying to convict me on trafficking, when I never sold to anyone, nor could they prove beyond a reasonable doubt that the pot was even mine. Even if Roxie was here to take the stand, they could not prove it. I vowed that in the civil action, I was going to sue them for false arrest and nail their little heads to the wall. And I do mean their 'little' heads.

I got to Brian's office and went in with an attitude. How could the prosecutor renege on a deal that they offered. It was almost like they were looking to see if I'd take their deal, to determine whether it went to court or not.

"I want the prosecutor's balls," I told Brian. "What the fuck kind of bullshit is this anyway?"

"Now don't get all hot, Mr. Casey," Brian said, "we still have a chance at talking to the Judge on Tuesday and based on the evidence, I don't think the Commonwealth is going to be able to prove anything against you. I wanted you here to grill you on strategy, just in case they move forward with a trial."

"OK," I said, "but what can I tell you that I haven't already told you?"

"They are going to say that you came down from New York, bought the pot and were going to sell it."

"And I guess my answer to that would be, who am I going to sell it too? I don't know anyone. Who did I buy it from? Where was I going to get customers? How much does pot sell for down here? If I've only been here 6 weeks, why did the Sheriff find plants growing on Roxie's land?"

"Very good Mr. Casey," Brian said, "Those are the kinds of answers that put questions in the jurors minds. Remember, they have to convict you beyond a reasonable doubt. Every time you make them question something, it will help your case."

Brian asked me 2 more questions that day. Have I ever been arrested before and was I honorably discharged from the Navy. I answered that 'Yes" I have an honorable discharge and 'Yes" I had several arrests in New York for drunk driving, but that was over 10 years ago. Then he said,

"Well, I think we are in good shape. You know how to conduct yourself in court and I will lead you toward the answers when I cross-examine you."

"I want you to drill the Sheriff's Deputy that arrested me Brian," I told him. "This guy is the same one that I believe was having an affair with Roxie. The same one who arrested her ex-husband and got him deported, the same one who allowed her to get away with the murder of Terry Jacoby and the same one who told all those lies to the Grand Jury that resulted in my indictment."

"Oh, don't worry Mr. Casey," he said, "He's going to be on the hot seat. Now, I have another appointment waiting so I'll see you at 8:30 sharp on Tuesday the 2nd, Right?"

I told him I'd be there with bells on my feet, waiting for him to crush the opposition. I had wanted to talk more about strategy; more than the 15 minutes that he allotted me. It seemed strange that I spent over 2 hours in travel back and forth to his office, for a strategy meeting that lasted only 15 minutes. I had a whole list of potential questions on my sheet that I wanted to be heard in court but he more or less told me not to worry, he would take care of it on Tuesday.

I left his office, buoyed by his positive attitude towards the outcome but still troubled by the fact that he really hadn't spent a lot of time working on this case. But, he was the highly paid expert who was going to get me off all the charges and make sure that justice was done.

I was still pissed at the antics of the prosecutor. On the drive home, I wondered if there was the possibility of suing him for misconduct. It just didn't seem right that he could dangle a carrot out and then snatch it away. I had heard that he was a real slime bag anyway and the only reason he got the Commonwealth Attorney position was because his 'daddy' had a lot of political pull. As I pulled into my yard that night, after driving over 180 miles, I decided that I would draft up my own set of questions for Brian to ask in court. That way, I knew the elements of the case that were important, would be covered.

And so would be my happy little ass.

* * *

48) Luck be a Lady Tonight

Burkesville, KY—March 1, 2010

The day before my court date, I put a call into Brian's office again. I knew that he had told me that he would be in court that day, but I wanted to cover some last minute details with him and I wasn't sure if we would have time tomorrow. To my surprise, he was in the office and picked up my call.

"Mr. Casey," he said, "are you getting excited?"

"I don't know if excited would be the word I'd use," I told him, "more like antsy with a bit of jangled nerves mixed in."

"Oh, that's normal son," he reassured me, "it's like stage fright. But I know that you'll do just fine tomorrow. What can I do for you?"

"Well Brian, I know that you are optimistic," I continued, "but I was wondering about my taking my car to court. If, on the outside chance that I get convicted, I don't want it sitting on Main Street in Burkesville. Do you think you could pick me up on your way in?"

"Hey, I've got it covered. Don't worry, go ahead and drive your car. Tomorrow at this time, you'll be a free man and all this worry will seem silly."

"OK," I said, "you know that my fate is in your hands and I'm counting on an acquittal. I just wish I had your level of confidence in this."

"Son, I've been dealing with these good 'ol boys for a long time. We all have been through the battles of court a million times. Some of us even drink together. Just get a good night's sleep and make sure that you are at the courthouse on time. I'm going in early and try to work my magic on the judge."

"OK, Brian," I said, "I'll see you tomorrow."

I hung up, filled a bit more with confidence that this would soon be over. I sat at my desk and wrote out the questions that I wanted to be introduced into court. Even though Roxie was not going to be there, I had to make the jury understand her past record of doing this to men and that this trial was not because of something I did.

I knew that I could not ask questions that directly related to her actions because she would not be there to answer or defend herself. All that would do would be to raise a lot of objections by the prosecution. So I worded the questions that Brian would ask me in such a way, that I could tell the whole story as a factual series of events, which the prosecution would find difficult to argue.

How long have you lived here, Mr. Casey?

Besides Ms. Patrick, how many other local people do you know here?

Have you ever been arrested for drugs before?

What kind of work do you do?

What kind of work did Ms. Patrick do?

How long had she lived here that you know of?

Have you ever seen her do drugs?

Did you bring property down from New York when you moved in with Ms. Patrick?

What happened to that property while you were incarcerated?

I ended up with 45 questions designed to make any reasonable juror understand that I was not the guilty party. Even though Roxie would not be available and could not be cross-examined, I hoped that it would be enough to cause reasonable doubt, which would lead to acquittal.

As soon as I finished I reviewed all the questions, answered them aloud and made any changes I needed to, I finally finished about midnight and went to bed. As I lay there, before dropping off to sleep, I prayed.

Holy Father; tomorrow comes the conclusion of this nightmare I have been in for so long. I pray for your guidance and strength and hope that the jury will be merciful in my case. I know that I have not always been the best of son's but I hope that you will find me worthy of escaping these false charges. Thank you for your presence Lord, in my life. Amen.

I got back up and went to my computer. I had to write some kind of letter about my final thoughts, based on the 'worst case' assumption that I would be convicted. I also had to send a set of instructions to Maggie because I knew that if I went to jail tomorrow, it would be immediate. No stopping at GO to pick up my $ 200 or any personal possessions and no chance to call anyone.

I finished and printed out my letter and instructions, put it in a stamped envelope and would mail it tomorrow on the way to court. If I didn't get convicted, which didn't seem feasible now, I could call Maggie and let her know the good news and to ignore the mail she was going to receive. Then I went back to bed.

I laid there thinking of a million thoughts of things I needed to do, things that were done and things that I had no control over. As sleep found me, the sounds of Frank Sinatra rang through my head. I hoped that the song was an indicator of what tomorrow would bring.

They call you lady luck, But there is room for doubt
At times you have a very un-lady-like way, of running out
You're on this date with me, The pickin's have been lush
And yet before this day is over,
You might give me the brush

You might forget your manners,
You might refuse to stay,
And so the best that I can do is sit and pray
Luck be a lady tonight, Luck be a lady tonight,

Luck if you've been a lady to begin with,
Luck be a lady tonight.

* * *

End of Book 1, PINNED!

Epilogue and Acknowledgments

I started writing this story, more or less as a warning to others, that there are truly unscrupulous people living among us. I have always considered myself a fair and just man; one who looks at the glass as half full rather than being half empty. I am generally quick to give the benefit of the doubt to others, until I am proven wrong. Within the pages of this book, one can easily see where I was wrong. I was wrong a lot, and about a great many things.

There are readers out there that my find the final ending of this book rather disappointing. That is because the original manuscript was written before the trial date and updated approximately a year and a half later. I have tried to keep all of the events in an orderly fashion; in exactly the way they have unfolded. After the trial came and went, there was enough material to allow me the opportunity to present the rest of the story in a subsequent, yet different novel. That novel, tentatively called "Stains on the Gavel" goes into more detail about the inner workings of the Kentucky Judicial system and will be available for review in 2013.

I have always held my friends in the highest esteem; valued more than any earthly possession. If it hadn't been for the support of my friends during this ordeal, I think I may have either cut the silver thread or at the very least found a rubber room. Getting bail money was a difficult task because I never travelled in circles where my friends were flush with cash. They were just ordinary 'working stiffs' like me. But I did benefit from the moral support and prayers of my friends and that kept me from coming unglued. I thank every one of them for all they did to help me.

Just to give you a peek into the sequel to this story, there was an incident that I found out about at a much later date that involved one of my friends. Unfortunately, because of the trust people generally had in me, one of my friends had indeed put up my bail money early on; none of which got to me. I didn't find this fact out, until the friendship was destroyed and I could get no response to the numerous attempts I made at redeeming that past trust. It was another $5,000 loss that Roxie pocketed and I have to live with. As a result of trust in me, I lost my friend who thought that I had somehow betrayed him/her. Roxie got the gold and I got the shaft.

Then, there comes the question that I pondered for so long; the question WHY? Why did all this happen to me when I try everyday, to go through life giving and not taking? Why was the wall built so high? There is an undercurrent within this story about loss and gain. I lost many things during this time including my clothes, my music and almost, my mind. One of the first things to go was my sense of humor. While that had always been prevalent in my life, as soon as Roxie and I returned to Kentucky, I was never called 'Funny Man" anymore.

But there were gains too. After careful analysis, I have come to 2 conclusions; the first being that this whole ordeal has brought me closer to the Lord than I was before all these events. I was never evil or malicious, I prayed periodically and I considered myself a Christian. But somewhere along the road, I had lost my way with the spirit. I rarely took the time to thank God for all the wonderful things he has given to me in this life. These trials have put me back on solid ground and I am truly thankful for that. These were my keys to ascension.

The second reason may indeed be, to give the authorities a second bite at the apple, in regards to Roxie's nefarious dealings with the people that fall for her. It should be self-evident from her actions in the book that she is indeed a person who has mental and moral issues that need to be dealt with. Perhaps this will bring light to these issues or perhaps nothing will come about of it in this lifetime. But darkness has been lifted upon the subject. Perhaps soon, the darkness in her heart will be too.

All I can say is that I truly believe that God will have the final say in what happens, and to whom. It is not my place to judge, but to accept everything as being part of the plan.

I would like to take this opportunity to thank some very special people who have been influential in my life. Whether they are living or dead, liked or disliked me, entertained or irritated me, or helped or hurt me, I hope to always have contact with these souls, now and in the hereafter. I believe truly that we are all of one body and are all truly, God's children.

My gratitude goes out to Kathy Morris, Dave Keller, Laura McMahon, Cheryl Grome, Gus Grome, Gary Gove, Tony DiDominico, Aaron Ballard, Don Avery, Dawn Ebert, Linda Driscoll, Wally Russo, Donna Bernardus, Jack Knowlton, Charles Castano, Magi Astrologer Helena, Brian Ravas, Marc DiGiuseppe, Dr. Nicole Middleton, John Walker, my dad Charles Massie Jr, my mom Dorothy Massie, my sisters Sue and Sherry, Penny Pagano and lastly, Patriche Roser and John Lubeck. I know I've forgotten others that I should have included, but forgetting doesn't mean that they aren't still deep in my heart.

A very special Thank You goes out to my copy editor, Ms. Judy Reveal, who is the owner of the Just Creative Writing and Indexing, who without her expert knowledge and ability, this book would never have seen the light of day and would probably be found balled up in my circular file. Thank you Judy.

Celebrities who had a part in shaping my life through the entertainment media include Rod Serling, Pablo Picaso, Jamie Lee Curtis, Frank Sinatra, Chevy Chase, Ronald Reagan, Monty Python, Lewis Black, Sean Connery, Firesign Theatre, Sam Kinesen, Arnold Schwarzenegger, Bill Bixby, Rodney Dangerfield, Jon Anderson, Bob Crane and countless others, who brought me drama, humor and spirituality.

Some of the music influences that rang through my head during the long days and nights of incarceration include *"Behind Blue Eyes"—The Who, "The Lady Lies"—Genesis, "Fella in the Cellar"—John Miles, "I Can't Quit You"—Blood-Sweat and Tears, "And You and I"—YES, "Snake Eyes"—Alan Parsons Project, "The Devil's Got My Throat"—Spock's Beard, "Stand Tall"—Burton Cummings, "Poor Boy"—Mike and the Mechanics, "Lost in a Lost World"—Moody Blues, "Lucky Man"—Emerson, Lake and Palmer, "Wind Up"—Jethro Tull, "Just Get through This Night"—Styx, "The Pass"—Rush, "Dust"—Mr. Mister* and so many, many more.

Last but certainly not least, I give praise to my Lord and Savior, Jesus Christ. Without his strength and guidance through dark alleys, I never would have survived. Many people believe that the essence of Karma is mainly an Eastern philosophy. I believe that Karma is the Lords way of correcting one's soul and bringing it closer towards fulfillment. There is a lot of Karma related to this book and I hope that this odyssey has, at least, helped to balance the scales. Thanks to everyone who has read my novel. The sequel is currently unfolding and will be available 2013. You can keep up to date with my writings at: StarShow Publications.

Charles W. Massie
July, 2012

Charles Massie grew up in upstate New York, the oldest of 4 children. After finishing high school, he enlisted in the United States Navy and served a total of six years at various ports around the world. Upon his return to civilian life, he continued his education at Syracuse University and eventually worked for a number of engineering firms, before finding his calling in the sales field.

Having an entrepreneurial spirit, he decided to go off on his own and has been instrumental in overseeing such companies as Massie Engineering Associates, InfoTech Consulting, LLC and CaterCats Catering. The call of creative expression was always in the background of his life and over the years, he has submitted articles and stories to Twilight Zone Magazine, Readers Digest, Analog Publications and others.

Pinned! – A Kentucky True Crime Story is his first novel and is the first book of the 'BlueGrass' series. Currently he is writing book two of the series, tentatively called ***Stains on the Gavel*** to be published in 2013, as well as working on a young adult adventure novel entitled ***The Boy in the Bin***, a series of cookbooks and a collection of jokes and other humorous stories.

His hobbies, when he is not writing, include progressive rock music, computers and other toys, travelling and enjoying the gifts that he has been blessed with. He loves animals, humor, exotic cars and practicing random acts of kindness. He currently lives in the Commonwealth of Kentucky.

StarShow Publications (www.starshowpublications.com) is a website that provides access to up and coming authors such as Charles W. Massie. Currently we have 3 books in the catalog, with another 9 in various stages of production and publication. The site, which is constantly updated, offers a reader the ability to download excerpts and full electronic copies of books, in a variety of formats.